D0209345

They're Never Too Young for Books

They're Never Too Young for Books

A Guide to Children's Books for Ages 1 to 8

•

•

•

•

•

Edythe M. McGovern & Helen D. Muller

Prometheus Books

59 John Glenn Drive
Buffalo, NewYork 14228-2197

Published 1994 by Prometheus Books

Library of Congress Cataloging-in-Publication Data

McGovern, Edythe M.
    They're never too young for books : a guide to children's books for ages 1–8 /
by Edythe M. McGovern and Helen D. Muller.
        p.   cm.
    Includes bibliographical references.
    ISBN 0-87975-858-9
    1. Children's literature—Bibliography. 2. Children—Books and reading.
I. Muller, Helen D. II. Title.
Z11035.A1M415   1994
[PN1009.A1]
016.8088'99282—dc20   93-33855
                                                                    CIP
                                                                    AC

Contents

Introduction

No one who has any contact, permanent or transitory, with young children denies that exposure to books is beneficial. It is almost a subconscious feeling, substantiated by formal research, that when literature in the broadest sense of that term is made part of a child's life from the onset, positive results are predictable. However reassuring and pleasant this assertion may be, it does seem to be something of a broad generalization. Therefore, the first purpose of this book will be to delineate these "positive results" as precisely as possible.

Once adults involved with small children have been convinced of the value of reading to those not yet able to read to themselves, these adults need to become aware of how to select books appropriate to each age level from infancy to about seven or eight years of age. If we consider that thousands of new titles come on to the market every year and add to this the number of worthwhile old favorites, it is clear that some attempt at establishing criteria for selection can be valuable and, indeed, may be almost mandatory.

Children's librarians can and do give expert assistance, of course, but having some basic idea of what books to select without professional advice is important. Parents and teachers will want to know how to differentiate between books of high calibre and those so readily available in supermarkets, drug and variety stores. The second purpose of this book, therefore, will be to assist the reader in establishing his or her own guidelines for wise selection.

Next, convinced that exposure has specific positive value and that there are some objective standards for book choice, the adult will be concerned with the presentation of the material: the best times and places to read aloud, the differences between reading to one or two children and reading to a group, the actual techniques involved in presenting picture books to small children, and the use of certain reinforcement aids, such as creative dramatics, story boards, and puppets.

And, finally, there is the matter of specific titles—guideposts, really—which the adult may find useful as he expands his familiarity with children's books. For this purpose, in Part Two, "Book Selection," there are various *categories of books,* and under each, lists of books alphabetically arranged by *title*, with author, illustrator, and annotation. For example, under "First Books" there is "*Goodnight Moon* by Margaret Wise Brown, illustrated by Clement Hurd," followed by a short description of the book.

In categories where there are some titles more appealing to the older child (ages six to eight), stars before each title will alert the adult reader.

At the end of the book, beginning on page 283, there is an alphabetical bibliography by author, with a separate entry for each title included in the text, the publisher, and date of publication.

Books that have become "classics" are included in this source book, but there is an emphasis on those published since the original *They're Never Too Young for Books* appeared (1980). However, the framework and philosophy that first engendered the publication remain basically the same because it is more important than ever to persuade adults to introduce children to the magic of books at the very earliest age and to keep reading aloud even after children have learned to read independently.

Part One

Positive Results

If there were no discernible benefit of reading aloud except the opportunity for the warm interaction which takes place between the adult reader and the child or children, exposing them to literature would still remain a very important activity, unique and satisfying. However, since there are quite a number of "positive results" which can be specifically identified, we need to examine them in some detail. They may be roughly divided into two categories: outcomes in terms of meeting immediate needs, and salutary effects in terms of future requirements. As we shall see, there will be some overlap here, since, to paraphrase William Wordsworth, "The child is parent to the adult."

One word of caution: No thinking person would claim that "meeting needs" of small children through exposure to literature is in any sense a complete program for their development. What most emphatically is asserted is that reading aloud can reasonably be expected to add dimension to that program in a way which cannot be fulfilled as well by any other activity.

IMMEDIATE NEEDS OF YOUNG CHILDREN

Although they are stated and explicated in various ways and in differing orders of importance by experts in the field of child development, a consensus regarding the requirements of a healthy, happy child would include the following:

1. Material Security
2. Safety
3. Emotional Security
4. Competence or Self-Esteem
5. A Need to Belong
6. A Need to Accept One's Uniqueness
7. A Need to Play and Escape
8. Aesthetic Satisfaction
9. Intellectual Stimulation

Along with a brief explanation of each of these categories, we shall investigate the connection between reading to young children and meeting these needs.

1. Material Security

Obviously, every child requires at least a minimum of material security in his "real world" in order to survive. A hungry child cannot be expected to pay much attention to anything which does not satisfy his immediate appetite for food. Recognition of this truism, of course, has led to many programs for amelioration, such as providing breakfasts and lunches for preschoolers and elementary school children as well. But what of the child who is literally deprived in the socioeconomic sense, lacking even some necessities? Can books make up in any way for indigence? Probably not. But this child has other needs, common to all children, and meeting these may help to make his material lack more bearable. Also, pragmatically, a broad exposure to the written word from a very early stage of intellectual development may well prepare that child for a more materially secure adulthood in terms of future requirements, such as literacy.

2. Safety

Child psychologists stress the small child's need for a predictable, somewhat proscribed world up to a point, a world which, as the toddler grows, includes to a greater and greater degree a need for new experience, excitement, and exploration, always with the knowledge that there is a home base to which he may return. As we shall see, there are a number of books which have this concept as their main idea or theme.

3. Emotional Security

Closely tied in with safety is the notion of emotional security, which means quite simply that no matter how far afield a child may wander—actually or in terms of his behavior—that child is still accepted and loved, usually by a parent. Later, he needs to become aware of the mutual trust which underlies secure relationships with his peers and/or adults outside the immediate family circle.

4. Competence or Self-Esteem

To a small child this means that he/she can do it, whatever "it" may be, sometimes against great odds. Since we recognize that even adults utilize role models in this way, albeit unconsciously, it is easy to recognize the function of books which picture examples for effectively interacting with one's environment to gain, first, self-esteem, and then the respect of others.

5. A Need to Belong

The first evidence of this need can be seen in the very young child's relationship with those who minister to his initial demands for the provision of his physical comforts. As he becomes less egocentric, he wants to feel a part of a close group, his family, and in this sense the "need to belong" is very much tied in with the desire for emotional security. However, there is a broader concept here as well: as the child matures and his world expands, he requires reassurance that he belongs in his neighborhood, is part of his ethnic/racial group, and ultimately assumes membership in the human race in the total sense.

6. A Need to Accept One's Uniqueness

Although he needs to belong to a group, the small child also needs to accept himself as a unique individual and to be reassured that being one's own self does not preclude acceptance by others who may be quite unique also.

7. A Need to Play and Escape

Books which can be included in this category may be equated with "escape" literature for adults. Even the most thoughtful grown-up enjoys humor for its own sake, amusement per se, without any intent beyond momentary pleasure, recreation in its original sense. Not surprisingly, even the youngest child has this same desire, which may be satisfied by nonsense words, rhyming jingles, humorous pictures, and preposterous exaggeration within a story.

8. Aesthetic Satisfaction

If we agree that "taste," particularly in the area of graphic art, is developed through repeated exposure to superior work, we have to look at picture books for children in a very special way. In no other genre of literature is there as great an opportunity for consistent presentation of the best as there is in books illustrated in many styles by artists of note. And youngsters under seven or eight favor books that are copiously illustrated. However, we need not choose books for their aesthetic quality in terms of art work alone; on the contrary, for the most part, superior choices incorporate outstanding illustration, which simplifies matters.

Since it is so significant, the topic of illustration will be dealt with in great depth in the section on book selection.

9. Intellectual Stimulation

At first glance, this may seem a low priority need for very young children, but many psychologists have concluded that curiosity itself is almost inborn, and certainly the need to know and then to understand is generally evident from the time a toddler begins to investigate the kitchen cupboards. To meet this need may mean giving a city child his first (and perhaps only) view of farm animals; it may entail reinforcing numerical concepts; it could include showing a five-year-old how to look for a word in his first picture dictionary. In short, what is involved here is the stimulation and the satisfaction of areas which can be primarily designated as intellectual, rather than aesthetic or emotional.

FUTURE EFFECTS

To examine needs which are not immediately apparent is not as simple a matter as looking at those which present themselves on a day-to-day basis when one has contact with young children. Nevertheless, certain topics clamor for consideration because they have application not only to the far-distant period of adulthood, but also because they have pertinence to the not-so-far-away times of later childhood and adolescence. In terms of long-range needs and results, what are the potentially "positive effects" of reading to children under the age of eight? Let us consider seven categories.

1. Literacy

For at least the last thirty years there has been an alarming increase in illiteracy among school-age children and young adults who somehow have not mastered the basic skills involved in reading—and consequently, writing—even by the time of their graduation from high school. We do not need to search out scholarly articles in professional journals to become aware of this problem. It is brought to our attention daily in news articles, in popular magazines, and whenever education is the subject of a radio or television broadcast. We are told, "Johnny—and his sister, Mary—can't read!" and along with a statement of the problem, we are frequently offered a plethora of solutions: Teach reading by this or that method; hire more dedicated teachers; hold them accountable; teach bilingually; decrease the number of students in each classroom; get back to basics; provide special services for remediation even into the college level; offer basic adult literacy programs in the community. None of these suggestions is in itself without merit. No one would dispute the contention that if a person has not learned to read by the time he or she is in the upper grades or has reached adulthood, something must be done. However, there may be an even simpler response than remediation, one which becomes quite obvious if we look back to a time when this condition (euphemistically called "functional illiteracy") did not exist or at least was not so widespread. The answer may lie in the reply to the question of why it is that people who grew up in an era when "reading aloud" was a fairly common family activity could usually master this somewhat complicated process quite easily. It is ironic that with all of the progress we have made during the last quarter century in diagnosing the "illness," with all of our attempts to "cure the patient," and with the ever increasing need to make him "well," that is, literate, we are more and more frequently having to admit that he died! Could it be that in our very efficient and fast-paced world we have overlooked one possible remedy? Again and again, formal studies show that children who can read are children who have been exposed to books from infancy, and adults who enjoy reading are adults who have been exposed to the printed word from early childhood.

It would seem, then, that there is a very practical purpose involved in presenting literature to young children. Reading to them will obviously not obliterate completely the problem of illiteracy. But it might well prove a less expensive and frustrating solution than any other proposal meant to stem the tide in a society which requires that more and more people read well.

2. Language Development

Closely tied to the actual process of reading is the area of language development, which may be further subdivided as (a) the acquisition of vocabulary, (b) a feeling for syntactical structure, (c) an appreciation of underlying meanings— implicit as contrasted with explicit—and (d) a sensitivity to one's mother tongue in an overall way.

(a) Vocabulary

We are all aware that we have a vocabulary much more extensive than we use in daily conversation. For example, most adults probably have not used the word "moat" once this month, yet they do not require a dictionary to understand that term. Few adults have thought specifically about a lion's "mane" or "curds and whey" in the past few days; still, there is no need to consult a dictionary to know what these words mean. But the acquisition of this nonworking vocabulary is no mystery. We all learned the meanings of a great many words by hearing them and/or reading them within the context of a story, and even if we do not have occasion to use them in everyday conversation, they are safely stored in the "computer" of our minds, to be recalled at will. To understand the significance of this process, try to think in an unfamiliar foreign language, in which even the simplest words are not "available for retrieval," and the handicap becomes clear.

In the same way, children who have not been given the opportunity to hear words which are not used in the ordinary circumstances of their lives cannot hope to fill these gaps in their understanding. What is really alarming about this paucity of vocabulary is that this lack can never be completely made up, even with remediation, since, as research shows, almost half of one's adult language skill is dependent upon what has been "learned" before the age of five!

(b) Syntactical Structure

Here we are talking at the simplest level about the way words are put together, the types and lengths of word groups or sentences. A more complicated view of syntax involves the notion of *style* too. Think how boring it would be if every sentence in the world were either a simple declarative statement or a simple interrogative sentence. Again, to grasp this concept we need only consider a beginning class in a foreign language, where all the verbs are conjugated in the present tense and there is little possibility of constructing sentences beyond the first-grade level even if the student is a doctoral candidate.

By exposure to an almost boundless variety of syntactical constructions as he is being read to, even the small child subconsciously becomes aware of the many, many ways in which language can be ordered to best express shades of meaning. These diversities are also stored in the computer of the mind to be savored, retrieved at will, and perhaps used later in his own writing, whether it is in an essay for a tenth-grade English class or in a letter of condolence to a friend whose mother has died.

(c) Implicit Meaning

To discuss the understanding of what is not explicitly written on the page, but is merely meant or implied, we really have to consider another literary term, *tone*. Is the author serious, or does he mean for us to chuckle with recognition of absurdity? As a test for sensitivity to this aspect of the printed word, discuss with any secondary school teacher what happens when an Art Buchwald column is assigned to a class of high school seniors. Without the instructor's prompting, few students realize the author's mode of getting the point across. Few will recognize the sly comic tone, and therefore most of the students may well misinterpret completely what has been written. It then becomes apparent that even when they have mastered the mechanics of deciphering words on a page, many young people are not able to recognize or assess underlying meaning. And this is not the case for the comic mode alone.

To further validate this conclusion, ask the same high school English teacher what happens when the group is faced with a passage from Mark Twain's *Huckleberry Finn* or John Steinbeck's *The Pearl.* Without direction from the instructor, few teenagers understand the criticism of unfair social systems implied by these authors, and instead tend to read only the literal stories, thereby missing the point entirely. It might be a possibility that had they been exposed to literature as three-year-olds, the notion of tone might have been imbibed effortlessly with a carryover at a later time. For instance, a child may never be made aware of the political implications of *Mother Goose,* and "Humpty-Dumpty" may be taken at face value by a toddler, but he will store the jingle in his mind without consciously thinking about it until finally the idea comes clear that if one "sits on a wall," falls off, and damages his "wholeness," nothing can ever put him together again—not even "all the king's horses and all the king's men." With maturation, the child might well consider less obvious interpretations.

(d) Sensitivity to the Mother Tongue

This concept, of course, involves a number of ideas, such as idiomatic speech, clichés, and catch phrases as opposed to thoughtful prose and nuances of expression. When we discuss this area of language development, we cannot ignore the preceding divisions of vocabulary and diction, syntax or style, and awareness of tone. Actually, an overall sense of language is a totality; those who are most literate as adults have without question acquired and enlarged this competence by early, frequent, and continued exposure to the printed word.

If we agree that the reading process itself with all that is implied—from word recognition to a sensitivity to language—is increased by exposing very young children to literature, we may count language development as the second positive result for the future.

3. Attitude Change

Undeniably, there are many factors involved in determining the way children perceive the universe, other people, behavioral standards, and so on. Indeed, it would be simplistic to ignore the major stimulus of the toddler's home environment—taken as a totality to include socio-economics, race, parental example, and the many other elements which help shape each person's world. Also, we must consider what surrounds the child when he goes outside his immediate family circle to interact with the community in the broadest sense of that term. How, then, can exposure to books alter attitudes which may be considered "undesirable"? For example, if the child is growing up in an environment where violence is more acceptable than gentleness, can exposure to a book wherein nonviolent behavior is rewarded change his attitude? Of course, there is no simple answer possible. But what we do know is that books offer a great potential for enlarging the child's horizons so that he may realize that there are alternatives to violence, choices to be made.

An interesting study done by Dr. Mark Taylor* at the University of Southern California in 1976 attempted to determine the efficacy of literature in this regard by presenting three books to six hundred first-grade children of the Montebello (California) School District, pre-testing and then post-testing for attitude change (and also for vocabulary acquisition). After exposure to these books, the children showed most encouraging changes in attitude about an important social behavior, sharing. Admittedly, no one can be certain how long-lasting these changes were, but at least there were new insights gained by the children, and once any person has looked at a situation from a fresh angle, it is improbable that he will revert completely to a less desirable attitude, at least as far as that particular area of behavior is concerned.

In effecting this kind of change, we must consider the development of empathy as a primary tool. How can books help here? If we assume that

---

*Mark Taylor, "A Study of the Effects of Presenting Literature to First-Grade Students by Means of Five Visual-Verbal Presentation Modes" (diss., University of Southern California, June 1976).

even sophisticated adults need exposure to the lives of others before they can truly empathize with them, how much truer it must be for small children whose worlds are necessarily circumscribed. We have all heard that children can be very cruel to their peers, tending, for instance, to make fun of those who seem "different" in some way. But if they have met other children through books, vicariously experiencing some of these "differences," there is some chance that whether the problem is inconsequential (such as wearing glasses or being unusually short) or serious (such as being mentally or physically handicapped) the child may have begun to develop enough feeling for "otherness" to behave with empathy.

In regard to attitudinal change we must also consider role models in books and the effect they can have in shaping future life-goal expectancy. For example, if little girls see female characters in books pictured as women engaged in activities other than homemaking, they may begin to think of themselves as Doctor Nancy rather than Nurse Nancy. And in the same way, if little boys see male characters in books working in fields not traditionally considered "masculine," they may begin to consider becoming nursery school teachers or ballet dancers without feeling strange about those choices.

When we discuss attitude, we should also consider such a prosaic matter as the attitude toward books themselves as primary learning tools. If the small child is encouraged to seek information at the very simplest level by looking at a picture dictionary or encyclopedia, this behavior might well illustrate the notion that we "look things up" if we are unsure about them, which is certainly a useful habit to acquire for future academic achievement.

4. Development of Imagination

We have spoken of empathy as part of attitudinal modification, but feeling as others feel relates also to the idea of developing the imagination. If a child is encouraged to formulate mental images, unreal as well as literal, stimulated by the books which are read to him, it is reasonable to expect that he will enlarge the ability to "put himself in another's shoes," and, of course, to escape from the mundane world as well, when that is his primary need.

Furthermore, genuinely creative thinking involves being able to synthesize extant ideas imaginatively, so that it is mandatory that a small child's powers of imagination be encouraged in preparation for learning to think creatively.

5. Specific Problems

Even when a youngster's world is quite secure in regard to basic necessities, he may still have "problems," some transitory, some more serious. For instance, many small children have very real fears about the dark; many are jealous of siblings (younger or older); some are afraid of animals. Other children have to come to terms with adoption, divorce, even death. Now, books in which characters deal successfully with these matters may not help a three- or four-year-old to attack the issue directly, as those who are enthusiastic abut bibliotherapy sometimes assert. However, what they can do for the child is to substantiate the fact that other people have these problems too, and hopefully provide a way for the child to talk about his own situation. Also, dealing with some of these areas obviously connects to empathy and attitudinal changes referred to above. For instance, reading a story about a child who is sure there are monsters under his bed may help the child who has the same fear to realize that he is not alone in being afraid.

6. Gaining Insight Through Vicarious Experience

This positive result of reading to young children is closely related to both the development of imagination and the ability to empathize with others. When presented with a great variety of books, the child must see a concomitant variety of options open to those who face identical or similar situations. Even a very young child can assimilate (at this age primarily through illustrations) that in parts of the world he has never seen people may live in surroundings totally different from his own, while at the same time sharing experiences common to all. Children in Alaska or Japan or Africa also feel loneliness or jealousy or happiness, but the only ways a child living in today's America can ever realize such commonality is through exposure to books. It may be obvious—perhaps too obvious to notice—but to a child who has never seen snow, even the simple antics of a toddler playing solitary games in that cold, white stuff may provide a broadening experience. Such insight is surely valuable.

7. Television

Closely connected to all we have said about "positive results" to be gained by reading to children is television watching, which unfortunately has become in some homes a substitute for reading. Realistically, the tube is such a convenient "baby sitter" that the temptation is great to use it that way. And as our society becomes increasingly violent, there has been a great deal of discussion about the negative effects of particular programs. However, regardless of programming and advertising (with which we may be concerned as well), the best that can be said of the "one-eyed monster" is that even at its least offensive, television engenders *mental passivity*.

In an article in *The Education Digest* by Jane M. Healy, even "Sesame Street" comes under attack. As she puts it:

> Children immersed from birth in the spicy sensory bouillabaisse of visual immediacy will not become readers unless they have soaked up the rich broth of language and reflection. Preschoolers who have been sold gimmicks in the name of learning and school-age children whose minds are habituated

to the "easy" pleasures of viewing may well find the culture of the school an alien one. Their brains, shaped by visual novelty, may gradually lose the ability to bend themselves intelligently around the written word.*

There have been several excellent books, such as Marie Winn's *The Plug-In Drug*† and Jerry Mander's *Four Arguments for the Elimination of Television*‡ that deal most convincingly with this aspect of media watching. And there have also been a great many articles written that present scientific data in support of the hypothesis that watching television produces an "alpha" state in the viewer, which in common terms means a semi-comatose condition, regardless of the program being viewed. While this may seem desirable to some adults who choose to "unwind" after a hard day's work by turning off their minds—especially for people who do not enjoy reading—it is certainly not advisable as an activity for young children who have so much of the world to absorb and are so eager to participate in experience.

It is charitable to label television watching for these youngsters only as a "waste of time." That this activity—or really lack of activity—literally teaches inattentiveness, that it fosters dependence on "being entertained," that it dulls emotional perception, and that it quite possibly plays a greater role in our current state of illiteracy than we will admit have become subjects on which most experienced school teachers could dwell at length. Certainly, when accused of "not teaching" properly in our schools, teachers might well cite the fact that by the time the average young person completes twelve grades of formal education, he or she will have spent 11,000 hours in classrooms and over 15,000 hours watching television.

Of course, with careful monitoring by adults both in regard to programs viewed and time spent in front of the set, some of the negative aspects can be minimized. If a family watches a specific program and discusses it or enjoys a particular program simply to laugh together, that is certainly not going to harm the children. However, realistically, many households keep the television on all the time without selectivity, which exacerbates the problem. What is incontrovertible is that the key word in television viewing is *passivity* as contrasted with the *interaction* which occurs when the child is being read to. Coming full circle, this interaction with a caring adult may be the most significant result of all.

---

*Condensed from *Education Week* 10 (September 19, 1990), p. 32. From Ms. Healy's book *Endangered Minds: Why Our Children Don't Think* (New York: Simon and Schuster, 1990).

†Marie Winn, *The Plug-In Drug* (New York: Viking Press, 1977).

‡Jerry Mander, *Four Arguments for the Elimination of Television* (New York: William Morrow, 1978).

Part Two

Book Selection

DEFINITIONS

Before beginning a detailed discussion of books for children in terms of specific criteria for selection, let us first define some basic terms. Webster's *Third International Unabridged Dictionary* reads: "Literature: writings in prose or verse, especially writings having excellence of form or expression and expressing ideas of permanent or universal interest." This seems acceptable if we emphasize the first clause—that is, [All] "writings in prose or verse," and then add, "specifically designed for children." Realistically, we must recognize that not all of the books under consideration will be of "permanent or universal interest," and unfortunately some of them may not even meet completely the criterion of "excellence of form or expression." Nevertheless, we will want to formulate some standards for evaluation in order to make the best choices from available materials.

Terms which will be used through the rest of this book include:

Fiction: a made-up story, usually written in prose.

Non-fiction: works offering facts or theories, usually written in prose.

Note: In some books there may be an overlap in modes, such as informational books which also tell a "fictional" story.

Poetry: a work in metrical form.

Plot: events arranged in a particular order; what "happens" in a work of fiction.

Climax: the high point in the story; in books for small children this is commonly near the end.

Characters: creations in fiction through which the author "works out" the story; in children's books, these may be human beings, animals, or inanimate objects, such as dolls, toys, articles in the environment, or those which do not exist in reality but are purely imagined.

Note: in juvenile fiction particularly, animals are frequently anthropomorphized (given the attributes of human beings so that they can talk and so on) and frequently inanimate objects are presented in this way as well.

Conflict: the struggle taking place between a character and an obstacle in the environment; or the struggle taking place between two

25

or more characters; or the struggle taking place between two opposing forces within a single character.

Theme: the main idea of a work.

Style: the mode of expression in terms of vocabulary, syntax, and so on; in books for young children, this must be expanded to include illustration.

Setting: the time or period in which the story takes place and the locale in which it happens.

Tone: the writer's attitude toward his subject.

Point of View: the "voice" in which fiction is written. Varieties would include the first-person storyteller, or, most often utilized in books for small children, the omniscient viewpoint wherein the storyteller (author) knows and reveals what every character is thinking at all times.

Rhythm: a uniform or patterned recurrence of a beat or accent.

Rhyme: identity of sound, especially used with the ends of words or lines of verse.

Motif: a theme, character, or verbal pattern which recurs.

GENERAL EXPECTATIONS BY AGE LEVELS

Keeping in mind that each child is a unique individual, it is still possible to schematize in a general way what may be expected of most children from birth to the time they are in first or second grade. In this way, we can formulate an overall view of what kinds of materials should be of interest to them at each stage of development.

AGE	CHARACTERISTICS	TYPES OF MATERIAL
0–1 year	Gradually becomes aware of environment and people from first eye-focusing to overt reactions.	May begin to show interest in large, brightly colored pictures. By end of first year should enjoy some simple Mother Goose rhymes, such as "patty cake."

AGE	CHARACTERISTICS	TYPES OF MATERIAL
1–2 years	Begins to understand constancy of objects; starts to grasp idea of "cause and effect." May begin to use words connecting them to objects or people.	By eighteen months should be interested in books picturing familiar objects (such as ball, dog, doll, etc.) one or two on a page. Heavy cardboard or washable cloth books best at this age. By age two should enjoy tactile books in which he can actually "touch" objects pictured and get sense of texture. Should enjoy simple rhymes, especially accompanied by actions.
2 years	Verbal fluency shows marked increase.	Likes books with repetitions, cumulative stories with simple plot-lines. May enjoy books requiring response and involvement.
2–2½ years	Further verbal fluency develops; may talk to himself, repeating phrases from books.	Enjoys "funny" books; simple nonsense verse. May pretend characters in books are alive (pat dog, kiss doll, and so on). Wants same book repeated again and again. Begins to examine books independently.
2½–3 years	Begins to talk in phrases and even sentences. May make up stories; may "read" to others; some memorization evident.	Books can be longer, more complex. Child can now listen in a "group." Enjoys verbal humor and imaginative stories about "real" people. Begins to show interest in simple informational books, such as alphabet or concept books.

AGE	CHARACTERISTICS	TYPES OF MATERIAL
3½–4 years	Imagination develops; language becomes more sophisticated. May ask for explanations. Wants to be independent; sometimes explores outside immediate environment. Plays more with others in group, rather than parallel play. May become aware of problems, such as illness, divorce, death. May show definite preferences about what he wants to hear.	Longer stories with more plot involvement become popular toward end of period. Enjoys folktales and fairy tales. Enjoys books with explanations of how things work, natural phenomena, and so on. Likes exaggeration and understands difference between reality and fantasy. Begins to enjoy unrhymed verse.
4–5 years	May have imaginary playmates. Shows interest in other children's activities. Interest in puppets, felt-board pieces, and so on grows. May begin to recognize words in books and on signs. Can usually count aloud. Interested in animals, wild and domestic.	Enjoys a wide variety of books. Tends to "study" illustrations carefully and critically. Enjoys books about unfamiliar people and places. By age five may show "reading readiness" through voluntary recognition of words and numerals. May like wordless picture books that "tell a story," which child may then "read" to other, younger children.
5–6 years	Depending on school experience, may be very social. Shows growing interest in world outside the immediate environment. May memorize story and repeat as though "reading." Enjoys participatory activities such as making puppets, doing creative dramatics, and so on.	Likes old favorites, but may readily accept new books. May enjoy books in series if the first one has been especially enjoyable. May accept "chapter" concept—progressing from one chapter (or story) to next after a time lapse. Likes to make personal choices in library, for instance. May actually begin to read books independently.

As a glance at these very general schemata will show, there is an entirely logical rule applicable to selecting books appropriate to the age of the child or children being read to. This may be condensed to: "The younger the child, the simpler and more literal the material should be." However, we must allow for variations from child to child, and from group to group, depending on past experience with books. It is to be expected that a preschooler who has been exposed to books from infancy, for example, will be interested in more complicated plots and be ready to spend longer periods of time being read to at age three than a child to whom read-alouds are a totally new experience. However, even within individual families with identical exposure patterns, there may be discernible differences from child to child and strong preferences without apparent cause. The task of the concerned adult is to make appropriate materials available and enjoy them with the developing child at each level.

INAPPROPRIATE MATERIALS

1. Condensations and Bowdlerized Versions.

In an effort to give children "the best," at the earliest possible time, we are sometimes tempted to offer condensed or bowdlerized versions of classics which seem too complicated in their original form. However, this should be avoided, since if we give youngsters the opportunity to enjoy being read to from their earliest years, they will in all probability grow into appreciation of more complex works as they mature. Watered-down versions have the same relationship to the originals as one-page plot summaries have to complete works in adult literature, with even less reason for their use.

2. Readers

In discussing inappropriate materials, we must mention the understandable temptation, especially toward the end of the preschool years, when a child seems ready to read, and may in fact actually *be* reading at a very simple level, to use "beginning readers" for read-alouds. However, in general, it is wise to avoid these "I Can Read" books for a very logical reason. Even the best of them have been created for a very specific purpose, one quite different from literary goals. These readers are primarily designed for reinforcement of word recognition; many of them feature lists of words at the end, showing the exact number of times a given word has been repeated in the text. And there is nothing wrong with this format—*for the practice of reading skills.* However, the vocabulary in such books must be kept within the grasp of a young child reading to himself, so the words used are not chosen to enrich his stock of more complicated expressions, but to reinforce instead what he already knows.

This same appropriate simplicity applies to sentence structure, style, and other literary elements as well. Granted we have come a long way from "See Spot run. Spot is running. See." Nevertheless, books classed as beginning readers should not be placed in competition with those written to be read *to children* who are not yet able to read them independently, but are entirely able to understand, appreciate, and enjoy more advanced materials. There is one notable exception to the suggestion that "readers" not be used as books to read aloud, and that is in the area of certain nonfictional books, particularly those dealing with aspects of scientific information. In order to keep the level of material simple enough for a four- or five-year-old child to understand— say, *Where does the rain come from?* or *What makes a seed grow into a flower?*—and still keep it entirely accurate, it is necessary to turn to books which are written rather simply, planned for first or second graders to read independently.

3. Books in Series

Sometimes a character is created (such as Harry the Dirty Dog or Babar the Elephant) which is so appealing to children that the author continues to use him as protagonist in additional books. Many of these are a source of continued delight as the child looks forward to adventure after adventure in which his familiar friend is pictured. One note of caution, however, is in order. If after reading two or three books in such a series, it seems to the discerning adult that the books no longer meet the standards of the original in terms of other literary elements—plot, theme, and so on—it might be wise to suspect that it is only commercialism at work, not literature. Unfortunately, some very well-known "characters" have been vulgarized in certain modern series so that even though the original was delightful, the current renditions are not the same calibre, although at first sight this may not be apparent. As always, it is necessary to check carefully before making assumptions about quality.

4. What About Stereotypes?

Without going deeply into the negative aspects of stereotypes as a means of setting up "standardized conceptions" of various groups, ideas which are frequently erroneous and often denigrating, we will want to avoid stereotypes if only to give children the widest view possible, allowing maximum opportunity for choices and options. Therefore, it is incumbent on the adults who select books for and with youngsters to exercise judgment about and avoidance of books which disparage any group—racial, ethnic, religious, or sexual. The label "censorship" has little meaning when we are talking about books for youngsters, unless we want to consider the elimination of some material, usually published before our society was sensitized to racism, for example, as censorship. Few adults today would want to read aloud from such a piece as *Stories of Little Brown Koko,* published in 1940, which begins:

> Once there was a little brown boy named Little Brown Koko. He was the shortest, fattest little Negro you could ever imagine. He had the blackest, little woolly head and great big round eyes, and he was the prettiest brown color, just like a bar of chocolate candy. Little Koko's Mammy thought him the most beautiful little boy in the whole wide world. Oh, he was a beautiful little brown boy, all right, but he had one bad habit. He was greedy. Why, compared to Little Brown Koko, a pig should be called a well-mannered gentleman. One day Little Brown Koko's nice, good, ole, big, black Mammy made a big seven-layer cake. . . .*

This example and others equally blatant seem to leap out from the page. However, sometimes more subtle writing may make it a little more difficult to recognize prejudice. We must, therefore, be constantly aware of the possibility even by inference of stereotypes, since a small child with limited experience may well accept what is presented to him as "the way things/people are."

Certainly we must avoid didacticism too, because books written primarily to "teach" a particular point of view or to illustrate a principle of "correct" behavior may have little literary value. It would seem that the wisest course is to select books which do not covertly or overtly attempt to make statements about groups of people, but instead meet other criteria for excellence.

5. Sexist Books

Much more widespread than the pejorative views of races, ethnic groups, or religions, and also crossing all lines, we find what we may label "sexism." This means the arbitrary assignment of lifelong roles based on reproductive organs alone. During the past three decades particularly there has been a growing awareness of women's rights and with it an emphasis on girls participating in sports traditionally reserved for boys, of girls and women engaged in activities formerly assumed to be exclusively masculine, and so on. There is little doubt that even our language, which calls for the masculine to be used as the third person singular pronoun, has tended to make females seem the *other* sex.

Unfortunately, in an effort to ameliorate the situation, some of the books which came on the scene in the early years of the women's movement tended to emphasize sexual equality at the expense of literary quality, and some still do. Also, significantly, these books omitted for the most part one of the most repugnant results of sexual stereotyping—its effect on boys and men. Many

---

*Blanche Seale Hunt, *Stories of Little Brown Koko* (New York: Colortype Company, 1940).

writers were so busy declaring that girls and women did not have to accept their customary "feminine" roles that they failed to make an equally strong case for boys and men who chose to behave in ways not traditionally designated as "masculine." What about boys who like to play with dolls? What about boys who enjoy cooking or doing macrame? What about boys who cry when they are hurt (just as girls do!), or those who prefer ballet to football? The point, of course, is that in order to combat sexism for both girls and boys we must emphasize general human characteristics, common to males and females alike, while refusing steadfastly to accept predetermined stereotypes as though they were immutable, confusing physiological differences with role determination.

Through literature we have a unique opportunity to present nonsexist role models to children to reinforce what they should be learning in their homes and schools regarding choices open to both sexes. We must recognize, however, the unhappy fact that many of our best titles in every other respect can be considered sexist in that the male characters dominate numerically, that female characters are frequently minor and/or passive, and that even adults as pictured in these books reinforce somewhat unrealistic stereotyped views of modern men and women. Since it is impractical to eliminate every book which with careful scrutiny could be considered somewhat sexist, the next best solution seems to be the cultivation of *awareness* concerning the problem, so that as new titles which eschew all traces of covert sexism appear, we choose those books, provided, of course, that they meet other criteria for high quality. Meanwhile, frank discussion with the children themselves can help clarify the situation for them. As one four-year-old boy said after hearing a story which involved a girl playing baseball, "My brother's team has won more games since my cousin Barbara pitches for them."

A VERY SPECIAL CONSIDERATION: ILLUSTRATION

As indicated previously, all books which are useful for young children must be profusely illustrated, and so it is pointless to designate them as anything but picture books. In this sense they are quite different from books meant for older children or adults, books which may or may not have pictures, but which (except for particular titles, such as *Life's Book of World War II,* for example), in no way depend on illustration to tell a story or clarify a concept. Therefore, for young children's books, we should consider the illustrations as intrinsic and carefully judge the artwork along with the other elements of style. And let us state quite frankly that *art* is the correct term here, since some of the foremost graphic artists create their work for superior children's books. It is a very purposeful creation, too, since young children themselves in an unhampered environment show a wide range of responses to the elements of art and demonstrate wide acceptance of various "styles," showing great aesthetic sensitivity. By the same token, if they are presented with a preponderance of inferior visual impressions, a negative effect upon the development of taste and aesthetic enjoyment may result. It is once more a matter of standards. We must know what constitutes superior work in order to recognize it and to avoid inferior varieties.

Possibly the most prevalent characteristic of poor artwork is the stereotyped illustration. MacCann and Richard in *The Child's First Books* describe it vividly:

> The illustrator is usually conforming to derivative criteria. He duplicates a formula already known and familiar to himself and to the consumer. . . . Animals are either anthropomorphized or drawn so that they resemble their stuffed-toy counterparts. Children and adults are drawn in costumes designed to defy period labeling; little girls have very full skirts and boys have short pants or are schematized in some similar fashion. The individualization of characters is accomplished by a cartoon-like overstatement of features.*

Further, they quote illustrator Nicholas Mordinoff, who says, ". . . sweetness has often been used as a substitute for feeling and intelligence."†

In stereotyped illustration, outlining is usually done in uniform black (like a coloring book), there is very little attention paid to spatial relationships, and blatant color is used to indicate the "center of interest." However, as MacCann and Richard point out, this stereotyped illustration has the broadest public acceptance since it is "familiar."

To comprehend the difference between inferior and superior illustration, one need only look at a scene showing Snow White and the seven dwarfs in a Walt Disney version of that story and then look at the edition which features illustrations done by Nancy Ekholm Burkert. In the first, Snow White bears more than a faint resemblance to Cinderella in another Disney book, whereas in Burkert's picture we have not only a more aesthetically pleasing illustration, but also one evocative of the individual characters in *this* story, set in *this* unique time and place. It is no wonder that this is so—since the Burkert illustrations are based on authenticity of detail, even down to the embroidery on Snow White's apron and the patterns of crockery on the table, whereas the Disney version merely reproduces the cartoon-like characters and setting from the movie.

But if we reject the stereotype, how shall we judge what may be unfamiliar and unique? First, we must realize that each artist has his/her own highly individual view of reality, his own interpretation, as it were, and by objectifying

---

*Donnarae MacCann and Olga Richard, *The Child's First Books: A Critical Study of Pictures and Texts* (New York: H. W. Wilson Company, 1973).

†Nicholas Mordvinoff, "Caldecott Award Acceptance," *Horn Book* (August 1952): 222.

for us his most subjective feelings, he creates a work which is truly nonrepeatable. It may be done in many colors, shades of one color, black and white, or sepia tones; it may be objective, nonobjective, or abstract; it may use light and shadow in completely realistic or entirely unrealistic ways. In short, the artist may use color, shape, line, texture, and the arrangement of these components in any way which seems appropriate. He may elect to use any one of the available media from woodcuts to pastels, from collage to gouache, or any combination of these. And he may even prefer to use creative photography or to combine that mode with drawings or paintings. Whatever the style utilized, the test for superior illustration must hinge on the question of whether or not the pictures are *complementary to the other elements of composition.*

What does this concept imply? First, the total "feeling" of the work must be considered. If the book has as its basic purpose the setting forth of concepts, such as "above-below" or "empty-full," realistic portrayals would be appropriate. If the book has as its core humor for its own sake, the drawings might well be more fanciful. If the story is set in a fairy-tale world inhabited by princesses and fairy godmothers, the illustrations should give the reader a sense of that world. If, on the other hand, it is set in Harlem where children play in the streets outside tenements, a very different style would seem more in order.

Next, since we know that children pay very close attention to pictures in their books, we need to make sure that if the illustrations are supposed to be "realistic," they represent reality accurately. For example, if a text reads that a character is wearing a red dress, the dress had better be red and not orange! This does not mean, however, that illustrations need represent reality at all. What it does suggest is that illustrations must be consistent and accurate within their own frame of reference.

Finally, young children seem to prefer pictures which are integrated into the page design so that they appear above or alongside the written text which is being illustrated, not on the page following.

The same rules apply to illustration as to other matters of style in regard to differences within the two-to-eight age range. In general, very small children may not be able to appreciate illustrations which are abstract or those which are too "busy." Most youngsters below two and a half may be puzzled by the notion of perspective since they need experience to acquire visual literacy in order to "understand" that a small tree in the distance is supposed to be farther away than a larger one in the foreground. However, with exposure and perhaps explication by the adult, they catch on rather quickly.

What we want to look for in picture books then are illustrations which are not stereotyped, which vary according to the demands of each individual book, and which provide a galaxy of fresh and original artwork for the child's enjoyment and aesthetic development. Beni Montresor defines a picture book as "A book whose content is expressed through its images,"* and this rule-of-thumb seems applicable to all books we select. Exposure to superior imagery seems a sensible way to reinforce verbal content as the adult presents books to small children.

Closely related to this subject of illustration is the topic of the format of these books. Title pages are important as they frequently give an idea of the book's subject. Generally, large type, widely spaced, with generous margins on all sides is inviting, and double-page spreads are popular. Sometimes a particular book will lend itself to an unusual treatment, as in Virginia Lee Burton's *The Little House* where the type follows the winding road described in the text, or the very special calligraphy so effectively used in the Babar books.

If possible, strong binding and high quality paper are desirable to insure long life, and even in paperback editions there are differences of quality in these respects which should be noted. For the infant-toddler, cardboard or washable cloth books are a necessity, and where there are participatory activities involved, as in *Pat the Bunny,* damage can be minimized only by sturdy construction. Pop-up books giving the effect of three dimensions can be fun too, but these and some other novel formats are less durable than more conventionally bound books. Fortunately, most books which are worth selecting are well designed, an important consideration since small children do not have the experience to realize that "You can't tell a book by its cover."

USE YOUR LIBRARY

It is a good idea to begin taking toddlers to the public library on a regularly scheduled basis so that the widest possible choice is made available to them from the beginning. Unfortunately, some adults hesitate to make use of this facility because they fear embarrassment when the two- or three-year-old behaves in a normally "noisy" manner. Be assured that children's sections do not require the solemn quiet of adult reading rooms, and, in fact, most public libraries plan story hours, puppet shows, and other activities specifically designed to involve small children in the world of literature as soon as possible.

A child should have his own personal library too, made up first of baby books and then augmented by those titles which the individual child has chosen repeatedly when presented with a broad selection.

Many of the very best books have been reproduced in paperback also, and some excellent titles are published as inexpensive paperback editions from the first. These books are less durable than the cloth-bound editions, of course, but less costly and quite satisfactory for ordinary home use. The same standards

---

*Beni Montresor, "Caldecott Award Acceptance," *Horn Book* (August 1965): 371.

for book selection should be applied to the paperbacks as to all other books, so that they are not chosen for price alone.

SOME SPECIFICS FOR SELECTING FICTION

As a first major division, let us consider the broad category that would include all stories, generally written in prose, without any specific teaching goals in mind. Informational books written as "stories" for young children will be discussed separately since these books have certain characteristics different from storybooks, although, as we shall see, they may share some of the same elements.

Keeping in mind the general rule about increased complexity as the child matures, let us look in some detail at the literary elements briefly defined earlier. To illustrate specifically how these "operate" we will use an old favorite, *The Story of Ferdinand* by Munro Leaf, published in 1936, as an example.

1. Plot

Just as in any good fiction, plots for children's books should be clearly arranged and come to a climax. If the book merely recounts events with no particular high point, the typical response could be, "So what?" The major difference between a story line for an adult book and a child's (in addition to intricacy and length, of course) is that in books for young children there is no use made of flashbacks or any other literary device which interferes with the clear line from beginning through the middle to the end. *Ferdinand* begins when the bull is young, growing up with his brothers, and tells of his early preference for "sitting under a cork tree and just smelling the flowers," rather than behaving as the other bulls do—butting and snorting and fighting. It explains how he grows up, still wanting only to sit peacefully under his favorite tree, then goes on to recount how the "men in funny hats" come from Madrid looking for the fiercest bull to fight in the bullfights. Not interested in the competition to be chosen, Ferdinand starts to walk toward his tree when he unknowingly sits on a bee who stings him. This leads logically to his overtly "fierce" behavior, which in turn causes the men to choose him and cart him away to Madrid.

Next, the human participants at the arena are shown and briefly explained. There are "the lovely ladies with flowers in their hair" in the grandstands; there are the *Banderilleros* "with long sharp pins with ribbons on them to stick in the bull and make him mad." Then come the *Picadores* "who rode skinny horses and had long spears to stick in the bull and make him madder." And finally, the *Matador*, who "had a red cape and a sword and was supposed to stick the bull last of all." All of the human participants are terrified of "Ferdinand the Fierce," who hesitantly comes into the ring, only to sit down and smell the ladies' flowers, refusing to fight and frustrating the blood-thirsty men who had anticipated a battle. The climactic line could be, "The *Matador* was so mad he cried because he couldn't show off with his cape and sword." Following quickly, the story's conclusion shows Ferdinand returning to his home, resuming his usual activity—just sitting under his favorite cork tree, "smelling the flowers." The final line reads: "He is very happy."

2. *Characters*

As the *protagonist* (main character) this bull is created with a distinct personality, or what we would term in adult literature, dimension. He is very briefly anthropomorphized in an early scene which shows his mother concerned because Ferdinand is "different" from her other children, asking him, "Why don't you run and play with the other little bulls and skip and butt your head?" But because she is a wise mother, she accepts his reply, "I like it better here where I can sit just quietly and smell the flowers." Except for this short episode, Ferdinand behaves like a bull, albeit a rather unusual one, rather than a human being.

3. *Conflict*

In this fairly simple tale there is an obvious difference between Ferdinand's desire for peace and tranquility and the presumptions made by those in his environment that he will welcome conflict by participating in the bullfight. He is not shown to be afraid, merely uninterested in combative behavior, as his siblings are. And of course, he has his way in the end; in other words, he wins the conflict.

4. *Theme*

Without explication the average three-year-old understands quite clearly the main idea of this story; namely, that each of us is a unique individual and should be allowed to follow his own inner voice to fulfill himself. In this particular book too, the main character is a bull, commonly stereotyped as somewhat fierce, but behaving here quite differently, whereas the traditionally macho men connected with bullfighting are at one point afraid, and later frustrated because they cannot "perform" according to expectation.

5. *Style*

In *Ferdinand* linguistic and illustrative styles are completely integrated. For example, when the men from Madrid first come to look over the potential fighting bulls, Ferdinand is on his way to his favorite cork tree to sit down. On the following page, the text reads, "He didn't look where he was sitting and instead of sitting on the nice cool grass in the shade, he sat on a bumble bee." The accompanying picture has as its center of interest the bee sitting on a flower, looking balefully toward a view of Ferdinand's rear end, followed on the next page by text that reads, "Well, if you were a bumble bee and a bull sat on you, what would you do? You would sting him. And that is just what this bee did to Ferdinand." The illustration here shows only the startled face of the bull, a few hairs standing up on his neck, nostrils dilated, and one eye (in profile) wide open. Then Leaf writes, "Wow! Did it hurt! Ferdinand jumped up with a snort. He ran around puffing and snorting, butting and pawing the ground as if he were crazy," and the accompanying illustration shows the deflated bee at the lower left hand corner of the page with the flying hoofs of the bull *above* the cloud formation which appeared in normal position on the preceding page. While the language level is not unduly complicated, words like "puffing," "snorting," "butting," and "pawing" are very descriptive and are made meaningful to the small child through the accompaniment of pictures which show Ferdinand in action.

6. Setting

The time factor is indefinite, so it is introduced in this book by the familiar phrase, "Once upon a time . . ." and continues with a statement of locale,"in Spain. . . ." Robert Lawson, the illustrator, using black India ink drawings with plenty of white space where appropriate, creates the world of rural Spain so precisely that each picture is informative, expertly combining realistic elements with such fanciful ones as having the corks hang from the tree in bunches like fruit.

7. Tone

Munro Leaf, the author, tells a straightforward story in an appropriate narrative style with no overt attempt to criticize bullfighting. Still, one gets the strong impression that his sympathy does not lie with the "five men in very funny hats," and again Lawson's pictures of these characters reinforces this judgment, thus complementing the text superbly. One of the men resembles a pig; another has a black patch over one eye; a third has a trim on his hat picturing an angel ministering to a dead bull. Ferdinand, on the other hand, is always shown as though content—except when stung by the bee—and even then he is only startled, not belligerent.

8. Point of View

So that the reader (and the listener) is aware at all times of what all the characters think and what motivates their actions, an omniscient point of view is used throughout.

Like so many other children's stories which have become "classics" because youngsters have continued to enjoy them for a very long time, *The Story of Ferdinand* meets all of the standards for selection. It tells an exciting story; it never preaches its theme, but makes the point clear instead through context; it has a main character with whom a child can identify and empathize; and it exemplifies the principle of text and illustration perfectly blended.

We can all think of many other books which have stood the test of time, noting that although Beatrix Potter's *Tale of Peter Rabbit,* Watty Piper's *The Little Engine That Could,* and Margaret Wise Brown's *Goodnight Moon* (as examples) differ in every way from *The Story of Ferdinand* and from each other, each qualifies as a superior picture book because each in its own way meets the same criteria for excellence.

A CHECK LIST FOR EXCELLENCE

To test for high quality in new fictional books, we might make judgments based on answers to the following questions:

1. Does the book have an interesting plot?
2. Is that plot the correct level of complexity to match the age of the child or children to whom the story is being read?
3. Does the story have a clear line of development—beginning, middle, climax, then ending?
4. Is the theme or main idea made clear within the context of the book, not by didactic insistence?
5. Are the characters, or at least the main characters, well-rounded and unique?
6. If these characters are really "people in fur," is this done without condescension?
7. Is the setting—time and place—adequately described verbally? pictorially?
8. Is the style appropriate to this particular book both verbally and pictorially?
9. Are the illustrations complementary to the text? Are they on the same page as the verbal text, especially for very young children?
10. Are the illustrations aesthetically pleasing in themselves?
11. Does the book avoid stereotyping of every kind?

And, when all is said and done, does the child *enjoy* the book? If it is requested over and over again, the question is adequately answered. Generally, if the adult reading the book likes it and is enthusiastic, the child will take a positive view. However, if for any reason (sometimes one not known to the child himself), a youngster seems uninterested or negative even about a book beloved by the parent or teacher, it is wise to lay that book aside, at least temporarily. Conversely, if a child selects a book in the library which seems inappropriate, but to which he seems attracted, the adult should respect that choice. After all, if enough variety is presented from the beginning, children tend to develop a taste for superior works, and if one child's preference varies from another child's, that very individuality has value in itself.

ANNOTATED FICTIONAL BOOK LISTS

In the following sections many titles are listed and annotated to fulfill specific areas of interest. However, these are in no sense intended as prescriptions, only as guidelines. In most of the sections, books suitable for the upper end of the age range are marked with two asterisks (**), but all titles should be used with flexibility to allow for individual differences, keeping in mind that although human beings share a great many characteristics in common, they also present an almost infinite variety within that commonality, and that is as it should be.

First Books and Nursery Rhymes

Among these there are several varieties. There are the "baby" books which are generally very short, simple, and printed on virtually indestructable heavy board. Such books may have no story line at all, but they do serve an important purpose. At the very simplest level they give the small child notions which adults take for granted. For example, the child will begin to understand right side up versus upside down; he will get the idea of how to turn pages; and he will start to see the connection between pictures—even one to the page— and the real world around him. Some of these also include tactile experiences which are stimulating to even the youngest child.

Also included in "first" books are those that tend to be short, but that usually tell a story, albeit a simple one, and that are printed on paper, not board. At this level children seem to enjoy repetition of both ideas and words. A good example would be *Little Gorilla* by Ruth Bornstein. On each page the little gorilla is shown loved by all the animals of the forest; then he grows up and has his first birthday, and all the animals show their continued affection for him by giving him a party.

One caveat: For these "first" books, it seems natural to read them to toddlers as bedtime stories, which is fine, but we must be sure not to inadvertently connect the idea of reading and going to sleep! To avoid this pitfall, it is advisable to offer books to the child from the earliest age at which he or she will sit quietly even for five or ten minutes and then reread a favorite book at bedtime.

Alphie's Feet, by Shirley Hughes. Alphie is proud of being able to put his new boots on by himself, but wonders why they feel funny. An "R" and an "L" help him to correct the error.

All Gone!, by Sarah Garland. A favorite expression of the very young with illustrations that show why it's so popular.

Are You My Mother?, by P. D. Eastman. A tiny bird tumbles out of his nest and goes on a search for his mother, asking everyone and everything the question until he finally ends up back in the nest.

Ask Mr. Bear, by Marjorie Flack. Danny asks each animal in turn what he should give his mother for her birthday. Finally, Mr. Bear gives him the answer which pleases his mother.

Avocado Baby, by John Burningham. The Hargraves' baby simply does not grow until he eats an amazing avocado which appears mysteriously in the family fruit bowl. Then everything changes.

The Baby Blue Cat Who Said No, by Ainslie Pryor. One little cat in a family of four knows only one word—NO. But Mother Cat deals with her playful baby with love.

Baby in the Box, by Frank Asch. A first book which rhymes box, fox, and ox.

The Baby's Catalogue, by Janet and Allan Ahlberg. With great humor the authors have pictured all the people, objects, and activities of babies, from eating to playing, from looking in the mirror to bathing.

The Baby's Lap Book, by Kay Chorao. A beautifully illustrated anthology of familiar nursery rhymes.

Bear, by Juan Wijngaard. A board book with almost no words shows a bear doing things which are typical activities for a baby.

Bear Shadow, by Frank Asch. Bear tries to get rid of his shadow, but without success until the sun changes its position in the sky and he can "make a deal" with his shadow.

Benny Bakes a Cake, by Eve Rice. Benny helps his mother make his birthday cake, but Ralph, his dog, pulls it off the table. Benny's daddy saves the day when he comes home with a birthday cake.

The Best Toy of All, by Fran Manushkin, illustrated by Robin Ballard. A book for the very young who discover that Mama and Papa are the best toys of all.

Betsy and the Chicken Pox, by Gunilla Wolde. Betsy's baby brother has chicken pox, so Betsy paints spots on herself to get some attention. When they are washed off, there are real spots underneath. Now both Betsy and her brother must stay in bed.

Betsy's Baby Brother, by Gunilla Wolde. An accurate reflection of a small girl with a new baby brother.

Betsy's First Day at Day Care, by Gunilla Wolde. Betsy is about three years old and her experiences in this and other Betsy books will seem familiar to this age group.

Better Not Get Wet, Jesse Bear, by Nancy White Carlstrom, illustrated by Bruce Degen. Despite Mama and Papa's repeated warnings, Jesse tries everything to get wet. Finally he is allowed to go into his little plastic pool and Papa Bear uses the hose on him.

Bright Eyes, Brown Skin, by Cheryl Willis Hudson and Bernette G. Ford, illustrated by George Ford. Four African-American children romp through this book, telling about their physical characteristics. Based on a poem written by Ms. Hudson in 1979.

The Box with Red Wheels, by Maud and Miska Petersham. The garden gate is open and all the curious animals come in to look into the strange red box. What's in it?

Brown Bear, Brown Bear, What Do You See?, by Bill Martin, Jr., illustrated by Eric Carle. A great book to teach colors with humor. A companion book to *Polar Bear, Polar Bear, What Do You Hear?*

Busy, Busy Toddlers, by Phoebe Dunn. Using the first person, each page shows a toddler doing things such as coloring, splashing in a puddle, making friends, eating, bathing, and greeting a turtle.

The Carrot Seed, by Ruth Krauss, illustrated by Crockett Johnson. Everyone said the carrot seed would not come up, but the little boy faithfully tends it, and has his reward.

The Chick and the Duckling, translated by Mirra Ginsburg, illustrated by Jose and Ariane Aruego. The chick and the duckling eggs hatch at the same time, and the chick copies every action of the duckling even when the duckling decides to swim.

Dad's Car Wash, by Harry A. Sutherland, illustrated by Maxie Chambliss. Little John gets very dirty playing with his cars and trucks, and Dad gives him a bath paralleling a car wash, while John's dinosaur washes his little toy car.

Dear Zoo, by Rod Campbell. Each page of this book for the toddler has a foldout revealing various animals, each unsuitable for a pet, until the very last one—a puppy.

Dog, by Juan Wijngaard. A board book showing a dog with everyday objects makes a very simple story for a baby.

Duck, by Juan Wijngaard. A baby duck interacts with simple objects, such as a water hose, in this board book for a baby.

Early Morning in the Barn, by Nancy Tafuri. In a wordless book all of the barnyard animals are pictured making appropriate sounds.

Emma's Pet, by David McPhail. Emma, a little bear, is complaining that she has no soft cuddly pet; then she sees one—her dad—and she runs to him, getting back the hugs she gives him.

Friends, by Helen Oxenbury. A charming board book for use with the smallest child.

Going to Sleep on the Farm, by Wendy Cheyette Lewison, illustrated by Juan Wijngaard. Wonderful illustrations show how different animals go to sleep standing, lying down, sitting on eggs, cuddled with a brood, or, if one is a small boy, in bed with some favorite toy animals.

Golden Bear, by Ruth Young, illustrated by Rachel Isadora. Golden Bear and his human companion learn to play the violin, talk to a ladybug, make mudpies, and dream together. Done in simple rhymed verse.

The Golden Egg Book, by Margaret Wise Brown, illustrated by Leonard Weisgard. A little bunny who finds an egg tries hard to get it open, but falls asleep just as the little yellow duck emerges. The two become friends and "no one is ever alone again."

Good Morning, Chick, by Mirra Ginsburg, illustrated by Byron Barton. A very simple book for the toddler about a chick, her mother, and some other barnyard animals.

Goodnight Moon, by Margaret Wise Brown, illustrated by Clement Hurd. A little bunny says goodnight to the room, the moon, and the little dollhouse, while in each picture the little mouse watches from different positions.

Goodnight, Owl!, by Pat Hutchins. During the day all the sounds of the forest keep Owl awake, so when darkness falls, Owl screeches and wakes all his friends.

** *Granfa' Grig Had a Pig and Other Rhymes Without Reason from Mother Goose,* illustrated by Wallace Tripp. Without altering any of the original rhymes, the author has succeeded in making this a hilarious rendition of Mother Goose which will appeal even to adults.

Happy Birthday, Moon, by Frank Asch. Bear and Moon exchange birthday gifts and both are happy.

Happy Birthday, Sam, by Pat Hutchins. It is Sam's birthday, but he still cannot reach the light switch, the bathroom taps, or the front doorknob. Then his grandfather's gift arrives and solves his problem.

Have You Seen My Duckling?, by Nancy Tafuri. A mother duck with seven little ducklings suddenly has only six. She asks all her animal friends about the missing baby who finally shows up.

Here Are My Hands, by Bill Martin, Jr., and John Archambault, illustrated by Ted Rand. In rhyme, a very simple book naming parts of the body, ending with the skin "bundling me in."

Hickory Dickory Dock, illustrated by Carol Jones. This collection of well-known nursery rhymes features peephole illustrations which make it fun to read.

Ho for a Hat!, by William Jay Smith, illustrated by Lynn Munsinger. In this delightful, rhythmic celebration of hats, the reader will find every kind of hat ever dreamed of, all tried on by a boy and his adorable dog.

How Do I Put It On?, by Shigeo Watanabe, illustrated by Yasuo Ohtomo. A darling little bear experiments with dressing himself, and finally succeeds.

I Can Build a House!, by Shigeo Watanabe, illustrated by Yasuo Ohtomo. Little Bear's efforts with blocks and pillows fail, but he finds the right material and figures out how to succeed.

I Can Ride It!, by Shigeo Watanabe, illustrated by Yasuo Ohtomo. Bear is sure that he can ride a tricycle, a two-wheel bike, and anything else with wheels; he takes tumbles, but he is learning.

I Can Take a Walk!, by Shigeo Watanabe, illustrated by Yasuo Ohtomo. Bear decides to take a walk all by himself but must be rescued by his dad from the wall he's climbed on.

I Hear, by Rachel Isadora. A first book with lovely paintings of a baby hearing sounds to which she can respond, such as a bird's chirp, a tea kettle's whistle, and a lullaby.

I See, by Rachel Isadora. A first book which illustrates beautifully the items of a typical toddler's day—a teddy bear, a stroller, some blocks, and then a bottle and a crib—"Good night."

I See, by Helen Oxenbury. On each page the little boy sees one item or person. Other board books in this series are *I Can, I Hear, and I Touch.*

I Touch, by Rachel Isadora. This charming book is a fine introduction to tactile experience for the toddler.

If All the Seas Were One Sea, illustrated by Janina Domanska. This is an imaginative retelling of the old nursery rhyme.

In a Pumpkin Shell, by Joan Walsh Anglund. This is an alphabet book giving a Mother Goose rhyme for each letter, such as "Hickety Pickety, my black hen" for letter H.

It's My Birthday!, by Shigeo Watanabe, illustrated by Yasuo Ohtomo. It's Bear's fourth birthday and he looks through the family photo album to recall his former birthdays.

Jack Goes to the Beach, by Jill Krementz. The bright photos in this board book illustrate a typical day at the beach for a small child and his family.

Just for You, by Mercer Mayer. The first of a series about an endearing animal who just happens to do everything a toddler would do. He really tries very hard!

Just Like Daddy, by Frank Asch. A very simple book about a bear family, in which the little bear does everything his father does.

Ladybug, Ladybug, by Ruth Brown. A rhymed extension of the familiar "Ladybug, ladybug, fly away home!" The imaginative illustrations evoke the countryside on a sun-drenched day.

Little Blue and Little Yellow, by Leo Lionni. Personifying colors, Lionni has them hugging and becoming green, but their families don't recognize them, so they cry until they are all blue and yellow tears. Then everyone understands and all ends happily.

Little Gorilla, by Ruth Bornstein. All the jungle animals love the little gorilla when he is a tiny thing. Then he grows into a BIG gorilla, and his friends show their love by giving him a birthday party.

The Little Mouse, the Red Ripe Strawberry, and the Big Hungry Bear, by Don and Audrey Wood, illustrated by Don Wood. A comical story with double-spread pictures which very young children love.

Lullaby, by Jane Chelsea Aragon, illustrated by Kandy Radzinski. Lavish watercolors illustrate this book in which a mother's lullaby is carried by the wind over hills and meadows, over lakes and woods to the sea, finally being transformed into the morning chirp of birds which greet the mother and child.

Max's Bath, by Rosemary Wells. Max, being very small, is a bit untidy, so his sister Ruby decides to clean him up. Note: The titles in this board-book series are all very popular with very young children. Max and his sister are irresistible.

Moongame, by Frank Asch. Little Bear learns the game of hide and seek, which he plays with all his little animal friends. Then he tries it with the moon.

Moonlight, by Jan Ormerod. In this wordless book a little girl goes through the bedtime ritual, but it's Mommy and Daddy who fall asleep first.

Mother Goose, illustrated by James Marshall. With his own particular sense of the absurd, the illustrator makes these familiar verses great fun.

Mother Goose, illustrated by Tasha Tudor. A very traditional rendition of all the Mother Goose rhymes.

The Mother Goose Book, illustrated by Alice and Martin Provensen. A traditional rendition of Mother Goose, with English-style illustrations in the mode of earlier times.

The Mother Goose Treasury, illustrated by Raymond Briggs. In 1833, Mother Goose carried this inscription: "No, no, my melodies will never die, while nurses sing, or babies cry." In this very complete version, the artist has overlooked nothing to make these verses come to life.

The Napping House, by Audrey Wood, illustrated by Don Wood. This charming cumulative tale has a surprise ending, done with great humor.

Oh, Lewis!, by Eve Rice. Little Lewis has trouble keeping his boots buckled, his jacket zipped, and his mittens on. Then he has trouble getting them off. A universal problem of the very young.

Old Mother Hubbard, by Colin and Jacqui Hawkins. A "Lift the Flap" book. As the old rhyme proceeds, each page has a lift-up flap revealing a humorous picture beneath.

Old Mother Hubbard, by Alice and Martin Provensen. The traditional verse with nontraditional illustrations.

Old Mother Hubbard and Her Wonderful Dog, illustrated by James Marshall. A deliciously humorous version of the old nursery rhyme.

On Mother's Lap, by Ann Herbert Scott, illustrated by Glo Coalson. There are two versions of this story—one in sepia tones, the other in soft pastels. Both tell of little Michael who brings all his toys and his puppy to share mother's lap with him and his baby sister. There is always room on mother's lap.

Once a Lullaby, by B. P. Nichol, illustrated by Anita Lobel. Rhymed text and illustrations describe young animals and children in moments just before they fall asleep.

Pat the Bunny, by Dorothy Kunhardt. In this early tactile book the youngest child can participate in activities dear to the hearts of youngsters, such as playing peek-a-boo, smelling flowers, and so on.

Play Rhymes, collected and illustrated by Marc Brown. Old favorites with music at the end of the book makes this a handy collection.

The Poky Little Puppy, by Janette Sebring Lowrey, illustrated by Gustaf Tenggren. Five little puppies dig a hole and go for a walk in the wide, wide world, but when they count themselves, there is always one who lags behind and misses all the good things to eat.

Polar Bear, Polar Bear, What Do You Hear?, by Bill Martin, Jr., illustrated by Eric Carle. A companion book to *Brown Bear, Brown Bear, What Do You See?* Teaches animal sounds with humor.

Poppy the Panda, by Dick Gackenbach. Katie O'Keefe's panda, Poppy, will not go to sleep until he has something nice to wear. Katie tries everything to please him, but is unsuccessful until her mother picks the perfect thing.

The Real Mother Goose, by Blanche Fisher Wright. This has a complete list of the rhymes and an alphabetical list of first lines which makes it a very useful edition.

The Runaway Bunny, by Margaret Wise Brown, illustrated by Clement Hurd. Within a framework of mutual love, a little bunny tells his mother how he will run away, and she answers his challenge by indicating how she will follow. In the end, he decides he might just as well stay where he is and be her little bunny.

Sam's Car, by Barbro Lindgren, illustrated by Eva Eriksson. Sam doesn't want to share his car with Lisa and they have an argument until Mother comes with a second car for Sam's little friend; then all is well. (Part of a series with Sam)

Sam Who Never Forgets, by Eve Rice. At exactly three o'clock Sam feeds each zoo animal what that animal enjoys eating, and Sam never forgets.

Sick in Bed, by Anne and Harlow Rockwell. A simple story for very young children, telling how a child becomes ill, is treated, and recovers.

Skyfire, by Frank Asch. Little Bear and Little Bird do not agree. Is it a rainbow with a pot of golden honey at the end, or is the sky on fire? In any case, Little Bear has his fill of honey after he has put out the fire in the sky.

Sleep Tight, by B. G. Hennessy, illustrated by Anthony Carnabuci. A bedtime read-aloud, this gentle book shows all things sleeping as night falls.

Sleepy Book, by Charlotte Zolotow, illustrated by Ilse Plume. Using animals from bears to spiders, this book illustrates beautifully how various creatures sleep, coming finally to the child in his or her cozy bed.

Spot's First Walk, by Eric Hill. Each page features a foldout as Spot goes for his first walk. There are many popular books which feature this cute puppy.

Sunshine, by Jan Ormerod. No text is necessary to understand how one small girl wakes with the sun and helps get the whole family ready for the day.

The Tawny Scrawny Lion, by Kathryn Jackson, illustrated by Gustaf Tenggren. All the animals fear the lion, who is scrawny because he chases them for his food. They suggest to Little Rabbit that he talk to Lion, and when Lion goes home with the rabbit, he decides he can fill up on carrot stew and no longer needs to catch the other animals for food.

Ten, Nine, Eight, by Molly Bang. In this unusual bedtime book, a little girl counts backward from "ten small toes all washed and warm" through numbers to "one big girl all ready for bed."

This Is Betsy, by Gunilla Wolde. The first of the stories of a very little girl and her daily activities.

Three Little Kittens, illustrated by Paul Galdone. The traditional rhyme with great illustrations.

Throw a Kiss, Harry, by Mary Chalmers. Harry, the mischievous cat, wanders away from his mother, and it takes the fire department to get him down from a roof.

Titch, by Pat Hutchins. Titch's sister Mary and his brother Pete are both older than Titch, which makes him feel left out of their activities until his little plant changes their relationship.

Tom and Pippo Make a Friend, by Helen Oxenbury. One of a charming series of Tom and Pippo stories for very young children. In this one, two children play in a sandbox and share toys.

Tortillitas Para Mama and Other Nursery Rhymes (Spanish and English on each page), translated by Margot Griego, Betsy L. Bucks, Sharon S. Gilbert, and Laurel A. Kimball, illustrated by Barbara Cooney. A traditional collection of Latin-American nursery rhymes preserved through the oral tradition.

Umbrella, by Taro Yashima. Momo is impatient for the rain to come, and she is delighted when she can finally carry her umbrella to nursery school and walk home without holding either her mother or father's hand.

The Very Busy Spider, by Eric Carle. As a little spider begins her web, each of the farm animals tries without success to divert her. Each strand of the web provides a tactile experience for the very young child as the spider completes her web and catches a fly.

The Very Hungry Caterpillar, by Eric Carle. How do butterflies come into being? Here the author imaginatively combines the process of metamorphosis with the days of the week, numbers of fruits, and ten foods dear to the hearts of children.

What a Good Lunch!, by Shigeo Watanabe, illustrated by Yasuo Ohtomo. Bear struggles with food when he tries to eat without help and ends up using his hands.

What Is It?, by Tana Hoban. Showing one familiar item to a page, such as a bib, a cup, and keys, this board book pleases the very youngest child who can identify each colorful picture.

What Sadie Sang, by Eve Rice. Sadie can walk, but she prefers to ride in her stroller. Sadie can talk too, but she prefers to sing, which she does as she goes out to do errands with her mama.

What's Inside?, by Anthea Sieveking. Great photos of toddlers discovering what's inside of drawers, the changing bag, the picnic basket, and mother's purse.

Where Does the Brown Bear Go?, by Nicki Weiss. When the lights go down, each of the animals from the cat to the brown bear goes home to bed.

Where Is It?, by Tana Hoban. A very appealing little rabbit is looking for something, which he finally finds by the end of the book.

Where's My Daddy?, by Shigeo Watanabe, illustrated by Yasuo Ohtomo. A little bear tries to find his daddy, asking all the animals he sees; but no one has time to answer, except his mommy who kisses him. Then Daddy comes home.

Who Took the Farmer's Hat?, by Joan L. Nodset, illustrated by Fritz Siebel. When the wind takes the farmer's hat, he runs after it, but the wind runs faster. He asks each animal in turn about his hat, and finally decides to replace it after he finds it being used as a bird's nest.

The Wild Baby, by Barbro Lindgren, illustrated by Eva Eriksson, adapted from the Swedish by Jack Prelutsky. Baby Ben is reckless, loud and wild. He does all the naughty things most children only dream about, but his mother loves him as only a mother can.

Your New Potty, by Joanna Cole, photos by Margaret Miller. With helpful answers to questions often asked by parents, this book shows small babies who still wear diapers, then goes on to show the potty as a gift to be used as Steffie and Ben are ready.

Zoe's Windy Day, by Barbara Reid. This wordless book shows little Zoe in different activities with her family. Note: Others in this series include *Zoe's Sunny Day*, *Zoe's Rainy Day*, and *Zoe's Snowy Day*.

Wordless Books

Books that tell a story entirely through illustration constitute a special group with values different from those having text. They contribute to the development of the child's imagination, and additionally, they make it possible for a youngster to increase his verbal fluency, since even shy children often volunteer to "tell" the story of such a book to an adult or to a younger child.

Ah-Choo, by Mercer Mayer. An elephant's sneeze changes everything.

The Adventures of Paddy Pork, by John S. Goodall. A very clever wordless book with cut-away half pages to move the story forward. One of a series about Paddy Pork.

Alligator's Toothache, by Diane DeGroat. Alligator cannot enjoy himself at a party until after the dentist has pulled his aching tooth.

Bobo's Dream, by Martha Alexander. The small dachshund, Bobo, keeps his bone due to the efforts of his "boy," and the dog dreams of returning the favor.

A Boy, a Dog, and a Frog, by Mercer Mayer. In this one the frog follows the boy and the dog home.

Carl Goes Shopping, by Alexandra Day. Another imaginative book about the wonderful weimaraner, Carl, who is the world's best babysitter.

Carl's Afternoon in the Park, by Alexandra Day. Here Carl, an extraordinary dog, takes care of both his puppy and a human baby with great affection while the human mommies have tea together.

Changes, Changes, by Pat Hutchins. Wooden blocks and two small wooden dolls change from one thing to another through rearrangements on each page.

Deep in the Forest, by Brinton Turkle. In this wordless book the characters in the original Goldilocks story are reversed. Now it is the three bears who intrude in a human domicile deep in the woods.

Do You Want to Be My Friend?, by Eric Carle. In this one the preschooler learns that we read from left to right, as the little mouse follows the larger animals and finds another little mouse by the end of the story.

Early Morning in the Barn, by Nancy Tafuri. Here all the barnyard animals make appropriate sounds to greet the day.

First Snow, by Emily Arnold McCully. As the little mouse family is going to Grandma's through the first snow of the season, one timid little mouse is afraid to try sledding, but becomes an enthusiast before the story ends.

***Free Fall,* by David Wiesner. In a really beautiful wordless book a young boy dreams of daring adventures in the company of imaginary creatures inspired by the things surrounding his bed.

Hiccup, by Mercer Mayer. Mr. and Mrs. Hippo deal with the hiccups in this almost wordless and very funny book.

I See a Song, by Eric Carle. As a violinist plays, the music forms gorgeous colored images.

Look Again, by Tana Hoban. Each page features a cut-out, showing part of the next page. But when the child sees the entire page which follows, he gets the idea that all is not what it seems at first.

***Look Again!,* illustrated by April Wilson. The reader is encouraged to spot the difference in twelve seemingly identical pairs of illustrations depicting a variety of the world's plants and animals that use shape and color to ensure their survival. There's a key to answers at the end, if needed.

Moonlight, by Jan Ormerod. Here a little girl goes through the bedtime ritual, but it is Mommy and Daddy who fall asleep first.

Mouse Around, by Pat Schories. When a tiny mouse is separated from his family, we must find him in each picture until they are reunited.

New Baby, by Emily Arnold McCully. Mice children, like humans, can resent all the attention showered on a new baby. In this wordless book we see how the young mouse reacts.

On My Beach There Are Many Pebbles, by Leo Lionni. Without words the author shows imaginatively all the shapes that pebbles can assume.

Out! Out! Out!, by Martha Alexander. A harried mother finally gets a pigeon who has flown in through the window to leave.

Overnight Adventure, by Frances Kilbourne, illustrated by Ann Powell. When some children decide to "camp" overnight in the backyard, they imagine storms and all kinds of wild animals.

Paddy's Evening Out, by John S. Goodall. Again with half pages to carry the action, this is a very funny adventure for Paddy.

The Patchwork Farmer, by Craig Brown. The farmer rips his overalls again and again doing his daily chores, so he ends up with a colorful patchwork pair.

Picnic, by Emily Arnold McCully. One little mouse is missing from the family picnic, but she's found as the truck returns.

Rosie's Walk, by Pat Hutchins. The fox is after Rosie the hen, but she doesn't know it. Unwittingly she leads him into one disaster after the other, each funnier than the last.

School, by Emily Arnold McCully. When all the older children go to school, they leave the smallest mouse at home. Curiosity, however, drives the little one to go too, so Mother has to go and pick her up.

The Snowman, by Raymond Briggs. In this charming book a little boy makes a snowman, and the two do everything together.

Sunshine, by Jan Ormerod. No text is necessary to understand how one small girl wakes with the sun and helps get the whole family ready for the day.

Take Another Look, by Tana Hoban. With holes in the middle of the pages, one might guess at what's on the next page, and usually be wrong. Seeing the whole picture is the clue.

**Topsy-Turvies: Pictures to Stretch the Imagination,* by Mitsumasa Anno. A very unusual and challenging book for the elementary school child and his parents.

Trucks, by Donald Crews. A colorful wordless book about trucks.

***Tuesday,* by David Wiesner. A wordless book which shows how frogs rise on their lily pads at night and explore nearby houses while their inhabitants sleep. Very imaginative.

A Year in the Country, by Douglas Florian. Each month on a farm is shown with appropriate activities.

Folk and Fairy Tales

In the category of fiction, there are two rather special kinds of books for children: fairy tales and folktales. Strictly speaking, fairy stories would include characters such as elves, gnomes, witches, giants, and other supernatural figures, and would tell of all manner of impossible events and fantastic outcomes.

Folktales, on the other hand, are usually stories which have come down from the oral tradition of the common people—the folk—and have been set down on paper later, but they, too, frequently feature feats of magic and otherworldly happenings.

Cinderella, for example, is considered a folktale and has versions from all over the world. In Judy Sierra's book* she retells twenty-five "Cinderella" stories from places as distant as India, Iran, Japan, and ancient Egypt, most predating the Perrault version (French, 1697), and there are a dozen more which Sierra omits for various reasons.

In addition to the well-known folk and fairy tales, there are a number

---

*Judy Sierra, *Cinderella,* illustrated by Joanne Caroselli (Oryx Press, 1992). This book, a part of the Oryx Multicultural Series, presents twenty-five versions of the tale from all over the world with notes and essays about their origins.

of noteworthy modern stories which seem also to belong in one or both of these sub-genres.

What we have done then is to combine in the list titles of both folk and fairy tales, and included more recent stories as well if they seem to belong in this category.

Many of these books involve a number of motifs which are worth mentioning.

The Youngest Child

Since quite frequently the youngest child was not thought to be a valuable addition to the family, particularly in societies which set great store by the tradition of the first-born being rather special (see any dictionary definition of "primogeniture"), it is understandable that stories would evolve to exalt the youngest member. Quite often he or she turns out to be the best-natured, the smartest, and the most fortunate, usually in a family of three children.

The Gullible Innocent

Closely connected to being the youngest child is the notion that a virtuous person may be temporarily outsmarted, but that he will eventually emerge victorious because he is "good." Tied into this motif also is the need which every small child has to triumph over those who rule him merely because they are the giants (adults) in his real world.

The Clever Animal

Sometimes this animal outsmarts other animals. If he is evil, he may come to a bad end; if he is good, all ends well for him. At times also he assists a human being who deserves his help.

The Evil Stepmother

Stemming from the fear of losing one's main source of protection through her death, the child projects what a substitute for his mother would be like. Unfortunately, this character never likes the stepchildren and frequently attempts to eliminate them completely from the family circle.

There is an element of sexism here, too, since the father never seems to protest the ill treatment of his children, but passively accepts the situation. Then, when the evil stepmother is punished (usually through death), the father who allowed her to mistreat his children is shown reunited with them—no questions asked.

Evil Is Ugly—Good Is Beautiful

Another motif which may seem negative must be carefully explained by the adult reader in terms not of physical appearance alone, but of how inner beauty equates with "good." For instance, Cinderella's stepmother and stepsisters are not pictured as ugly people in the physical sense, but their behavior makes them seem so when compared to Cinderella whose virtue makes her seem beautiful even in her ragged clothing.

Tears as a Way to Break a Spell

There may be a connection here to water as a means of purification, or this may be looked upon as an objectification of the idea that compassion itself can thwart evil and release beneficence, personified as a beautiful or handsome person. When Beauty in *Beauty and the Beast* sheds tears at the sight of the Beast dying because she has not returned from her father's home as she promised she would, he becomes the handsome prince who has been under an evil spell.

The Magical Solution to a Problem

The human desire to find a way out of a situation which seems hopeless has no doubt evoked this motif throughout a wide range of stories. Along with this goes the galaxy of characters from leprechauns to fairy godmothers who can call forth such "miracles" for the deserving.

The Pourquoi or "Why" Story

In response to natural curiosity and the need to explain phenomena in terms understandable to all, these stories which border on myth or legend appear in many cultures. Since they attempt to answer questions concretely (although the explanations are usually fantastic in the literal sense of that word), they are designated "pourquoi" stories.

The Cumulative Repetitive Story

This motif is a great favorite with small children, possibly because they can feel a sense of their own ability in that they can correctly guess what will come next, even before it is read to them. Also, of course, the rhythm that is part and parcel of the repetitive mode is pleasing in itself and sometimes quite humorous.

*   *   *

There is always the question of violence in folk and fairy tales, and there is some concern on the part of today's adults in regard to "telling children the truth," which these stories cannot be said to do. However, according to the late Dr. Bruno Bettleheim, the world-renowned child psychologist, and explained in detail in his book *The Uses of Enchantment,** there is no need for worry on either score.

In regard to violence, Dr. Bettleheim felt that these tales often meet the child's need for release of negative feelings which he is not able to express in any other way. And regarding veracity, he asserts that fairy and folktales have a different kind of "truth" from modern, realistic books, and that they meet the child's deep psychological needs better than any other type of literature.

In any case, these kinds of stories have been very popular with children for a very long time in many, many societies and have spawned a great number of modern-day books in the same mode.

Aesop's Fables, selected and illustrated by Michael Hague. Thirteen of Aesop's Fables are gorgeously illustrated in this collection, with capsulated advice at the end of each.

Akimba and the Magic Cow: An African Folktale, retold by Anne Rose, illustrated by Hope Meryman. Akimba, the poorest man in his village, is given a magic cow which gives gold coins, then a magic sheep which gives silver coins, and finally a chicken which gives eggs. Each time he leaves the animals in the care of his friend Bumba, they are stolen. How Akimba uses his magic stick to get his animals back is a very satisfying ending.

Aladdin and the Wonderful Lamp, retold by Andrew Lang, illustrated by Errol LeCain. This book recounts the tale of a poor tailor's son who becomes a wealthy prince with the help of a magic lamp that he finds in an enchanted cave.

***All of You Was Singing,* by Richard Lewis, illustrated by Ed Young. An Aztec myth told lyrically about the world's creation and the advent of music.

Always Room for One More, by Sorche Nic Leodhas, illustrated by Nonny Hogrogian. This is an old Scottish song about a generous family which keeps growing by inviting all passing travelers to join them. Then when the house literally bursts, all the strangers rebuild the house—twice the size as it was. Music at the end of the book.

The Amazing Bone, by William Steig. Little Pearl, an adorable pig, finds a talking bone in the woods, a bone which has apparently fallen out of the basket of a witch. They become friends and the bone ultimately saves Pearl's life.

---

*Bruno Bettleheim, *The Uses of Enchantment* (New York: Alfred A. Knopf, 1976).

The Amazing Pig, by Paul Galdone. In his attempt to marry the princess, the poor peasant boy makes up outrageous stories of what his pig can do. The king, who has promised his daughter to anyone who can tell him a story which he cannot believe, goes along with the tall tale, until. . . .

Anansi and the Moss-Covered Rock, retold by Eric Kimmel, illustrated by Janet Stevens. Anansi the Spider is walking through the forest when a strange moss-covered rock with magic powers catches his eye. Anansi then uses the rock to fool Lion, Elephant, Rhinoceros, Hippopotamus, Giraffe, and Zebra. But Little Bush Deer is not fooled and uses the rock to teach Anansi a lesson.

Anansi Goes Fishing, retold by Eric Kimmel, illustrated by Janet Stevens. With a "pourquoi" motif showing why spiders spin webs, this folktale tells how the lazy spider Anansi is fooled by his friend Turtle into making a net to catch a fish, which is then eaten by Turtle.

Anansi the Spider: A Tale from the Ashanti, adapted and illustrated by Gerald McDermott. The trickster Anansi has six good sons, each with a special talent that he uses to rescue Kwaku Anansi when he is in trouble. When Anansi calls upon Nyame, the God of All Things, to help him decide which son shall be rewarded with the globe of white light, Nyame decides it should remain in the sky for all to see, so we have the moon.

**Anancy and Mr. Dry-Bone,* by Fiona French. Miss Louise was very clever and very beautiful, but she had never laughed in her whole life, so she vowed to marry the first man who could make her laugh. Mr. Dry-Bone does conjuring tricks, but they don't work. Then Anancy comes along with a weird outfit, and Miss Louise makes her decision.

And Sunday Makes Seven, by Robert Baden, illustrated by Michelle Edwards. Carlos and Anna are poor, but happy; cousin Ricardo is rich, but selfish. When Carlos makes up a rhyme about the days of the week, he is richly rewarded by twelve witches, but Ricardo is punished when he tries to do the same thing (from Costa Rica).

The Ant and the Elephant, by Bill Peet. A charming story of animals, from a tiny ant to a huge elephant, who need help at one time or another, but it's only the ant and the elephant who are gracious and grateful.

Arrow to the Sun: A Pueblo Indian Tale, retold and illustrated by Gerald McDermott. A Native-American version of Christ's birth and rebirth as Boy, child of the Lord of the Sun.

**Atariba and Niguayona,* adapted by Harriet Rohmer and Jesus Guerrero Rea, illustrated by Consuelo Mendez Castillo. With both Spanish and English on each page, this is a legend of a miraculous cure from the native people of Puerto Rico.

Awful Aardvark, by Mwenye Hadithi, illustrated by Adrienne Kennaway. Why do aardvarks sleep all day and eat termites at night? In this "pourquoi" story we find the answer when aardvark's snoring annoys his larger fellow animals, who fail to dislodge him from his branch of a tree.

** *Baba Yaga: A Russian Folktale,* retold by Eric Kimmel, illustrated by Megan Lloyd. A kind little girl, Marina, is sent into the forest by her stepmother to have Baba Yaga remove the horn from her forehead. But Baba Yaga is an evil witch who plans to eat Marina. The girl escapes, but when her lazy stepsister, Marusia, tries to outwit Baba, the witch puts the horn on her forehead instead.

Baboushka and the Three Kings, by Ruth Robbins, illustrated by Nicolas Sidjakov. In this Russian folktale a poor old woman, Baboushka, decides to follow the three kings to seek the newborn Christ child, but she loses the path in the snow. Now every year she travels through the land with her gifts for small children.

Baby Rattlesnake: An Indian Tale, adapted by Lynn Moroney, illustrated by Veg Reisberg. Willful baby rattlesnake throws tantrums because he wants a rattle before he's ready, and he misuses it, learning a valuable lesson.

** *Beauty and the Beast,* retold by Deborah Apy, illustrated by Michael Hague. Through her great capacity to love, a kind and beautiful maiden releases a handsome prince from the spell which has made him an ugly beast.

** *Beauty and the Beast,* illustrated by Jan Brett. This is the same story with magnificent illustrations.

** *Beauty and the Beast,* retold and illustrated by Carol Heyer. Full-page paintings make this a truly beautiful retelling of the traditional tale.

** *Beauty and the Beast,* retold and illustrated by Warwick Hutton. In this version of the story the costumes and settings are more modern than in the traditional books.

** *Beauty and the Beast,* retold by Marianna Mayer, illustrated by Mercer Mayer. In this version, Beauty has three brothers as well as two selfish sisters, but the basic story of how goodness and love breaks the evil spell remains. A little longer than some other editions, but with truly gorgeous paintings.

Big Anthony and the Magic Ring, by Tomie De Paola. This time Big Anthony, Strega Nona's helper, steals her magic gold ring so that he can become a handsome lothario, dance the tarantella, and have a little nightlife. But when he cannot remove the ring, he's in trouble again.

Bony-Legs, by Joanna Cole, illustrated by Dirk Zimmer. Baba Yaga, the traditional Russian witch, is outwitted by Sasha, a kind little girl who has help from animal friends.

Borreguita and the Coyote, by Verna Aardema, illustrated by Petra Mathers. A Mexican folktale which tells how a clever little lamb repeatedly outwits the coyote who plans to eat her.

The Boy Who Held Back the Sea, by Lenny Hort, illustrated by Thomas Locker. Here the traditional tale of the boy who saved Holland by putting his finger in the dike is illustrated in the manner of the great Dutch artists.

The Bremen Town Musicians, by the Brothers Grimm, illustrated by Josef Palecek. The traditional tale of the donkey, dog, cat, and rooster who escape from their homes when they are in danger of being killed. They then scare robbers from a house which they take over.

The Bremen Town Musicians, retold and illustrated by Ilse Plume. With quite modern illustrations, this is the traditional tale of the four animals who, on their way to Bremen, scare away the robbers and take over the little house in the woods.

Bringing the Rain to Kapiti Plain, by Verna Aardema, illustrated by Beatriz Vidal. In rhyme and using the rhythm of "The House That Jack Built," this African folktale tells of a man who shoots an arrow into a big black cloud to end the severe drought that is causing havoc on Kapiti Plain.

Burgoo Stew, by Susan Patron, illustrated by Mike Shenon. Five rough, dirty, naughty boys decide they will take whatever food Billy Que has, even if they have to steal it. But Billy shows them (with a magic stone) how to make Burgoo Stew instead and they eat heartily.

Caleb and Kate, by William Steig. An amusing tale of the carpenter Caleb, who, after quarreling with his wife Kate, angrily leaves his house and goes into the woods where a wicked witch turns him into a dog.

Caps for Sale, retold and illustrated by Esphyr Slobodkina. This story of the peddler, his caps, and the monkeys who take them while he is asleep has everything young children love: plot, drama, suspense, humor, warmth, and simplicity.

The Cat Who Loved to Sing, by Nonny Hogrogian. By making one trade after another the cat finally gets what he really wants and needs—a mandolin with which he can accompany himself.

**Chanticleer and the Fox: From Chaucer's Canterbury Tales,* adapted and illustrated by Barbara Cooney. The traditional tale of the conceited rooster who believes the fox's flattery and sings with his eyes closed, which nearly costs him his life.

**The Chinese Mirror,* adapted from a Korean folktale by Mirra Ginsburg, illustrated by Margot Zemach. A villager returns home from a voyage to China with a strange treasure which he keeps in his trunk—a mirror. When his family discovers it, there is wild confusion as each person sees a different stranger peering out.

The Child's Story Book, by Kay Chorao. A number of old favorites, such as "Jack and the Beanstalk," "The Wonderful Teakettle," and "Hansel and Gretel" are simply told and beautifully illustrated.

Cinderella, by Charles Perrault, illustrated by Marcia Brown. The traditional story of the stepdaughter who marries the prince, but here she forgives her stepsisters and they marry two lords of the court on the day of her wedding.

Cinderella, adapted and illustrated by Paul Galdone. The two stepsisters mistreat Cinderella, but she ends up with the prince and she forgives her sisters by the story's end.

Clever Kate, adapted from a story by the Brothers Grimm by Elizabeth Shub, illustrated by Anita Lobel. A very funny tale of how honest, well-meaning Kate, who does not think too logically, truly earns the title "clever."

Clever Tom and the Leprechaun, retold and illustrated by Linda Shute. Tom Fitzpatrick is determined to make the little leprechaun he catches tell him where there is gold, and the little man agrees, taking Tom to a field of boliauns. "Under this one," says the leprechaun, "is the gold." Tom goes to get his shovel, first tying a bright red garter to the plant, but when he returns, all plants have red garters, so he is foiled.

**The Contest: An Armenian Folk Tale,* adapted and illustrated by Nonny Hogrogian. This very amusing story tells of two robbers who discover that they are both engaged to the same girl. They decide to hold a contest with the young lady as the prize for the robber who is the cleverest. She, however, has other ideas.

Could Anything Be Worse?, retold and illustrated by Marilyn Hirsh. Here the man goes to the rabbi for advice about having a peaceful, quiet home, and is told to bring in the chickens, the cow, his fat brother, and nagging sister-in-law. When it becomes unbearable, the rabbi advises the man to reverse the situation, and the family finds their life is wonderful.

Crackle Gluck and the Sleeping Toad, by Dick Gackenbach. The Gluck family is convinced that a two-hundred-year-old toad is their lucky charm, but their daughter, Crackle, proves to her reluctant parents and brother that he's a hoax.

**Crow Chief,* by Paul Goble. An Indian legend and also a "pourquoi" story of why crows which were originally white are now black. It is a punishment for warning the buffalo so that they would not be caught by the Plains Indian hunters who need them to survive.

Deep in the Forest, by Brinton Turkle. A wordless book in which the characters appearing in the original Goldilocks story are reversed. Here it is the three bears who intrude in a human domicile deep in the woods.

**Dick Whittington and His Cat*, told and illustrated by Marcia Brown. A very poor lad has nothing to send to sea when his master sends a ship with goods to trade, so he reluctantly sends his cat. As it turns out, the cat rids the Barbary court of vermin and the king there sends back great riches for Dick, who then prospers and eventually becomes Lord Mayor of London.

Don't Tell the Whole World, by Joanna Cole, illustrated by Kate Duke. In order to keep his wife Emma from telling their mean landlord about the money they've found, John rigs up other "miracles," like fish in a tree and a cider jug in the weeds. Mr. Snood then concludes that Emma just dreams about everything, including the money.

The Dragon Nanny, by C. L. G. Martin, illustrated by Robert Rayevsky. When the King decides that Nell Hannah is too old to continue as the royal nanny, he sends her into the forest where she takes on two new charges— baby dragons, Cinder and Sparky—to save herself from their mother's wrath.

Dragonfly's Tale, by Kristina Rodanas. The people waste food and stage a mock battle with it to show off to their neighbors, but the Corn Maidens, disguised as old beggar women, see what is going on and punish the tribe with poor harvests. Then two Ashivi children must regain the blessings of the Maidens, which they do with the aid of a dragonfly.

Dreamcatcher, by Audrey Osofsky, illustrated by Ed Young. A story of the Ojibway Indians of the Great Lakes, who put great store in dreams. There is a dream net to catch the bad dreams, so that only the good dreams get through to the sleeping infant. Illustrated with dreamlike pastels.

A Drop of Honey: An Armenian Folktale, by Djemma Bider, illustrated by Armen Kojoyian. After a quarrel with her brothers, Anayida falls asleep and learns in her dream that small quarrels can lead to big troubles. Book includes recipe for baklava.

**Duffy and the Devil*, by Harve and Margot Zemach. Based on a Cornish folk play with its origins in the Rumpelstiltskin story, this book tells of Squire Lovel who looks for a maid's helper and chooses Duffy, who bluffs about knowing how to spin and knit. The girl then makes a pact with the devil who does all the work. If she can't guess his name after three years, she will be his. Married now to the squire, Duffy through trickery learns the name, but as the devil goes up in a puff of smoke, so does all the knitting, leaving Squire Lovel nude.

The Egyptian Cinderella, by Shirley Climo, illustrated by Ruth Heller. In this version of Cinderella, set in Egypt in the sixth century B.C., Rhodopis, a slave girl, eventually comes to be chosen by the pharaoh to be his queen.

The Elephant's Child, by Rudyard Kipling, illustrated by Jan Mogensen. Really a "pourquoi" story showing why elephants have long trunks, but also a cumulative tale about the little elephant who is full of "satiable curtiosity," a quality unappreciated by his relatives.

The Elves and the Shoemaker, retold and illustrated by Paul Galdone. This is a shortened version of the story, best suited to very young children.

The Elves and the Shoemakers, retold and illustrated by Jada Rowland. Set in nineteenth-century England, and told as Dickens might have told it, this is the traditional tale of a good but poor shoemaker and his ailing wife who are saved by the "little people" that come during the night and make exquisite shoes.

The Emperor's New Clothes, by Hans Christian Andersen, illustrated by Virginia Lee Burton. A vain and foolish emperor believes what two thieves tell him about their talent for weaving wonderful cloth for clothes which only the wise will be able to see. Everyone is afraid to tell the emperor the truth, so he leads a parade naked; then a little child blurts out the truth.

The Empty Pot, by Demi. A charming tale of Ping, a small Chinese boy whose honesty is rewarded by his emperor.

Everyone Knows What a Dragon Looks Like, by Jay Williams, illustrated by Mercer Mayer. The poor boy Han is courteous to the little rotund man who claims to be the dragon come to save the city of Wu from the Wild Horsemen who are threatening. No one else treats him well, but he saves the city anyway for Han's sake. Then he turns into a traditional dragon.

***Fables,* by Arnold Lobel. Deliciously droll illustrations of animals would be enough to recommend this book, but the twenty original fables with their humorous admonitions make it a don't-miss selection.

Favorite Nursery Tales, illustrated by Tomie De Paola. In his inimitable style, De Paola illustrates a collection of the most familiar nursery stories from Aesop, the Brothers Grimm, Hans Christian Andersen, Joseph Jacobs, and others.

Fin M'Coul, the Giant of Knockmany Hill, retold and illustrated by Tomie De Paola. A charming Irish folktale with the giant's wife Oonagh carrying out the plan by which Fin outwits the evil giant.

***The Firebird,* retold by Robert D. San Souci, illustrated by Kris Waldherr. Based on the story of the famous ballet danced to the music of Igor Stravinsky, this lavishly illustrated book tells of Prince Ivan, the enchanted garden, and the rescue of Princess Elena from the evil sorcerer Kastchei with the help of the Firebird's magic feather.

Five Bad Boys, Billy Que, and the Dustdobbin, by Susan Patron, illustrated by Mike Shenon. The Dustdobbin lives in an old slipper under Billy Que's bed, and when Billy steps on the tiny thing, he shrinks Billy down to the size of a teaspoon. To regain his normal size, Billy must receive five gifts freely given. The five bad boys save Billy although this is not their intention.

**The Flame of Peace: A Tale of the Aztecs,* by Deborah Nourse Lattimore. To prevent the outbreak of war, a young Aztec boy, Two Flint, must outwit nine evil lords of the night to obtain the flame of peace from Lord Morning Star. He succeeds, and a great Alliance of Cities marks the beginning of many peaceful decades.

**The Fool of the World and the Flying Ship: A Russian Folktale,* retold by Arthur Ransome, illustrated by Uri Shulevitz. Ignored by his parents, who prefer their two elder clever sons, Fool decides to build a flying ship and marry the Czar's daughter. Because he is kind and generous, Fool gathers many allies on the way to the czar's palace and achieves his desires.

The Frog Prince, by the Brothers Grimm, illustrated by Robert Baxter. In this version the princess tries to avoid keeping her promise of friendship to the frog after he has gotten her golden ball out of the well. But the king insists that she do as she promised. When she throws the frog against the wall in anger, he turns into a handsome prince whom she marries.

The Frog Prince, retold by Edith Tarcov, illustrated by James Marshall. This is the traditional story, but the illustrations make the princess quite portly, which makes the story even funnier than originally intended.

The Funny Little Woman, retold by Arlene Mosel, illustrated by Blair Lent. This Japanese folktale begins with the funny little woman chasing her rice dumpling, reminding the reader of the gingerbread boy who ran away. However, in this story the woman is captured by the evil Oni who make her cook for them until she escapes, returns home, and cooks rice dumplings with the Oni's magic paddle, becoming the richest woman in Japan.

Giant John, by Arnold Lobel. John must go into the world to earn money, and he does work successfully for the royal family, that is, until the fairies come and make him dance to their music.

***Gidja the Moon,* by Percy Trezise and Dick Roughsey. This is the Aboriginal story that explains the moon and its cycles as it grows "fat," then wanes, only to be reborn again. Gidja's wife becomes the Evening Star, his daughter the Morning Star.

The Gingerbread Boy, illustrated by Paul Galdone. Here the naughty ginger-bread boy escapes until the wily wolf tricks and eats him.

**The Girl Who Loved Wild Horses,* by Paul Goble. Though this Indian girl loves her family, she prefers to live with the wild horses, and Sioux tradition holds that she becomes one of them.

Goldilocks and the Three Bears, retold and illustrated by Jan Brett. This well-known tale is enhanced by the exquisitely wrought illustrations.

Goldilocks and the Three Bears, illustrated by Penny Ives. A Peek-Through-the-Window Book. A charming version of the familiar story for the very young child who will enjoy the cut-out pages.

Goldilocks and the Three Bears, retold and illustrated by James Marshall. In this version of the story Goldilocks is a disobedient, pushy little girl and the three bears live in a Victorian house and ride bicycles.

The Gunniwolf, retold by Wilhelmina Harper, illustrated by William Wiesner. This folktale recounts Little Girl's forays into the jungle to pick flowers although she has been warned by her mother to fear the Gunniwolf who lives there. Her sweet songs lull the creature to sleep and she escapes unharmed.

Hansel and Gretel, by the Brothers Grimm, illustrated by Susan Jeffers. The traditional tale, done with a gingerbread house that looks good enough to eat. It is Gretel who solves the problem of escaping from the witch by pushing her into the oven meant for Hansel.

Hansy's Mermaid, by Trinka Hakes Noble. After a severe storm, the Klumperty girls find a mermaid washed up on their farm near the Zuider Zee. Their father insists on keeping her because as he tells Hansy, his son, "Don't you know that to be like us is the best you can be." But the boy sympathizes with Seanora's desire to return to the sea and figures a way to help her do so.

The Hare and the Tortoise, retold by Caroline Castle, illustrated by Peter Weevers. In this retelling of La Fontaine's fable, new animal characters are added: a wise Badger, a flamboyant Frog, an industrious Mole, and others. But it is the health-nut Hare and the scholarly Tortoise who still hold center stage.

The Hare and the Tortoise, by Jean de La Fontaine, illustrated by Brian Wildsmith. This traditional fable, gorgeously illustrated, tells of the virtue of being slow and steady rather than quick and careless.

Harlequin and the Gift of Many Colors, by Remy Charlip and Burton Supree, illustrated by Remy Charlip. Based on a Commedia dell' Arte character who originated in Bergamo, Italy, poor Harlequin cannot go to the Carnival without a costume, but when his friends give him many scraps from their costumes he has the most beautiful costume of all.

Harvey the Foolish Pig, by Dick Gackenbach. A poor pig is determined to go on a journey to ask the great king for wealth, but fails to recognize the riches offered to him on the way.

***Heckedy Peg,* by Audrey Wood, illustrated by Don Wood. With wonderful oil paintings as illustrations, this story of a mother with seven children is a modern fairy tale in the style of the Brothers Grimm. The mother goes to town and promises each child a gift of choice when she returns; the children are kidnapped by a witch who turns them into various foods, but their mother rescues them, and Heckedy Peg drowns.

Henny Penny, retold and illustrated by Paul Galdone. In this simple cumulative tale, Henny Penny's friends all believe her warning that the sky is falling. All, that is, except Foxy Loxy, who with his family makes a fine feast of them all.

The Hole in the Dike, retold by Norma Green, illustrated by Eric Carle. Originally told by Mabel Mapes Dodge over 100 years ago in her book *Hans Brinker or The Silver Skates,* this story of Peter, the little Dutch boy who saved Holland from a flood by putting his finger in the dike, seems as fresh as ever.

Hot Hippo, by Mwenye Hadithi, illustrated by Adrienne Kennaway. An African "pourquoi" story which tells why hippos live in water during the day, but come out to eat grass nightly.

The House That Jack Built, illustrated by Rodney Peppe. The traditional tale with the repetition that children love is beautifully illustrated here.

The House That Jack Built, illustrated by Jenny Stow. This familiar cumulative nursery rhyme is transposed here to a lush Caribbean setting which works rather well.

How the Birds Changed Their Feathers: A South American Indian Folktale, by Joanna Troughton. In the "pourquoi" tradition, this brightly colored book "explains" how all birds that were completely white in the beginning became so richly colored.

***How We Came to the Fifth World,* adapted by Harriet Rohmer and Mary Anchondo, illustrated by Graciela Carrillo. This book tells an Aztec creation story, using both English and Spanish on each page. Each of the worlds is ruled and eventually destroyed by gods of the four elements: water, air, fire, and earth because of evil in the hearts of people.

The Hungry Leprechaun, by Mary Calhoun, illustrated by Roger Duvoisin. In very hard times in Ireland, even the leprechauns are poor, but Patrick O'Michael O'Sullivan O'Callahan does not believe that the little leprechaun Tippery cannot remember his magic. The result: potatoes for all of Ireland.

It Could Always Be Worse, by Margot Zemach. The story of a man who cannot stand the noise of a wife and six children in his one-room hut. The rabbi advises bringing in all the animals. Then when they leave, all seems quiet and peaceful by contrast.

Jack and the Beanstalk, retold by Susan Pearson, illustrated by James Warhola. The traditional story of the poor boy, the magic beans, and the giant. Nicely illustrated.

***The Jade Stone: A Chinese Folktale,* adapted by Caryn Yacowitz, illustrated by Ju-Hong Chen. When the Great Emperor of All China commands him to carve a Dragon of Wind and Fire in a piece of perfect jade, Chan Lo discovers that the stone wants to be something else. He braves the displeasure of the emperor by carving what he "hears" from the jade and almost loses his life.

Jamie O'Rourke and the Big Potato: An Irish Folktale, illustrated by Tomie De Paola. Lazy Jamie O'Rourke doesn't know how he and his wife Eileen will eat after she becomes too ill to dig potatoes. Jamie, however, catches a leprechaun who gives him a seed which solves all his problems for good.

Jim and the Beanstalk, by Raymond Briggs. A humorous modern retelling of the boy who climbs the beanstalk. This giant has no teeth, can no longer see without glasses, and is bald. Jim solves all these problems and is rewarded with a huge gold coin.

Journey Cake, Ho, by Ruth Sawyer, illustrated by Robert McCloskey. In this version a dour old man and a merry old woman send their "bound-out" boy Johnny away when there is not enough food for three. He takes a journey-cake which then falls out of his knapsack and leads all the farm animals back home. The journey-cake then becomes a Johnny-cake for the lad.

King Midas and the Golden Touch, retold and illustrated by Kathryn Hewitt. The traditional tale of the greedy king who wishes that everything he touches should turn to gold is told with humor in this version.

***King of the Cats,* by Joseph Jacobs, retold and illustrated by Paul Galdone. A great ghost story about a gravedigger who tells his wife his strange experience, and then finds that it is his own cat who solves the mystery about the identity of Tim Tildrum.

The King's Shadow, by Robert D. Larranaga, illustrated by Joe Greenwald. The little king, fearing his own shadow, tries unsuccessfully to get rid of it. Finally forced to face a fiery dragon, the little king overcomes his fear when the dragon flees at the sight of the shadow that he believes is a giant.

***The Knee-High Man and Other Tales*, retold by Julius Lester, illustrated by Ralph Pinto. In these folktales personified animals subtly represent human relationships, particularly among rural African Americans of earlier times.

***The Legend of Food Mountain*, adapted by Harriet Rohmer, illustrated by Graciela Carrillo. With very colorful illustrations and both Spanish and English on each page, we learn the legend of how the great god Quetzalcoatl solves the problem of how to feed his people when the great red ant brings corn, but not before he tames the rain god Tlaloc.

The Legend of the Indian Paintbrush, retold and illustrated by Tomie De Paola. A dramatically told story of a young Indian boy's Dream-Vision, which when realized results in a magnificent painting of the sunset and the wildflowers called Indian Paintbrush that still cover the hills of Wyoming in spring.

Leprechauns Never Lie, by Lorna Balian. Lazy Ninny Nanny and her Gram live in a hut, and they have a poor life because Ninny won't do any of the chores. She wants only to catch a leprechaun and get his gold. She does find one, and he tricks her into repairing the roof, digging the potatoes, and getting water into the rain barrel before he leaves, his gold intact.

The Lion and the Rat, by Jean de La Fontaine, illustrated by Brian Wildsmith. A lion allows a rat to escape and is surprised to find later that although none of the large beasts can free him from a trap, the little rat is able to gnaw through the ropes that hold him and repay the lion's kindness. Gorgeous illustrations.

The Little Girl and the Big Bear, retold by Joanna Galdone, illustrated by Paul Galdone. This is a retelling of a traditional Slavic tale in which a clever little girl outwits a huge bear who is holding her captive by hiding in a basket of pies.

The Little Red Hen, retold and illustrated by Paul Galdone. This cautionary tale is done with great humor even though the Little Red Hen eats the whole cake.

Little Red Riding Hood, by the Brothers Grimm, illustrated by Harriet Pincus. In this traditional version the huntsman saves both Red Riding Hood and her grandmother by cutting open the wicked wolf and then filling his body with stones.

Little Red Riding Hood, retold and illustrated by Paul Galdone. Again the traditional story, but with pictures typical of this artist.

Little Red Riding Hood, illustrated by John S. Goodall. Here the heroine of this tale is a mouse. A charming wordless rendition with half pages to help move the story along.

***Little Sister and the Month Brothers,* retold by Beatrice Schenk De Regniers, illustrated by Margot Tomes. This Slavic fairy tale shows the twelve month brothers helping Little Sister to thwart the schemes of her stepmother and stepsister. There are interesting small pictures with added dialogue on each page, which makes this ideal for use in a creative dramatics group.

Liza Lou and the Yeller Belly Swamp, by Mercer Mayer. This version of the Little Red Riding Hood story has the quick-thinking Liza Lou outsmarting all the "haunts, gobblygooks, witches, and devils" in the Yeller Belly Swamp as she carries food to her grandmother's house.

Llama and the Great Flood: A Folktale from Peru, by Ellen Alexander. In this version of the Great Flood story, it is a llama who warns his owner of the coming disaster, and so all the animals go to the top of Willka Qutu, the only peak in the Andes which remains above the surging waters that cover the earth.

Lon Po Po, translated from the Chinese and illustrated by Ed Young. In this version of Little Red Riding Hood, it is the mother who goes to visit grandmother, leaving her three daughters at home to be visited by the wolf who gets into their house by pretending to be Grandma. The eldest girl, however, outsmarts the wolf and saves them all.

The Magician, adapted and illustrated by Uri Shulevitz. On the eve of Passover the prophet Elijah comes to a small village disguised as a magician and gives a poor family everything they need to celebrate the holiday.

The Man Who Kept House, retold by Kathleen and Michael Hague, illustrated by Michael Hague. A farmer claims that while he toils all day his wife does nothing. They exchange jobs with hilarious results: the cow is hanging from the roof, the baby is tied to a chair, and the husband is in the hearth with his head in a pot.

***Many Moons,* by James Thurber, illustrated by Louis Slobodkin. The Court Jester is wiser than the Lord High Chamberlain and the Royal Wizard when the Princess Lenore demands that her father get her the moon. But the wisest of all is the little princess herself.

Mary Mary, by Sarah Hayes, illustrated by Helen Craig. Mary Mary is indeed "contrary," but she is also very brave and has considerable skill at managing the lonely giant who lives on the hill.

The Miller, the Boy and the Donkey, by Jean de LaFontaine, illustrated by Brian Wildsmith. An amusing tale of advice given, ignored, and taken as the miller and the boy take the donkey to town to be sold. Magnificent illustrations.

Millions of Cats, by Wanda Gag. When a little old man goes to select a pet kitten, there is fierce competition to be "the chosen one." One little kitten who believes itself homely remains outside the fray and is selected. In its new home the kitten grows into a sleek, beautiful cat.

The Mitten, adapted and illustrated by Jan Brett. In this Ukrainian version the story is slightly different from the Tresselt book described below. Both are charming for young children.

The Mitten, by Alvin Tresselt, illustrated by Yaroslava Mills. Like the famous shoe that housed the Old Woman and her too many children, a mitten, lost in the woods by a little boy, magically holds almost all of the forest creatures that come crowding in.

***Molly Whuppie,* retold by Walter de la Mare, illustrated by Errol Le Cain. A very smart and brave girl outwits the giant and his wife and thereby helps herself and her two sisters to the king's three sons as a reward.

Momotaro the Peach Boy: A Japanese Tale, retold and illustrated by Linda Shute. The kind and courteous peach boy with his dog, his monkey, and his pheasant beat the wicked Oni and bring back all the silver and gold which the Oni had taken from the poor peasants.

The Monkey and the Crocodile: A Jataka Tale from India, illustrated by Paul Galdone. In the conflict between the monkey and the crocodile who wants to eat him, the monkey outwits the greedy predator.

The Monster and the Tailor, by Paul Galdone. An unreasonable grand duke insists that the tailor stitch his trousers in the graveyard, and the poor man barely escapes the monster who pursues him, but he finishes the "lucky" trousers and gets his bag of gold.

***Moss Gown,* by William H. Hooks, illustrated by Donald Carrick. Here the characters of Cordelia from Shakespeare's "King Lear" and Cinderella blend seamlessly with the magic of the black gris-gris woman acting as catalyst. Really gorgeous paintings bring it all to life.

Mufaro's Beautiful Daughters: An African Folktale, told and illustrated by John Steptoe. Inspired by an African story collection of 1895, this book illustrates kindness rewarded, greed and pride punished, when two sisters travel to the court of their king who is searching for a worthy bride.

Mushroom in the Rain, by Mirra Ginsburg, illustrated by Jose Aruego and Ariane Dewey. Like the mitten which expands to house all the animals that get into it, the mushroom grows large enough to shelter the ant, the butterfly, the mouse, the sparrow, and even the rabbit.

***The Nightingale,* by Hans Christian Andersen, translated by Eva Le Gallienne, illustrated by Nancy Ekholm Burkert. When the emperor of China hears the wonderful song of the nightingale, he has the bird brought to him, and he tries to keep it prisoner. Later the emperor of Japan sends him a magnificent jeweled replica, and he banishes the living bird. Near death, the emperor is saved by the song of the real bird, who promises to remain with him as long as he may come and go freely.

The North Wind and the Sun, by Jean de La Fontaine, illustrated by Brian Wildsmith. The North Wind and the Sun make a wager. Which of them can make the horseman shed his coat? The Sun, of course, by warmth and gentleness achieves what the North Wind in all his strength and fury cannot do. Extravagantly illustrated.

The Old Woman and the Willy Nilly Man, by Jill Wright, illustrated by Glen Rounds. The ninety-two-year-old woman can't sleep because her shoes insist on dancing all night, so she goes to the scary willy-nilly man, who eventually helps her after she makes him laugh.

Once a Mouse, by Marcia Brown. An East-Indian fable illustrates the consequences of conceit as an old hermit with magic powers changes a mouse into a cat, then a dog, and finally a tiger—each time to save the mouse from harm. When the tiger threatens to kill the old hermit, he is turned back into a mouse.

Once in a Wood: Ten Tales from Aesop, adapted and illustrated by Eve Rice. Some very well-known fables and a few less popular ones are included in this book.

One Fine Day, by Nonny Hogrogian. A cumulative tale that begins with a fox lapping up an old woman's milk and having his tail cut off in punishment. Now he must replace the milk to have his tail sewed back, which involves a cow, a jug, a blue bead, an egg, and an old miller.

The Pancake Boy: An Old Norwegian Folktale, by Lorinda Bryan Cauley. Mother Goody Poody makes a pancake to feed her seven children, but the pancake boy successfully runs away until a clever piggy wiggy catches him.

Peach Boy, by William H. Hooks, illustrated by June Otani. Found floating on the river inside a peach, Momotaro is a blessing to his childless parents. Then when he is grown, he sets out to rid the village of the evil Oni monsters, and, with the help of a dog, a monkey, and a hawk, Momotaro succeeds.

Perez y Martina: A Puerto Rican Folktale, by Pura Belpre, illustrated by Carlos Sanchez. Martina, a beautiful cockroach, is sought by many animals, but chooses Perez, a debonair mouse.

Peter and the Wolf, by Sergei Prokofiev, translated by Maria Carlson, illustrated by Charles Mikolaycak. The story of the ballet is illustrated here by double-spread pictures of all the characters as they act out this familiar drama.

***The Pied Piper of Hamelin.* Each edition of this book, based on the old legend, is unique because of the different styles of illustration. The Brothers Grimm retold it as *The Rat Catcher* and Robert Browning wrote a poem about the Pied Piper. Three illustrators of note, Errol Le Cain, Annegert Fuchshuber, and Mercer Mayer, have all created unique versions of the tale of the piper who fulfilled his promise to rid Hamelin of rats, and had his revenge when he was not paid as promised.

Potato Pancakes All Around, by Marilyn Hirsh. In this variation of the traditional folktale in which a stranger comes into a quarrelsome situation and demonstrates making food without using the common ingredients, here a peddler shows both Grandma Yetta and Grandma Sophie that potato pancakes for Hanukkah can be made from an old crust of rye bread, plus, of course. . . .

Prince Bertram the Bad, by Arnold Lobel. Incorrigible little Prince Bertram finally meets his match when he hits a blackbird with a stone; the bird is really a witch who turns Prince Bertram into a dragon. All ends happily when the dragon saves the witch's life, and she turns him back into a boy— this time Good Prince Bertram.

The Princess and the Pea, by Hans Christian Andersen, illustrated by Paul Galdone. A prince who wants to marry only a genuine princess searches the world to find her; then out of a storm comes a bedraggled maiden who proves she is a princess by having a sore back after sleeping on a single pea put under twenty mattresses and twenty featherbeds by the queen.

Princess Horrid, by Erik Christian Haugaard, illustrated by Diane Dawson Hearn. With all the trappings of a traditional fairy tale, and some very modern witty critiques of royalty, this story of an extremely bad little princess who is turned into a kitten and then rescued by the lowliest scullery maid of the realm will amuse readers of all ages.

The Principal's New Clothes, by Stephanie Calmenson, illustrated by Denise Brunkus. A hilarious updated version of *The Emperor's New Clothes* has Mr. Bundy falling for the lies told by Ivy and Moe, tricksters, not tailors, and appearing at the school assembly in his underwear because he's been told that anyone who can't see the suit is stupid. A kindergarten child yells out the truth.

Puss in Boots, by Paul Galdone. A very poor young man gains a fortune and marries a princess when his cat, the clever Puss, outwits an evil giant.

The Queen Who Couldn't Bake Gingerbread, by Dorothy Van Woerkom, illustrated by Paul Galdone. King Pilaf wants a wife who can bake gingerbread, and Queen Calliope wants a husband who can play the slide trombone. They compromise on their deficiencies at first, but then they begin to quarrel until each learns to fulfill these needs by himself and herself.

Rapunzel, by the Brothers Grimm, retold by Amy Ehrlich, illustrated by Kris Waldherr. The traditional tale of the wicked witch who holds the beautiful Rapunzel prisoner, then abandons her in the wilderness when she finds the girl has fallen in love with a prince.

Rapunzel, retold and illustrated by Jada Rowland. This version of the story has the wicked enchantress who imprisons Rapunzel turning from her evil ways, returning the girl to her parents after she has reunited her with the blinded Prince, and welcoming many children to play on the castle grounds.

Red Riding Hood, retold and illustrated by James Marshall. The same tale, but told with a bit more irreverent humor than in other versions.

Rosa and Marco and the Three Wishes, by Barbara Brenner, illustrated by Megan Halsey. A magical fish grants the traditional three wishes to a boy and girl who are fishing. They waste them in comical fashion.

***The Rough-Face Girl,* by Rafe Martin, illustrated by David Shannon. This is the Algonquin version of the Cinderella story, where the heroine and her two beautiful but heartless sisters compete for the affections of the Invisible Being. Here the wise sister of the Invisible Being replaces the fairy godmother, seeing the inner beauty of the rough-face girl.

Ruby, by Michael Emberley. While taking cheese pies to her granny, Ruby, a small but determined mouse, forgets her mother's advice never to talk to strangers, especially cats. When a smooth-talking feline saves her from a foul reptile, she tells him Granny's address. A really droll retelling of the Red Riding Hood story.

Rumpelstiltskin, by the Brothers Grimm, retold and illustrated by Jonathan Langley. The story of Ruby, a miller's daughter, who promises her firstborn to Rumpelstiltskin when he helps her spin straw into gold remains the same, but this edition has humorous drawings and now it is the Queen who rules alone after the greedy King falls into the Royal Crocodile Pool at the end.

Rumpelstiltskin, by the Brothers Grimm, retold and illustrated by Paul O. Zelinsky. Illustrated with oil paintings of the medieval setting, this retelling of the popular story is truly a work of art.

***Saint George and the Dragon,* retold by Margaret Hodges from Edmund Spenser's *Faerie Queene,* illustrated by Trina Schart Hyman. The brave Red Cross Knight fights the dragon for the fair Princess Una to save her land, and after three days he is finally victorious. He marries Una, but must keep fighting for the Fairy Queen as he promised, at last earning his name, St. George of Merry England.

**Salt: A Russian Tale,* adapted by Harve and Margot Zemach, illustrated by Margot Zemach. In this folktale the youngest of the merchant's three sons, called Ivan the Fool, outsmarts his two wicked brothers, marries the princess of his choice, and shows a giant what happiness means.

The Secret of the Hawaiian Rainbow, by Stacy Kaopuiki, illustrated by Bob Wagstaff. A wizard and a legendary race of small elves gather colors from native sources and make a rainbow to remind the people of how important and beautiful are water and rain.

Seven in One Blow, by Friere Wright and Michael Foreman. A little tailor swats seven flies in one blow, then goes on to slay seven giants through trickery and is able to marry the princess when the king believes he has saved the city.

***Sidney Rella and the Glass Sneaker,* by Bernice Myers. A really novel take-off on the traditional Cinderella theme when Sidney wants to play football and is helped by a "small person" who gives him the uniform, including glass sneakers. Sidney ends up being the star of the team and then more.

***A Single Speckled Egg,* by Sonia Levitin, illustrated by John Larrecq. Three superstitious farmers worry about losing their farms, but their wives go to the teacher, who tells the women to sympathize and worry even more. Abel, Nagel, and Zeke then decide that women exaggerate and stop their fretting.

Six Foolish Fishermen, by Benjamin Elkin, illustrated by Katherine Evans. When each of the six brothers counts, he forgets to include himself, so all agree that one brother must have drowned. A young boy sets them straight, and they give him their fish in gratitude.

The Sleeping Beauty, by the Brothers Grimm, retold and illustrated by Trina Schart Hyman. With lavish medieval paintings to illustrate the tale of enchantment, this book vividly recreates the story of the bewitched princess who is awakened by the kiss of her true love.

***Sleeping Ugly,* by Jane Yolen, illustrated by Diane Stanley. This hilarious turnabout tale of a beautiful but nasty princess, a fairy godmother, a prince without means, and a one-hundred-year spell, after which Plain Jane marries the prince, will elicit laughter from children already familiar with the basic plot of *Sleeping Beauty*.

Snow White and Rose Red, by the Brothers Grimm, illustrated by Gennady Spirin. Two lovely sisters save a half-frozen bear who comes to their mother's cottage and are repaid when he saves them from an evil gnome. He then sheds his bearskin and tells the girls that he is really the prince under the spell of the wicked gnome. Snow White marries him, and Rose Red marries his brother.

Snow White and the Seven Dwarfs, by the Brothers Grimm, translated by Randall Jarrell, illustrated by Nancy Ekholm Burkert. A really magnificent rendition of this fairy tale with illustrations done with great attention to accurate detail. Note: See discussion in Book Selection-Illustration.

Snow White, by the Brothers Grimm, translated by Paul Heins, illustrated by Trina Schart Hyman. From the German, as written originally, this rendition illustrated with attention to details of the medieval period makes the story of the wicked queen and Snow White with the dwarfs who befriend her really come to life.

**The Squire Takes a Wife,* by Eve Feldman, illustrated by Bari Weissman. A rich squire is determined to marry the farmer's daughter Kate, but with the help of the stableboy, she tricks him and avoids the marriage.

**The Stonecutter: A Japanese Folktale,* by Gerald McDermott. When the stonecutter gets his wish to become first, the prince, then the sun, the cloud, and finally, the mountain, he must fear the new stonecutter chiseling away at his base.

Stone Soup, retold and illustrated by Marcia Brown. Three hungry soldiers come toward a French village, but find nobody to feed or house them until they show the stingy villagers how to make soup from a stone.

Stone Soup, retold by Carol Pasternak and Allen Sutterfield, illustrated by Hedy Campbell. In this version of the story the setting is a classroom of children who are "noisy" and those who don't speak English and are "quiet." The school janitor, Mr. O'Leary, makes "stone soup," which brings the children and their families together.

Stone Soup, retold and illustrated by John Warren Stewig. In this story it is a clever girl, Grethel, who discovers the way to make life easier for her mother and herself by showing villagers how to make soup with only a stone.

A Story, A Story: An African Tale, retold and illustrated by Gail E. Haley. This Spider Man or Ananse story tells how Ananse fulfills the requirements of the sky god in order to earn the god's golden box filled with stories and bring it back to earth, scattering the stories everywhere.

Strega Nona, retold and illustrated by Tomie De Paola. A very popular Italian folktale—one of many with the same theme—this story tells of a "Grandma Witch" with a magic pasta pot and Big Anthony, a disobedient boy who is her helper. When Big Anthony tries to show off, there are catastrophic results as pasta covers almost the entire town.

Strega Nona's Magic Lessons, by Tomie De Paola. This time it's Bambolona, the baker's daughter, who comes to Strega Nona to learn some magic, but, as always, it is Big Anthony who gets into trouble trying to outsmart Strega Nona.

The Table, the Donkey and the Stick, by the Brothers Grimm, retold and illustrated by Paul Galdone. Three sons of a tailor are driven from home because of a greedy goat, but each son finds a trade and is given a magic gift by his master. When an evil innkeeper steals both the table and the donkey, it is the third son's stick that sets things right.

The Talking Eggs, by Robert D. San Souci, illustrated by Jerry Pinkney. A colorful folktale of the American South, this story deals with two sisters, Rose, who is spoiled and lazy but her mother's favorite, and Blanche, who is forced to fetch and carry and do all the hard work. When Blanche meets a strange old lady in the woods and behaves with her usual kindness, everything is reversed for her, her sister Rose, and their mother.

***Tattercoats,* retold by Margaret Greaves, illustrated by Margaret Chamberlain. This version of the story ends with her grandfather being reunited with Tattercoats after she has married her prince.

***Tattercoats,* edited by Joseph Jacobs, illustrated by Margot Tomes. In this nontraditional variation on the Cinderella theme, the child is rejected by her grandfather, but finds a friend in the gooseboy. This version ends happily for Tattercoats, but her grandfather remains estranged.

Teeny Tiny, retold by Jill Bennett, illustrated by Tomie De Paola. This is the same ghost story as *The Teeny Tiny Woman.*

The Teeny Tiny Woman, retold and illustrated by Paul Galdone. This is an old English ghost story with a humorous twist.

The Teeny Tiny Woman: An Old English Ghost Tale, retold and illustrated by Barbara Seuling. This amusing story features repetition which small children enjoy and a surprise ending.

The Three Bears, retold and illustrated by Paul Galdone. A more modern mode of illustration than Jan Brett's makes this version of the Goldilocks story seem simpler, perhaps preferable for younger children.

The Three Billy Goats Gruff, by P. C. Asbjornsen, illustrated by Marcia Brown. The traditional tale of the troll and the billy goats is enhanced by lovely artwork.

The Three Billy Goats Gruff, by P. C. Asbjornsen, illustrated by Paul Galdone. Only the style of illustration differentiates these two books. This is slightly more comic than Ms. Brown's.

Three Fox Fables, by Aesop, illustrated by Paul Galdone. With a little story for each, certain truisms come clear, such as the fox flattering the crow until she sings, thereby dropping her cheese. Moral: Never trust a flatterer.

The Three Little Pigs. One version illustrated by Paul Galdone, and a second by Margot Zemach, each charming in its own way, tell the story of how the third little pig outwits the big bad wolf. A real favorite.

The Three Little Pigs and the Fox, by William H. Hooks, illustrated by S. D. Schindler. In this Appalachian version of the story, Hamlet, a female runt, and the youngest of the three pigs, saves her two greedy brothers from the clutches of the "mean, tricky old drooly-mouth fox."

The Three Wishes: An Old Story, by Margot Zemach. A poor woodcutter and his wife free an imp from under a fallen tree and are granted three wishes which they don't use wisely.

Thumbelina, by Hans Christian Andersen, retold by Amy Erlich, illustrated by Susan Jeffers. The traditional story of the girl less than one-inch tall who is first stolen away by the toad, then taken in for the winter by the mouse, who wants her to marry the mole. She is finally rescued by the swallow whose life she saved and marries the king of the flowers, so she becomes queen.

Thumbelina, by Hans Christian Andersen, retold by Deborah Hautzig, illustrated by Kaarina Kaila. This is the same story, just with a different but equally attractive style of illustration.

Tico and the Golden Wings, by Leo Lionni. Tico, born without wings, has his dream of golden wings granted, but his friends resent his being different. Tico then meets a number of needy people, and to each he gives one of his golden feathers. Now he has black wings like his friends, but he knows that he, like everyone else, is really unique.

Tikki Tikki Tembo, retold by Arlene Mosel, illustrated by Blair Lent. A delightful "explanation" for the Chinese custom of giving children short names, and a subtle reprimand to parents who show favoritism to one child over another.

Tim O'Toole and the Wee Folk, by Gerald McDermott. Tim and his wife Kathleen are very poor, but Tim gets some magic help from the "wee folk." However, a dishonest neighbor, McGoon, takes both the goose that lays golden eggs and the tablecloth which will furnish food. Then the little people give Tim a hat, and that fixes everything.

**Toad Is the Uncle of Heaven: A Vietnamese Folk Tale,* retold and illustrated by Jeanne M. Lee. In Vietnam, "Uncle" is a term of respect, and this folktale explains how the toad earns that title when all the animals on earth are dying from a drought. The toad leads the bees, rooster, and tiger to beg the King of Heaven for rain, which he grants, so when Uncle Toad croaks, it is a sign of rain for the Vietnamese.

Tom Thumb, retold and illustrated by Richard Jesse Watson. Truly gorgeous illustrations make this traditional tale of the boy hero who is only as big as his father's thumb a very appealing book. Children can relate to a world where all adults seem like giants.

Too Much Noise, by Ann McGovern, illustrated by Simms Taback. Peter is concerned with the noises in his house, so he goes to the village wise man who advises the addition of various animals. Each, of course, makes his own noise. Small children love the repetition and get the joke when Peter is told to get rid of the animals and can now have a quiet dream.

The Town Mouse and the Country Mouse, retold and illustrated by Lorinda Bryan Cauley. Two mice cousins exchange visits, and each decides that his way of life is best for him.

The Town Mouse and the Country Mouse: Adapted from Aesop, illustrated by Janet Stevens. The city mouse is bored when she visits her country cousin, but when he visits her in the city he is nearly eaten, so he decides that "It's better to have beans and bacon in peace than cakes and pies in fear."

**The Treasure,* retold and illustrated by Uri Shulevitz. Poor Isaac dreams three times of a treasure at the bridge near the royal palace in the capital, but after an arduous journey he finds that the bridge is guarded, so he cannot search. A captain of the guard then tells Isaac about *his* dream, and when Isaac returns home, he finds treasure under his own stove.

A Treeful of Pigs, by Arnold Lobel, illustrated by Anita Lobel. This fanciful story tells of a lazy farmer whose hard-working wife finally gets her husband to do his share of work as he had promised he would.

Turramulli the Giant Quinkin, by Percy Trezise and Dick Roughsey. An Australian Aboriginal myth from the Stone Age, this story tells of the bad Quinkins, the good Quinkins, and most dangerous of all, the single giant who is eventually overcome with the help of the good Quinkins.

The Turtle and the Monkey: A Philippine Tale, illustrated by Paul Galdone. In order to get her fair share of the banana tree she finds in the river, Turtle must outwit the very greedy Monkey.

Two Ways to Count to Ten: A Liberian Folktale, retold by Ruby Dee, illustrated by Susan Meddaugh. King Leopard decides to test all the other animals to see who will succeed him. The one who throws the king's spear into the air and counts to ten before it comes down shall win. How the clever antelope outwits the other animals makes a delightful story.

The Ugly Duckling, by Hans Christian Andersen, retold and illustrated by Lorinda Bryan Cauley. His mother and all the other animals and humans he meets reject the large and ugly duckling, and he spends his first winter of life in misery. Then he finds the flock of swans and realizes that he is a beautiful swan and not a duck at all.

The Ugly Duckling, by Hans Christian Andersen, retold by Lilian Moore, illustrated by Daniel San Souci. This is the same story with different illustrations.

Uncle Nacho's Hat, adapted by Harriet Rohmer, illustrated by Veg Reisberg. This simple Nicaraguan folktale tells of a lovable old man who tries without success to get rid of his old hat after his niece has bought him a new one. It is a metaphor for all the bad habits he cannot discard until he changes his ways of thinking. Spanish and English on each page.

**Vasilissa the Beautiful: A Russian Folktale,* retold by Elizabeth Winthrop, illustrated by Alexander Koshkin. With elements of both the Cinderella and the Hansel and Gretel stories, plus the unique Russian witch, the evil Baba Yaga, this folktale, illustrated in full-page color, tells of a girl, her stepmother and stepsisters, and a magic little doll left to Vasilissa by her mother just before the woman dies.

**Vassilisa the Wise: A Tale of Medieval Russia,* retold by Josepha Sherman, illustrated by Daniel San Souci. When the merchant and musician Staver boasts of his wife's beauty and wisdom, he angers Prince Vladimir and is thrown into a dungeon. But his clever wife saves him and the prince must admit that Staver is right.

The Village of Round and Square Houses, by Ann Grifalconi. A grandmother explains to her listeners why in their village on the side of a volcano in the remote hills of the Cameroons (in Central Africa) the men live in square houses and the women live in round ones.

The Wave, adapted from Lafcadio Hearn's *Gleanings in Budda Fields* by Margaret Hodges, illustrated by Blair Lent. In this Japanese folktale Ojiisan, the grandfather who lives at the top of the mountain with his grandson Tada, burns his rice field in order to get the attention of four hundred villagers who live near the shore, so that they may run up the mountain and thereby escape the tidal wave which will wreck their little village.

Why Mosquitoes Buzz in People's Ears: A West African Tale, retold by Verna Aardema, illustrated by Leo and Diane Dillon. Children enjoy the sequential repetition in this beautifully illustrated "pourquoi" story.

Why Rat Comes First: A Story of the Chinese Zodiac, by Clara Yen, illustrated by Hideo C. Yoshida. When the Jade King calls all the animals to heaven, twelve come, so there is a twelve-year cycle of years. The Jade King then decides to let earthly children choose which animal will be first, and in a contest between the ox and the rat, through cleverness the rat wins.

Why the Sun and the Moon Are in the Sky: An African Folktale, by Elphinstone Dayrell, illustrated by Blair Lent. When the water comes to visit the sun and the moon in their house, it fills the house to overflowing and so forces the hosts to go up into the sky, where they have remained ever since.

Who's in Rabbit's House?: A Masai Tale, retold by Verna Aardema, illustrated by Leo and Diane Dillon. Written as though it were a staged play, with masks to show various emotions, this tale tells of Rabbit who cannot get into his house because "the long one" has taken possession of it. Finally, after threatening other animals, the "ferocious creature" opens the door. It is only a caterpillar.

Wiley and the Hairy Man, by Molly Garrett Bang. A folktale from the American South about a boy and his mother who live on a swamp near the Tombigbee River. To avoid the evil of the Hairy Man and get rid of him forever, the two have to trick him three times—and they do.

Yeh-Shen, retold by Ai-Ling Louie, illustrated by Ed Young. This unique version of the Cinderella story dates back to tenth-century China, so that it has historic interest, as well as being an exquisite book on its own.

Zeralda's Ogre, by Tomi Ungerer. In the town people are terrified by a typical ogre who eats children, but the farmer's daughter Zeralda, who is an extraordinary cook, meets the ogre and changes his eating habits with her delightful cuisine.

Tall Tales

A subgroup of folktales are *tall tales,* that is, stories which are unrealistic, frequently comic, and largely American. Many have heroes and heroines who are larger-than-life, who might in another time be called legendary figures.

Andy and the Lion, by James Daugherty. This is a retelling of the classic story of Androcles and the Lion. A boy bravely removes a thorn from the paw of a lion and is later remembered by the same lion who breaks loose at the circus.

Burt Dow, Deep-Water Man, by Robert McCloskey. A rollicking tall tale of a retired seaman who fishes from his leaky boat, almost drowns, and is saved by being swallowed by a whale.

Charlie Drives the Stage, by Eric Kimmel, illustrated by Glen Rounds. In this story "Charlie" Drummond, a stagecoach driver with real moxie, promises to get Senator McCorkle on the train to Washington in spite of an avalanche, road agents, Indians on the warpath, and a raging river between Grass Valley and LeGrande. It's quite a ride, but Charlene gets the senator there in time.

Cloudy With a Chance of Meatballs, by Judith Barrett, illustrated by Ron Barrett. Life is delicious in the town of Chewandswallow where it rains soup and juice, snows mashed potatoes, and blows storms of hamburgers—until the weather takes a turn for the worse. Then, as Grandpa tells it, the people have to abandon the town.

The Giant Vegetable Garden, by Nadine Bernard Westcott. In their desire to win the prize for the finest vegetables at the county fair, the townspeople overdo it, and Peapack is almost ruined by the plants which have overgrown everything.

Grandpa's Too-Good Garden, by James Stevenson. Grandpa tells Mary Ann and Louie about a garden he had years ago that his baby brother Wainey "helped" him with. A really funny tall tale.

John Henry: An American Legend, by Ezra Jack Keats. The great steel-driving man was unusual even as an infant. His life comes alive on these pages.

Johnny Appleseed: A Tall Tale, retold and illustrated by Steven Kellogg. This book presents the life of John Chapman, better known as Johnny Appleseed, and tells of his kindness to animals, as well as his extraordinary physical fortitude.

Paul Bunyan: A Tall Tale, retold and illustrated by Steven Kellogg. Paul and his extraordinary blue ox Babe have outlandish adventures from Paul's infancy in Maine through his long life from coast to coast.

Pecos Bill, by Steven Kellogg. This is a wonderfully illustrated tall tale of the hero raised by a coyote. He invents lassos, cattle roping, rodeos, and finally marries Slewfoot Sue after he rescues her from her long descent from the moon where she had bounced because of her bustle.

Rocks in My Pockets, by Marc Harshman and Bonnie Collins, illustrated by Toni Goffe. The rocks around their mountain farm serve all of the Woods family very well in many ways. Then some ladies from the city come and change their lives, but not entirely.

Three Strong Women: A Tall Tale from Japan, by Claus Stamm, illustrated by Jean and Mou-sien Tseng. Forever-Mountain is the best wrestler in Japan, but he learns what real strength is when he meets Maru-me, her mother, and her grandmother. Stunningly illustrated with authentically detailed landscapes.

Security and Safety

Children all have need for security and safety, physical and psychological, which suggests that titles which emphasize these areas are important. There are many fears relating to a child's well-being which can be assuaged by the right book, since children identify with characters (even nonhuman ones) that they meet in stories.

For example, when Mother Rabbit talks to her little bunny about safety in Margaret Wise Brown's *The Runaway Bunny,* the theme comes across clearly. In the same way, vague nameless fears about going to sleep in a darkened room are speedily defused when the small hero in Mercer Mayer's *There's a Nightmare in My Closet* courageously takes complete charge of the terrified and comical creatures who beg him to comfort them. Some books which are in this category follow.

Alfi and the Dark, by Sally Miles, illustrated by Errol Le Cain. On a night when he cannot get to sleep, Alfi talks to The Dark and learns where Dark goes when someone turns on the light.

Alfie Gives a Hand, by Shirley Hughes. Alfie goes to his first birthday party at Bernard's, but since his mother and little sister are not going, Alfie takes what is left of his security blanket with him. Then he puts it down to help little Min, another preschooler, and finds he doesn't need the blanket at all.

Angus and the Ducks, by Marjorie Flack. A curious Scotch terrier decides to investigate the strange noise coming from the other side of the hedge and almost regrets his curiosity.

Angus Lost, by Marjorie Flack. Angus is tired of the same house, the same cat, and the same yard, so he escapes to find that being lost is no fun. He is glad to return home.

Are You My Mother?, by P. D. Eastman. A tiny bird tumbles out of his nest and goes on a search for his mother, asking everyone and everything the question until he finally ends up back in the nest.

Beady Bear, by Don Freeman. Beady tries to "go it alone" in a cave after he learns that bears live in caves. But he is happy when his boy rescues him and takes him home to his own little bed.

The Bear's Bicycle, by Emilie Warren McLeod, illustrated by David McPhail. A little boy and his bear ride bicycles; the bear does all the wrong things whereas the child illustrates safe bike rules. Then they both have a cookie and milk at home.

A Better Safe Than Sorry Book, by Sol and Judith Gordon, illustrated by Vivien Cohen. This book touches on a subject most people would rather ignore—sexual assault, but it does so tastefully, with a guide for parents at the end. Unhappily, there is more of this aberrant behavior than most parents want to think about, but the idea is "better safe (warned) than sorry."

Boris and the Monsters, by Elaine Macmann Willoughby, illustrated by Lynn Munsinger. In order to protect Boris from the monsters which come to his room each night, his father buys him a "fierce watchdog," but Ivan the Terrible is still a puppy who is afraid of the dark himself.

Clyde Monster, by Robert L. Crowe, illustrated by Kay Chorao. Clyde is a nice little monster, but he's afraid of humans. However, his parents reassure him, "A long time ago monsters and people made a deal. Monsters don't scare people—and people don't scare monsters."

Dinosaurs, Beware! A Safety Guide, by Marc Brown and Stephen Krensky. With a comic book format, this funny book makes some important points about physical safety.

Fang, by Barbara Shook Hazen, illustrated by Leslie Holt Morrill. A young boy selects the biggest, fiercest-looking dog he can find to protect him from danger. Then he finds that Fang is frightened of everything, even his own image in the mirror, but when the youngster reassures Fang, he loses his own fears.

First Pink Light, by Eloise Greenfield, illustrated by Moneta Barnett. Tyree's mother does not understand why he wants to hide and surprise his daddy who has been away a whole month, but he follows her suggestion and waits for the dawn in a big comfortable chair with his pillow and blanket. Then Daddy comes home and carries him to his bed.

Ghost's Hour, Spook's Hour, by Eve Bunting, illustrated by Donald Carrick. Scary incidents at midnight give Jake and his dog Biff a frightening time, but all turn out to have good explanations when Jake finds his parents on the couch-bed in the living room.

Going to Sleep on the Farm, by Wendy Cheyette Lewison, illustrated by Juan Wijngaard. Wonderful illustrations show how different animals go to sleep standing, lying down, sitting on eggs, cuddled with a brood, or, if one is a small boy, in bed with some favorite toys.

Hazel's Amazing Mother, by Rosemary Wells. Hazel and her doll Eleanor get lost on the way back from the store, and are waylaid by some very destructive bullies. Then Hazel's mother, almost like magic, appears and saves them both.

Hildilid's Night, by Cheli Duran Ryan, illustrated by Arnold Lobel. Hildilid lives high in the hills near Hexham, and she hates the night. She tries unsuccessfully to get rid of it and finally decides just to turn her back. Then it becomes day.

Ira Sleeps Over, by Bernard Waber. When Ira is invited to sleep at his friend Reggie's house, he anticipates a really good time, but he has a problem. Should he take his teddy bear or not? A wonderful warm story for preschoolers.

The Island of the Skog, by Steven Kellogg. On National Rodent Day the mice all decide to escape from their predators and sail away to find a safe place to live. When they finally moor near an island, they are frightened of the Skog who lives there, but after they trap him, they discover that he's tiny too and is afraid of them.

The King's Shadow, by Robert D. Larranaga, illustrated by Joe Greenwald. The little king, fearing his own shadow, tries unsuccessfully to get rid of it. Finally forced to face a fiery dragon, the little king overcomes his fear when the dragon flees at the sight of the shadow that he believes is a giant.

Klippity Klop, by Ed Emberley. Prince Krispin, a knight, goes for a ride on his horse Dumpling, and all is well until a dragon frightens the horse. The prince then decides that being safe at home is a fine thing.

Laney's Lost Momma, by Diane Johnston Hamm, illustrated by Sally G. Ward. Laney loses her mother in a large department store, but she remembers what to do and what to avoid, and she finds her lost mother quite quickly.

Left Behind, by Carol Carrick, illustrated by Donald Carrick. When Christopher's class goes into the city to visit the aquarium, they also travel on the subway. When the boy gets separated from the group, he is afraid he will never be reunited with them.

Little Fox Goes to the End of the World, by Ann Tompert, illustrated by John Wallner. As Little Fox's mother is fitting her jacket, Little Fox explains how she will go to the end of the world, meet strange animals, and face many dangers. Her mother is frightened, but not Little Fox. At the end she will come home, and, says her mother, "I shall be waiting for you with your favorite dinner."

Little Gorilla, by Ruth Bornstein. All the jungle animals love little gorilla when he is a tiny thing. Then he grows into a BIG gorilla, and his friends show their love by giving him a birthday party.

Maggie and the Monster, by Elizabeth Winthrop, illustrated by Tomie De Paola. Mysteriously a little monster comes to Maggie's room each night and finally admits she is looking for her mama, so Maggie takes her down the hall to the broom closet where her mother lives.

Make Way for Ducklings, by Robert McCloskey. In this gentle tale of a duck family trying to find a safe place to raise their brood, the Mallard family causes quite a stir in Boston before they settle on an island in the Public Garden.

Maybe She Forgot, by Ellen Kandoian. Jessie is happy to go to her first ballet class, but she becomes fearful when her mother is late picking her up. Mother has had a flat tire and is late, but she assures Jessie that she could never forget her.

Poinsetta and the Firefighters, by Felicia Bond. Poinsetta is delighted to have her own room at last, but she hears some sounds in the night; then what she thinks is the sunrise is a fire in the telephone wires outside, so her being awake turns out well.

Rooster's Off to See the World, by Eric Carle. Original title *Rooster Who Set Out to See the World.* In this cumulative story the rooster adds other gorgeously colored animals as he sets out to travel. But when night falls, the animals, including the rooster, decide to go back to their homes.

The Runaway Bunny, by Margaret Wise Brown, illustrated by Clement Hurd. Within a framework of mutual love a little bunny tells his mother how he will run away, and she answers his challenge by indicating how she will follow him. In the end, he decides he might just as well stay where he is and be her little bunny.

Scuffy the Tugboat, by Gertrude Crampton, illustrated by Tibor Gergely. Scuffy thinks he is too big to play with the little boy in the bathtub, so he goes on an adventure down the stream which goes into the river, then is almost lost at sea, but he is rescued by the boy and his dad and then decides that the bathtub is the place "for a red-painted tugboat" after all.

The Something, by Natalie Babbitt. Mylo's fear of the dark leaves him after he's modeled the "something" he fears out of clay.

The Story About Ping, by Marjorie Flack, illustrated by Kurt Wiese. Ping and his family, who live on a Yangtze River boat, go ashore each day to hunt for snails. But when the boat master calls, they must return. And Ping is always late. To avoid being last back on board, Ping decides to hide, but he finds that life alone is quite dangerous for a small duck and returns to his family.

The Summer Night, by Charlotte Zolotow, illustrated by Ben Shecter. A father and his little daughter share a walk in the moonlight; then the little girl goes happily to sleep.

Sylvester and the Magic Pebble, by William Steig. Sylvester has a pebble which can grant his every wish, but when he meets a lion, he panics and wishes himself turned into a large stone. No one can find him, and his parents are devastated until by a happy accident they are able to free him and reunite their family.

There's a Nightmare in My Closet, by Mercer Mayer. A small boy prepares to confront his nightmare, wearing his helmet and carrying his toy gun. But the nightmare is so frightened that he crawls into bed with the boy for comfort.

Thunder Cake, by Patricia Polacco. A little girl's fear of thunder turns into an adventure when her grandma (Babushka) shows her how to bake a thunder cake. The recipe is included.

The Town Mouse and the Country Mouse: Adapted from Aesop, illustrated by Janet Stevens. The city mouse is bored when she visits her country cousin, but when he visits her in the city, he is nearly eaten, so he decides that "It's better to have beans and bacon in peace than cakes and pies in fear."

The Two Bad Ants, by Chris Van Allsburg. An unusual view of the world from the perspective of two naughty ants who desert their colony and try to get all they want to eat instead of taking the "crystals" back to the queen ant. They escape and are glad to return to their family.

The Underbed, by Cathryn Clinton Hoellwarth, illustrated by Sibyl Graber Gerig. Tucker's mother helps him get rid of the monster that lives under his bed when she tells him how she had the very same trouble when she was a little girl.

Wake Up, Vladimir, by Felicia Bond. Vladimir Groundhog runs away from his home in late autumn and, after a long winter's sleep, wakes up, scares away a monster (his shadow), and runs home never to leave again.

The Way Home, by Judith Benet Richardson, illustrated by Salley Mavor. Unable to convince her baby to leave the beach where they have spent the day playing, a mother elephant uses inventive means to draw her young one away to home and safety. Unusual three-dimensional art illustrates this book.

Where the Wild Things Are, by Maurice Sendak. Max in his wolf suit makes mischief of every kind, and he is sent to his room without supper. But he "sails out of his room" and goes where the wild things live. He becomes their king, but decides to go home again to his very own room where his supper is waiting, "and it's still hot."

Willy Bear, by Mildred Kantrowitz, illustrated by Nancy Winslow Parker. A small boy about to go to school projects his feelings about having a night light, cuddling with a toy, and being "grown up" on to his pet teddy bear.

You're My Nikki, by Phyllis Rose Eisenberg, illustrated by Jill Kastner. Nikki needs reassurance when her mother goes out to work, and she gets it.

Family Life

Since the typical child's world is centered in the family, we must consider a number of relationships with siblings and parents. There is the two- or three-year-old faced with a new baby who seems suddenly to have usurped center stage. There are the everyday interactions among all siblings. There are the unusual brothers and sisters, perhaps with a handicap which requires special care. There are single parents of both sexes, and there are circumstances involving adoption.

Then, of course, there are just general family relationships. Some titles which seem broadly appropriate appear first, followed by more narrowly focused subject matters. None of the lists should be considered exhaustive.

Alexander and the Terrible, Horrible, No Good, Very Bad Day, by Judith Viorst, illustrated by Ray Cruz. Told in the first person, Alexander decides to go to Australia when everything goes wrong, but as his mom tells him, "Some days are like that. Even in Australia." A humorous look at modern family life.

All Kinds of Families, by Norma Simon, illustrated by Joe Lasker. This book explores in words and pictures what a family is and how families vary in makeup and lifestyles. It includes in a quiet fashion some troubled relationships, as well as some happy ones.

And My Mean Old Mother Will Be Sorry, Blackboard Bear, by Martha Alexander. Anthony tries to feed honey to his teddy bear, and when his mother gets angry, he "runs away" to the woods with his blackboard bear.

Are You My Mother?, by P. D. Eastman. A tiny bird tumbles out of his nest and goes on a search for his mother, asking everyone and everything the question, until he finally ends up back in his nest.

Ask Mr. Bear, by Marjorie Flack. Danny asks each animal in turn what he should give his mother for her birthday. Finally, Mr. Bear gives him the answer which pleases Danny's mom.

Aunt Nina's Visit, by Franz Brandenberg, illustrated by Aliki. Six nieces and nephews have fun trying to do a puppet show with six tiny kittens running all over the place. They are Aunt Nina's gift to the children.

The Baby Blue Cat Who Said No, by Ainslie Pryor. One little cat out of four knows only one word—NO. But Mother Cat deals with her playful baby with love.

Bedtime for Frances, by Russell Hoban, illustrated by Garth Williams. One of a series about a badger family, this book emphasizes the excuses the typical toddler makes to avoid going to bed. All of the Frances books are favorites with young children.

Better Not Get Wet, Jesse Bear, by Nancy White Carlstrom, illustrated by Bruce Degen. Despite Mama and Papa's repeated warnings, Jesse tries everything to get wet. Finally he is allowed to go into his little plastic pool and Papa Bear uses the hose on him.

Black Is Brown Is Tan, by Arnold Adoff, illustrated by Emily A. McCully. A small child's view of his mixed parentage: an African-American mother and a Caucasian father, apparently a happy home.

Blueberries for Sal, by Robert McCloskey. Little Sal and her mother go to Blueberry Hill and have quite an adventure when they "get all mixed up" with a bear and her cub.

Bread and Honey, by Frank Asch. Little Bear paints a picture of his mother, but he keeps adjusting it as each animal he meets makes suggestions. When he gets home with the resulting hodgepodge, his mother hangs it on the refrigerator anyway.

Bread and Jam for Frances, by Russell Hoban, illustrated by Lillian Hoban. Mother Badger gives Frances just what she wants for every meal—bread and jam—until Frances decides to try some other foods and finds she likes them.

A Chair for My Mother, by Vera B. Williams. All their furniture is burned in a fire, and it takes a large jar full of carefully hoarded coins to buy a soft, comfortable chair for a little girl, her mother, and her grandmother.

The Circus Baby, by Maud and Miska Petersham. Mother Elephant tries to teach her baby to do what the clown's baby does, but try as hard as Baby Elephant can, it just does not work because Baby Elephant *is* an elephant.

Cousins Are Special, by Susan Goldman. A simple explanation of the relationship which exists between the daughters of two adult sisters.

Daddy Makes the Best Spaghetti, by Anna Grossnickle Hines. A very modern father picks Corey up at day care, shops for dinner, and makes the best spaghetti. Then he acts as Bathman. Corey and his parents have a really great time, reading before bedtime and ending the day with warm kisses.

Daddy's Roommate, by Michael Willhoite. A young boy learns to like Frank, his father's roommate, and to understand that gay couples are just like other people. Love is the all-important ingredient of a relationship.

Dads Are Such Fun, by Jakki Wood, illustrated by Rog Bonner. Animal children and human children share experiences which make dads such fun. Warm and loving for youngsters.

Evan's Corner, by Elizabeth Starr Hill, illustrated by Sandra Speidel. A reissue with contemporary illustrations, this story tells of Evan's desire for a corner of his own in the two-room flat he shares with his family.

Family Pictures, by Carmen Lomas Garza. Told in the first person, with both Spanish and English on each page, this book tells about life in rural Texas from the viewpoint of a child and her family.

First Pink Light, by Eloise Greenfield, illustrations by Moneta Barnett. Tyree's mother does not understand why he wants to hide and surprise his daddy,who has been away a whole month, but he follows her suggestion and waits for the dawn in the big comfortable chair with his pillow and blanket. Then Daddy comes home and carries him to his bed.

Fish Fry, by Susan Saunders, illustrated by S. D. Schindler. Elaborate pastoral watercolors capture rural East Texas of seventy years ago as Edith, her family, and her friend Eugene go to a fish fry and nearly have an encounter with an alligator.

Friday Night is Papa Night, by Ruth Sonneborn, illustrated by Emily A. McCully. Papa must have two jobs so that he can take care of his family, but he is able to come home on Friday nights. Mama, Manuela, Carlos, and Ricardo all wait patiently when Papa does not come by dark. But it is Pedro, the youngest child, who lights up the kitchen and greets his father.

Gregory, the Terrible Eater, by Mitchell Sharmat, illustrated by Jose Aruego and Ariane Dewey. Most goats will eat anything, but Gregory decides he must have healthy foods, such as fruits, vegetables, milk, bread, and butter. This finicky behavior upsets his parents who consult Doctor Ram about Gregory's eating habits.

Growing Vegetable Soup, by Lois Ehlert. A child and her father decide to grow everything they will need to make vegetable soup, and they do.

Harry and the Terrible Whatzit, by Dick Gackenbach. Harry warns his mother not to go into the basement to get a jar of pickles, and when she doesn't return, he goes down to save her from the Whatzit.

He's My Brother, by Joe Lasker. Jamie suffers from "the invisible handicap." He is not retarded, but he has difficulties adjusting to the normal lifestyle of a child in the early grades. His family is very supportive and loving.

How My Parents Learned to Eat, by Ina R. Friedman, illustrated by Allen Say. An American sailor courts a Japanese girl and each tries, in secret, to learn the other's way of eating. They succeed, and the little girl says her parents now use chopsticks some days and knives, forks, and spoons at other times.

I Wish Daddy Didn't Drink So Much, by Judy Vigna. Although her father has made her a beautiful sled for Christmas, a little girl is disappointed in his behavior, which is due to his addiction to alcohol. Her mother tries to explain that he must get help before he can get better.

Jeremy's First Haircut, by Linda Walvoord Girard, illustrated by Mary Jane Begin. Jeremy's dad thinks it's time for Jeremy to have his hair cut, but his mother thinks he's too young for a barbershop, so his parents cut his hair and he feels like a big little boy. It is fun.

Just Like Daddy, by Frank Asch. A very simple book about a bear family in which the little bear does everything his father does.

Just Us Women, by Jeanette Caines, illustrated by Pat Cummings. A young girl and her Aunt Martha drive to North Carolina, doing whatever suits them enroute. It's a lovely trip.

Like Jake and Me, by Mavis Jukes, illustrated by Lloyd Bloom. Alex discovers that even his "tough guy" stepfather Jake can panic in fear when the boy tells him that a spider has crawled into his clothing. With great humor, Alex helps Jake to strip down and capture the spider.

Little Bear, by Else Holmelund Minarik, illustrated by Maurice Sendak. Four short stories about Little Bear, his wise mother, and some of his little friends.

Little Fox Goes to the End of the World, by Ann Tompert, illustrated by John Wallner. As Little Fox's mother is fitting her jacket, Little Fox explains how she will go to the end of the world, meet strange animals, and face many dangers. Her mother is frightened, but not Little Fox. At the end, she will come home, and says her mother, "I shall be waiting for you with your favorite dinner."

Little Fur Family, by Margaret Wise Brown, illustrated by Garth Williams. A day in the life of a little fur family from morning when the little fur child goes off to play until he comes home for supper and his warm bed.

Little Nino's Pizzeria, by Karen Barbour. Tony likes to help his father at their small family restaurant, but everything changes when Little Nino's Pizzeria becomes a fancier place. Now Tony just seems to be in the way. Then Nino decides to return to the smaller place, but now it is to be called Little Tony's Pizzeria.

Mara in the Morning, by C. B. Christiansen, illustrated by Catherine Stock. Moving quietly through her house, this little girl enjoys the peaceful sounds of early morning and then shares this special time with her mother.

Maybe She Forgot, by Ellen Kandoian. Jessie is happy to go to her first ballet class, but she becomes fearful when her mother is late picking her up. Mother has had a flat tire and is late, but she assures Jessie that she could never forget her.

Mr. Rabbit and the Lovely Present, by Charlotte Zolotow, illustrated by Maurice Sendak. A little girl consults her rabbit friend about a birthday gift for her mother and takes his advice about giving something of each color her mother likes—a basket of fruit.

** *Molly's Pilgrim,* by Barbara Cohen, illustrated by Michael J. Deraney. When Molly is told to make a doll like a Pilgrim for the Thanksgiving display at school, Molly's mother dresses the doll as she herself dressed before leaving Russia to seek religious freedom. Molly is embarrassed; her classmates laugh at her, but Ms. Stickely, a wise teacher, makes things right.

Mooch the Messy, by Marjorie Weinman Sharmat, illustrated by Ben Shecter. Mooch, a rat, lives in a lovely hole under Boston. He likes to be messy, but he cleans up when his father comes to visit. After Papa leaves, however, Mooch reverts to his old habits.

Mother Makes a Mistake, by Ann Dorer, illustrated by Ellen Anderson. Knowing Kate would rather play than bathe, Mother purposely substitutes words for bathtub until Kate finally asks to be put in the tub.

My Daddy Don't Go to Work, by Madeena Spray Nolan, illustrated by Jim LaMarche. A family nearly breaks up because the father is out of work and thinks perhaps he should go elsewhere to look for a job, but his wife and little girl persuade him to stay.

My Mama Says There Aren't Any Zombies, Ghosts, Vampires, Creatures, Demons, Monsters, Fiends, Goblins or Things, by Judith Viorst, illustrated by Kay Chorao. Nick's mother assures him that there are no scary things coming to get him. Of course, Mommies sometimes do make mistakes. But sometimes they don't.

** *Nadia the Willful,* by Sue Alexander, illustrated by Lloyd Bloom. When her favorite brother Hamed disappears in the desert forever, Nadia refuses to let him be forgotten, despite her father's decree that his name shall not be uttered. Finally Tarik, the sheik, realizes that Nadia is not willful, but wise.

A New Coat for Anna, by Harriet Ziefert, illustrated by Anita Lobel. After World War II there are no coats in the stores, so to keep her promise to Anna, her mother exchanges things she owns for wool, weaving, spinning, and sewing until the child has her pretty new red coat.

No Nap, by Eve Bunting, illustrated by Susan Meddaugh. Susie is tired, but decides against a nap. Daddy has a battle plan, but little Susie wins the war.

Obadiah the Bold, by Brinton Turkle. Obadiah Starbuck wants to be a pirate when he grows up, but who ever heard of a Quaker pirate? He changes his mind when his father shows him his seafaring grandfather Obadiah's chronometer given to him in 1798 for bravery.

On a Hot, Hot Day, by Nicki Weiss. Mama and her young son Angel find nice things to do together, no matter the weather.

One Morning in Maine, by Robert McCloskey. A simple family story revolving around little Sal and her loose tooth, which she loses when digging clams with her father. Life as it was in the 1950s.

One of Three, by Angela Johnson, illustrated by David Soman. The youngest of three sisters tells how there are always the three of them doing everything together, except when the two older sisters must leave her behind. Then there are still three of them: the little girl, her mama, and her daddy.

**Our Home Is the Sea,* by Ricki Levinson, illustrated by Dennis Luzak. A Chinese boy hurries home from school to his family's houseboat in Hong Kong's harbor. He is very anxious to get back to the sea with his father and his grandfather and wishes to remain on the sea for the rest of his life.

Owl Moon, by Jane Yolen, illustrated by John Schoenherr. On a winter's night, under a full moon, a father and daughter trek into the woods to see the Great Horned Owl.

Papa's Panda, by Nancy Willard, illustrated by Lillian Hoban. James and his dad discuss the problems a real panda would cause if James got one as a birthday present, after which James is very pleased with his gift of a toy panda.

The Perfect Spot, by Robert J. Blake. A young boy and his artist father walk in the woods for quite a while before they find "the perfect spot" for both of them.

Peter's Pockets, by Eve Rice, illustrated by Nancy Winslow Parker. Peter's new pants don't have any pockets, so Uncle Nick lets him use his until Peter's mother solves the problem in a clever and colorful way.

Piggybook, by Anthony Browne. When Mrs. Piggott unexpectedly leaves one day, her demanding husband and two sons begin to realize just how much she does for them. When she returns, things change radically.

Planting a Rainbow, by Lois Ehlert. A child and her mother plant a flower garden with bulbs, seeds, and seedling plants, and every year they reap a rainbow of colors.

Poems for Fathers, edited by Myra Cohn Livingston, illustrated by Robert Casilla. Some serious, some comical poems about fathers of all kinds and their behavior.

The Quarreling Book, by Charlotte Zolotow, illustrated by Arnold Lobel. A rainy day makes everyone feel grumpy, but the sun comes out and all the children (and their parents) decide to be pleasant.

Rain, by Peter Spier. A wordless book showing with splendid illustrations all the activities of a family when it rains.

Sam, by Ann Herbert Scott, illustrations by Symeon Shimin. Sam is lonely as each family member is too busy to pay attention to him. Then when he cries, they all understand, and his mother lets him make his own tart with raspberry jam.

Sam Goes Trucking, by Henry Horenstein. Using photographs, this book shows a young boy going with his trucker father on a sixteen-wheeler as they haul fish to the big city, a full day's round-trip ride.

She's Not My Real Mother, by Judith Vigna. When Miles spends the weekend in the city with his daddy and his stepmother, he refuses all her overtures until they go to the Ice Capades, and she doesn't tell his father how he pretended to be lost and frightened her. Then he agrees to be her friend, but she's still not his *real* mommy.

Stevie, by John Steptoe. Robert is not too thrilled when he hears that little Stevie is coming to stay with his family on weekdays, and Stevie does prove something of a pest. Then Stevie's family moves away, and Robert finds he misses the little guy.

Story Hour—Starring Megan!, by Julie Brillhart. When Megan's mother, the librarian, can't read at story hour because Megan's little brother Nathan is too noisy, Megan takes over and does a great job.

The Summer Night, by Charlotte Zolotow, illustrated by Ben Shecter. A father and his little daughter share a walk in the moonlight, and then the little girl goes happily to sleep.

Take Time to Relax!, by Nancy Carlson. Tina the beaver and her family are constantly "on the go" until a snowstorm keeps them home, and they rediscover how much fun they can have, just the three of them.

The Terrible Thing That Happened at Our House, by Marge Blaine, illustrated by John C. Wallner. A little girl is sorely discomforted when her mother goes back to being a science teacher, and things change in the household. Then the family realizes that they can manage so they will have more time together, and they do.

Tight Times, by Barbara Shook Hazen, illustrated by Trina Schart Hyman. A little boy's dad tries to explain the term "tight times" when he has to refuse getting the child the dog he wants. But his parents do allow him to keep the kitten he's found, and he names it "Dog."

Time of Wonder, by Robert McCloskey. A simple, restful, and poetic description of life on a New England island during summer as the family explores and enjoys all that nature offers.

The Underbed, by Cathryn Clinton Hoellwarth, illustrated by Sibyl Graber Gerig. Tucker's mother helps him get rid of the monster that lives under his bed when she tells how she had the very same trouble when she was a little girl.

The Way Home, by Judith Benet Richardson, illustrated by Salley Mavor. Unable to convince her baby to leave the beach where they have spent the day playing, a mother elephant uses inventive means to draw her young one away to home and safety. Unusual three-dimensional works of art illustrate this story.

What Mary Jo Shared, by Janice May Udry, illustrated by Eleanor Mill. Mary Jo can't find a thing to share with her classmates. When she finds one grasshopper, Jimmy brings in a jar full. When she thinks of her umbrella, she finds it is one of many. Finally, she shares something no one else has thought of.

When Daddy Had the Chicken Pox, by Harriet Ziefert, illustrated by Lionel Kalish. Three children have had the chicken pox. Now it's Daddy's turn. A reassuring look at a sick parent who recovers.

When I Have a Little Girl, by Charlotte Zolotow, illustrated by Hilary Knight. A small girl tells her mother all the things she will allow her small girl to do, things which are forbidden by her mother, such as going out in the snow without shoes, letting her hair grow as long as she wants it, and feeding all the stray cats in the neighborhood even if they stay around.

Where's Chimpy?, by Berniece Rabe, illustrated by Diane Schmidt. Misty, a little girl afflicted with Down's Syndrome, can't go to sleep without her little monkey. She and her dad search everywhere and find many other misplaced items before they find Chimpy under a towel near the bathtub.

Where's My Daddy?, by Shigeo Watanabe, illustrated by Yasuo Ohtomo. A little bear tries to find his daddy, asking all the animals he sees, but no one has time to answer except his mommy who kisses him. Then Daddy comes home.

***White Dynamite and Curly Kidd,* by Bill Martin, Jr., and John Archambault, illustrated by Ted Rand. Lucky Kidd watches her dad ride a mean bull and dreams of becoming a rodeo rider herself.

Why Do Grown-Ups Have All the Fun?, by Marisabina Russo. Hannah and her doll Aggie can't go to sleep, thinking that Hannah's parents are eating ice cream, playing with blocks, or molding play dough. When she sees her parents reading, writing, and folding laundry, Hannah decides to turn in.

William's Doll, by Charlotte Zolotow, illustrated by William Pene Du Bois. William wants a real baby doll like the one Nancy has. His father buys all the typical "boy" toys for him, and William plays with them, but when his grandmother comes, he asks her for the doll and he gets it.

***Yonder,* by Tony Johnston, illustrated by Lloyd Bloom. With very effective artwork this book shows the cycle of life in nature and for humans as well.

Books About the New Baby

Aren't You Lucky?, by Catherine Anholt. A little girl goes through the waiting for her baby brother to arrive and suffers through the usual feelings of being displaced, but finally begins to enjoy the new addition.

Arthur's Baby, by Marc Brown. D. W., Arthur's little sister, takes charge of the new baby, Kate, and that's all right with Arthur. Then it is he who must come to the rescue when Kate won't stop crying.

A Baby for Max, by Kathryn Lasky and Maxwell B. Knight, illustrated by Christopher G. Knight. Very realistic treatment of how a little boy is prepared for the arrival of his sister, recognizing all the ambivalent feelings of a first child.

A Baby Sister for Frances, by Russell Hoban, illustrated by Lillian Hoban. Of course, Frances resents her baby sister Gloria. That is, until her very wise parents help her to understand that there is pleasure in being the big sister in a family.

Betsy's Baby Brother, by Gunilla Wolde. An accurate reflection of a small girl with a new baby brother.

Billy and Our New Baby, by Helene S. Arnstein, illustrated by M. Jane Smyth. Feeling jealous of his new baby brother, Billy wants to behave like an infant but realizes that it's more fun to be a big boy.

Changes, by Anthony Browne. As he waits for his parents to return home, a young boy with a vivid imagination tries to figure what his father meant when he said, "Things are going to change around here."

Everett Anderson's Nine Month Long, by Lucille Clifton, illustrated by Ann Grifalconi. Everett, first a one-parent child after his father's death, learns to love Mr. Perry, his new daddy, and to welcome baby Evelyn Perry who arrives to complete their family.

Jack and the Monster, by Richard Graham, illustrated by Susan Varley. Jack's new baby brother seems like a monster to him, howling and making messes all over the house, until Jack learns to view the addition to his family in a more positive light.

Katie Morag and the Tiresome Ted, by Mairi Hedderwick. Jealous of her new baby sister, Katie decides in a fit of temper to throw her teddy bear into the sea, but is delighted to have it back, washed up onshore along with other treasures from the sea.

New Baby, by Emily Arnold McCully. Mice children, like humans, can resent all the attention showered on the new baby. In a wordless book we see how the young mouse reacts to the new center of attention.

Nobody Asked Me if I Wanted a Baby Sister, by Martha Alexander. Oliver tries every way he can to give away his new baby sister, but he takes her home when he finds that it is he she wants.

On Mother's Lap, by Ann Herbert Scott, illustrated by Glo Coalson. There are two versions of this book—one in sepia tones, the other in soft colors. Both tell the story of little Michael who brings all his toys and his puppy to share mother's lap with him and his new baby sister. There is always room on mother's lap.

Peter's Chair, by Ezra Jack Keats. Now Peter feels displaced by his new baby sister Susie, and so he decides to "run away" by going outside with his dog Willie and his little chair. However, he does not fit in the chair any more! He has outgrown it.

Our Teacher's Having a Baby, by Eve Bunting, illustrated by Diane De Groat. As the months pass during the first-grade teacher Mrs. Neal's pregnancy, her class gets involved writing letters to the baby, thinking up possible names, and designing a baby room on the bulletin board. Then Isabel arrives, and the children understand that teachers can be mothers and that mothers can be teachers too, as Mrs. Neal assures the class that she will return.

Sam Is My Half Brother, by Lizi Boyd. Hessie's dad and her stepmother have a new baby, and Hessie is fearful that little Sam will now get all the attention, but she is reassured by her father and thinks positively about her new role as "big sister."

She Come Bringing Me That Little Baby Girl, by Eloise Greenfield, illustrated by John Steptoe. Kevin asked for a baby brother, not a wrinkled little sister who is now the focus of attention for all visitors. But his mother makes it clear that he must help her with the baby, and that his mother has two arms, one for each child.

Waiting for Hannah, by Marisabina Russo. A mother explains to her small daughter how she was expected through a hot summer and finally arrived, round and perfect, with "lots of brown hair."

What Comes in Spring?, by Barbara Savadge Horton, illustrated by Ed Young. As a mother goes through the four seasons with her small child, she also tells gently the story of the child's own birth.

When You Were a Baby, by Katherine Ross, illustrated by Phoebe Dunn. A parent describes for a child all the things experienced in babyhood from the first perceptions of sight and sound to the beginning of crawling and walking.

Books About Adoption

Abby, by Jeanette Caines, illustrated by Steven Kellogg. Adopted as an infant, Abby is very happy with her parents and her big brother Kevin, who wants to take her to school for his show-and-tell.

The Chosen Baby, by Valentina P. Wasson, illustrated by Glo Coalson. Really the seminal book on adoption, how the process works, and how to share the idea of "being chosen" with the newly adopted child. Lovely warm illustrations.

I Am Adopted, by Susan Lapsley, illustrated by Michael Charlton. A basic book about a boy and his little sister whose parents brought them home to make a family.

***We Don't Look Like Our Mom and Dad,* by Harriet Langsam Sobel, illustrated by Patricia Agre. With photographs the author shows the lives of two Korean boys adopted at different times into an American Caucasian family. The boys, Eric and Joshua, sometimes wonder about their birth mothers, but the family, including the grandparents, are a truly loving group.

Books About Siblings and Sibling Rivalry

Belinda's Balloon, by Emilie Boon. The bear family is on a picnic. Then Lucy takes her little sister to the balloon man and gets a magic balloon.

Big Brother, by Charlotte Zolotow, illustrated by Mary Chalmers. Big brother teases little sister until she realizes that he is only fooling, and they play nicely together.

Big Sister and Little Sister, by Charlotte Zolotow, illustrated by Martha Alexander. Little Sister is tired of always tagging after Big Sister, so she goes off on her own and hides. Surprised that Big Sister cries when she can't find her, Little Sister decides that they need each other.

A Birthday for Frances, by Russell Hoban, illustrated by Lillian Hoban. It's not Frances's birthday, it's Gloria's, and Frances has to borrow two weeks' allowance to buy her sister some bubble gum and a tasty Chompo bar. It's hard to be an unbirthday girl.

Christina Katerina and the Time She Quit the Family, by Patricia Lee Gauch, illustrated by Elise Primavera. Christina rebels when she is blamed for what her brother John and his friends do to her room, so she becomes "Agnes" for a week and does exactly as she pleases. Then she returns to the family—when she pleases, of course.

The Coolest Place in Town, by Kathy Caple. When Hank and Zoey's sister Dory kicks them out of their wading pool on a hot summer day, the boys find a way to get even.

D. W. All Wet, by Marc Brown. Arthur tricks his little sister D. W. into trying the water, and she finds it fun.

Harvey's Hideout, by Russell Hoban, illustrated by Lillian Hoban. Harvey Muskrat has a secret club and he won't include his sister Mildred, who then won't invite him to her secret parties. But they are both really alone, and decide that they need each other as playmates.

I Can! Can You?, by Carol Adorjan, illustrated by Miriam Nerlove. A little girl tells what her older sister is able to do that she cannot, but then she relates what she CAN do, which gets to be more every day.

I Have a Sister; My Sister Is Deaf, by Jeanne Whitehouse Peterson, illustrated by Deborah Ray. Little sister says with her face what many people cannot say in words, and she reads people's eyes. Warm intimate pictures and a poetic text evoke an appealing and perceptive portrait of a young deaf child.

I Wish I Was Sick Too!, by Franz Brandenberg, illustrated by Aliki. Elizabeth envies Edward because the family is concerned about his illness. Then she becomes ill, and when they have both recovered, they agree that being well is best.

If It Weren't for You, by Charlotte Zolotow, illustrated by Ben Shecter. A young boy explains to his younger brother what advantages he would have as an only child: his own room, unshared toys, and so on. But, he says, he would have to spend all his time with grownups, which is not an attractive thought.

I'll Fix Anthony, by Judith Viorst, illustrated by Arnold Lobel. There isn't much a younger brother can do about a mean big brother, but there's a lot he can think. "When I'm six. . . ."

I'm the Big Sister Now, by Michelle Emmert, illustrated by Gail Owens. Michelle tells of her sister Amy, who has cerebral palsy. It is a loving picture, but, of course, since it is factual, it may prove sad for some readers.

Jack and Jake, by Aliki. People confuse Jack for Jake and Jake for Jack, but there are differences, even between twins. Can you find them?

Jamaica Tag-Along, by Juanita Havill, illustrated by Anne Sibley O'Brien. When her older brother Ossie won't let Jamaica play basketball with him and his friends, she helps a younger child build a sand castle as she realizes what it feels like to be considered a "tag-along."

Jo, Flo and Yolanda, by Carol De Poix, illustrated by Stephanie Soveney. A subtle picture of a warm, loving Puerto Rican family living in New York; each of the triplets has her own dream of the future.

***Jumanji,* by Chris Van Allsburg. Left on their own for the afternoon, Peter and Judy find more excitement than they bargain for in a mysterious jungle-adventure board game when the animals come alive.

** *My Sister's Silent World,* by Catherine Arthur, illustrated by Nathan Talbot. Eight-year-old Heather is deaf. Her older sister explains her hearing aid, her lip-reading, and her sign language; unfortunately, other children are not always understanding.

One Ballerina Two, by Vivian French, illustrated by Jan Ormerod. A little sister copies her older sister's ballet movements, counting backward ten to one.

One of Three, by Angela Johnson, illustrated by David Soman. The youngest of three sisters tells how there are always the three of them doing everything together except when the two older sisters must leave her behind. Then there are still three of them—the little girl, her mama, and her daddy.

Patrick's Dinosaurs, by Carol Carrick, illustrated by Donald Carrick. Hank and Patrick go to the zoo, and when Hank tells his younger brother about dinosaurs, the younger boy's imagination goes wild.

Peabody, by Rosemary Wells. The little bear, Peabody, belongs to Annie, who almost forgets their closeness when she gets a "talking" doll for her birthday. Then her baby brother Robert gets hold of the doll and ruins its innards, so Peabody is back in the number-one spot.

Poinsetta and Her Family, by Felicia Bond. There are just too many sisters and brothers for Poinsetta to have any private space to read her book. So when her family leaves, she remains behind, but is only too happy when they return.

Princess Pooh, by Kathleen M. Muldoon, illustrated by Linda Shute. Patty Jean Piper is jealous of her sister Penelope Marie, because Penelope has a wheelchair and crutches and, in Patty's eyes, is treated like a princess. However, a trial run with Princess Pooh's wheelchair changes Patty's mind.

The Real Hole, rev. ed., by Beverly Cleary, illustrated by Mary Stevens. With interference and suggestions from his twin sister Janet, four-year-old Jimmy sets out to dig the biggest hole in the world. Then his father finds a use for it.

**Spin a Soft Black Song, by Nikki Giovanni, illustrated by Charles Bible. This is a very unusual book, celebrating African-American life in poems based on what children say from infancy through age ten. The author uses her own experience and that of her brother Charles for verisimilitude.

Titch, by Pat Hutchins. Titch's sister Mary and his brother Pete are both older than Titch, which makes him feel left out of their activities until his little plant changes their relationship.

We're Very Good Friends, My Brother and I, by P. K. Hallinan. Two small boys illustrate the ways they share playtime and enjoy being friends as well as brothers.

Which Witch Is Which?, by Pat Hutchins. A simple book about twin girls at a birthday party. Since all the children are in costume, it's difficult to tell which witch is Ella and which witch is Emily. Trying to decide is fun.

Books About Single-Parent Families

Emily and the Klunky Baby and the Next-Door Dog, by Joan M. Lexau, illustrated by Martha Alexander. Poor Emily. Her mother is busy trying to do taxes, Emily and the baby try to find Daddy's apartment but get lost, and the next-door dog is no help in getting home. Finally she finds her house, but the baby's nap doesn't materialize.

A Father Like That, by Charlotte Zolotow, illustrated by Ben Shecter. A little boy talks with his mother about the father he's never had, imagining how he'd help with the dishes, play checkers, empathize when the boy is feeling blue, and so on. His mother assures him that when he grows up, he can become "a father like that."

Fly Away Home, by Eve Bunting, illustrated by Ronald Himler. Andrew and his father are homeless, so they live in the airport. They are clever about being inconspicuous, and they do manage, but Andrew longs for the day they can have an apartment again. All too sad and true.

I Love My Mother, by Paul Zindel, illustrated by John Melo. A single parent tries to give her young son a good life, but they both miss the boy's father.

I Speak English for My Mom, by Muriel Stanek, illustrated by Judith Friedman. A Mexican widow and her young daughter share life, with the child translating for her mom. Then the woman decides that to get a better job she has to learn English and starts night school.

Mama One and Mama Two, by Patricia MacLachlan, illustrated by Ruth Lercher Bornstein. A really beautiful story of a little girl whose mother becomes seriously depressed, so the child lives with a wonderful foster-mother (Mama Two) until Mama One comes home from where she is being helped to recover.

My Mother Lost Her Job Today, by Judy Delton, illustrated by Irene Trivas. Barbara Ann, age six, imagines real tragedy when her mother comes home depressed because of losing her job. But her mother reassures her that she will find another job and there will still be birthdays, Christmas, and trips to the zoo.

My Mother the Mail Carrier, by Inez Maury, translated into Spanish by Norah Allemany, illustrated by Lady McCrady. A little girl tells about her mother's life as a mail carrier and describes their warm relationship.

My Mother's House, My Father's House, by C. B. Christiansen, illustrated by Irene Trivas. With warmth and honesty this book affirms a young child's feelings about divorced parents who have shared custody. What she wants as an adult is one house with no suitcases.

My Mother's Getting Married, by Joan Drescher. Katy's mother is marrying Ben and everyone is happy about it except Katy, who shows her displeasure by wearing her blue jeans under her flower-girl dress. Katy catches her mother's bouquet, and no one notices the jeans. However, Katy still exhibits jealousy when she finds she is not included in the honeymoon. Her mother lovingly reassures her that all will be well, and she will always remain her mother's "Katydid."

One More Time, by Louis Baum, illustrated by Paddy Bouma. In a very subtle way we learn that little Simon is spending a visitation day with his dad, who takes him back to his mom when the day ends.

**Wagon Wheels, by Barbara Brenner, illustrated by Don Bolognese. This is a true story of the Muldie family, African-American pioneers, who travel to Kansas after the Civil War to take advantage of the Homestead Act. The father and his three children start in Nicodemus, Kansas, but the boys must follow their father to a place 150 miles farther on where the farming is good.

You're My Nikki, by Phyllis Rose Eisenberg, illustrated by Jill Kastner. Nikki needs reassurance when her mother goes out to work, and she gets it.

Books About Children and the Older Generation

Abuela, by Arthur Dorros, illustrated by Elisa Kleven. While riding on a bus with her Spanish-speaking grandmother, a little girl imagines that they are flying over New York City, seeing the sights. A glossary is at the end of the book.

Always Gamma, by Vaunda Micheaux Nelson, illustrated by Kimanne Uhler. A little girl has a really warm relationship with her grandparents, particularly her grandmother. Then that lady begins to act strangely (Alzheimer's), and goes into a nursing home, but the child remembers all their time together with deep love.

** *Annie and the Old One,* by Miska Miles, illustrated by Peter Parnall. In this Najavo family Annie and her grandmother have a very special relationship, so the child tries very hard to avoid the fact that her grandmother will die. She tries to hold back time, but then her grandmother explains the idea of life as a cycle, and Annie takes up her weaving stick again.

Apt. 3G, by Ezra Jack Keats. Ben and Sam investigate the sound of music in their tenement and meet the blind man downstairs who plays the harmonica. A touching but unsentimental look at his world.

Aunt Flossie's Hats (and Crab Cakes Later), by Elizabeth Fitzgerald Howard, illustrated by James Ransome. Sara and Susan enjoy going to their great-great-aunt's house to hear her reminisce about the past, evoked by each of her hats which the little girls try on. Then they all go to eat crab cakes.

Bigmama's, by Donald Crews. Visiting his grandmother's house—she is Bigmama—in Cottondale, the author remembers all the fun he had as a boy spending a whole summer vacation with his family on the old-fashioned farm.

Babushka's Doll, by Patricia Polacco. It's a very special doll, as Babushka's granddaughter Natasha discovers when she takes it down from the shelf and finds it uncontrollably selfish and demanding.

Better With Two, by Barbara M. Joosse, illustrated by Catherine Stock. Mrs. Brady and her old dog Max have a young friend Laura who sometimes joins them for "elevenses," or tea. Then Max dies, and Laura tries to make Mrs. Brady feel better by letting her know how sorry she is about Max's death.

A Birthday Basket for Tia, by Pat Mora, illustrated by Cecily Lang. Cecilia and her cat, Chica, prepare a special surprise for Tia's ninetieth birthday. In the basket Cecilia puts all the special things she shares with her great-aunt.

Blow Me a Kiss, Miss Lilly, by Nancy White Carlstrom, illustrated by Amy Schwartz. A sweet story about a little girl's friendship with an older woman who dies, but is always remembered with deep affection by the child.

The Cat Next Door, by Betty Ren Wright, illustrated by Gail Owens. Told in the first person, a little girl describes her typical summer visit to her grandparents' cabin near a lake, and a little cat who always greets her. Then her grandmother dies, and the child is comforted by the cat and her two newly born kittens.

Cherry Tree, by Ruskin Bond, illustrated by Allan Eitzen. A story from India in which Rakhi, a six-year-old girl, heeds her grandfather's advice and plants the seed of a cherry which survives many mishaps and grows into a lovely tree.

***Cornrows,* by Camille Yarbrough, illustrated by Carole Byard. Mama and Great Grammaw tell stories of African history as they braid Shirley Ann and her brother Mike's hair in cornrows, making meaningful patterns and giving the cornrows names of famous African Americans.

Could Be Worse!, by James Stevenson. Everything is always the same at Grandpa's house, even the things he says—until one unusual morning when Grandpa tells the children about his dream.

The Crack-of-Dawn Walkers, by Amy Hest, illustrated by Amy Schwartz. Sadie and her grandfather take their every-other-Sunday walk through the snowy city streets. On alternate weeks, her little brother Ben has his turn to take the walk. A very warm relationship exists between Grandpa and his grandchildren.

Dawn, by Uri Shulevitz. An old man and his grandson sleep by a lake and awake to put their rowboat into the water. Then everything dramatically turns green because of the sunrise.

***The Day Before Christmas,* by Eve Bunting, illustrated by Beth Peck. A really wonderful story of seven-year-old Allie, who goes to the city on the train with her grandfather for her first view of *The Nutcracker.* The ballet itself is gorgeous, but even more memorable is that her grandfather tells her how her deceased mother had enjoyed the same ballet when she was seven. Magnificent illustrations.

Digging to China, by Donna Rawlins. Hearing her friend Marj, the elderly lady next door, speak wistfully of China, Alexis digs a hole all the way through the earth to that exotic country and brings back a postcard for Marj on her birthday.

From Me to You, by Paul Rogers, illustrated by Jane Johnson. A grandmother born in 1906 tells her granddaughter of life in earlier times and gives her a momento with lace which had been used when she was young.

Grandpa, by Barbara Borack, illustrated by Ben Shecter. A very warm story of a girl's love for her grandparents, and especially her closeness to her grandpa.

Grandpa's Song, by Tony Johnston, illustrated by Brad Sneed. Jolly, rotund, and exuberant Grandpa, always fun to be with, is becoming a bit forgetful, but his loving grandchild helps him by singing their favorite song.

Grandpa's Too-Good Garden, by James Stevenson. Grandpa tells Mary Ann and Louie about a garden he had years ago that Wainey, his baby brother, "helped" him with. A tall tale, really, and lots of fun.

Granny Is a Darling, by Kady MacDonald Denton. Granny comes to visit the family and shares a room with Billy. Her snoring teaches him about "things that make noise in the night."

Ganzy Remembers, by Mary Grace Ketner, illustrated by Barbara Sparks. A little girl and her grandmother visit her great-grandmother in a nursing home, and the lady remembers when she was a girl called Daphne in Texas. She tells many stories, and some of them, as her daughter says, are true.

Happy Birthday, Grampie, by Susan Pearson, illustrated by Ronald Himler. Martha makes a special birthday card for her Swedish grandfather's eighty-ninth birthday since he is blind. The family goes to visit him in the nursing home, and he "reads" her card, saying in English, "I love you too, Martha."

I Dance in My Red Pajamas, by Edith Thacher Hurd, illustrated by Emily Arnold McCully. Jenny's parents don't understand, but when Jenny goes to spend the night at grandma and grandpa's house, they enjoy a lively, noisy time together.

I Go With My Family to Grandma's, by Riki Levinson, illustrated by Diane Goode. New York at the turn of the century is the scene for five families coming by different means of transportation (from each of the boroughs) to gather at Grandma's house in Brooklyn.

I Have Four Names for My Grandfather, by Kathryn Lasky, illustrated by Christopher G. Knight. Pop or Poppy, Gramps or Grandpa, it makes no difference. Tom has a real friend in his grandfather, and they both enjoy this relationship.

I Know a Lady, by Charlotte Zolotow, illustrated by James Stevenson. Sally describes a loving and lovable old lady in her neighborhood who grows flowers, waves to children when they pass her house, and bakes cookies for them.

Katie Morag and the Two Grandmothers, by Mairi Hedderwick. Katie has two very different grandmothers, plain Grannie Island and sophisticated Grandma Mainland. They don't seem to like each other until Grandma Mainland's secret beauty formula saves the day for Grannie Island's prize sheep.

Kevin's Grandma, by Barbara Williams, illustrated by Kay Chorao. Kevin's grandma is decidedly different! She used to work in a circus; now she rides a Honda 90, gives judo lessons, and skydives. The writer believes everything Kevin tells him about his grandma, except that she makes peanut butter soup. That's just too much!

****Knots on the Counting Rope,* by Bill Martin, Jr., and John Archambault, illustrated by Ted Rand. On a cool, dark night under the stars, a Native-American boy sits with his grandfather before a campfire. "Tell me who I am, Grandfather," pleads the boy and the old man does. The counting rope is a metaphor for the passage of time and for the boy's emerging confidence in facing the challenge of his blindness. A very moving, poignant story.

Maxie, by Mildred Kantrowitz, illustrated by Emily A. McCully. On the day Maxie, an elderly woman who lives alone, stays in bed because she thinks her dull routines are of no use to anyone, she discovers how many people rely on her performing them.

Miss Rumphius, by Barbara Cooney. Alice Rumphius wants to grow up to travel the world and then live by the sea, as her grandfather had. But first she must make the world more beautiful, which she does by scattering flower seeds everywhere so that the countryside is ablaze with color every spring.

**The Moon Lady,* by Amy Tan, illustrated by Gretchen Schields. Nai-Nai tells her granddaughters the story of her outing as a seven-year-old in China to see the Moon Lady and being granted a secret wish.

Mother Told Me So, by Carol A. Marron, illustrated by George Karn. Melissa Sue Albina McCormick is not a perfect child, so she sits in her room and thinks about all the unwise things she has done, things like drowning the plants in orange juice and spilling oatmeal on the window ledge. Her mother tells Melissa that she had never done such things. *But* Grandma tells Melissa about what her Mother did do when she was a little girl. She was not a perfect child either.

Music, Music for Everyone, by Vera B. Williams. Grandma is ill and the money which used to be saved in the glass jar must be spent to make her well. But Rosa and her friends form the Oak Street Band (Rosa on accordian, Jenny on fiddle, Mae on flute, and Leora on drums) and are successful in their first engagement for money, so they will continue.

My Grammy, by Marsha Kibbey, illustrated by Karen Ritz. Amy's grandmother, who has Alzheimer's Disease and can no longer stay on her farm alone, moves in with her daughter, son-in-law, and granddaughter, Amy. At first the girl is resentful of the intrusion and puzzled by Grammy's rather strange behavior. However, Amy finally understands what is causing Grammy's problem and the two form a loving attachment.

My Grandma's in a Nursing Home, by Judy Delton and Dorothy Tucker, illustrated by Charles Robinson. Jason and his mother visit Grandma in a nursing home, and the boy begins to understand the reasons for people being in Meadowbrook. A realistic book.

My Grandpa Retired Today, by Elaine Knox Wagner, illustrated by Charles Robinson. As she helps her grandfather clean and lock his barber shop one final time, Margery senses the pain he feels, even though they have lots of plans about how to spend his days.

My Grandson Lew, by Charlotte Zolotow, illustrated by William Pene Du Bois. Lew's mother is surprised that her six-year-old remembers his grandfather, who died when Lew was only two. But the boy does have memories of his grandpa which he shares with his mother.

Nana Upstairs and Nana Downstairs, by Tomie De Paola. Tommy has a grandmother and a great-grandmother, and he has a very special relationship with both of them. After his great-grandmother dies, he sees a star falling from the sky, and then when he has grown up, his grandmother dies and the second star makes him think that they are both "upstairs."

**Nessa's Fish,* by Nancy Luenn, illustrated by Neil Waldman. Nessa, a brave Eskimo girl, goes fishing with her grandmother, who becomes ill during the night. This leaves Nessa with the responsibility of watching over the woman and frightening away the animal poachers who try to get the fish. She succeeds, but is glad to see her family in the morning.

Now One Foot, Now the Other, by Tomie De Paola. Bobby learns how to walk when his beloved grandfather Bob teaches him. Then Bob has a stroke, and the tables are turned as Bobby helps his grandfather regain his mobility.

Oma and Bobo, by Amy Schwartz. Grandma Oma is not in favor of Alice getting a dog. But Bobo and Oma become fast friends by the time Bobo is in the dog show put on by Mr. Benjamin's Training School for Dogs.

On the Pampas, by Maria Cristina Brusca. A personal account of the author's summer spent with her grandparents at the Argentine equivalent of a ranch. Life is very different from her world in Buenos Aires, but she learns a lot and she loves it.

The Patchwork Quilt, by Valerie Flournoy, illustrated by Jerry Pinkney. Tenderly told, this is the story of the patchwork quilt that Grandmother is making; when she becomes unable to finish it, her granddaughter completes the masterpiece.

The Purple Coat, by Amy Hest, illustrated by Amy Schwartz. When Gabrielle and her mother go into the city to visit Grandpa, who is a tailor, Gabby is determined that this year the coat he makes for her will be purple, not navy. Grandpa manages to make both Gabrielle and her mother happy.

Rechenka's Eggs, by Patricia Polacco. An injured goose, rescued by Babushka, unintentionally breaks the painted eggs intended for the Easter Festival in Moscva, but lays thirteen marvelously colored ones to replace them, then leaves one last egg before rejoining her flock.

Song and Dance Man, by Karen Ackerman, illustrated by Stephen Gammell. When his grandchildren follow Grandpa up the attic stairs, a dazzling show is about to begin! Grandpa gets out his old costumes, dances, and sings; vaudeville is back.

A Special Trade, by Sally Wittman, illustrated by Karen Gundersheimer. Nelly, a little girl, has Bartholomew, a grandfatherly man, as a friend. In a very gentle way Nelly is able to reciprocate when Bartholomew is in a wheelchair, pushing him as he had pushed her in her stroller years before.

There's Nothing to Do, by James Stevenson. When Mary Ann and Louie tell Grandpa how bored they are, it reminds him of a time when he and his brother Wainwright were visiting their grandfather's farm, not a boring time.

Thunder Cake, by Patricia Polacco. A little girl's fear of thunder turns into an adventure when her grandma (Babushka) shows her how to bake a thunder cake. Recipe is included.

The Two of Them, by Aliki. A tenderly told tale of a little girl and the grandfather who loves her from the day of her birth. They share many things; then he becomes old and ill, and she takes care of him. When he dies, she is very sad, but she always remembers her Papouli with love.

The Village of Round and Square Houses, by Ann Grifalconi. A grandmother explains to her listeners why in their village on the side of a volcano (in the remote hills of the Cameroons in Central Africa) the men live in square houses and the women live in round ones.

The Wall, by Eve Bunting, illustrated by Ronald Himler. A boy and his father come from far away to visit the Vietnam Veterans Memorial in Washington and they find the name of the boy's grandfather, who was killed in the conflict.

Watch Out for the Chicken Feet in Your Soup, by Tomie De Paola. Joey is embarrassed to take his friend Eugene to visit his old-fashioned Italian grandma—but she and Eugene get along very well indeed.

***The Wednesday Surprise,* by Eve Bunting, illustrated by Donald Carrick. Anna and her grandmother have a very close relationship, especially since Anna is helping Grandma prepare a surprise for Anna's father at his birthday party. Grandma has learned to read.

We'll Ride Elephants Through Brooklyn, by Susan L. Roth. Grandpa is ill, but his grandchildren are planning a great circus-type parade to celebrate his recovery, and they do it!

What Goes Around Comes Around, by Sally G. Ward. Little Isabel accompanies her eccentric grandmother on a fun-filled journey through the neighborhood to give away Grandma's famous soup, and they return with treasures from all Grandma's friends.

When I Am Old With You, by Angela Johnson, illustrated by David Soman. A little girl imagines being old with her beloved Grandaddy and joining him in such activities as playing cards all day, visiting the ocean, and eating bacon on the porch.

William's Doll, by Charlotte Zolotow, illustrated by William Pene Du Bois. William wants a real baby doll like the one Nancy has. His father buys all the typical "boy" toys for him, and William plays with them, but when his grandmother comes, he asks her for the doll and he gets it.

Books About Competence and Self-Esteem

Another requirement of a happy child usually involves a feeling of self-worth achieved through mastery or competence. The list of books exemplifying that even the least likely to succeed can emerge triumphant with sufficient perseverence should probably begin with one of the very early books in this vein, the still-popular *Little Engine That Could* by Watty Piper. And as time has gone on, the recognition of this need has grown and with that recognition more and more books have been written which illustrate these qualities.

Ada Potato, by Judith Caseley. When Ada plays the violin in the school bandestra, she is teased by a group of bullies. After her mother tells her how she was teased as a child, Ada solves her problem with wit.

The Adventures of Isabel, by Ogden Nash, illustrated by James Marshall. Meet the inimitable Isabel who handles hair-raising encounters with ease and aplomb. Nash's verses are delightful.

Amazing Grace, by Mary Hoffman, illustrated by Caroline Binch. Grace loves to act and is determined to play Peter Pan in the school play. Her classmates say that she cannot do it because she is African-American and a girl, but Grace discovers that she can do anything she sets her mind to.

Anatole, by Eve Titus, illustrated by Paul Galdone. The most contented mouse in France, Anatole is upset when he hears people saying unkind things about mice, and he devises a way to do something to change their minds.

Andy—That's My Name, by Tomie De Paola. Andy is too young to read but he knows his name, and when the big kids start fooling with the letters, making other words out of Andy—but won't let him play—he goes home.

Angelina Ballerina, by Katherine Holabird, illustrated by Helen Craig. A pretty little mouse wants to become a ballerina more than anything in the world, and she does.

Anna Banana and Me, by Lenore Blegvad, illustrated by Erik Blegvad. Anna Banana is a fearless girl who plays with the little boy who is telling the story. He is really quite timid, but with Anna's help he becomes as brave as she is.

Anton B. Stanton and the Pirats, by Colin McNaughton. A very tiny boy (about the size of a rat) is captured by pirats, made to walk the plank, is saved by water rats, and then volunteers to rescue the princess who is being held for ransom.

Arthur Meets the President, by Marc Brown. Winning an essay contest takes Arthur and his whole class to Washington, D.C. But Arthur must memorize his speech for the President, which makes him nervous. D. W., his sister, turns out to be a help for a change.

The Balancing Girl, by Berniece Rabe, illustrated by Lillian Hoban. Margaret is a first grader who is very good at balancing objects while in her wheelchair and on crutches. In spite of Tommy who tries to knock everything down, Margaret builds a project which benefits the school carnival.

**Ben's Trumpet, by Rachel Isadora. Young Ben wants to be a trumpeter, but he plays only an imaginary instrument and is ridiculed by his friends. Then one of the musicians in a neighborhood nightclub discovers his ambition and rectifies the situation.

The Boy Who Held Back the Sea, by Lenny Hort, illustrated by Thomas Locker. Here the traditional tale of the boy who saved Holland by putting his finger in the dike is illustrated in the manner of the great Dutch artists.

Brave Irene, by William Steig. Irene Bobbin's mother is ill, but little Irene braves the snow and a windstorm to get the duchess's gown to her palace and then gets to attend the party there.

Bravo, Tanya, by Patricia Lee Gauch, illustrated by Satomi Ichikawa. Tanya loves to dance, but in class, with the teacher's loud clapping to keep time, she can barely hear the piano, so she almost gives up ballet, but not really.

Broderick, by Edward Ormondroyd, illustrated by John Larrecq. With tongue-in-cheek the author writes the story of a mouse who chooses surfing as his way to fame and wealth. However, he sends donations to libraries because he regrets having chewed up so many books before learning to read them.

By George, Bloomers!, by Judith St. George, illustrated by Margot Tomes. In the mid-nineteenth century no women wore slacks. Then Mrs. Amelia Bloomer started something as an early feminist. In this fictional story a little girl, Hannah, is able to save her little brother Jamie because she can climb onto the roof in her "bloomers."

The Carrot Seed, by Ruth Krauss, illustrated by Crockett Johnson. Everyone said the carrot seed would not come up, but the little boy faithfully tends it and has his reward.

Chocolate Chip Cookies, by Karen Wagner, illustrated by Leah Palmer Preiss. Twin boys follow a recipe for chocolate chip cookies step by step, and so can the reader.

Charlie Needs a Cloak, by Tomie De Paola. In this introduction to the way wool becomes cloth and cloth becomes clothing, Charlie, a shepherd, and his favorite sheep humorously take all needed steps so that when winter comes, Charlie has a new red cloak.

A Color of His Own, by Leo Lionni. The sad chameleon has a problem—unlike all other animals, he has no color of his own, but he finds a partner and they change color together.

Come Away from the Water, Shirley, by John Burningham. Shirley's parents sit at the seaside and say the usual things to their little girl on the left-hand pages, while on the right-hand pages we see that Shirley is thinking about boarding a pirate ship, capturing it, and finding treasure, returning triumphant with her dog.

Cornelius, by Leo Lionni. Cornelius, a crocodile who walks upright, sees things no crocodile has ever seen before and learns to do tricks the monkey teaches him. The other crocodiles pretend that they don't care, but they do.

Crackle Gluck and the Sleeping Toad, by Dick Gackenbach. The superstitious Gluck family is convinced that a two-hundred-year-old toad is their lucky charm, but their daughter Crackle proves to her reluctant parents and brother that he's a hoax.

Cross-Country Cat, by Mary Calhoun, illustrated by Erick Ingraham. A very clever Siamese cat, Henry, finds when he is left behind by accident in the snow-covered mountains that he can use the skis his children have made for him.

**Crow Boy,* by Taro Yashima. A very tender story of an unusual boy, Chibi, who seems to be slower than the other children in his school, but who has a very special talent.

Custard the Dragon, by Ogden Nash, illustrated by Linell Nash Smith. In verse typical of Nash, this story tells of the girl, Belinda, and her pets, including the cowardly dragon Custard who behaves bravely when faced with an evil pirate.

Dance, Tanya, by Patricia Lee Gauch, illustrated by Satomi Ichikawa. Tanya's older sister Elise takes ballet lessons and dances in a recital, but little Tanya also has talent and shows how she too can be a ballerina.

Effie, by Beverley Allinson, illustrated by Barbara Reid. When Effie the ant saves other ants from being trampled by an elephant, her loud voice is suddenly appreciated by her friends.

Flossie and the Fox, by Patricia C. McKissack, illustrated by Rachel Isadora. Told in rural Southern dialect, this is the story of a wily fox notorious for stealing eggs who meets his match when he encounters a bold little girl in the woods. Flossie insists that she must have proof that he is a fox before she will be frightened.

Frederick, by Leo Lionni. A refreshing view of the work ethic that we may remember from the fable "The Ant and the Grasshopper." Frederick's contribution of imagination and poetry is as valuable as the food-gathering done by his fellow mice.

Garth Pig and the Ice Cream Lady, by Mary Rayner. When Garth Pig goes out to buy Whooshes for himself and nine siblings, he finds the ice cream lady is really a wolf who has other ideas.

The Goat in the Rug, by Charles L. Blood and Martin Link, illustrated by Nancy Winslow Parker. Geraldine, a goat, describes each step as she and her Navajo friend make a rug from her hair, clipping, carding, dyeing, and actually weaving a traditional Navajo rug.

Grover, Grover, Come on Over, by Katherine Ross, illustrated by Tom Cooke. Picturing many of the familiar characters from Sesame Street, we see Grover making a kite for the others. It flies.

Growing Vegetable Soup, by Lois Ehlert. A child and her father decide to grow everything they will need to make vegetable soup, and they do.

The Hare and the Tortoise, retold by Caroline Castle, illustrated by Peter Weevers. In this retelling of Aesop's fable, new animal characters are added: a wise Badger, a flamboyant Frog, an industrious Mole, and others. But it is the "health-nut" Hare and the scholarly Tortoise who still hold center stage.

The Hare and the Tortoise, by Jean de La Fontaine, illustrated by Brian Wildsmith. The traditional fable, gorgeously illustrated, tells of the virtues of being slow and steady, rather than quick and careless.

Hattie, the Backstage Bat, by Don Freeman. The only occupants of the Lyceum Theatre are Hattie and the stage doorman, Mr. Collins. That is, until a show is being rehearsed and Hattie has to stay out of sight. On opening night, however, she appears, thrills the audience, and makes the play a success.

High-Wire Henry, by Mary Calhoun, illustrated by Erick Ingraham. The further adventures of Henry, the smart Siamese cat who can walk on his hind legs. Here he saves the new puppy Buttons when the dog gets stuck out on a ledge of the house.

Horton Hatches the Egg, by Dr. Seuss. Horton, the elephant, has promised to sit on Mayzie's egg while she takes a vacation, and he is true to his word even when she doesn't return. After a number of adventures, the egg hatches near Palm Beach and the good-for-nothing Mayzie swoops down and claims it. However, it is an elephant-bird.

Horton Hears a Who!, by Dr. Seuss. As Horton the elephant is bathing, he hears a small speck of dust calling for help, and the adventure goes on from there, in rhyme, until the end—when all the Whos in Whoville are protected forever.

How Do I Put It On?, by Shigeo Watanabe, illustrated by Yasuo Ohtomo. A darling little bear experiments with dressing himself and finally succeeeds.

How Many Trucks Can a Tow Truck Tow?, by Charlotte Pomerantz, illustrated by R. W. Alley. A sturdy little tow truck comes to the rescue when three other tow trucks in town all break down on the same day. Rhyme and colorful illustrations make this book comical.

How My Garden Grew, by Anne and Harlow Rockwell. With pride and pleasure, a little girl describes how she plants and takes care of a vegetable garden all by herself. A very first look at gardening.

Howie Helps Himself, by Joan Fassler, illustrated by Joe Lasker. Though he enjoys life with his family and attends school, Howie, a child with cerebral palsy, wants more than anything else to be able to move his wheelchair by himself.

I Can Build a House!, by Shigeo Watanabe, illustrated by Yasuo Ohtomo. Little Bear's efforts with blocks and pillows fail, but he finds the right material and figures out how to succeed. Part of an excellent series with appeal for the toddler who says, "I do it by myself."

I Can Ride It!, by Shigeo Watanabe, illustrated by Yasuo Ohtomo. Bear is sure he can ride a tricycle, a two-wheel bike, and anything else with wheels, and he takes tumbles trying, but he is learning.

****I Hate English!*, by Ellen Levine, illustrated by Steve Bjorkman. When her family moves to New York from Hong Kong, Mei Mei finds it difficult to adjust to school and the sounds of English until her teacher, Nancy, tries a new tactic.

I Like Me!, by Nancy Carlson. By admiring her finer points and showing that she can take care of herself and have fun even when there's no one else around, a charming pig proves the best friend you can have is yourself.

I Speak English for My Mom, by Muriel Stanek, illustrated by Judith Friedman. A Mexican widow and her young daughter share life, with the child translating for her mom. Then the woman decides that to get a better job she has to learn English and starts night school.

Just for You, by Mercer Mayer. The first of a series about an endearing animal who just happens to do everything a toddler would do. He really tries very hard!

Katy and the Big Snow, by Virginia Lee Burton. A valiant (female) tractor saves the town when no other vehicle can get through the deep snow.

The King's Shadow, by Robert D. Larranaga, illustrated by Joe Greenwald. The little king, fearing his own shadow, tries unsuccessfully to get rid of it. Finally forced to face a fiery dragon, the little king overcomes his fear when the dragon flees at the sight of the shadow which he believes to be a giant.

**Knots on the Counting Rope, by Bill Martin, Jr., and John Archambault, illustrated by Ted Rand. On a cool, dark night under the stars, a Native-American boy sits with his grandfather before a campfire. "Tell me who I am, Grandfather," pleads the boy, and the old man does. The counting rope is a metaphor for the passage of time and for the boy's emerging confidence in facing the challenge of his blindness. A very moving and poignant story.

Leo the Late Bloomer, by Robert Kraus, illustrated by Jose Aruego. Leo the tiger can't do anything right. He can't read or write or draw. He is a sloppy eater, and he never says a word. Then one day in his own good time Leo blooms!

Let's Go Swimming with Mr. Sillypants, by M. K. Brown. After Mr. Sillypants has a dream of falling into the water and not being able to save himself, he decides to go ahead with swimming lessons.

The Lion and the Rat, by Jean de La Fontaine, illustrated by Brian Wildsmith. A lion allows a rat to escape, and is surprised to find later that although some of the other large beasts cannot free him from a trap, the little rat is able to gnaw through the ropes and repay the lion's kindness. Beautiful color illustrations.

The Little Engine That Could, by Watty Piper. When the train filled with toys and goodies breaks down, the Passenger Train and the Freight Train feel too important to help, and the Rusty Old Engine is too tired, so it is the Little Blue Engine who saves the day.

The Little Red Hen, retold and illustrated by Paul Galdone. This well-known cautionary tale is done with great humor even though the Little Red Hen eats the whole cake.

The Little Wood Duck, by Brian Wildsmith. His mother and all the woodland animals make fun of the little duck who swims in circles instead of in a straight line until his peculiar way of swimming saves the family.

The Long Red Scarf, by Nettie Hilton, illustrated by Margaret Power. Grandpa's friend Jake has a blue scarf to keep him warm when the two men go fishing, and Grandpa wants a long red scarf to wear on these outings, but he can't find anyone to knit it for him. Maude can't knit; Isabel doesn't have time; so he asks Jake for advice and learns to knit himself.

Mary Mary, by Sarah Hayes, illustrated by Helen Craig. Mary Mary is indeed "contrary," but she is also very brave and has considerable skill at managing the lonely giant who lives on the hill.

Matthew's Dream, by Leo Lionni. Matthew's parents are poor, but they have high hopes for their son. He, however, wants to see the world, which he discovers in a museum. So he decides to become a painter, marries Nicoletta, and achieves success as an artist.

Mike Mulligan and His Steam Shovel, by Virginia Lee Burton. Mary Anne, Mike's steam shovel, has dug canals, cut through mountains, and dug deep holes for the cellars of skyscrapers. But now Mary Anne is considered old-fashioned, until in Popperville she digs the cellar for the new town hall and remains there as the new furnace.

Mik's Mammoth, by Roy Gerrard. A great story told in rhyme of a little boy who is left behind when the rest of the tribe of cavemen go off in search of food. He finds a baby mammoth, Rumm, and the two survive very well, saving the tribe from fierce warriors who pursue them when they return.

Mirandy and Brother Wind, by Patricia C. McKissack, illustrated by Jerry Pinkney. To win first prize in the Junior Cakewalk, Mirandy tries to capture the wind for her partner, and she succeeds. Of course, Ezel, who is usually clumsy, helps a lot.

**Mirette on the High Wire,* by Emily Arnold McCully. In nineteenth-century Paris the widow Gateau and her daughter Mirette run a high-class board-inghouse for actors and performers of many kinds. When the Great Bellini, famed high-wire walker, comes to Mme Gateau's, he agrees to teach Mirette, but also confesses that he now has a fear of performing. However, with Mirette's help, he regains his courage.

**Miss Fanshawe and the Great Dragon Adventure,* by Sue Scullard. A truly novel book about an intrepid British lady who successfully traps a dragon by traveling to the center of the earth in a hot-air balloon, circa late-nineteenth century.

Miss Nelson Has a Field Day, by Harry Allard, illustrated by James Marshall. The notorious Viola Swamp, the meanest teacher in the world, reappears at the Horace B. Smedley School, this time to shape up the football team and make them win at least one game.

**Mr. and Mrs. Pig's Night Out,* by Mary Rayner. When Mother and Father announce to their ten piglets that there will be a babysitter for the evening, they get the usual chorus of groans, but when she turns out to be Mrs. Wolf, the piglets outsmart her plan to eat them.

Mouse Soup, by Arnold Lobel. A very clever mouse convinces a weasel, by telling four stories, that he needs certain ingredients to make mouse soup. By the time the weasel has gathered the ingredients, the mouse has escaped.

Music, Music for Everyone, by Vera B. Williams. Grandma is ill and the money which used to be saved in the glass jar must be spent to make her well. But Rosa and her friends form the Oak Street Band (Rosa on accordian, Jenny on fiddle, Mae on flute, and Leora on drums) and are successful in their first engagement for money, so they will continue.

My Ballet Class, by Rachel Isadora. A girl about eight years old explains facts about ballet, including the barre, the five basic positions, and some simple terminology.

My Mother and I Are Growing Strong, by Inez Maury, translated into Spanish by Anna Munoz, illustrated by Sandy Speidel. A bilingual story of a family whose father is in prison for hitting someone who had insulted him. Emilita and her mother bravely carry on the father's gardening route alone.

Nattie Parson's Good-Luck Lamb, by Lisa Campbell Ernst. When her grandfather decrees that her cherished pet lamb Clover must be sold, Nattie figures a way out, and the shawl that she weaves from his special wool brings enough money for the next winter's hay.

**Nessa's Fish,* by Nancy Luenn, illustrated by Neil Waldman. Nessa, a brave Eskimo girl, goes fishing with her grandmother, who becomes ill during the night. This leaves Nessa with the responsibility of watching over the woman and frightening away the animal poachers who try to get the fish. She succeeds but is glad to see her family in the morning.

A New Coat for Anna, by Harriet Ziefert, illustrated by Anita Lobel. After World War II there are no coats in the stores, so to keep her promise to Anna her mother exchanges things she owns for wool, weaving, spinning, and sewing until the child has her pretty new red coat.

Noel the Coward, by Robert Kraus, illustrated by Jose Aruego and Ariane Dewey. Coward-powered Noel (and his cowardly father) change their lives after attending Charlie's School of Self-Defense. They have no need to fight back because they know they can.

Norman the Doorman, by Don Freeman. The artistic little mouse, Norman, lives in the attic of the Majestic Museum of Art, where he acts as doorman at a well-hidden hole in the back of the place. But Norman creates a masterpiece for a sculpture contest which wins first prize.

Oh, Lewis!, by Eve Rice. Little Lewis has trouble keeping his boots buckled, his jacket zipped, and his mittens on. Then he has trouble getting them off when he comes home. A universal problem of the very young.

Opening Night, by Rachel Isadora. Heather is very excited about her first professional appearance in *A Midsummer Night's Dream,* in which she and her friend dance in the ballet.

Otto Is Different, by Fritz Brandenberg, illustrated by James Stevenson. Otto the octopus learns the advantages of having eight arms instead of just two as he does household tasks, plays hockey, and gets goodnight hugs from his parents.

Owliver, by Robert Kraus, illustrated by Jose Aruego and Ariane Dewey. A baby owl who likes to act is encouraged by his mother, but his father would prefer that he follow a more secure profession and become a doctor or a lawyer. However, when he is grown, Owliver makes his own choice.

Pancakes, Pancakes, by Eric Carle. Jack wants a big pancake for breakfast, but first he must get the ingredients: wheat made into flour, eggs, milk, butter, wood for the fire, and also some jam for topping. Colorful illustrations make this book a delight.

Pelle's New Suit, by Elsa Beskow, translated from the Swedish by Marion Letcher Woodburn, illustrated by Elsa Beskow. Pelle's little lamb provides the wool, but it needs to be carded, dyed, woven into cloth, and sewn into a suit. The boy exchanges his services for each step of the process.

The Plant Sitter, by Gene Zion, illustrated by Margaret Bloy Graham. When his family decides not to go away for the summer, Tommy invents his own job, "sitting" with people's plants. He does a great job—almost too good. The plants grow so big that there is little room for his family until Tommy gets a library book with instructions for transplanting.

Playing Marbles, by Julie Brinckloe. A little girl draws a circle to play marbles and proves her skill against two boys who don't remain condescending for long.

**Ragtime Tumpie,* by Alan Schroeder, illustrated by Bernie Fuchs. Tumpie, a young African-American girl who will later become famous as the dancer Josephine Baker, longs to find the opportunity to dance amid the poverty and vivacious street life of St. Louis in the early 1900s, and she wins a silver dollar for her first public appearance in a contest.

Roland the Minstrel Pig, by William Steig. Roland, who plays the lute and composes songs and sings them beautifully, is urged by his friends to go into the world and share his talents. He is too trusting when he meets Sebastian, a fox, but escapes being a victim when the king saves him and takes him to court where he becomes famous.

Sabrina, by Martha Alexander. A little girl would like to exchange her name for a more common one, but decides that if it's the name of a princess she will keep it after all.

**Sam, Bangs and Moonshine,* by Evaline Ness. Samantha has a reckless habit of lying, which her father calls "moonshine." She also has a cat, Bangs, and a little friend, Thomas. Sam's bad habit almost causes tragedy when she sends Thomas and Bangs into danger, which teaches her the difference between "moonshine" and reality.

Sam Johnson and the Blue Ribbon Quilt, by Lisa Campbell Ernst. While mending the awning over the pigpen, Sam discovers that he enjoys sewing pieces together, but he meets with ridicule when he asks to join his wife's quilting club, so he forms his own. The two clubs cooperate at the county fair. Genuine quilt patterns border each page.

**Silent Lotus,* by Jeanne M. Lee. Lotus, who is born deaf, cannot speak, and she is a lonely child, playing only with the herons, cranes, and white egrets. Her parents take her to the palace in the Khmer Kingdom, and she learns to dance so well that she becomes the most famous dancer in the court. Gorgeous illustrations.

Someday Rider, by Ann Herbert Scott, illustrated by Ronald Himler. Kenny longs to be a cowboy like his dad, and he practices by trying to ride every animal on the ranch. Finally his mom teaches him how to ride a horse and he is able to join the group going to a roundup.

Story Hour—Starring Megan!, by Julie Brillhart. When Megan's mother, the librarian, can't read at story hour because Megan's little brother Nathan is too noisy, Megan takes over and does a great job.

The Story of Ferdinand, by Munro Leaf, illustrated by Robert Lawson. When the men "in funny hats" come to find the fiercest bull for the bullring in Madrid, Ferdinand is uninterested, but when he reacts to a bee sting, he seems a good candidate. However, once in the bullring, he refuses to fight, frustrating all the macho men who finally give up and return him to his home where he sits under the cork tree smelling the flowers.

Swimmy, by Leo Lionni. The only survivor after all the other small fish have been gobbled up by a big fish, the scared, lonely, and very sad Swimmy goes through his deep wet world seeking others like him. Then he shows them how to swim in a formation which looks like a giant fish so that they are safe from predators.

There's an Alligator Under My Bed, by Mercer Mayer. A sequel to *There's a Nightmare in My Closet,* the alligator under his bed makes the boy's bedtime a hazardous operation, but he lures it out of the house and into the garage.

There's Something in My Attic, by Mercer Mayer. Convinced that there is something making noise in the attic at night, a brave little girl sneaks upstairs, lasso in hand, to capture whatever it is.

Three Brave Women, by C. L. G. Martin, illustrated by Peter Elwell. Mama and Grammy's humorous childhood anecdotes help Caitlin to deal with her fear of spiders. When she realizes that Billy Huxley is afraid of her little dog Muffy, that helps too.

Three Days on a River in a Red Canoe, by Vera B. Williams. A little girl describes in detail a camping trip she takes with her mother, her Aunt Rosie, and her cousin Sam. Makes camping sound like fun.

Titch, by Pat Hutchins. Titch's sister Mary and his brother Pete are both older than Titch, which makes him feel left out of their activities until his little plant changes their relationship.

A Visit to the Sesame Street Library, by Deborah Hautzig, illustrated by Joe Mathieu. Big Bird goes to a bookstore, and when he finds he doesn't have enough money to buy the book he wants, he goes to the library and learns all about services that libraries provide, such as books of all kinds, puppet shows, a reading corner, tapes, books for the blind, and many more.

We Never Get to Do Anything, by Martha Alexander. A little boy is determined to go swimming, and he finally thinks up a way to get his wish right in his own backyard.

***The Wednesday Surprise,* by Eve Bunting, illustrated by Donald Carrick. Anna and her grandmother have a very close relationship, especially since Anna is helping Grandma prepare a surprise for Anna's father at his birthday party. Grandma has learned to read.

What's the Matter, Sylvie, Can't You Ride?, by Karen Born Anderson. A little girl experiences the trials and tribulations of learning to ride a two-wheel bike.

When Will I Read?, by Miriam Cohen, illustrated by Lillian Hoban. Jim is impatient to read and finally realizes that he can read some words when he tells the teacher about the sign on the hamsters' box.

Whistle for Willie, by Ezra Jack Keats. Little Peter wants to be able to whistle to call his dog Willie, but he simply can't make the sound. However, practice makes perfect, so Peter finally learns to whistle.

Willy the Champ, by Anthony Browne. Willy, a chimpanzee, is not very good at sports or fighting, but when the local bully shows up, Willy wins the battle.

Books About Behavior and Misbehavior

When considering the element of conflict in children's books, sometimes the protagonist (main character) is in conflict with an antagonist, at other times the protagonist is in conflict with the environment, and finally, he may be in conflict with himself. This is no different than the types of conflict found in adult literature. However, most books for young children can simply group these conflicts under a heading entitled "Books About Behavior and Misbehavior."

If a bully is threatening the protagonist, it is a conflict with an antagonist who is "misbehaving," as in the first title listed, *Ada Potato*. If the protagonist cannot resist shoplifting, as in *Arnie and the Stolen Markers*, it is a conflict with his own conscience that must be resolved. In the great majority of children's books, the protagonist wins the conflict.

Ada Potato, by Judith Caseley. When Ada plays the violin in the school bandestra, she is teased by a group of bullies. After her mother tells how she was teased as a child, Ada solves her problem with wit.

All About You, by Catherine and Laurence Anholt. A charming first look at life for a child: How do you feel? Who lives in your house? Where do you like to go? and other questions of this type give a child an opportunity to compare his or her life with the lives of other children.

An Anteater Named Arthur, by Bernard Waber. Arthur is a sweet little anteater who doesn't always understand that he must tidy up his room, eat what his mother puts on the table, and not forget what he needs to take with him when he goes to school.

Angus and the Ducks, by Marjorie Flack. A curious Scotch terrier decides to investigate the strange noise coming from the other side of the hedge and almost regrets his curiosity.

Arnie and the Stolen Markers, by Nancy Carlson. Arnie simply cannot resist the set of markers in Harvey's toy and candy store where he and his friend Louanne go every Saturday morning. So he steals them and feels very guilty and frightened. Then Harvey lets him work until he earns the price of the coveted markers and even gives him paper on which to paint.

Babushka's Doll, by Patricia Polacco. It's a very special doll, as Babushka's granddaughter Natasha discovers when she takes it down from the shelf and finds it uncontrollably selfish and demanding.

The Baby Blue Cat Who Said No, by Ainslie Pryor. One little cat out of four knows only one word—NO. But Mother Cat deals with her playful baby with love.

Bear Party, by William Pene Du Bois. A charming story about koalas who become unfriendly toward each other until they don costumes and masks and have a wonderful party, keeping part of their costumes on afterward so that they will recognize each other.

The Bear's Bicycle, by Emilie Warren McLeod, illustrated by David McPhail. A little boy and his bear ride bicycles; the bear does all the wrong things whereas the child illustrates safe bike rules. Then they both have a cookie and milk at home.

Bedtime for Frances, by Russell Hoban, illustrated by Garth Williams. One of a series about a badger family, this book emphasizes the excuses the typical toddler makes to avoid going to bed. All of the Frances books are favorites with young children.

Better Not Get Wet, Jesse Bear, by Nancy White Carlstrom, illustrated by Bruce Degan. Despite Mama and Papa's repeated warnings, Jesse tries everything to get wet. Finally he is allowed to go into his little plastic pool and Papa Bear uses the hose on him.

Big Bad Bruce, by Bill Peet. Bruce, a bully bear, never picks on anyone his own size until he is diminished in more ways than one by a small but very independent witch.

Big Brother, by Charlotte Zolotow, illustrated by Mary Chalmers. Big brother teases little sister until she realizes that he is only fooling, and they play nicely together.

A Big Fat Enormous Lie, by Marjorie Weinman Sharmat, illustrated by David McPhail. When a little boy lies about eating a jar of cookies, his conscience makes him visualize the lie as a green blob, getting bigger and uglier all the time, so he confesses to his parents and the enormous monstrosity disappears.

The Biggest House in the World, by Leo Lionni. A little snail learns how to make his shell really extraordinary, but when it grows so large that its owner cannot move to get food, all is lost.

Bread and Jam for Frances, by Russell Hoban, illustrated by Lillian Hoban. Mother Badger gives Frances just what she wants for every meal—bread and jam—until Frances decides to try some other foods and finds she likes them.

A Cake for Barney, by Joyce Dunbar, illustrated by Emilie Boon. Barney the bear has a little cake with five cherries on it, but he can't eat it because one bully after another demands one cherry after another. Finally Barney defies a really big bully and just eats the whole cake at one gulp.

The Cat in the Hat, by Dr. Seuss. An early classic by Dr. Seuss who rhymes the unbelievable antics of the cat who comes to amuse the children on a rainy day, wrecks everything, and then remedies all damage by the time Mother comes home.

The Circus Baby, by Maud and Miska Petersham. Mother Elephant tries to teach her baby to do what the clown's baby does, but try as hard as Baby Elephant can, it just does not work because Baby Elephant *is* an elephant.

Curious George, by H. A. Rey. The first of a series about a mischievous little monkey and "the man in the yellow hat" who brings him home from the jungle.

Curious George Goes to the Hospital, by Margaret and H. A. Rey. This time the little monkey has swallowed a piece of a jigsaw puzzle and must have it removed. Of course, he gets into the usual scrapes in the hospital.

The Cut-Ups, by James Marshall. Spud Jenkins and Joe Turner get away with every kind of prank until they meet Mary Frances Hooley. She lets them ride in her rocket, which gets them involved with Lamar J. Spurgle, the vice-principal who "never forgets a face." One of a series starring Spud and Joe.

Doctor Rabbit's Foundling, by Jan Wahl, illustrated by Cyndy Szekeres. A fanciful tale about a very small tadpole who grows into Tiny Toad and leaves Doctor Rabbit to be with other toads. Mother Rabbit explains, "Every child must go away at last."

Don't Call Me Names!, by Joanna Cole, illustrated by Lynn Munsinger. Nell is afraid of Mike and Joe because they always tease her and make fun of her until she stands up to them for her little friend, Nicky. Then she can defend herself, too.

Don't Touch!, by Suzy Kline, illustrated by Dora Leder. When all grown-ups constantly tell Dan not to touch this and that, the boy finds something he can safely squeeze, smash, and pound to his heart's content.

Elbert's Bad Word, by Audrey Wood, illustrated by Audrey and Don Wood. Elbert snatches a bad word out of the air one day at an elegant garden party and shocks everyone. Then he is cured by a wizard gardener, so that when Elbert next has occasion to use "the word," it comes out as "My stars! Thunder and Lightning!" and other acceptable expressions, and he gets three cheers.

Feelings, by Aliki. This book explains with simple drawings what feelings are, and tells when people experience anger, shyness, pride, jealousy, sadness, and other emotions.

Finders Keepers, by William Lipkind and Nicolas Mordvinoff. Nap and Winkle argue about who the bone they've found belongs to—the one who saw it first or the one who touched it first. After almost losing it, they decide to share the bone.

First Flight, by David McPhail. A naughty teddy bear, in contrast with his well-behaved owner, ignores all the rules and disrupts a boy's first airplane trip to visit his grandmother.

Gladys Told Me to Meet Her Here, by Marjorie Weinman Sharmat, illustrated by Edward Frascino. Gladys and Irving are best friends, but now Irving can't find Gladys, so he goes to look for her, which causes the problem. She is waiting where she said she would wait.

The Good-Bye Book, by Judith Viorst, illustrated by Kay Chorao. A child whose parents are going out to a French restaurant comes up with a variety of pleas and excuses for not staying at home with a babysitter, but when they've gone. . . .

The Gorilla Did It, by Barbara Shook Hazen, illustrated by Ray Cruz. A little boy blames his messy room on his mischievous friend the gorilla, who then helps him clean everything up and promises to be a good gorilla in the future.

The Green-Tailed Mouse, by Leo Lionni. An innocent group of mice frolicking in the woods are persuaded by a strange mouse to devise costumes for a Mardi Gras celebration. They start to behave in aggressive ways to live up to their frightening new images. Then a second mouse advises them to burn all the masks and return to their original state. However, one mouse who has dyed his tail green is unable to remove the paint.

Gregory, the Terrible Eater, by Mitchell Sharmat, illustrated by Jose Aruego and Ariane Dewey. Most goats will eat anything, but Gregory decides he must have healthy foods, such as fruits, vegetables, milk, bread, and butter. This finicky behavior upsets his parents who consult Doctor Ram about Gregory's eating habits.

The Grizzly Sisters, by Cathy Bellows. Mama Bear is careful, but her cubs don't listen to her admonitions. They delight in scaring beavers and wolves, but when they meet humans, Mama must rescue them from the people and their cameras.

The Grouchy Ladybug, by Eric Carle. A novel book with cutaway pages as the grouchy ladybug wants to fight with larger and larger animals.

Harry the Dirty Dog, by Gene Zion, illustrated by Margaret Bloy Graham. The first of the "Harry" books explains that Harry hates a bath, so he runs away but gets so dirty during his meanderings that he is not recognized by his family when he returns. He then brings his bath brush, gets bathed, and all is well.

Hazel's Amazing Mother, by Rosemary Wells. Hazel and her doll, Eleanor, get lost on the way back from the store and are waylaid by some very destructive bullies. Then Hazel's mother, almost like magic, saves them both.

Henry and the Red Stripes, by Eileen Christelow. Henry, the rabbit, insists that painting red stripes on himself is fine until he is taken by Mr. Fox and almost cooked. After a narrow escape, he's happy to be just a plain brown rabbit—except when he's at home.

Henry the Explorer, by Mark Taylor, illustrated by Graham Booth. Henry, a small boy, and his dog Angus decide to explore the world. They get lost, but since Henry has put an "H" on everything he has discovered, the search party is able to find him rather promptly.

Herman the Helper, by Robert Kraus, illustrated by Jose Aruego and Ariane Dewey. A very small octopus, Herman, helps everyone, and when the day is done, helps himself to mashed potatoes at dinner.

Hound and Bear, by Dick Gackenbach. Three short stories about two very good friends. Hound, however, nearly ruins their relationship with his practical jokes.

I Want to Sleep in Your Bed!, by Harriet Ziefert, illustrated by Mavis Smith. It is time for everyone to go to bed, but Susan can't fall asleep in her own bed until she puts her doll's bed next to her own and tells her a story about a little girl who didn't want to sleep in her own bed.

I Was So Mad!, by Norma Simon, illustrated by Dora Leder. Illustrating valid reasons for anger—blame for a mess you didn't make, frustration when you can't turn a somersault, having to take a rest when you're not tired—but concluding, "It's not bad to get mad—sometimes." It's reassuring.

I'm Telling You Now, by Judy Delton, illustrated by Lillian Hoban. Little Artie behaves beautifully, and never does anything his mother tells him not to do. But he does not always read her mind in advance about no-noes.

I'm Terrific, by Marjorie Weinman Sharmat, illustrated by Kay Chorao. Jason Bear thinks he's terrific and awards himself gold stars for superior performance, but his friends don't like to be around him, so he tries the other extreme. Then finally he understands the happy medium in behavior.

Jerome the Babysitter, by Eileen Christelow. Jerome's sister Winifred gives him the job of sitting with the Gatorman kids who behave abominably until Jerome tames them.

Keep Your Mouth Closed, Dear, by Aliki. Charles, a young crocodile, cannot help swallowing everything in sight. His parents try all kinds of remedies, even putting a zipper on his mouth, but nothing works until he helps his mother with the cleaning and uses the vacuum.

King of the Playground, by Phyllis Reynolds Naylor, illustrated by Nola Langner Malone. Sammy is a bully who won't let Kevin share any playground equipment. He uses threats, which Kevin's father turns around to teach Kevin problem solving. The two boys end by playing cooperatively.

Laney's Lost Momma, by Diane Johnston Hamm, illustrated by Sally G. Ward. Laney loses her mother in a large department store, but she remembers what to do and what to avoid, and she finds her lost mother quite quickly.

Little Toot, by Hardie Gramatky. Little Toot comes from a long line of tugboats, but he doesn't like work and he is frightened of the sea which lies outside the channel. All he wants to do is blow smoke bubbles. Then when he changes his mind, no ship wants him until he becomes a hero by saving a huge liner stuck between two rocks.

Madeline and the Bad Hat, by Ludwig Bemelmans. When the Spanish Ambassador and his family move next door to Madeline's school, the twelve girls and Miss Clavel have to deal with Pepito, the ambassador's son, who is a holy terror.

Max's Dragon Shirt, by Rosemary Wells. On a shopping trip to the department store, Max's determination to get a dragon shirt leads him away from his distracted sister Ruby and into trouble, but he gets what he wants.

Messy, by Barbara Bottner. Her real name is Harriet, but she likes to be called Harry, and she is a lovable girl, but messy. For a week before her ballet recital she tidies everything up and when she appears in her white tutu, she's a big success. Then she and her parents go for ice cream. . . .

Mine's the Best, by Crosby N. Bonsall. Two boys argue about the merits of two rubber fish, but after both toys are deflated, the children finally agree.

Miss Nelson Is Back, by Harry Allard, illustrated by James Marshall. When Miss Nelson has to have her tonsils out, and her class is bored with Mr. Blandsworth the principal, they figure out a way to do what they wish on school time. However, they are foiled by Viola Swamp, the substitute teacher.

Miss Nelson Is Missing!, by Harry Allard and James Marshall, illustrated by James Marshall. The kids in Room 207 take advantage of their teacher's good nature until she disappears and they are faced with a vile substitute, Miss Viola Swamp.

Mr. Gumpy's Outing, by John Burningham. Mr. Gumpy lives near a river and has a boat. He agrees to take the children and then a number of animals for a boat ride, and all goes well until they start misbehaving.

***Molly's Pilgrim,* by Barbara Cohen, illustrated by Michael J. Deraney. When Molly is told to make a doll like a Pilgrim for the Thanksgiving display at school, Molly's mother dresses the doll as she herself dressed before leaving

Russia to seek religious freedom. Molly is embarrassed; her classmates laugh at her, but Ms. Stickely, a wise teacher, makes things right.

Monty, by James Stevenson. Monty the alligator takes a duck, a rabbit, and a frog across the river to school, but he gets tired of their constant criticism, and goes on "vacation" until they appreciate him again.

Mooch the Messy, by Marjorie Weinman Sharmat, illustrated by Ben Shecter. Mooch, a rat, lives in a lovely hole under Boston. He likes to be messy, but he cleans up when his father comes to visit. After Papa leaves, however, Mooch reverts to his old habits.

Mother Told Me So, by Carol A. Marron, illustrated by George Karn. Melissa Sue Albina McCormick is not a perfect child, so she sits in her room and thinks about all the unwise things she has done, things like drowning the plants in orange juce and spilling oatmeal on the window ledge. Her mother tells Melissa that she had never done such things. *But* Grandma tells the child about what Mother did do when she was a little girl. She was not a perfect child either!

No Nap, by Eve Bunting, illustrated by Susan Meddaugh. Susie is tired, but decides against a nap. Daddy has a battle plan, but Susie wins the war.

No Nap for Benjamin Badger, by Nancy White Carlstrom, illustrated by Dennis Nolan. Mama Badger tells her son Benjamin in rhyme how all creatures take naps, but he is nearly three and doesn't want to take one. In the heat of the afternoon, Benjamin finally falls asleep and Mama Badger joins him for a nap.

No Peas for Nellie, by Chris L. Demarest. Nellie explains that she would rather eat really horrible things like a crocodile or water buffalo than eat a pea. Then when she has given in (to get dessert), her dad asks her to finish her milk—same routine. Great, funny illustrations.

Noisy Nora, by Rosemary Wells. In this rhymed book everyone ignores little Nora, who then makes every kind of noise to get attention.

Nosey Mrs. Rat, by Jeffrey Allen, illustrated by James Marshall. Shirley Rat is really nosey and is considered the neighborhood plague until she finally gets her due when she crosses young Brewster Blackstone and he gets his revenge.

Oh, Were They Ever Happy!, by Peter Spier. Mr. and Mrs. Noonan leave their house, and their children paint everything in sight, inside and out, with every color paint they find in the garage and basement.

Ollie Forgot, by Tedd Arnold. Ollie's rather unreliable memory, which loses whatever he has in mind whenever he hears something new, gets him into all kinds of trouble on the way to the market. Even after all is well, he has a problem remembering his way home.

Owl at Home, by Arnold Lobel. Four very short humorous stories about Owl who has some difficulty figuring things out.

Perfect Pigs: An Introduction to Manners, by Marc Brown and Stephen Krensky. Using a comic-book format with pigs as characters, this book is really quite comical with manners a side issue.

Petunia, by Roger Duvoisin. A silly goose learns that just carrying a book doesn't make her wise after all her barnyard friends follow her advice with negative results. She decides to learn to read.

Pig Pig Grows Up, by David McPhail. The youngest of the pig family continues to act like a baby until a near catastrophe gives him a chance to "grow up" in a hurry. Then he does.

Pinkerton, Behave, by Steven Kellogg. A large, lovable Great Dane, Pinkerton, gets all commands confused, and when he is taken to obedience school, he confuses all the other dogs as well. But he does come through in a real situation when a burglar breaks into the house.

A Pocket for Corduroy, by Don Freeman. Lisa's little bear thinks he needs a pocket for his overalls, so he tries to find one in the laundromat, getting into all kinds of scrapes until Lisa finds him the next day and makes him a pocket with his name tucked inside.

The Popcorn Dragon, by Jane Thayer, illustrated by Lisa McCue. Dexter is a real show-off and he loses his friends, the elephant, the zebra, and the kangeroo, by blowing smoke at them. Then he finds he can use his special talent to pop corn.

Prince Bertram the Bad, by Arnold Lobel. Incorrigible little Prince Bertram finally meets his match when he hits a blackbird with a stone; the bird is really a witch who turns Prince Bertram into a dragon. All ends happily when the dragon saves the witch's life, and she turns him back into a boy— this time Good Prince Bertram.

Princess Horrid, by Erik Christian Haugaard, illustrated by Diane Dawson Hearn. With all the trappings of a traditional fairy tale, and some very modern witty critiques of royalty, this story of an extremely bad little princess who is turned into a kitten, then rescued by the lowliest scullery maid of the realm will amuse readers of all ages.

The Quarreling Book, by Charlotte Zolotow, illustrated by Arnold Lobel. A rainy day makes everyone feel grumpy, but the sun comes out, and all the children and their parents decide to be pleasant.

Rabbit's New Rug, by Judy Delton, illustrated by Marc Brown. Rabbit is so fond of his new rug that he almost loses his friends because he is afraid they will spoil it in some way. He changes his mind and has a party.

Rotten Ralph, by Jack Gantos, illustrated by Nicole Rubel. Sarah's cat Ralph is really rotten, so the family decides to leave him at the circus. There he is badly treated and runs away, ending up in a trash can where Sarah finds him. He returns to the family, vowing never to be rotten again, except. . . .

**Sam, Bangs and Moonshine, by Evaline Ness. Samantha has a reckless habit of lying, which her father calls "moonshine." She also has a cat, Bangs, and a little friend, Thomas. Sam's bad habit almost causes tragedy when she sends Thomas and Bangs into danger, which teaches her the difference between "moonshine" and reality.

Say Thank You, Theodore, by Wendy Cheyette Lewison, illustrated by Jili Kangas. This book of manners features some little "people in fur," including Theodore, who finally becomes mannerly—most of the time.

Shy Charles, by Rosemary Wells. Being painfully timid and shy doesn't keep Charles from rescuing his baby sitter, Mrs. Block, after she's fallen down the stairs. Done in amusing verse.

The Signmaker's Assistant, by Tedd Arnold. Norman is the signmaker's apprentice and he's good at his job, but when he gets the idea of making some signs on his own, signs which cause havoc in the town, it's another matter.

Silly Fred, by Karen Wagner, illustrated by Normand Chartier. A darling, happy-go-lucky, little pig Freddy sings silly songs to himself and turns somersaults on his bed. Then the serious beaver tells him he doesn't like him, so Freddy tries to behave differently, but it doesn't work.

Skip to My Lou, illustrated by Nadine Bernard Westcott. When his parents leave a young boy in charge of the farm for a day, chaos erupts as the animals take over the house, beginning with flies in the sugarbowl. But he gets it all cleaned up before Mom and Dad return.

Slinky Malinki, by Lynley Dodd. Slinky is an average cat during the day, but at night he turns into a thief. One fateful night he gets carried away and steals so much that he gets caught. He then vows to behave properly. Done in humorous rhymed verse.

Squawk to the Moon, Little Goose, by Edna Mitchell Preston, illustrated by Barbara Cooney. Little Goose, who is supposed to stay in bed, goes out to see the moon and is caught by the fox; she cleverly escapes him, but not Mother Goose's spanking.

The Tale of Benjamin Bunny, by Beatrix Potter. Benjamin, Peter's cousin, is as naughty as Peter, but his father, old Mr. Benjamin Bunny, is more severe than Peter's mother when it comes to corporal punishment.

The Tale of the Flopsy Bunnies, by Beatrix Potter. Benjamin Bunny is now grown up and married to his cousin Flopsy, with an improvident large family. When the Flopsy Bunnies eat too many lettuces from Mr. McGregor's garden, they almost become rabbit pie, but are saved by Thomasina Tittlemouse, another wonderful character from the classic collection of more than twenty books by this author-artist.

The Tale of Peter Rabbit, by Beatrix Potter. Mischievous Peter almost ends up in a pie when Mr. McGregor nearly catches him in his garden eating lettuce, French beans, and radishes. The original drawings and text are not to be missed.

Throw a Kiss, Harry, by Mary Chalmers. Harry, the naughty cat, wanders away from his mother, and it takes the fire department to get him down from a roof.

***The True Francine,* by Marc Brown. Francine and Muffy are good friends until Muffy lets Francine take the blame for cheating on a math test when it is she who is guilty.

Two Bad Ants, by Chris Van Allsburg. An unusual view of the world from the perspective of two disloyal ants who desert their colony and try to get all they want to eat instead of taking the "crystals" back to the queen ant. They escape and are glad to return to their family.

Two Greedy Bears, by Mirra Ginsburg, illustrated by Jose Aruego and Ariane Dewey. Two bear cubs, determined to outdo each other, continue their rivalry until a clever fox teaches them a hilarious lesson by dispensing surprising, but absolutely equal, justice.

The Tyrannosaurus Game, by Steven Kroll, illustrated by Tomi De Paola. On a boring day the children play a game giving each child in turn a chance to say what the tyrannosaurus did. When the cops come, after the creature has done a lot of mischievous things, the tyrannosaurus has disappeared.

Use Your Head, Dear, by Aliki. Charles is a very forgetful crocodile who has trouble at home and in school too. He means well, but he can't keep his mind on what he's doing until his father gives him an invisible thinking cap for his birthday.

Veronica, by Roger Duvoisin. This hippopotamus feels that she isn't noticed among all the other hippos on the mud bank where she lives, so she runs away to the city where she is conspicuous and famous, but gets into a lot of trouble. She is glad to go home again.

Wally the Worry-Warthog, by Barbara Shook Hazen, illustrated by Janet Stevens. Wally, a warthog who worries about everything, finally meets Wilberforce Warthog, who he thinks must have horrible claws inside the gloves he wears. Then Wally discovers that Wilberforce is a worrier too.

Walter the Wolf, by Marjorie Weinman Sharmat, illustrated by Kelly Oechsli. Walter is perfect until he is temporarily corrupted by Wyatt the Fox, but when Walter finds out that biting really hurts, he returns to being, well, almost perfect.

The Wild Baby, by Barbro Lindgren, illustrated by Eva Eriksson, adapted from the Swedish by Jack Prelutsky. This baby Ben is reckless, loud, and wild. He does all the naughty things most children only dream about, but his mother loves him as only a mother can.

Willy the Wimp, by Anthony Browne. Willy is mild-mannered until he decides to do some body building and saves Milly from an attack by the urban gorillas. Now he's not a wimp anymore.

SOCIALIZATION OUTSIDE THE HOME

After the toddler has begun to attend nursery school or at least has begun to go beyond his immediate family circle, other needs become evident. There is the question of belonging to the group, and, as the child begins to interact with other children, the topic of friendship becomes important. The youngster may consider what can happen if he "fights" with his friend, or how he will feel if he or his friend moves away from the neighborhood.

In addition, the small child will have to deal with adults who are technically "strangers." Most of these people will, of course, be a positive force, but, unfortunately, the child will also have to be prepared to respond appropriately to any adult whose intention or behavior could be considered negative or harmful.

Books About Friendship and the Need to Belong

Alexander and the Wind-Up Mouse, by Leo Lionni. Alexander, a mouse, meets the wind-up toy mouse Willy, and they become friends. But when Alexander goes to the Magic Lizard to be changed into a toy mouse, he decides that having Willy changed into a live mouse is preferable.

All I See, by Cynthia Rylant, illustrated by Peter Catalanotto. A lovely story of the friendship that develops between an artist and a young, shy boy who wants to become a painter also.

Amos and Boris, by William Steig. Amos, a mouse, loves the ocean, builds a boat, and sails out to sea. All goes well until he falls overboard and nearly drowns. Then he is saved by the whale, Boris. Years later, Amos saves Boris's life in return.

And I Mean It, Stanley, by Crosby Bonsall. The mystery of who or what is behind the fence is finally cleared up happily by a little girl who talks to Stanley about the "really neat thing" she has made.

Angel Child, Dragon Child, by Michelle Maria Surat, illustrated by Vo-Dinh Mai. Ut, a little Vietnamese girl attending school in the United States, is very lonely for her mother who is still in Vietnam. She finds it very difficult to adjust to our country. But an "enemy" becomes a friend and all ends happily.

Anna . . . Anya: A Month in Moscow, by Irene Trivas. A five-year-old is confused when she goes to Moscow with her parents, who will work there for a month. Even the circus does not make her change her "Nyet" about Russia until she goes to a day-care center where she meets Anya and starts to learn the language. She then sees that things which really matter—like family love—are the same everywhere.

A Bargain for Frances, by Russell Hoban, illustrated by Lillian Hoban. Thelma, Frances's little friend, almost gets the best of Frances, but Frances ends up getting the best of the bargain when she holds Thelma to "no backsies" in their tea set deal.

Beady Bear, by Don Freeman. Beady tries to "go it alone" in a cave after he learns that bears live in caves. But he is happy when his boy rescues him and takes him home to his own little bed.

Benjamin and Tulip by Rosemary Wells. Tulip is a bully, but Benjamin's aunt thinks she is a sweet little thing. The first of a series about these endearing little animals.

The Best-Ever Good-Bye Party, by Amy Hest, illustrated by DyAnne DiSalvo-Ryan. Jason is moving and his best friend Jessica is very upset, as he is, about the separation. Then Jessica throws a two-person party and things seem a bit better.

Best Friends, by Miriam Cohen, illustrated by Lillian Hoban. Jim is not really sure that Paul is his best friend until the light in the classroom's incubator goes out. Then the two boys cooperate to save the baby chicks—and know they're really best friends.

Best Friends, by Steven Kellogg. Kathy feels lonely and betrayed when her best friend goes away for the summer and leaves her alone, but she changes her mind after Louise returns.

Best Friends for Frances, by Russell Hoban, illustrated by Lillian Hoban. Frances shows Albert how to be a "best friend" instead of a macho badger, and solves her sister Gloria's problem of being too small to join the group for baseball at the same time.

The Best Trade of All, by Nina Bourque, illustrated by Jackie Urbanovic. Two women, the trader Bevin and the shopkeeper Kumi, from widely separated areas of the world, embark on a cooperative career of adventure and friendship.

Blackboard Bear, by Martha Alexander. When he is told by the older children that he is too small to play their games, this boy draws a huge bear on the blackboard to replace his little teddy bear. Suddenly he is sought after by the others.

Can I Keep Him?, by Steven Kellogg. A fantasy about a small boy in search of companionship. Refused a pet of every sort, the child settles realistically for a new boy next door.

Cecily G. and the 9 Monkeys, by H. A. Rey. Both Cecily and the monkeys are lonely, so they join forces to play wonderful games and live happily together.

A Color of His Own, by Leo Lionni. The sad chameleon has a problem: unlike all other animals, he has no color of his own. But he finds a partner and they change colors together.

Corduroy, by Don Freeman. The little brown bear has lost a button on his overalls, and tries unsuccessfully to find it at night after the department store has closed. But little Lisa loves him just as he is and takes him home.

Dandelion, by Don Freeman. When Dandelion gets an invitation to Jennifer Giraffe's party, he gets so "gussied up" that he is not recognized by his hostess who shuts the door in his face. Then it rains: his mane becomes straight; he loses his fancy jacket, cap, and cane; and now that he is no longer a stylish dandy, he is welcomed by his friends at the party.

Ernest and Celestine, by Gabrielle Vincent. Ernest, a bear, and Celestine, a mouse, lose Celestine's stuffed bird Gideon in the snow. But Ernest fixes everthing. A sweet story for a very young child.

Everett Anderson's Friend, by Lucille Clifton, illustrated by Ann Grifalconi. Everett learns that a little girl, Maria, can be fun to play with, even though she wins when Everett and his three boyfriends let her play ball with them.

Everybody Knows That!, by Susan Pearson, illustrated by Diane Paterson. Patty and Herbie are friends, and now they are starting kindergarten together. But suddenly sexism raises its ugly head. Patty, however, turns the tables on Herbie and teaches him that both boys and girls can be pilots and make cookies.

The Friend, by John Burningham. A very simple look at two small boys who are "best friends" even though they sometimes quarrel.

Frog and Toad Together, by Arnold Lobel. These two endearing animals have humorous adventures in this and other books in this series. Older children can read this independently.

George and Martha, by James Marshall. Five very short stories about two friends—hippopotami—who find it's best to tell the truth.

Gladys Told Me to Meet Her Here, by Marjorie Weinman Sharmat, illustrated by Edward Frascino. Gladys and Irving are best friends, but now Irving can't find Gladys, so he goes to look for her, which causes the problem. She is waiting where she said she would wait.

The Golden Egg Book, by Margaret Wise Brown, illustrated by Leonard Weisgard. A little bunny who finds an egg tries hard to get it open, but falls asleep just as the little yellow duck emerges. The two become friends, and "No one is ever alone again."

Goodbye Rune, by Marit Kaldhol, illustrated by Wenche Yen, translated by Michael Crosby-Jones. Little Sara loses her good friend Rune when he drowns, and she tries hard to understand what "dead" means. A very tender look at a difficult subject.

The Greatest Treasure, by Arcadio Lobato. It is time for the witches to choose a new queen, and she will be the witch who finds the most special treasure. Meera and her raven friend Ernest crash on an island, which is really a whale. Ernest implores Meera to stop for treasure, but she prefers to make friends with the whale because a friend is the greatest treasure of all; so Meera wins.

The Guest, by James Marshall. As Mona is practicing her scales, she feels Maurice, a little snail, crawling up her back. He becomes her guest, but one day he disappears. When he returns, he brings some little friends with him.

Harlequin and the Gift of Many Colors, by Remy Charlip and Burton Supree, illustrated by Remy Charlip. Based on a Commedia dell' Arte character who originated in Bergamo, Italy, poor Harlequin cannot go to the Carnival without a costume, but his friends give him many scraps from their costumes with the result that he has the most beautiful costume of all.

Harvey's Hideout, by Russell Hoban, illustrated by Lillian Hoban. Harvey Muskrat has a secret club, and he won't include his sister Mildred, who then won't invite him to her secret parties. But they are both really alone and decide that they need each other as playmates.

The Hating Book, by Charlotte Zolotow, illustrated by Ben Shecter. In simple rhyme a little girl ponders her friend's sudden unfriendliness, and finally asks the reason, finding a simple explanation, and all ends well.

Hound and Bear, by Dick Gackenbach. Three short stories about two very good friends. Hound, however, nearly ruins their relationship with his practical jokes.

I Had a Friend Named Peter, by Janice Cohn, illustrated by Gail Owens. With a foreword about children's reactions to death, this tender story tells of Betsy and her friend Peter, who dies. Betsy and her parents talk about death and burial, so that she understands that Peter will continue to live in the memories people have of him.

I Know What I Like, by Norma Simon, illustrated by Dora Leder. Each child is a unique, developing individual who may have specific likes and dislikes, and these may change as he/she grows. This book emphasizes that people can be friends even if they choose some very different things to like.

I Was All Thumbs, by Bernard Waber. Legs, as Dr. Pierre calls him, is an octopus who is being returned to the sea from the laboratory. At first he has a hard time adjusting to this new world, but he finally feels less lonely after he meets Knuckles, another alumnus of the lab.

Ida and Betty and the Secret Eggs, by Kay Chorao. Vacationing in the country, Ida is "best friends" with Betty and they share a secret. Then along comes Lucinda and trouble brews.

I'm Terrific, by Marjorie Weinman Sharmat, illustrated by Kay Chorao. Jason Bear thinks he's terrific and awards himself gold stars for superior performance, but his friends don't like to be around him, so he tries the other extreme. Then finally he understands the happy medium in behavior.

Ira Says Goodbye, by Bernard Waber. In this sequel, Ira's older sister taunts him with the news that his best friend Reggie is moving away. Then Reggie acts happy about going, which devastates Ira completely. All ends well as Ira prepares to spend the weekend at Greendale, Reggie's new home.

Ira Sleeps Over, by Bernard Waber. When Ira is invited to sleep at Reggie's house, he anticipates a really good time, but he has a problem. Should he take his teddy bear or not? A wonderful warm story for preschoolers.

Jamaica Tag-Along, by Juanita Havill, illustrated by Anne Sibley O'Brien. When her older brother Ossie won't let Jamiaca play basketball with him and his friends, she helps a younger child build a sand castle as she realizes what it feels like to be considered a "tag-along."

Let's Be Enemies, by Janice May Udry, illustrated by Maurice Sendak. John thinks that his friend James always wants to be the boss, so John goes to tell him that they are enemies, but they decide that's not much fun; it's better to be friends.

Little Blue and Little Yellow, by Leo Lionni. Personifying colors, Lionni has them hugging and becoming green, but their families don't recognize them, so they cry until they are all blue and yellow tears. Then everyone understands and all ends happily.

Louie, by Ezra Jack Keats. Gussie, the mouse puppet, really appeals to Louie, who usually doesn't speak to anyone. His young friends realize that Louie needs to keep Gussie, and they arrange it.

Magical Hands, by Marjorie Barker, illustrated by Yoshi. A lovely warm story of four men who are friends. William, the barrel maker, secretly does the morning chores for each of his friends on their birthdays, and when his own birthday comes, he finds himself rewarded.

Mr. McGill Goes to Town, by Jim Aylesworth, illustrated by Thomas Graham. Mr. McGill wants to go to the town fair, but he has so many repairs to make on his mill that he thinks he won't get there. However, his friends Mr. McRae, Mr. McCall, Mr. McNeil, and Mr. McGrew all want to go too, but also have chores to finish. By helping each other, the work is finished and they can all go happily together.

**Molly's Pilgrim,* by Barbara Cohen, illustrated by Michael J. Deraney. When Molly is told to make a doll like a Pilgrim for the Thanksgiving display at school, Molly's mother dresses the doll as she herself dressed before leaving Russia to seek religious freedom. Molly is embarrassed; her classmates laugh at her, but Ms. Stickely, a wise teacher, makes things right.

Moving Molly, by Shirley Hughes. Molly is lonely after her family's move from the city to the country, but she adjusts with the help of her new next-door neighbors, the twins Kathy and Kevin.

My Friend John, by Charlotte Zolotow, illustrated by Ben Shecter. A pleasant story about two little boys who know everything about each other and always stick together.

My Friend William Moved Away, by Martha Whitmore Hickman, illustrated by Bill Myers. When Jimmy's very close friend William moves away, he is devastated. When Jimmy goes by William's old house, he thinks about going a few doors farther, and he finds a new friend, Mary Ellen, so he feels a little better.

Old Henry, by Joan Blos, illustrated by Stephen Gammell. When Henry moves into an old house that has been vacant for years, his neighbors expect him to do some fixing, but he does nothing, so they nag him until he leaves. Then they miss him, and strangely, he misses them too. People do not have to have the same lifestyle to get along.

Our Veronica Goes to Petunia's Farm, by Roger Duvoisin. At first Veronica the hippopotamus seems welcome at the farm; then the other animals treat her like an outsider, and she pines away until they show her friendship once again.

Overnight at Mary Bloom's, by Aliki. A child has a wonderful time when she spends the night at her grown-up friend's apartment. Where else are there pets, a baby, and permission to make a loud rumpus?

Pet of the Met, by Lydia and Don Freeman, illustrated by Don Freeman. *The Magic Flute* as performed at the Metropolitan Opera changes the lives of Maestro Petrini, a mouse who turns pages for the prompter, and his mortal enemy Mefisto, the cat who loves opera but hates mice.

Rachel Parker, Kindergarten Show-Off, by Ann Martin, illustrated by Nancy Poydar. Five-year-old Olivia's new neighbor Rachel is in her kindergarten class, and the two girls must overcome feelings of jealousy to become friends. They succeed.

Rolling Harvey Down the Hill, by Jack Prelutsky, illustrated by Veronica Chess. A collection of humorous poems about the narrator's four friends, one of whom is the obnoxious Harvey.

Sam, by Ann Herbert Scott, illustrated by Symeon Shimin. Sam is lonely as each family member is too busy to pay attention to him. Then when he cries, they all understand, and his mother lets him make his own tart with raspberry jam.

Somebody Loves You, Mr. Hatch, by Eileen Spinelli, illustrated by Paul Yalowitz. Mr. Hatch is a somber, solitary figure until he receives a mysterious heart-shaped box of chocolates for Valentine's Day. After that, he becomes outgoing, happy, and helpful to all his neighbors. Then the postman confesses that he had delivered the box to Mr. Hatch by mistake.

Soup for Supper, by Phyllis Root, illustrated by Sue Truesdell. A wee small woman catches Giant Rumbleton taking vegetables from her garden and finds they can share both vegetable soup and friendship. With music for the soup song at the end.

A Special Trade, by Sally Wittman, illustrated by Karen Gundersheimer. Nelly, a little girl, has Bartholomew, a grandfatherly man, as a friend. In a very gentle way Nelly is able to reciprocate when Bartholomew is in a wheelchair, just as she had been in her stroller years before.

Stevie, by John Steptoe. Robert is not too thrilled when he hears that little Stevie is coming to stay with his family on weekdays, and Stevie does prove to be something of a pest. Then Stevie's family moves away, and Robert finds that he misses the little guy.

Susie and Alfred in the Knight, the Princess and the Dragon, by Helen Craig. Susie and Alfred are best friends, but Susie wants more. She wants Alfred to save her from imagined dangers. Then eventually Alfred has the chance to fight a dragon for her, and Susie is a very happy little pig.

Theodore, by Edward Ormondroyd, illustrated by John M. Larrecq. Lucy's mother accidentally includes Theodore, a pet bear, in the laundry, and Lucy's father doesn't notice him in the washer or dryer. After his adventures, he is reunited with Lucy.

Tillie and the Wall, by Leo Lionni. A curious mouse wonders what is on the other side of the big wall, and finally gets the idea of digging under it, only to find other little mice on the other side, so they join together for a party.

Timothy Goes to School, by Rosemary Wells. Timothy learns about being accepted and making friends during the first week of his first year at school.

Together, by George-Ella Lyon, illustrated by Vera Rosenberry. "You cut the timber and I'll build the house" starts this tale of how two girls cooperate even in their dreams.

Tom and Pippo Make a Friend, by Helen Oxenbury. One of the series of Tom and Pippo stories for very young children. In this book two children play in a sandbox and share toys.

Visiting Pamela, by Norma Klein, illustrated by Kay Chorao. Carrie doesn't like to visit other children's houses, but she is finally persuaded to go to Pamela's after school. By the time her mother comes to pick her up, Carrie has begun to find the visit pleasant and will do it again.

Watch Out for the Chicken Feet in Your Soup, by Tomie De Paola. Joey is embarrassed to take his friend Eugene to visit his old-fashioned Italian grandma, but she and Eugene get along very well indeed.

We're Very Good Friends, My Brother and I, by P. K. Hallinan. Two small boys illustrate the ways they share at play time and enjoy being friends as well as brothers.

What Goes Around Comes Around, by Sally G. Ward. Little Isabel accompanies her eccentric grandmother on a fun-filled journey through the neighborhood to give away her famous soup, and they return with treasures from all Grandma's friends.

Who's Going to Take Care of Me?, by Michelle Magorian, illustrated by James Graham Hale. When Eric and Karin go to day care together, Karin takes care of her brother. But when Karin goes on to school, Eric feels small and alone until he finds a little friend who needs his care.

Will I Have a Friend?, by Miriam Cohen, illustrated by Lillian Hoban. Jim's father assures him on the first day of school that he will have a friend, but he finds they are all "taken" until he finds Paul.

Willis, by James Marshall. Willis is a sad creature because he needs sunglasses and does not have the money for them. His friends, Bird, Snake, and Lobster help him in very humorous ways.

Willy and Hugh, by Anthony Browne. Willy is lonely until he makes a friend, Hugh Jape, who helps him against Butter Nose, just as Willy helps Hugh to read.

Books That Emphasize Sexual Identity

Particularly in the past thirty years there has been an increased awareness of changing sexual roles in our society. What deserves emphasis is not the changing view of females alone, but also alternate views regarding stereotypical behavior by males. Attitudes based on gender alone are established very early in every child's life—perhaps even before birth—which may in itself be inconsequential. What it may mean, however, is that a human being may not be free to develop uniquely without being locked into a particular kind of behavior, interest, and later, professional goal based solely on gender.

Following are titles that can introduce and reinforce views which allow free development and applaud the extraordinary.

The Adventures of Isabel, by Ogden Nash, illustrated by James Marshall. Meet the inimitable Isabel who handles the most hair-raising encounters with ease and aplomb. Nash's verses are delightful.

Anna Banana and Me, by Lenore Blegvad, illustrated by Erik Blegvad. Anna Banana is a fearless girl who plays with the little boy telling the story. He is really quite timid, but with Anna's help he becomes as brave as she.

Best Friends for Frances, by Russell Hoban, illustrated by Lillian Hoban. Frances shows Albert how to be a "best friend" instead of a macho badger, and solves her sister Gloria's problem of being too small to join the group for baseball at the same time.

Brave Irene, by William Steig. Irene Bobbin's mother is ill, but little Irene braves the snow and a windstorm to get the duchess's gown to her palace, and then gets to attend the party there.

By George, Bloomers!, by Judith St. George, illustrated by Margot Tomes. In the mid-nineteenth century no women wore slacks. Then Mrs. Amelia Bloomer started something as an early feminist. In this fictional story a little girl, Hannah, is able to save her little brother Jamie because she can climb onto the roof in her "bloomers."

Charlie Drives the Stage, by Eric Kimmel, illustrated by Glen Rounds. In this great tall tale, "Charlie" Drummond, a stagecoach driver with real moxie, promises to get Senator McCorkle on the train to Washington in spite of an avalanche, road agents, Indians on the warpath, and a raging river between Grass Valley and LeGrande. It's quite a ride, but Charlene gets the senator there in time.

Come Away from the Water, Shirley, by John Burningham. Shirley's parents sit at the seaside and say the usual things to their little girl on the left-side pages, while on the right-hand pages we see that Shirley is thinking about boarding a pirate ship, capturing it, and finding treasure, returning triumphant with her dog.

The Cut-Ups, by James Marshall. Spud Jenkins and Joe Turner get away with every kind of prank until they meet Mary Frances Hooley. She lets them ride in her rocket, which gets them involved with Lamar J. Spurgle, the vice-principal who "never forgets a face." One of the series starring Spud and Joe.

Daddies at Work, by Eve Merriam, illustrated by Eugenie Fernandes. A companion book to *Mommies at Work,* this book shows daddies at many kinds of jobs, some of which are nontraditional, and also tending and loving their children.

Do Not Open, by Brinton Turkle. The intrepid Miss Moody and her cat Captain Kidd live at Land's End, where Miss Moody fills her cottage with things she has picked up on the beach. One day after a storm Miss Moody and Captain find a bottle labeled "Do Not Open," but the kindly woman can't resist a child's voice begging to be let out, so she ignores the warning, and the trouble starts.

Everett Anderson's Friend, by Lucille Clifton, illustrated by Ann Grifalconi. Everett learns that a little girl, Maria, can be fun to play with, even though she wins when Everett and his three boyfriends let her play ball with them.

Everybody Knows That!, by Susan Pearson, illustrated by Diane Paterson. Patty and Herbie are friends, and now they are starting kindergarten together. But suddenly sexism raises its ugly head. Patty, however, turns the tables on Herbie and teaches him that both boys and girls can be pilots and also make cookies.

Free to Be You and Me, collected by Marlo Thomas. A good collection of nonsexist stories and poems, most with illustrations.

I Want to Be a Firefighter, by Edith Kunhardt. Holly's father is a volunteer firefighter, and she learns all about fighting fires, which helps her to choose her future job.

Jerome the Baby Sitter, by Eileen Christelow. Jerome's sister Winifred gives him the job of sitting with the Gatorman kids, who behave abominably until Jerome tames them.

Just Us Women, by Jeanette Caines, illustrated by Pat Cummings. A young girl and her Aunt Martha drive to North Carolina, doing whatever suits them enroute. It's a lovely trip.

Katy and the Big Snow, by Virginia Lee Burton. A valiant (female) tractor saves the town when no other vehicle can get through the deep snow.

Kevin's Grandma, by Barbara Williams, illustrated by Kay Chorao. Kevin's grandma is decidedly different! She used to work in a circus; now she rides a Honda 90, gives judo lessons, and skydives. The writer believes everything Kevin tells him about his grandma, except that she makes peanut butter soup. That's too much!

The Long Red Scarf, by Nettie Hilton, illustrated by Margaret Power. Grandpa's friend Jake has a blue scarf to keep him warm when the two men go fishing, and Grandpa wants a long red scarf to wear on these outings, but he can't find anyone to knit it for him. Maude can't knit; Isabel doesn't have time; so he asks Jake for advice and learns to knit himself.

Madeline's Rescue, by Ludwig Bemelmans. Intrepid Madeline almost drowns, but is saved by a dog, Genevieve, who then returns with Miss Clavel's girls to the boarding school. She fits in well until Lord Cucuface, a trustee, insists that she be turned out. The girls have their revenge when Genevieve comes back and has eleven puppies—one for each student.

The Man Who Kept House, retold by Kathleen and Michael Hague, illustrated by Michael Hague. A farmer claims that while he toils all day, his wife does nothing. They exchange jobs with hilarious results: the cow is hanging from the roof, the baby is tied to a chair, and the husband is in the hearth with his head in a pot.

Mary Mary, by Sarah Hayes, illustrated by Helen Craig. Mary Mary is indeed "contrary," but she is also very brave and has considerable skill at managing the lonely giant who lives on the hill.

Maybelle, the Cable Car, by Virginia Lee Burton. Set in San Francisco, the cable cars reminisce about the "old days" before competition from the buses almost eliminated them. But the citizens vote to keep the cable cars, and, freshly painted, they still run up and down the steep hills with a merry "clang, clang."

Mike Mulligan and His Steam Shovel, by Virginia Lee Burton. Mary Anne, Mike's steam shovel, has dug canals, cut through mountains, and dug deep holes for the cellars of skyscrapers. But now Mary Anne is considered old-fashioned, until in Popperville she digs the cellar for the new town hall and remains there as the new furnace.

** *Miss Fanshawe and the Great Dragon Adventure,* by Sue Scullard. A truly novel book about an intrepid British lady who successfully traps a dragon by traveling to the center of the earth in a hot air balloon, circa late-nineteenth century.

** *Molly Whuppie,* retold by Walter de la Mare, illustrated by Errol Le Cain. A very smart and brave girl outwits the giant and his wife and thereby helps herself and her two sisters to the king's three sons as a reward.

Mommies at Work, by Eve Merriam, illustrated by Eugenie Fernandes. This book illustrates a great many occupations and professions now commonly open to working women who are also mothers.

Mommy's Office, by Barbara Shook Hazen, illustrated by David Soman. Emily accompanies her mother downtown to see where she works. A very friendly look at an executive mother.

Mothers Can Do Anything, by Joe Lasker. The text and illustrations demonstrate many occupations of modern mothers, including plumber, dentist, subway conductor, and others.

My Mother and I Are Growing Strong, by Inez Maury, translated into Spanish by Anna Munoz, illustrated by Sandy Speidel. A bilingual story of a family whose father is in prison for hitting someone who had insulted him. Emilita and her mother bravely carry on the father's gardening route alone.

My Mother the Mail Carrier, by Inez Maury, translated into Spanish by Norah Allemany, illustrated by Lady McCrady. A little girl tells about her mother's life as a mail carrier and describes their warm relationship.

Piggybook, by Anthony Browne. When Mrs. Piggott unexpectedly leaves one day, her demanding husband and two sons begin to realize just how much she does for them. When she returns, things change radically.

Playing Marbles, by Julie Brinckloe. A little girl draws a circle to play marbles and proves her skill against two boys who don't remain condescending for long.

The Queen Who Couldn't Bake Gingerbread, by Dorothy Van Woerkom, illustrated by Paul Galdone. King Pilaf wants a wife who can bake gingerbread, and Queen Calliope wants a husband who can play the slide trombone. They compromise on their deficiencies at first, but then begin to quarrel until each learns to fulfill his need for him or her self.

Rachel and Obadiah, by Brinton Turkle. Obadiah Starbuck has earned a silver coin by spreading the news of a ship returning to Nantucket after a long absence. His little sister Rachel wants to be sent as the messenger when a second ship arrives, but first she has to prove that she can win a race with Obadiah. The boy (like the hare in the old fable) stops to eat blackberries, thinking he can easily beat Rachel. She wins and earns two silver coins, but only keeps one.

Sam Johnson and the Blue Ribbon Quilt, by Lisa Campbell Ernst. While mending the awning over the pigpen, Sam discovers that he enjoys sewing patches together, but he meets with ridicule when he asks to join his wife's quilting club, so he forms his own. The two clubs cooperate at the county fair. Genuine quilt patterns border each page.

***The Squire Takes a Wife,* by Eve Feldman, illustrated by Bari Weissman. A rich squire is determined to marry the farmer's daughter Kate, but with the help of the stableboy, she tricks him and avoids the marriage.

The Terrible Thing That Happened at Our House, by Marge Blaine, illustrated by John C. Wallner. A little girl is sorely discomforted when her mother goes back to being a science teacher, and things change in the household. Then the family realizes that they can manage so that they will have more time together, and they do.

There's Something in My Attic, by Mercer Mayer. Convinced that there is something making noise in the attic at night, a brave little girl sneaks upstairs, lasso in hand, to capture whatever it is.

Three Brave Women, by C. L. G. Martin, illustrated by Peter Elwell. Mama and Grammy's humorous childhood anecdotes help Caitlin to deal with her fear of spiders. When she realizes that Billy Huxley is afraid of her little dog Muffy, that helps too.

The Three Little Pigs and the Fox, by William H. Hooks, illustrated by S. D. Schindler. In this Appalachian version of the story, Hamlet, a female runt, and the youngest of the three, saves her two greedy brothers from the clutches of the "mean, tricky, old drooly-mouth fox."

A Treeful of Pigs, by Arnold Lobel, illustrated by Anita Lobel. This fanciful story tells of a lazy farmer whose hard-working wife finally gets her husband to do his share of the work as he had promised he would.

A Visit to the Police Station, by Dotti Hannum, illustrated by Romie Flanagen. This book describes the activities that take place at a police station and explains the various duties of the policemen and policewomen.

When We Grow Up, by Anne Rockwell. Pictures demonstrate the various jobs that children want when they grow up. Nonsexist and nondidactic.

White Dynamite and the Curly Kidd, by Bill Martin, Jr., and John Archambault, illustrated by Ted Rand. Lucky Kidd watches her dad ride a mean bull and dreams of becoming a rodeo rider herself.

William's Doll, by Charlotte Zolotow, illustrated by William Pene Du Bois. William wants a real baby doll like the one Nancy has. His father buys all the typical "boy" toys for him, and William plays with them, but when his grandmother comes, he asks her for the doll and he gets it.

Zeralda's Ogre, by Tomi Ungerer. In the town people are terrified by a typical ogre who eats children, but the farmer's daughter Zeralda, who is an extraordinary cook, meets the ogre and changes his eating habits with her delightful cuisine.

Changes

Changes come into all lives from birth through death. That is simply the nature of things. Some of these changes are temporary, some permanent. By the time we consider ourselves adults, most of us are able to deal with the alterations which we experience and make the appropriate responses. Children, however, with their limited view of the world, sometimes suffer some trauma even when a friend moves away, or there is a new school situation to face. Certainly a major change in the life of a child, such as a divorce or the death of a loved one, can be traumatic, and requires great care in trying to ease the pain for the youngster. Can books help in the healing process? Not as much as an empathetic adult, it's obvious, but perhaps just knowing that others have come through a similar experience can offer some solace. It's certainly worth a try.

Books About Moving

The Best-Ever Good-Bye Party, by Amy Hest, illustrated by DyAnne DiSalvo Ryan. Jason is moving and his best friend Jessica is very upset, as he is, about the separation. Then Jessica throws a two-person party and things seem a bit better.

Goodbye House, by Frank Asch. Just before leaving with his family for the move to their new home, Little Bear says goodbye to all his favorite places in and around his old house.

I'm Not Moving, Mama!, by Nancy White Carlstrom, illustrated by Thor Wickstrom. Little Mouse simply does not want to move, and he gives his mother many reasons, but Mother Mouse overcomes his objections and says, "It's better being all together."

Ira Says Goodbye, by Bernard Waber. In this story Ira's older sister taunts him with the news that his best friend Reggie is moving away. Then Reggie acts happy about going, which devastates Ira completely. All ends well as Ira prepares to spend the weekend at Greendale, Reggie's new home.

Moving Day, by Tobi Tobias, illustrated by William Pene Du Bois. Big changes for a small child mean happy thoughts and sad ones too. Goodbye to familiar friends and places, and hello to new friends and places.

Moving Molly, by Shirley Hughes. Molly is lonely after her family's move from the city to the country, but she adjusts with the help of her new next-door neighbors, the twins Kathy and Kevin.

My Friend William Moved Away, by Martha Whitmore Hickman, illustrated by Bill Myers. When Jimmy's very close friend William moves away, he is devastated. When Jimmy goes by William's old house, he thinks about going a few doors farther, and he finds a new friend, Mary Ellen, so he feels a little better.

People, People, Everywhere!, by Nancy Van Laan, illustrated by Nadine Bernard Westcott. It's the city! And all over town there are people doing city things, scurrying to city places, moving to the country. One family does move, but they're not alone for long. In verse, this is an amusing look at the hectic life we all live.

Books About Starting a New Chapter: School

Alice Ann Gets Ready for School, by Cynthia Jabar. Alice Ann experiences both fun and anxiety as she gets ready for the biggest event in her young life.

Betsy's First Day at Day Care, by Gunilla Wolde. Betsy is about three years old and her experiences in this and other Betsy books are very popular with those in this age group.

Everybody Knows That!, by Susan Pearson, illustrated by Diane Paterson. Patty and Herbie are friends, and now they are starting kindergarten together. But suddenly sexism raises its ugly head. Patty, however, turns the tables on Herbie and teaches him that both boys and girls can be pilots and make cookies too.

Going to Day Care, by Fred Rogers. With realistic photographs, Mr. Rogers gives a young child a reassuring picture of day care.

Going to My Nursery School, by Susan Kuklin. With excellent photographs, and told in the first person, a little boy shows all that he does at nursery school. There is a page to parents at the end, "What to look for in a Nursery School."

My Brown Bear Barney, by Dorothy Butler, illustrated by Elizabeth Fuller. A little girl tells what she takes everywhere she goes, which always includes her stuffed bear. But Mother says that when she goes to school next year, Barney can't go. We'll see.

My Nursery School, by Harlow Rockwell. One of a practical series for the preschooler, this book illustrates typical nursery school activities and situations in a realistic and inviting way.

The New Teacher, by Miriam Cohen, illustrated by Lillian Hoban. A typical group of first graders speculate about the new teacher. Then they meet her and all is well.

Off to School, by Ann Schweninger. Button Brown, a little rabbit, has an exciting first day at school as he and his classmates play games, draw pictures, have a snack, and hear a story.

Rachel Parker, Kindergarten Show-Off, by Ann Martin, illustrated by Nancy Poydar. Five-year-old Olivia's new neighbor Rachel is in her kindergarten class and the two girls must overcome feelings of jealousy to become friends. They succeed.

School, by Emily Arnold McCully. A wordless book shows all the older children going to school and leaving the smallest mouse at home with Mother. Curiosity, however, drives the little one to go to school too, and Mother Mouse has to come and get her.

**School Days,* by B. G. Hennessy, illustrated by Tracey Campbell Pearson. In this book there is a look at an entire day in a school setting for elementary school children, perhaps in first or second grade.

Shawn Goes to School, by Petronella Breinberg, illustrated by Errol Lloyd. A colorfully illustrated book shows a youngster who cries when he first goes to nursery school, but then likes it.

Starting School, by Muriel Stanek, illustrated by Betty and Tony De Luna. The young narrator describes the preparations for going to school and the classroom activities on the first day.

Timothy Goes to School, by Rosemary Wells. Timothy learns about being accepted and making friends during the first week of his first year at school.

Toad School, by Cathy Bellows. Polly Wog is a toad who doesn't want to go to school, but after Miss Lilywart, her teacher, has given her some lessons in how to croak, to puff, and to leap, she is convinced that there is importance to education.

We Laughed a Lot, My First Day at School, by Sylvia Root Tester, illustrated by Frances Hook. Scared to go to his first day of kindergarten, Jon discovers it's not so bad—he even laughs a lot. Noteworthy is the teacher, Mr. Green.

Who's Going to Take Care of Me?, by Michelle Magorian, illustrated by James Graham Hale. When Eric and Karin go to day care together, Karin takes care of her brother. But when Karin goes on to school, Eric feels small and alone until he finds a little friend who needs his care.

Will I Have a Friend?, by Miriam Cohen, illustrated by Lillian Hoban. Jim's father assures him on his first day of school that he will have a friend, but he finds they are all "taken" until he finds Paul.

Willy Bear, by Mildred Kantrowitz, illustrated by Winslow Parker. A small boy about to go to school projects his feelings about having a night light, cuddling with a toy, and being "grown up" on to his pet teddy bear.

Books About Divorce

Dinosaurs Divorce, by Laurene Krasny Brown and Marc Brown. This book says many of the same things set down in serious books about divorce, but using dinosaurs and a light touch makes this emotional subject more palatable to children.

Emily and the Klunky Baby and the Next-Door Dog, by Joan M. Lexau, illustrated by Martha Alexander. Poor Emily. Her mother is busy trying to do taxes. Emily and the baby try to find daddy's apartment, but get lost, and the next-door dog is no help in getting home. Eventually she finds her house but the baby's nap doesn't materialize.

**Me Day,* by Joan Lexau, illustrated by Robert Weaver. It's Rafer's birthday, but his parents are divorced and the boy thinks his father has forgotten him. A realistic, rather somber picture of a ghetto family, even though his dad does come to take him for a "long, long day."

My Mother's House, My Father's House, by C. B. Christiansen, illustrated by Irene Trivas. With warmth and honesty this book affirms a young child's feelings about divorced parents who have "shared custody." What she wants as an adult is one house with no suitcases.

One More Time, by Louis Baum, illustrated by Paddy Bouma. In a very subtle way we learn that little Simon is spending a visitation day with his dad, who takes him back to his mom when the day ends.

She's Not My Real Mother, by Judith Vigna. When Miles spends the weekend in the city with his daddy and his stepmother, he refuses all her overtures until they go to the Ice Capades, and she doesn't tell his father how he pretended to be lost and frightened her. Then he agrees to be her friend, but she's still not his *real* mommy.

Books About Illness

Always Gamma, by Vaunda Micheaux Nelson, illustrated by Kimanne Uhler. A little girl has a really warm relationship with her grandparents, particularly her grandmother. Then that lady begins to act strangely (Alzheimer's) and goes into a nursing home, but the child remembers all their time together with deep love.

Betsy and the Chicken Pox, by Gunilla Wolde. Betsy's baby brother has chicken pox, so Betsy paints spots on herself to get attention. When they are washed off, there are real spots underneath. Now Betsy and her brother must both stay in bed.

Curious George Goes to the Hospital, by Margaret and H. A. Rey. This time the little monkey has swallowed a piece of a jigsaw puzzle and must have it removed. Of course, he gets into the usual scrapes in the hospital.

The Emergency Room, by Anne and Harlow Rockwell. A little boy who has sprained his ankle goes to a hospital emergency room. There he is examined, x-rayed, bandaged, given crutches, and shown how to walk on them until his ankle heals. A reassuring look at a place that might be frightening to some children.

I Wish I Was Sick Too!, by Franz Brandenberg, illustrated by Aliki. Elizabeth envies Edward because the family is concerned about his illness. Then she becomes ill, and when they have both recovered, they agree that being well is best.

Madeline, by Ludwig Bemelmans. In rhymed verse the author pictures twelve little girls in a Parisian boarding school, emphasizing the smallest and bravest, Madeline. Poor Miss Clavel must call a doctor in the middle of the night— Madeline has appendicitis. After a visit to the hospital, the other eleven want one too!

My Grammy, by Marsha Kibbey, illustrated by Karen Ritz. Amy's grandmother, who has Alzheimer's Disease and can no longer stay on her farm alone, moves in with her daughter, son-in-law, and granddaughter Amy. At first the little girl is resentful of the intrusion and puzzled by Grammy's rather strange behavior. However, Amy finally understands what is causing Grammy's problem and the two form a loving attachment.

My Grandma's in a Nursing Home, by Judy Delton and Dorothy Tucker, illustrated by Charles Robinson. Jason and his mother visit Grandma in a nursing home, and the boy begins to understand the reasons for people being in Meadowbrook. A realistic book.

Sick in Bed, by Anne and Harlow Rockwell. A simple story for very young children, telling how a child becomes ill, is treated, and recovers.

A Visit from Dr. Katz, by Ursula Le Guin, illustrated by Ann Barrow. A little girl, bored with being sick in bed, is amused by playing with her two little cats.

When Daddy Had the Chicken Pox, by Harriet Ziefert, illustrated by Lionel Kalish. Three children have had the chicken pox. Now it's Daddy's turn. A reassuring look at a sick parent who recovers.

Books About Death

The Accident, by Carol Carrick, illustrated by Donald Carrick. Christopher's dog Bodger is killed when he runs in front of a pickup truck. The driver is very sorry; Christopher's parents are devastated as well. But finally, the boy goes with his father to pick out a headstone to mark the dog's grave, and he is able to cry in grief.

**Annie and the Old One,* by Miska Miles, illustrated by Peter Parnall. In this Navajo family Annie and her grandmother have a very special relationship, so the child tries very hard to avoid the fact that her grandmother will die. She tries to hold back time, but then her grandmother explains the idea of life as a cycle, and Annie takes up the weaving stick again.

Better with Two, by Barbara M. Joose, illustrated by Catherine Stock. Mrs. Brady and her old dog Max have a young friend, Laura, who sometimes joins them for "elevenses," or tea. Then Max dies, and Laura tries to make Mrs. Brady feel better by letting her know how sorry she is about Max dying.

Blow Me a Kiss, Miss Lilly, by Nancy White Carlstrom, illustrated by Amy Schwartz. A sweet story about a little girl's friendship with an older woman who dies, but is always remembered with deep affection by the child.

The Cat Next Door, by Betty Ren Wright, illustrated by Gail Owens. Told in the first person, a little girl describes her typical summer visit to her grandparents' cabin near a lake, and a little cat who always greets her. Then her grandmother dies, and the child is comforted by the cat and her two newly born kittens.

The Dead Bird, by Margaret Wise Brown, illustrated by Remy Charlip. The children find a dead bird and give it an appropriate burial. A good introduction to death for young children.

Goodbye Rune, by Marit Kaldhol, illustrated by Wenche Yen, translated by Michael Crosby-Jones. Little Sara loses her good friend Rune when he drowns, and Sara tries very hard to understand what "dead" means. A very tender look at a difficult subject.

I Had a Friend Named Peter, by Janice Cohn, illustrated by Gail Owens. With a foreword about children's reactions to death, this perceptive story tells of Betsy and her friend Peter who dies. Betsy and her parents talk about death and burial, so that she understands that Peter will continue to live in the memories that people have of him.

Jim's Dog Muffins, by Miriam Cohen, illustrated by Lillian Hoban. Little Jim's dog Muffins is run over, and the boy is inconsolable until his best friend Paul makes him cry—and laugh—remembering Muffins.

My Grandson Lew, by Charlotte Zolotow, illustrated by William Pene Du Bois. Lew's mother is surprised that her six-year-old remembers his grandfather, who died when Lew was only two. But the boy does have memories of his grandpa, which he shares with his mother.

**Nadia the Willful, by Sue Alexander, illustrated by Lloyd Bloom. When her favorite brother Hamed disappears in the desert forever, Nadia refuses to let him be forgotten, despite her father's decree that his name shall not be uttered. In the end, Tarik, the sheik, realizes that she is not willful, but wise.

Nana Upstairs, Nana Downstairs, by Tomie De Paola. Tommy has a grandmother and a great-grandmother, and he has a very special relationship with both of them. After his great-grandmother dies, he sees a star falling from the sky, and then when he is grown, his grandmother dies and the second star makes him think that they are both now "upstairs."

The Saddest Time, by Norma Simon, illustrated by Jacqueline Rogers. This book explains death as the inevitable end of life and provides three situations in which children experience powerful emotions when someone close has died. Memories of the loved ones are precious.

The Tenth Good Thing About Barney, by Judith Viorst, illustrated by Erik Blegvad. A very tender story about a boy whose cat has died. At the funeral, he tells nine good things about Barney. Then he discovers the tenth: Barney in the ground will help to grow flowers, a pretty nice job for a cat.

The Two of Them, by Aliki. A tenderly told tale of a little girl and the grandfather who loves her from the day of her birth. They share many things; then he becomes old and ill, and she takes care of him. When he dies, she is very sad, but she always remembers her Papouli with love.

The Wall, by Eve Bunting, illustrated by Ronald Himler. A boy and his father come from far away to visit the Vietnam Veterans Memorial in Washington and find the name of the boy's grandfather, who was killed in the conflict.

"Special" Children

The Balancing Girl, by Berniece Rabe, illustrated by Lillian Hoban. Margaret is a first grader who is very good at balancing objects while in her wheelchair and on her crutches. In spite of Tommy, who tries to knock everything down, Margaret builds a project which benefits the school carnival.

He's My Brother, by Joe Lasker. Jamie suffers from the "invisible handicap." He is not retarded, but he has difficulties adjusting to the normal lifestyle of a child in the early grades. His family is very supportive and loving.

Howie Helps Himself, by Joan Fassler, illustrated by Joe Lasker. Though he enjoys life with his family and attends school, Howie, a child with cerebral palsy, wants more than anything else to be able to move his wheelchair by himself.

I Have a Sister: My Sister Is Deaf, by Jeanne Whitehouse Peterson, illustrated by Deborah Ray. Little sister says with her face what many people cannot say in words, and she reads people's eyes. Warm, intimate pictures and a poetic text evoke an appealing and perceptive portrait of a young deaf child.

I'm the Big Sister Now, by Michelle Emmert, illustrated by Gail Owens. Michelle tells of her sister, Amy, who has cerebral palsy. It is a loving picture, but, of course, since it is factual, it may prove sad for some readers.

**Knots on the Counting Rope,* by Bill Martin, Jr., and John Archambault, illustrated by Ted Rand. On a cool, dark night under the stars, a Native-American boy sits with his grandfather before a campfire. "Tell me who I am, Grandfather," pleads the boy and the old man does. The counting rope is a metaphor for the passage of time and for the boy's emerging confidence in facing the challenge of his blindness. A very moving and poignant story.

Lisa and Her Soundless World, by Edna S. Levine, illustrated by Gloria Kamen. Born deaf, Lisa gets some help from a hearing aid, and she has learned lip-reading and sign language as well, but she must work very hard to learn to sound like others when she speaks.

My Sister's Silent World, by Catherine Arthur, illustrated by Nathan Talbot. Eight-year-old Heather is deaf. Her older sister explains her hearing aid, her lip-reading, and her sign language; unfortunately, other children are not always understanding.

Princess Pooh, by Kathleen M. Muldoon, illustrated by Linda Shute. Patty Jean Piper is jealous of her sister Penelope Marie because Penelope has a wheelchair and crutches, and in Patty's eyes is treated like a princess. However, a trial run with "Princess Pooh's" wheelchair changes Patty's mind.

**Silent Lotus, by Jeanne M. Lee. Lotus, who is born deaf, cannot speak, and she is a lonely child, playing only with the herons, cranes, and white egrets. Her parents take her to the palace in the Khmer Kingdom, and she learns to dance so well that she becomes the most famous dancer in the court. Gorgeous illustrations.

Where's Chimpy?, by Berniece Rabe, illustrated by Diane Schmidt. Misty, a little girl afflicted with Down's Syndrome, can't go to sleep without her little monkey. She and her dad search everywhere and find many other misplaced items before they find Chimpy under a towel near the bathtub.

Peace-Related Books

The Alphabet Tree, by Leo Lionni. Each letter has a favorite leaf, but a strong wind blows them in every direction. Then the word bug shows them how letters can form words, after which the purple caterpillar shows them the next step, sentences, important sentences about "Peace on Earth."

The Butter Battle Book, by Dr. Seuss. With his usual humor, Dr. Seuss shows in this book the futility of war as the Yooks and the Zooks fight about which side of bread should be buttered.

Crafty Chameleon, by Mwenye Hadithi, illustrated by Adrienne Kennaway. Illustrated in bold and exciting patterns, this is a tale of brains over brawn, as the chameleon outwits both the leopard and the crocodile who are threatening him.

Drummer Hoff, by Barbara Emberley, illustrated by Ed Emberley. Highly stylized illustration and rhyme show a number of "military men" involved in firing a cannon, after which all is destroyed. A subtle plea for peace.

**The Flame of Peace: A Tale of the Aztecs, by Deborah Nourse Lattimore. To prevent the outbreak of war, a young Aztec boy, Two Flint, must outwit nine evil lords of the night to obtain the flame of peace from Lord Morning Star. He succeeds, and a great Alliance of Cities marks the beginning of many peaceful decades.

Harald and the Giant Knight, by Donald Carrick. Set in medieval times, this story tells of Harald, who gets a close-up view of the baron's knights when they take over his father's farm to train for summer tournaments. The family must take desperate measures to get rid of the interlopers.

Huge Harold, by Bill Peet. Harold is a rabbit who grows very large and has to escape pursuit by hunters in an amusing rhymed story. He finally meets Orville B. Croft, a gentle, kind farmer who helps him find his niche.

The Hunter and His Dog, by Brian Wildsmith. A hunter trains his dog to fetch ducks. The dog, however, hides the wounded ducks and fetches sticks instead. Then the hunter watches the dog secretly take bread to the wounded ducks, and, feeling ashamed, the man rescues the ducks and sets them free when they have recovered from the bullet wounds.

King of the Playground, by Phyllis Reynolds Naylor, illustrated by Nola Langer Malone. Sammy is a bully who won't let Kevin share any playground equipment. He uses threats, which Kevin's father turns around to teach Kevin problem solving. The two boys end by playing together cooperatively.

The Knight and the Dragon, by Tomie De Paola. As neophytes, the knight and the dragon both go to the library to get information on how to fight each other. Then, since they both fail, they decide on a better solution to the problem.

Millions of Cats, by Wanda Gag. When a little old man goes to select a pet kitten, there is fierce competition to be the "chosen one." One little kitten who believes itself to be homely remains and is selected. In its new home, the kitten grows into a sleek, beautiful cat.

Mine's the Best, by Crosby Bonsall. Two boys argue about the merits of rubber toy fish, but after both toys are deflated, the children finally agree.

A Peaceable Kingdom: The Shaker Abecedarius, illustrated by Alice and Martin Provensen. A quaintly illustrated alphabet rhyme that includes the animals from alligator to zebra.

The Pinkish, Purplish, Bluish Egg, by Bill Peet. The gentle dove Myrtle has no children left in her nest, and she is lonely. Then she spies a peculiar egg, which when hatched is a griffin, a mythical creature whom she calls Zeke. All the other birds are frightened of him, but he turns out to be peace-loving like the dove. Done in rhyme.

Potatoes, Potatoes, by Anita Lobel. A wise woman with two sons builds a wall around her land, so that the army of the East and the army of the West won't ruin her potato fields. But her sons grow up, and each becomes the leader of a warring force. They converge on the woman's land, fight a battle, and ruin everything in sight. Then she suggests an alternative peaceful way of living, and the wall comes down as all the soldiers and their mothers replant.

Sam the Minuteman, by Nathaniel Benchley, illustrated by Arnold Lobel. A young boy goes with his father, a Minuteman, at the beginning of the American Revolution, and sees firsthand how terrible fighting is when his friend is shot by a British soldier.

Six Crows, by Leo Lionni. The crows and the farmer are at war. The crows eat the farmer's wheat so he builds larger and larger scarecrows, while they frighten him with scarier and scarier kites. Finally the wise owl suggests that they talk, and they settle their differences peaceably before the crop is ruined.

The Story of Ferdinand, by Munro Leaf, illustrated by Robert Lawson. When the men "in funny hats" come to find the fiercest bull for the bullring in Madrid, Ferdinand is uninterested, but when he reacts to a bee sting, he seems a good candidate. However, once in the bullring, he refuses to fight, frustrating all the macho men, who finally give up and return him to his home, where he sits under the cork tree smelling flowers.

Terrible Things, by Eve Bunting, illustrated by Stephen Gammell. All is peaceful for the animals in the clearing until the Terrible Things come for the creatures with feathers, but when Little Rabbit protests, he is silenced by the others. As each group is taken in turn, Little Rabbit is left alone, certain now that no one must look away from the Terrible Things, but must protest together.

The Wall, by Eve Bunting, illustrated by Ronald Himler. A boy and his father come from far away to visit the Vietnam Veterans Memorial in Washington and find the name of the boy's grandfather, who was killed in the conflict.

Humorous Books

As an antidote to the more serious aspects of life, every child has a need to "escape," and, of course, folk and fairy tales listed earlier can draw the youngster into a never-never world to fulfill this desire. But there are several other kinds of books which also meet this need. As a special category, there are books designed primarily to be funny. Adults do not always recognize the extent to which children relish the absurd, whether it is a matter of a character who behaves ridiculously or only a repetition of silly sounds. This innate love of fun accounts for the continued popularity of Mother Goose, the early Dr. Seuss books, and the cumulative tale, as well as many nonsense rhymes listed later in the poetry section.

Alexander and the Terrible, Horrible, No Good, Very Bad Day, by Judith Viorst, illustrations by Ray Cruz. Told in the first person, Alexander decides to go to Australia when everything goes wrong, but as his mom tells him, "Some days are like that. Even in Australia." A good look at modern family life.

Amelia Bedelia, by Peggy Parish, illustrated by Fritz Siebel. Amelia means to follow directions exactly, but her literal interpretations make this a very funny book, and Amelia's great lemon meringue pie saves her job at the Rogers' house. First in a series of equally amusing stories of Amelia.

Animals Should Definitely Not Wear Clothing, by Judith Barrett, illustrated by Ron Barrett. Very amusing illustrations show why the book's title is true.

The Big Brown Bear, by Georges Duplaix, illustrated by Gustaf Tenggren. When his wife sends him down to the brook to catch a fish, she warns him against trying to rob the beehive, but he can't resist the smell of honey, and the bees get him.

Bill and Pete, by Tomie De Paola. William Everett Crocodile, who changes his name to Bill, and his talking "toothbrush" friend Pete get along very well, but one day the Bad Guy who makes suitcases out of crocodiles captures Bill. With Pete's help Bill escapes and has his revenge on the Bad Guy.

The Cat Who Wore a Pot on Her Head, by Jan Slepian and Ann Seidler, illustrated by Richard E. Martin. Bendemolena finds that a pot on her head shuts out the noise, but it also prevents her from hearing clearly, which leads to much confusion in a very humorous book.

Cecily G. and the 9 Monkeys, by H. A. Rey. Both Cecily and the monkeys are lonely, so they join forces to play wonderful games and live happily together.

Clever Kate, adapted from a story by the Brothers Grimm by Elizabeth Shub, illustrated by Anita Lobel. A very funny tale of how honest, well-meaning Kate, who does not think too logically, truly earns the title "clever."

Clocks and More Clocks, by Pat Hutchins. One day Mr. Higgins finds an old grandfather clock in his attic. In this very amusing tale, he tries to check the time by comparing it to many other clocks, running each time up to his attic.

Cloudy With a Chance of Meatballs, by Judith Barrett, illustrated by Ron Barrett. Life is delicious in the town of Chewandswallow where it rains soup and juice, snows mashed potatoes, and blows storms of hamburgers—until the weather takes a turn for the worse. Then, as Grandpa tells it, the people had to abandon the town.

Curious George, by H. A. Rey. The first of a series about a mischievous little monkey and "the man in the yellow hat" who brings him home from the jungle.

Curious George Goes to the Hospital, by Margaret and H. A. Rey. This time the little monkey has swallowed a piece of a jigsaw puzzle and must have it removed. Of course, he gets into the usual scrapes while in the hospital.

The Day Jimmy's Boa Ate the Wash, by Trinka Hakes Noble, illustrated by Steven Kellogg. The class visits a farm on their field trip, but when Jimmy brings along his pet boa constrictor, the result is mayhem. One thing leads to the next, with unpredictable results.

Dear Garbage Man, by Gene Zion, illustrated by Margaret Bloy Graham. Stan, the new garbage man, finds a horseshoe of flowers which says, "Best Luck to Emily," so he ties it on his truck instead of putting it into the chewer-upper. But it doesn't stop there. Stan saves all the things people put out and invites everyone to take what they want. The next day, however, he finds it all on the curb again, so this time he uses the chewer-upper.

Dog for a Day, by Dick Gackenbach. After transforming a football into a toaster and a cat into a canary, Sidney's new invention creates unexpected problems by changing Sidney into his dog Wally, and his dog into Sidney.

Don't Forget the Bacon!, by Pat Hutchins. Such a simple grocery list—just three items, and, of course, the bacon. But six farm eggs get confused with six fat legs, a pound of pears sounds like a flight of stairs, and "I forgot the bacon!"

Farmer Palmer's Wagon Ride, by William Steig. Farmer Palmer, a pig, and his hired hand Ebenezer go to town with a load of vegetables to sell, but they must use all the gifts which Farmer Palmer has for his family to get them back to the farm safely.

Father Fox's Pennyrhymes, by Clyde Watson, illustrated by Wendy Watson. With musical lilt these exuberant rhymes sing of American country life. There are lullabies, counting-rhymes, sly and funny jingles all set forth by Father Fox in overalls.

George Shrinks, by William Joyce. When George wakes up to find himself shrunk to the size of a mouse, he has a terrible time following instructions left in a note by his parents, but he tries to do everything with hilarious results.

The Giant Jam Sandwich, by John Vernon Lord and Janet Burroway. One hot summer in Itching Down, four million wasps fly into town. How to get rid of them? Bap the baker has the idea of making a giant jam sandwich, and the whole town cooperates.

The Gollywhopper Egg, by Anne Rockwell. Timothy Todd, a peddler, tries to get rid of a coconut by passing it off as a gollywhopper egg, and he succeeds.

A Great Big Ugly Man Came Up and Tied His Horse to Me: A Book of Nonsense Verse, by Wallace Tripp. Some of the poems are clever and mischievous, and others are just plain silly, but with wonderful illustrations all will touch a child's funny bone.

The Happy Hippopotami, by Bill Martin, Jr., illustrated by Betsy Everitt. In deliciously droll verse we see the happy hippos enjoying a day at the beach.

Hiccup, by Mercer Mayer. Mr. and Mrs. Hippo deal with the hiccups in this almost wordless and very funny book.

Horton Hatches the Egg, by Dr. Seuss. Horton the elephant has promised to sit on Mayzie's egg while she takes a vacation, and he is true to his word even when she doesn't return. After a number of adventures, the egg hatches near Palm Beach, and the good-for-nothing Mayzie swoops down and claims it. However, it is an elephant-bird!

Imogene's Antlers, by David Small. One Thursday Imogene wakes up with a pair of antlers on her head and causes a sensation wherever she goes.

Jimmy's Boa Bounces Back, by Trinka Hakes Noble, illustrated by Steven Kellogg. A pet boa constrictor wreaks havoc at a posh garden party. As Maggie tells it, the story becomes more and more fantastic, and it's a lot of fun.

John Patrick Norman McHennessy—The Boy Who Was Always Late, by John Burningham. A wickedly funny story of childish wisdom and adult foolishness as the teacher regrets his decision to disbelieve a student's outlandish excuses for being tardy.

** *The Judge: An Untrue Tale,* by Harve Zemach, illustrated by Margot Zemach. Five prisoners come before the judge. Their crime? They each want to warn of the Horrible Thing that is coming. Each is sent to jail. Then . . .

Keep Your Mouth Closed, Dear, by Aliki. Charles, a young crocodile, cannot help swallowing everything in sight. His parents try all kinds of remedies, even putting a zipper on his mouth, but nothing works until he helps his mother with the cleaning and uses the vacuum.

King Bidgood's in the Bathtub, by Audrey Wood, illustrated by Don Wood. Despite pleas from his court, the fun-loving King Bidgood will not get out of his bathtub to rule his kingdom until a little page solves the problem.

Lentil, by Robert McCloskey. Lentil and his harmonica are welcome everywhere in Alto, Ohio, except to Old Sneep, who doesn't like anything, and almost ruins the town's welcome to Colonel Carter by making it impossible for the band to play. Lentil saves the day.

The Man Who Kept House, retold by Kathleen and Michael Hague, illustrated by Michael Hague. A farmer claims that while he toils all day, his wife does nothing. They exchange jobs with hilarious results: the cow is hanging from the roof, the baby is tied to a chair, and the husband is in the hearth with his head in a pot.

McElligot's Pool, by Dr. Seuss. In his inimitable rhyme we learn why there's everything in the pool from whales to A THING-A-MA-JIGGER, which is why the boy keeps fishing there.

Meanwhile, Back at the Ranch, by Trinka Hakes Noble, illustrated by Tony Ross. A really hilarious book with a dead-pan look at the expression, "Meanwhile. . . ." Rancher Hicks drives eighty-four miles to Sleepy Gulch while his wife Elna stays on the ranch to dig potatoes. What happens is just what Elna deserves.

Mr. Gumpy's Motor Car, by John Burningham. With endless patience Mr. Gumpy takes his friends on another outing, this time in his red motor car. When it rains and they get stuck in the mud, the children and the animals are reluctant to get out and push, but all ends well.

Mr. Gumpy's Outing, by John Burningham. Mr. Gumpy lives near a river and has a boat. He agrees to take the children, and then a number of animals, for a boat ride and all goes well until they start misbehaving.

Mrs. Armitage on Wheels, by Quentin Blake. Mrs. Armitage and her faithful dog Breakspear start out on a bicycle, to which the lady adds so many items that it crashes, so she takes to roller skates, but she will add to these as well, so. . . .

Mr. Pig and Sonny Too, by Lillian Hoban. Four very short and funny stories about Mr. Pig, who always means well, but ends up in difficulties, which Sonny tries to help him solve.

Mole and Shrew Step Out, by Jackie French Koller, illustrated by Stella Ormai. Mole is overlooked when Mouse sends invitations for her swanky party, so Shrew invites him to escort her. Mole does misunderstand what "tails" means, but Shrew sticks by her new friend, and they plan a party of their own.

The Napping House, by Audrey Wood, illustrated by Don Wood. This charming cumulative tale has a surprise ending, done with great humor.

A Nice Walk in the Jungle, by Nan Bodsworth. Miss Jellaby is determined to take her class on a nature walk through the "jungle," and two by two they go, but Miss J. doesn't notice the boa constrictor eating the children, one by one.

The Pelican's Chorus and the Quangle Wangle's Hat, by Edward Lear, illustrated by Kevin W. Maddison. In two poems the grand King and Queen of the Pelicans live a joyous life on the banks of the Nile and a strange creature's vast hat attracts a wide variety of nesters. Nonsense verse with great pictures.

A Penny a Look, by Harve and Margot Zemach. A hilarious tale of two brothers who set out to catch a one-eyed man who they intend to exhibit. However, they find that he is not alone, and so the one-eyed men turn the tables and exhibit the red-haired two-eyed rascals instead.

Perfect Pigs: An Introduction to Manners, by Marc Brown and Stephen Krensky. Using a comic-book format with pigs as characters, this book is really quite comical, with manners a side issue.

The Piggy in the Puddle, by Charlotte Pomerantz, illustrated by James Marshall. A really catchy, rhymed story of pigs in the milieu they love best—mud.

Pierre: A Cautionary Tale, by Maurice Sendak. No matter what is said to Pierre, he has only one retort, "I don't care!" Then a lion changes his mind.

The Principal's New Clothes, by Stephanie Calmenson, illustrated by Denise Brunkus. A hilarious updated version of *The Emperor's New Clothes* has Mr. Bundy falling for Ivy and Moe, tricksters, not tailors, and appearing at the school assembly in his underwear because he has been told that anyone who can't see the suit is stupid. A kindergarten child yells out the truth.

The Quangle Wangle's Hat, by Edward Lear, illustrated by Helen Oxenbury. All of the traditional animals come to build on the Quangle Wangle's hat, with rhymed nonsense and great illustrations.

The Quicksand Book, by Tomie De Paola. This humorous look at the composition of quicksand and what to do should one fall in teaches jungle girl and jungle boy not to panic.

Rabbits on Roller Skates, by Jan Wahl, illustrated by David Allender. Rhymed text and humorous illustrations follow the progress of a group of rabbits on roller skates.

Randy's Dandy Lions, by Bill Peet. In humorous verse we learn how Randy's lions cannot perform in the circus because of cage fright. Nothing helps until they howl all one night, keeping all the animals awake, so they alone are available to do the show.

Rolling Harvey Down the Hill, by Jack Prelutsky, illustrated by Victoria Chess. A collection of humorous poems about the narrator's four friends, one of whom is obnoxious Harvey.

Rosie's Walk, by Pat Hutchins. In this wordless book the Fox is after Rosie the hen, but she doesn't know it. Unwittingly, she leads him into one disaster after the other, each funnier than the last.

**Sidney Rella and the Glass Sneakers,* by Bernice Myers. A really novel take-off on the traditional Cinderella theme when Sidney wants to play football and is helped by a "small person" who gives him the uniform, including glass sneakers. Sidney ends up being the star of the team and then more.

Squeeze a Sneeze, by Bill Morrison. Some very funny ways to use rhyming words, such as "Can you tickle a pickle for a nickel?" and "Hit a fly in the eye with a blueberry pie," make this a great way to start a game with children making up their own "funnies."

"Stand Back," Said the Elephant, "I'm Going to Sneeze," by Patricia Thomas, illustrated by Wallace Tripp. In funny rhymed verse, each animal asks the elephant not to sneeze, remembering what had happened the last time. The little mouse scares the elephant, so he doesn't sneeze. He laughs instead with the same terrible results.

The Stupids Step Out, by Harry Allard, illustrated by James Marshall. Hilarious illustrations show the Stupid family doing everything from riding on top of the car while their dog drives to taking a bath without any water. The first of a series which is very popular.

The Surprise Party, by Pat Hutchins. "I'm having a party tomorrow," Rabbit whispers to his friend, Owl. "It's a surprise." But Owl passes the news along to Squirrel. "Rabbit is hoeing the parsley tomorrow," he says. From Squirrel to Duck, from Duck to Mouse, and on and on the erroneous news spreads. Finally all is straightened out.

The Tale of Meshka the Kvetch, by Carol Chapman, illustrated by Arnold Lobel. A woman who spends all of her time complaining soon finds her complaints coming true. The rabbi tells her she has Kvetch's Itch and explains that she can cure herself by "praising the good in life."

** *Topsy-Turvies: Pictures to Stretch the Imagination,* by Mitsumasa Anno. A very unusual and challenging wordless book for the elementary school child and his parents.

The Trouble With Grandad, by Babette Cole. Everyone is jealous of Grandad because he wins all the prizes at the vegetable shows, so they give him a mysterious tomato plant which grows and grows and gets Grandad in real trouble.

Underwear!, by Mary Elise Monsell, illustrated by Lynn Munsinger. Bismark the buffalo sees no fun in anything, and he won't wear underwear. Then his friends who love wearing it change Bismark's mind, and his life as well.

** *Upside-Downers: More Pictures to Stretch the Imagination,* by Mitsumasa Anno. This is the sequel to *Topsy-Turvies.* Here the artist again uses rhyme, and with playing cards shows that what is up in one view is down in another.

Veronica, by Roger Duvoisin. This hippopotamus feels that she isn't noticed among all the other hippos on the mud bank where she lives, so she runs away to the city where she is conspicuous and famous, but gets into a lot of trouble. She is glad to go home again.

Who Sank the Boat?, by Pamela Allen. In rhymed verse and with great illustrations we learn how each animal gets into a rowboat until it is finally overloaded.

Willis, by James Marshall. Willis is a sad creature because he needs sunglasses and does not have the money for them. His friends Bird, Snake, and Lobster help him in very humorous ways.

The Wind Blew, by Pat Hutchins. A humorous cumulative story in delicious rhyme, this book illustrates what a mischievous wind can do.

The Wingdingdilly, by Bill Peet. Orvie's dog Scamp is tired of being just a dog, so he runs away and meets Zildy the witch, who turns him into a really fantastic combination animal, a wingdingdilly. Then he finds himself captured by C. J. Pringle for his Incredible Creature Show. But finally Zildy turns him back into Scamp and he returns to Orvie at the farm.

The Wizard, the Fairy and the Magic Chicken, by Helen Lester, illustrated by Lynn Munsinger. The competition is keen when these three vie to see who can do the zaniest magic. Then they are forced to cooperate when the monsters they've created get too scary.

Wombat Stew, by Marcia K. Vaughan, illustrated by Pamela Lofts. When the clever dingo catches a wombat on the banks of a billabong, he plans on stew, but he listens to the advice of other animals, such as the platypus, and adds all kinds of miscellany to the stew before putting the wombat in, so he ends up without his meal.

Yummers!, by James Marshall. Emily Pig, trying to lose weight, takes a walk with her friend Eugene the turtle. But enroute Emily eats so much that she becomes ill, which she blames on the walk.

Books About Monsters

As we can see in any amusement park, human beings seem to get a sense of escape and enjoyment through being frightened when they know there is no real danger.

Sometimes it's fun to be scared. In terms of children's literature this tendency can be seen by the increasing popularity of books about monsters. It is interesting to note that when Maurice Sendak's *Where the Wild Things Are* first appeared, adults were almost uniformly of the opinion that it would be "too scary" for preschoolers. However, "child pressure" soon changed their minds. As Sendak has said, the children send him pictures of the monsters they have drawn which make his look tame in comparison.

Boris and the Monsters, by Elaine Macmann Willoughby, illustrated by Lynn Munsinger. In order to protect Boris from the monsters that come to his room each night, his father buys him a "fierce watchdog," but Ivan the Terrible is still a puppy who's afraid of the dark himself.

Clyde Monster, by Robert L. Crowe, illustrated by Kay Chorao. Clyde is a nice little monster, but he's afraid of humans. However, his parents reassure him, "A long time ago monsters and people made a deal. Monsters don't scare people and people don't scare monsters."

Do Not Open, by Brinton Turkle. The intrepid Miss Moody and her cat Captain Kidd live at Land's End, where Miss Moody fills her cottage with things she has picked up on the beach. One day after a storm Miss Moody and Captain Kidd find a bottle labeled "Do not open," but the kindly lady can't resist a child's voice begging to be let out, so she ignores the warning, and the trouble starts.

Harry and the Terrible Whatzit, by Dick Gackenbach. Harry warns his mother not to go into the basement to get a jar of pickles, and when she doesn't return, he goes down to save her from the Whatzit.

The Island of the Skog, by Steven Kellogg. On National Rodent Day the mice all decide to escape from their predators, and sail away to find a safe place to live. When they finally moor near an island, they are frightened of the Skog who lives there, but after they trap him, they discover that he's tiny too and is afraid of them.

Mag the Magnificent, by Dick Gackenbach. A boy's drawing of a magical monster on his wall sets off a series of adventures for both of them, until his mother wants the wall cleaned off. He cleans it, but he draws the monster in miniature behind his mirror.

Maggie and the Monster, by Elizabeth Winthrop, illustrated by Tomie De Paola. Mysteriously a little monster comes to Maggie's room each night and finally admits that she is looking for her mama, so Maggie takes her down the hall to the broom closet where her mother lives.

The Monster and the Tailor, by Paul Galdone. An unreasonable Grand Duke insists that the tailor stitch his trousers in the graveyard, and the poor man barely escapes the monster who pursues him, but he finishes the "lucky" trousers and gets his bag of gold.

Monster Poems, edited by Daisy Wallace, illustrated by Kay Chorao. Seventeen poems by various authors describe different kinds of monsters.

My Mama Says There Aren't Any Zombies, Ghosts, Vampires, Creatures, Demons, Monsters, Fiends, Goblins or Things, by Judith Viorst, illustrated by Kay Chorao. Nick's mother assures him that there are no scary things coming to get him. Of course, mommies sometimes do make mistakes. But sometimes they don't.

The Spooky Tail of Prewitt Peacock, by Bill Peet. All the other peacocks make fun of Prewitt's scraggly tail and chase him away. But the tail looks scary when open, which saves all the peacocks from Travis the tiger.

The Terrible Troll, by Mercer Mayer. "I wish I lived a thousand years ago," says a young boy who is enthralled with the ideas of knights, dragons, and even a terrible troll to do battle against. But then he changes his mind as the fantasy ends.

There's a Nightmare in My Closet, by Mercer Mayer. A small boy prepares to confront his nightmare wearing his helmet and carrying his toy gun. But the nightmare is so frightened that he crawls into bed with the boy for comfort.

There's an Alligator Under My Bed, by Mercer Mayer. A sequel to *There's a Nightmare in My Closet*, the alligator under his bed makes the boy's bedtime a hazardous operation, but he lures it out of the house and into the garage.

There's Something in My Attic, by Mercer Mayer. Convinced that there is something making noise in the attic at night, a brave little girl sneaks upstairs, lasso in hand, to capture whatever it is.

The Underbed, by Cathryn Clinton Hoellwarth, illustrated by Sibyl Graber Gerig. Tucker's mother helps him get rid of the monster that lives under his bed when she tells him how she had the very same trouble when she was a little girl.

Where the Wild Things Are, by Maurice Sendak. Max in his wolf suit makes mischief of every kind and is sent to his room without supper. But he "sails out of his room," and goes where the wild things live. He becomes their king, but decides to go home again to his very own room where his supper is waiting, "and it's still hot."

Wiley and the Hairy Man, by Molly Garrett Bang. A folktale from the South about a boy and his mother who live on a swamp near the Tombigbee River. To avoid the evil of the Hairy Man, and get rid of him forever, the two have to trick him three times—and they do.

The Wizard, the Fairy and the Magic Chicken, by Helen Lester, illustrated by Lynn Munsinger. The competition is keen when these three vie to see who can do the zaniest magic. Then they are forced to cooperate when the monsters they've created get too scary.

You're the Scaredy-Cat, by Mercer Mayer. Two little boys decide to camp in the backyard, and one tells the story of the garbage can monster to frighten his friend, who just goes to sleep. Then the teller dreams of the monster and is the frightened one.

Zeralda's Ogre, by Tomi Ungerer. In the town people are terrified by a typical ogre who eats children, but the farmer's daughter, Zeralda, who is an extraordinary cook, meets the ogre and changes his eating habits with her delightful cuisine.

Flights of Fancy

Another way to "escape" serious problems and everyday trials and tribulations is by using one's imagination. Most children have this ability to the nth degree, and there are many books with their unusual illustrations which make it possible to exercise this ability.

Abuela, by Arthur Dorros, illustrated by Elisa Kleven. While riding on a bus with her Spanish-speaking grandmother, a little girl imagines that they are flying over New York City, seeing the sights. A glossary is at the end of the book.

Alistair's Elephant, by Marilyn Sadler, illustrated by Roger Bollen. Alistair Grittle is an unusual ten-year-old. He's very neat; he does his homework; he plays games which exercise his mind. However, his life changes radically when an elephant follows him home from the zoo.

Alistair's Time Machine, by Marilyn Sadler, illustrated by Roger Bollen. When Alistair builds a time machine for his entry in the school science competition, he takes on more than he bargains for. He has some strange encounters in past times, even saving cave people from the woolly mammoths, but the judges don't believe his contraption works.

And My Mean Old Mother Will Be Sorry, Blackboard Bear, by Martha Alexander. Anthony tries to feed honey to his teddy bear, and when his mother gets angry, he "runs away" to the woods with his blackboard bear.

And to Think That I Saw It on Mulberry Street, by Dr. Seuss. Marco embroiders what he sees on his way to school on Mulberry Street, but feels it is just too much for his dad to believe, so when he's asked what he has seen, he just says, "Nothing but a plain horse and wagon." But the readers know better!

Barn Dance!, by Bill Martin, Jr., and John Archambault, illustrated by Ted Rand. A country boy dreams of a barn dance with the scarecrow as fiddler and all the animals participating. Illustrations make the scene come alive.

The Bear's Toothache, by David McPhail. A small boy with a loose tooth has an adventure with a bear whose crying wakens him because of his toothache. All is solved when the child gets the bear's tooth out.

The Big Orange Splot, by Daniel Manus Pinkwater. When a seagull drops a can of orange paint on his neat house, Mr. Plumbean gets an idea that affects his entire neighborhood. First the neighbors protest, and then each house becomes the dream of its owner.

The Cat in the Hat, by Dr. Seuss. An early classic by Dr. Seuss who rhymes the unbelievable antics of the cat who comes to amuse the children on a rainy day, wrecks everything, and then remedies all damage by the time Mother comes home.

The Chalk Box Story, by Don Freeman. Eight sticks of magic chalk draw the sky, sea, an island, a turtle, and a boy waiting to be rescued. But the ship doesn't see the boy, so the turtle takes matters in hand.

Come Away from the Water, Shirley, by John Burningham. Shirley's parents sit at the seaside and say the usual things to their little girl on the left-side pages, while on the right-hand pages we see that Shirley is thinking about boarding a pirate ship, capturing it, and finding treasure, returning triumphant with her dog.

Could Be Worse!, by James Stevenson. Everything is always the same at Grandpa's house, even the things he says—until one unusual morning when Grandpa tells the children about his dream.

Digging to China, by Donna Rawlins. Hearing her friend Marj, an elderly lady next door, speak wistfully of China, Alexis digs a hole all the way through the earth to that exotic country and brings back a postcard for Marj on her birthday.

Dreams, by Ezra Jack Keats. Roberto and Archie, city children this author has created in other books, are here, dreaming that the huge shadow of Roberto's paper mouse sails down and scares away the dog that has cornered Archie's cat.

***Free Fall,* by David Wiesner. In a really beautiful wordless book a young boy dreams of daring adventures in the company of imaginary creatures inspired by the things surrounding his bed.

***The Garden of Abdul Gasazi,* by Chris Van Allsburg. Alan agrees to dog-sit with Miss Hester's mischievous dog Fritz, but when they go for a walk, they end up in the garden of Gasazi the Great, a magician who convinces Alan that he has turned Fritz into a duck. Maybe he has.

The Giant Jam Sandwich, by John Vernon Lord and Janet Burroway. One hot summer in Itching Down, four million wasps flew into town. How to get rid of them? Bap the baker has the idea of making a giant jam sandwich, and the whole town cooperates.

Goodness Gracious!, by Phil Cummings, illustrated by Craig Smith. A child celebrates herself while visualizing adventures with pirates, dogs, baboons, and witches. A fun book.

Harold and the Purple Crayon, by Crockett Johnson. With his wonderful purple crayon, Harold draws everything he's thinking and has fantastic adventures, but finally he draws his own room and his bed and gets into it to go to sleep.

Hey, Al, by Arthur Yorinks, illustrated by Richard Egielski. Al, a janitor, and his faithful dog Eddie share a very poor lifestyle in a single room. A mysterious bird offers to fly them to a paradise in the sky, but they find after a time that there is really no place like home.

Hey, Get Off Our Train, by John Burningham. A really clever book in which a young boy goes to bed and dreams that his toy train really runs. But as he and his dog are traveling around the world, an elephant, a seal, and other endangered animals board the train to avoid extinction. Simply wonderful imaginative illustrations and a surprise ending.

Humphrey's Bear, by Jan Wahl, illustrated by William Joyce. Humphrey is not too old to sleep with his teddy bear; they have wonderful adventures after he goes to bed, just as his father had before him.

I Meant to Clean My Room Today, by Miriam Nerlove. In rhyme a little girl tells all the reasons she is unable to clean her room: a big white lion, a yellow turtle, an orange lamb, a green kitten, and other exotic animals simply demand her attention.

I See a Song, by Eric Carle. A wordless book in which a violinist plays and the music forms gorgeous colored images.

I Took My Frog to the Library, by Eric A. Kimmel, illustrated by Blanche Sims. In a very imaginative story, a young girl brings her pets—a frog, a pelican, a giraffe, an elephant, and others—to the library with predictably disastrous results.

If Dinosaurs Came Back, by Bernard Most. A child imagines all the ways dinosaurs could be useful in this modern world. Different dinosaurs are accurately labeled at the back of the book.

If Dinosaurs Were Cats and Dogs, by Colin McNaughton. In rhymed verse a child imagines what it would be like if everyday pets were the size of dinosaurs. Havoc ensues!

In the Night Kitchen, by Maurice Sendak. Mickey has a dream which includes the baking of a morning cake, with a number of Oliver Hardys assisting. Great fun.

Jamberry, by Bruce Degen. A boy and an endearing rhyme-spouting bear go through a fantastic world of berries, and their adventure comes to a razzamatazz finale under a strawberry sky.

***Jumanji,* by Chris Van Allsburg. Left on their own for the afternoon, Peter and Judy find more excitement than they bargain for in a mysterious jungle-adventure board game, when the animals come alive.

Lullaby, by Jane Chelsea Aragon, illustrated by Kandy Radzinski. Lavish watercolors illustrate this book in which a mother's lullaby is carried by the wind over hills and meadows, over lakes and woods, to the sea, finally being transformed into the morning chirp of birds which greet the mother and child.

Mag the Magnificent, by Dick Gackenbach. A boy's drawing of a magical monster on his wall sets off a series of adventures for both of them, until his mother wants the wall cleaned off. He cleans it, but he draws the monster in miniature behind his mirror.

May I Bring a Friend?, by Beatrice Schenk De Regniers, illustrated by Beni Montresor. When invited to come to their palace first for tea, then for dinner, lunch, breakfast, Halloween, and Apple Pie Day, the little boy brings some unusual "friends" to the delight of the royal couple.

***Miss Fanshawe and the Great Dragon Adventure,* by Sue Scullard. A truly novel book about an intrepid British lady who successfully traps a dragon by traveling to the center of the earth in a hot-air balloon, circa late-nineteenth century.

***Nettie Jo's Friends,* by Patricia C. McKissack, illustrated by Scott Cook. Nettie Jo searches for a needle to sew a dress for Annie Mae, so she can take the doll to the wedding where Nettie Jo will be the flower girl. But the three animals she helps during the search do not seem inclined to reciprocate until the end.

Nothing Ever Happens on My Block, by Ellen Raskin. Chester Filbert imagines all kinds of excitement that could happen on his block, but as he sits on the curb, he misses all that really does happen.

On My Beach There Are Many Pebbles, by Leo Lionni. A wordless book showing imaginatively all the shapes that pebbles can assume.

One Monday Morning, by Uri Shulevitz. Skillfully juxtaposing the stark reality of a New York tenement with the make-believe world of a child who imagines royalty in the image of playing cards, this book creates an endearing young hero.

Overnight Adventure, by Frances Kilbourne, illustrated by Ann Powell. In this wordless book some children decide to "camp" overnight in the backyard and imagine storms and all kinds of wild animals.

The Paper Party, by Don Freeman. Jory is watching TV with his dog Peetza, and he imagines the puppets in the show invite him to join them, but it's all make-believe. He'd rather be a boy.

Patrick's Dinosaurs, by Carol Carrick, illustrated by Donald Carrick. Hank and Patrick go to the zoo, and when Hank tells his younger brother about dinosaurs, the younger boy's imagination runs wild.

***Rondo in C,* by Paul Fleischman, illustrated by Janet Wentworth. An extraordinary book which shows in lyrical language and sensitive pastel portraits the thoughts of each individual as he or she listens to a young girl playing Beethoven's "Rondo in C" at her piano recital.

Show and Tell, by Elvira Woodruff, illustrated by Denise Brunkus. Andy's offerings for show-and-tell always seem to bore his kindergarten class until one day he finds a magic bottle of bubbles that temporarily transports all of them on an aerial adventure.

The Snowman, by Raymond Briggs. In this charming wordless book a little boy personifies a snowman he has built, and they do everything together.

Tar Beach, by Faith Ringgold. The setting is a New York City apartment-house roof, and the story revolves around the quilt on which the girl lies, dreaming of flying over George Washington Bridge, over the ice-cream factory, and into the night sky filled with stars.

The Terrible Troll, by Mercer Mayer. "I wish I lived a thousand years ago," says a young boy who is enthralled with the idea of knights, dragons, and even a terrible troll to do battle against. But then he changes his mind as the fantasy ends.

That's Good! That's Bad!, by Margery Cuyler, illustrated by David Catrow. A little boy has a series of adventures and misadventures when he visits the zoo with his parents.

Time to Get Out of the Bath, Shirley, by John Burningham. During her bath Shirley is off on a series of imaginative adventures about which her mother has no idea.

The Trek, by Ann Jonas. A little girl "sees" large jungle animals on her way to school, animals no one else sees. A clever book with pictures of the "real" animals at the end.

***Tuesday,* by David Wiesner. A wordless book which shows how frogs rise on their lily pads at night and explore nearby houses while their inhabitants sleep. Very fanciful.

When the Sky Is Like Lace, by Elinor Lander Horwitz, illustrated by Barbara Cooney. This interesting book describes the strange and wonderful things that can happen on a "bimulous" night when the sky is like lace, and everything is "strange-splendid" and "plum-purple."

Where the Wild Things Are, by Maurice Sendak. Max in his wolf suit makes mischief of every kind and is sent to his room without his supper. But he "sails out of his room" and goes where the wild things live. He becomes their king, but decides to go home again to his very own room where his supper is waiting, "and it's still hot."

You Look Ridiculous, Said the Rhinoceros to the Hippopotamus, by Bernard Waber. When the Rhino tells the Hippo that she looks ridiculous because she doesn't have a horn on her nose, it starts Hippo dreaming. Then in her dream each animal she meets tells her she needs what he has—a lion's mane, tiger's spots, elephant's ears, and so on. Now she really looks ridiculous, so she's happy that it is only a dream. She's proud to be what she is.

You're the Scaredy Cat, by Mercer Mayer. Two little boys decide to camp in the backyard, and one tells the story of the garbage can monster to frighten his friend, who just goes to sleep. Then the teller dreams of the monster and he is the frightened one.

**Zoe's Tower,* by Paul and Emma Rogers, illustrated by Robin Bell Corfield. An imaginative story of a little girl who explores an old deserted tower near her home.

Books About Animals

Animals are favorite characters in children's stories, many times really representing human beings ("people in fur"), but also they appear simply as animals. The following titles combine several types of animals.

The Caterpillar and the Polliwog, by Jack Kent. Caterpillar explains to Polliwog that she will change into something else after she's spun her cocoon, and he waits patiently. By the time she emerges as a butterfly, he has become a frog.

Gobble, Growl, Grunt, by Peter Spier. Familiar and unfamiliar animals, wild and domesticated, tiny and huge, are all artfully reproduced by this well-known artist with typical sounds for each.

A Hippopotamusn't, by J. Patrick Lewis, illustrated by Victoria Chess. More than thirty mostly humorous poems about animals of every kind, with appropriately funny illustrations.

It Does Not Say Meow, by Beatrice Schenk De Regniers, illustrated by Paul Galdone. Rhymed riddles about animals, with the answer pictured on each page following the riddle.

My Red Umbrella, by Robert Bright. A little girl finds that her umbrella grows larger as more animals find shelter from the rain under it.

A Peaceable Kingdom: The Shaker Abecedarius, illustrated by Alice and Martin Provensen. A quaintly illustrated alphabet rhyme that includes the animals from alligator to zebra.

Roar and More, by Karla Kuskin. This colorful reissue of a notable book presents rhyming text showing behavior and noises of each animal.

Where Does the Brown Bear Go?, by Nicki Weiss. When the lights go down, each of the animals from the cat to the brown bear goes home to bed.

A Year of Beasts, by Ashley Wolff. Ellie and Peter go through the months, exploring with appropriate woodland animals for each. Shows the cycle in nature with lovely soft illustrations.

A Zooful of Animals, edited by William Cole, illustrated by Lynn Munsinger. A great collection of short poems about animals—all kinds—with delightful, humorous illustrations. For example, "The Raccoon" reads, "The raccoon wears a mask at night and has a brown-ringed tail. That's how I recognize him when he dumps my garbage pail."

Pets

The Accident, by Carol Carrick, illustrated by Donald Carrick. Christopher's dog Bodger is killed when he runs in front of a pickup truck. The driver is very sorry; Christopher's parents are devastated as well. But finally, the boy goes with his father to pick out a headstone to mark the dog's grave, and he is able to cry in grief.

The Adventures of Taxi-Dog, by Debra and Sal Barracca, illustrated by Mark Buehner. Maxi, a homeless dog, finds taxi driver Jim who invites him to come home and live with him. A humorous dog-eye view of New York, as Maxi goes everywhere with Jim.

Angus and the Cat, by Marjorie Flack. Angus is teased by a little cat who always jumps too high for the little terrier to reach. When she is gone, however, Angus realizes that he misses her, and he's glad when she returns.

Angus and the Ducks, by Marjorie Flack. A curious Scotch terrier decides to investigate the strange noise coming from the other side of the hedge and almost regrets his curiosity.

Angus Lost, by Marjorie Flack. Angus, a small Scotch terrier, is tired of the same house, the same cat, and the same yard, so he escapes to find that being lost is no fun. He is glad to return home.

Annie and the Wild Animals, by Jan Brett. When Annie's cat disappears, she attempts friendship with a variety of unsuitable woodland animals, but with the emergence of spring, everything comes right.

Archie, Follow Me, by Lynne Cherry. A little girl describes her very warm relationship with her pet cat.

At Mary Bloom's, by Aliki. The day the mouse has babies, all Mary Bloom's pets join in the celebration with Mary, her baby, and her little girlfriend.

Aunt Nina's Visit, by Franz Brandenberg, illustrated by Aliki. Six nieces and nephews have fun trying to do a puppet show with six tiny kittens running all over the place. They are Aunt Nina's gift to the children.

A Bag Full of Pups, by Dick Gackenbach. Mr. Mullins's dog has puppies, which he gives away to different people who want them to perform different tasks, but the last one goes to a boy who wants only a warm pet to love.

Benjy and the Barking Bird, by Margaret Bloy Graham. Benjy likes Aunt Tilly, but he is jealous of her parrot, who barks like a dog, so Benjy gets rid of her; then he gets her back by providing a mate.

Benjy's Boat Trip, by Margaret Bloy Graham. Benjy is supposed to stay home with Aunt Mary when his family goes on a cruise. But he accidentally ends up on another ship and has an adventure with a cat.

Benjy's Dog House, by Margaret Bloy Graham. Benjy wants to sleep with the children, Linda and Jimmy, and refuses to sleep outside in his dog house. After an adventure with the town baker, he gets to sleep inside again.

Benny Bakes a Cake, by Eve Rice. Benny helps his mother make his birthday cake, but Ralph, his dog, pulls it off the table. Benny's daddy saves the day when he comes home with a birthday cake for Benny.

Better With Two, by Barbara M. Joosse, illustrated by Catherine Stock. Mrs. Brady and her old dog Max have a young friend Laura, who sometimes joins them for "elevenses," or tea. Then Max dies, and Laura tries to make Mrs. Brady feel better by letting her know how sorry she is about Max dying.

Bobo's Dream, by Martha Alexander. The small dachshund Bobo keeps his bone due to the efforts of his boy, and the dog dreams of returning the favor. A wordless book.

Boris and the Monsters, by Elaine Macmann Willoughby, illustrated by Lynn Munsinger. In order to protect Boris from the monsters that come to his room at night, his father buys him a "fierce watchdog," but Ivan the Terrible is still a puppy who's afraid of the dark himself.

A Boy, a Dog, and a Frog, by Mercer Mayer. A wordless book shows the frog following the boy and the dog home.

Carl Goes Shopping, by Alexandra Day. Another imaginative wordless book about the wonderful weimaraner, Carl, who is the world's best babysitter.

Carl's Afternoon in the Park, by Alexandra Day. A wordless book which shows Carl, an extraordinary dog, taking care of both his puppy and a human baby with great affection while the human mommies have tea together.

The Cat Next Door, by Betty Ren Wright, illustrated by Gail Owens. Told in the first person, a little girl describes her typical summer visit to her grandparents' cabin near a lake, and a little cat who always greets her. Then her grandmother dies, and the child is comforted by the cat and her two newly born kittens.

The Cat Who Wore a Pot on Her Head, by Jan Slepian and Ann Seidler, illustrated by Richard E. Martin. Bendemolena finds that a pot on her head shuts out the noise, but it also prevents her from hearing clearly, which leads to much confusion in a very humorous book.

Clifford the Big Red Dog, by Norman Bridwell. The hard-back edition of Clifford commemorates twenty-five years since the first paperback Clifford appeared. There are many favorites in the series. This was the first.

Cross-Country Cat, by Mary Calhoun, illustrated by Erick Ingraham. A very clever Siamese cat, Henry, finds when he is left behind by accident in the snow-covered mountains that he can use the skis which the children have made for him.

Dear Zoo, by Rod Campbell. Each page of this book for the toddler has a fold-out, revealing various animals, each unsuitable for a pet, until the very last one—a puppy.

The Dog Who Had Kittens, by Polly M. Robertus, illustrated by Janet Stevens. When Eloise has kittens, Bassett Hound Baxter feels ignored. Then the kittens snuggle up to Baxter, so he misses them as much as Eloise when they leave for homes of their own.

Fang, by Barbara Shook Hazen, illustrated by Leslie Holt Morrill. A young boy selects the biggest, fiercest-looking dog he can find to protect him from danger. Then he finds that Fang is frightened of everything, even his image in the mirror, but as the youngster reassures Fang, he loses his own fear.

Finders Keepers, by William Lipkind and Nicholas Mordvinoff. Nap and Winkle argue about who the bone they've found belongs to—the one who saw it first or the one who touched it first. After almost losing it, they decide to share the bone.

The First Dog, by Jan Brett. Set in the Pleistocene Age, Kip the cave boy meets Paleowolf, who warns him just in time when fierce animals are in the area, and the first boy-dog friendship becomes reality. Imaginatively illustrated with bordered pages which reproduce cave drawings.

A Fish Out of Water, by Helen Palmer, illustrated by P. D. Eastman. A little boy does not follow Mr. Carp's feeding directions when he buys a goldfish, so Otto becomes gigantic, causing all kinds of problems.

The Foundling, by Carol Carrick, illustrated by Donald Carrick. Christopher still misses his dog, Bodger, who had been killed accidentally. But when his father takes him to the pound, he feels he doesn't want to replace Bodger. Then he realizes that the puppy which he thought belonged to the Tilton family next door really has no home, and he takes little Ben to his heart.

Friendship's First Thanksgiving, by William Accorsi. Friendship, a dog who has crossed the sea with the Pilgrims, describes the colony's first year in the New World, culminating in the first Thanksgiving.

**The Garden of Abdul Gasazi,* by Chris Van Allsburg. Alan agrees to dog-sit with Miss Hester's mischievous dog Fritz, but when they go for a walk, they end up in the garden of Gasazi the Great, a magician who convinces Alan that he has turned Fritz into a duck. Maybe he has.

Ghost's Hour, Spook's Hour, by Eve Bunting, illustrated by Donald Carrick. Scary incidents at midnight give Jake and his dog Biff a frightening time, but all turn out to have good explanations when Jake finds his parents on the couch-bed in the living room.

Go Away, Dog, by Joan L. Nodset, illustrated by Crosby Bonsall. Uncle George sends Jimmy a dog for his birthday, but Jimmy doesn't like dogs. Of course, the dog changes all of that.

Hairy Maclary–Scattercat, by Lynley Dodd. Hairy Maclary, a dog, goes looking for something to chase, and frightens one cat after another until he meets Scarface Claw, who chases Hairy all the way home.

Harry by the Sea, by Gene Zion, illustrated by Margaret Bloy Graham. Harry goes with his family to the beach and gets lost, is mistaken for a sea monster, but finally finds his family again.

Harry the Dirty Dog, by Gene Zion, illustrated by Margaret Bloy Graham. The first of the "Harry" books explains that Harry hates a bath, so he runs away, but gets so dirty during his meanderings that he is not recognized by his family when he returns. He then finds his bath brush, gets bathed, and all is well.

Have You Seen My Cat?, by Eric Carle. A little boy is looking for his cat and meets all the other "cats": a puma, a jaguar, a cheetah, and so on. Then he finds his cat.

He Wakes Me, by Betsy James, illustrated by Helen K. Davis. A small girl explains why her cat is so lovable and dear to her, how he wakes her in the morning and puts her to sleep at night.

Henry the Explorer, by Mark Taylor, illustrations by Graham Booth. Henry, a small boy, and his dog Angus decide to explore the world. They get lost, but since Henry has put an "H" on everything he has discovered, the search party is able to find him rather promptly.

Here, Kitty Kitty, by Maureen Roffey. A peep-through-the-hole book shows the family looking for the family cat.

Hey, Al, by Arthur Yorinks, illustrated by Richard Egielski. Al, a janitor, and his faithful dog Eddie share a very poor lifestyle in a single room. A mysterious bird offers to fly them to a paradise in the sky, but they find after a time that there is really no place like home.

Hi, Cat!, by Ezra Jack Keats. Archie only says, "Hi, Cat," but that's all the encouragement the stray cat needs to stick around.

High-Wire Henry, by Mary Calhoun, illustrated by Erick Ingraham. The further adventures of Henry, the smart Siamese cat who can walk on his hind legs. Here he saves the new puppy Buttons when the dog gets stuck out on a ledge of the house.

Hot-Air Henry, by Mary Calhoun, illustrated by Erick Ingraham. The sassy Siamese cat stows away on a hot-air balloon and ends up taking a fur-raising flight across the mountains.

If Dinosaurs Were Cats and Dogs, by Colin McNaughton. In rhymed verse a child imagines what it would be like if everyday pets were the size of dinosaurs. Havoc ensues!

I'm the Best, by Marjorie Weinman Sharmat, illustrated by Will Hillenbrand. A dog who has lived with many owners finally finds a home and a family that loves him and will keep him for the rest of his life.

Jim's Dog Muffins, by Miriam Cohen, illustrated by Lillian Hoban. Little Jim's dog, Muffins, is run over, and the boy is inconsolable until his best friend Paul makes him cry—and laugh—remembering Muffins.

The Josefina Story Quilt, by Eleanor Coerr, illustrated by Bruce Degen. While traveling west with her family in 1850, a young girl makes a patchwork quilt chronicling the experiences of the journey and reserves two special patches for her pet hen Josefina.

Kitten for a Day, by Ezra Jack Keats. A confused but friendly puppy joins four kittens for play and then suggests that next time they all be puppies for a day.

Lost in the Storm, by Carol Carrick, illustrated by Donald Carrick. Christopher and his dog Bodger go to play with his new friend Gray on a little island, but there is a storm and Gray's parents won't let the boys look for the dog until daylight when they find Bodger safely sheltered under some steps which have been washed up on the beach.

Madeline's Rescue, by Ludwig Bemelmans. Intrepid Madeline almost drowns, but is saved by a dog, Genevieve, who then returns with Miss Clavel's girls to the boarding school. She fits in well until Lord Cucuface, a trustee, insists that she be turned out. The girls have their revenge when Genevieve comes back and has eleven puppies—one for each student.

Marshmallow, by Clare T. Newberry. A true story of the author's cat Oliver, who had never met a rabbit until Marshmallow, a little white rabbit, joins the household. Cats are not supposed to cuddle bunnies like kittens, are they?

Maxi, the Hero, by Debra and Sal Barracca, illustrated by Mark Buehner. A follow-up to *Maxi, the Taxi-Dog,* this book shows him still riding with his friend Jim and becoming a hero when he catches a thief. Done in rhyme.

Millions of Cats, by Wanda Gag. When a little old man goes to select a pet kitten, there is fierce competition to be the "chosen one." One little kitten, who believes itself to be homely, remains and is selected. In its new home, the kitten grows into a sleek, beautiful cat.

Momo's Kitten, by Mitsu and Taro Yashima. The little kitten is now a grown cat with babies of her own, each one a distinct individual. Momo enjoys seeing them develop and grow.

Moses the Kitten, by James Herriot, illustrated by Peter Barrett. A true story by the famous vet about a stray kitten who finds a very strange mother at the farm.

My Cat Maisie, by Pamela Allen. The boy next door has a dog, Lobo, but Andrew doesn't have a pet until a stray cat comes to his house. At first she won't stay because Andrew plays too roughly. At night, however, she returns and as they cuddle gently in Andrew's bed, he names her Maisie.

My Puppy Is Born, by Joanna Cole, photos by Jerome Wexler. An informational book showing the first eight weeks in the life of a miniature dachshund, Sausage.

Nattie Parson's Good-Luck Lamb, by Lisa Campbell Ernst. When her grandfather decrees that her cherished pet lamb Clover must be sold, Nattie figures a way out, and the shawl that she weaves from Clover's special wool brings enough money for the next winter's hay.

No Roses for Harry!, by Gene Zion, illustrated by Margaret Bloy Graham. Because it has roses in the pattern, Harry tries every way he can to get rid of the sweater Grandma has knitted for him. Finally a bird helps him by unraveling it and making a nest. Grandma replaces it with a black and white sweater.

Nothing at All, by Wanda Gag. In a forgotten corner of an old forgotten farm stand three little doghouses in which three orphan puppies live. One has pointed ears, one has curly ears, the third is invisible. But Little-Nothing-At-All (on advice of a jackdaw with a book) repeats a magic chant for nine days, each day becoming more "real" until he can join his brothers and play with the children who have adopted them. Youngsters love his chant, "I'm busy getting dizzy," meanwhile whirling round and round, and will join in as the puppy works hard to materialize.

Oma and Bobo, by Amy Schwartz. Grandma Oma is not in favor of Alice getting a dog. But Bobo and Oma become fast friends by the time Bobo is in the dog show put on by Mr. Benjamin's Training School for Dogs.

Pet Show!, by Ezra Jack Keats. When the pet show starts, Archie cannot find his cat anywhere, so he brings a germ in a glass jar, and gets the prize for the quietest pet just as an old lady shows up with Archie's cat. The boy lets her keep the blue ribbon, but not his cat.

Pinkerton, Behave, by Steven Kellogg. A lovable Great Dane, Pinkerton, gets all commands confused, and when he is taken to obedience school, he confuses all the other dogs as well. But he does fine in a real situation when a burglar breaks into the house.

A Pocketful of Cricket, by Rebecca Caudill, illustrated by Evaline Ness. Jay is a boy who is really in touch with nature. He treasures all the items he saves—leaves, Indian arrowheads, and many others—but nothing is like the cricket Jay takes home and then to school.

The Poky Little Puppy, by Janette Sebring Lowrey, illustrated by Gustaf Tenggren. Five little puppies dig a hole and go for a walk in the wide, wide world, but when they count themselves, there is always one who lags behind and misses all the good things to eat.

Rotten Ralph, by Jack Gantos, illustrations by Nicole Rubel. Sarah's cat Ralph is really rotten, so the family decides to leave him at the circus. There he is badly treated and runs away, ending up in a trash can where Sarah finds him. He returns to the family, vowing never to be rotten again, except. . . .

**Sam, Bangs and Moonshine,* by Evaline Ness. Samantha has a reckless habit of lying, which her father calls "moonshine." She also has a cat, Bangs, and a little friend, Thomas. Sam's bad habit almost causes tragedy when she sends Thomas and Bangs into danger, which teaches her the difference between "moonshine" and reality.

Six-Dinner Sid, by Inga Moore. A black cat, Sid, lives on Aristotle Street at six different houses, but because these people don't speak to each other, each family thinks Sid is their cat until he has a cough, and the vet reveals

Sid's chicanery. So Sid switches to Pythagoras Place, where the people do speak to each other, but don't mind his having six dinners a day.

Slinky Malinki, by Lynley Dodd. Slinky is an average cat during the day, but at night he turns into a thief. One fateful night he gets carried away and steals so much that he gets caught. He then vows to behave properly. Done in humorous rhymed verse.

Some Swell Pup, by Maurice Sendak and Matthew Margolis, illustrated by Maurice Sendak. In a comic-book format this book illustrates how to train a pup, overlooking all his faults, with love. Actually a sly reminder of how parents ought to train children.

Spot's First Walk, by Eric Hill. Each page features a foldout as Spot goes for his first walk. There are many popular books which feature this cute puppy. Suitable for very young children.

The Tenth Good Thing About Barney, by Judith Viorst, illustrated by Erik Blegvad. A very tender story about a boy whose cat has died. At the funeral he tells nine good things about Barney. Then he discovers the tenth; Barney in the ground will help to grow flowers, a pretty nice job for a cat.

The Third-Story Cat, by Leslie Baker. Alice escapes from her apartment and meets a tiger cat who shows her the park and all its charms. However, Alice has a frightening experience with a dog, and then finds the window closed when she returns home.

Thy Friend, Obadiah, by Brinton Turkle. At first Obadiah is embarrassed to have one special seagull follow him everywhere, but after he is able to help the bird by taking a fishhook from its beak, he accepts the bird's friendship.

Tight Times, by Barbara Shook Hazen, illustrated by Trina Schart Hyman. A little boy's dad tries to explain the term "tight times" when he has to refuse getting the child the dog he wants. But his parents allow him to keep the kitten he's found and he names it "Dog."

Tom's Tail, by Arlene Dubanevich. Tom likes to sleep even when the mice are overrunning the place, but one day the mice go too far and Tom quickly restores order.

The Turkeygobbling Frog Show, by Janet Slater Redhead, illustrated by Tracey Clark. In rhymed verse we see Henrietta Hilda with her frog Matilda, Braggybottom Betty with her frog Spaghetti, and other braggarts who eat their words when Speckles, who belongs to the boy with the freckles, wins the frog-jumping contest.

A Visit from Dr. Katz, by Ursula Le Guin, illustrated by Ann Barrow. A little girl bored with being sick in bed is amused by playing with her two little cats.

What's Maggie Up To?, by Durga Bernhard. Maggie is an orange cat who lives in an apartment house where she has many friends. They are very concerned when she disappears, after stealing a ball of yarn, a stuffed bunny, and some striped socks. When the children find her in the attic, she has a family of ten kittens.

Whistle for Willie, by Ezra Jack Keats. Little Peter wants to be able to whistle to call his dog Willie. But he simply can't make the sound. However, practice makes perfect, so Peter finally learns to whistle.

William and Boomer, by Lindsay Barrett George. William and his dad find a baby goose, and when they can't find its parents, they take it home and raise it. At last it's warm enough for William to learn to swim with his animal friend.

The Wingdingdilly, by Bill Peet. Orvie's dog Scamp is tired of being just a dog, so he runs away and meets Zildy the witch, who turns him into a really fantastic combination animal, a wingdingdilly. Then he finds himself captured by C. J. Pringle for his Incredible Creature Show. Eventually Zildy turns him back into Scamp and he returns to Orvie back at the farm.

Winnie the Witch, by Valerie Thomas, illustrated by Korky Paul. Wilbur, Winnie's black cat, can't easily be seen in Winnie's all-black house, so she turns him green, but she falls over him in the grass. Then she tries a rainbow effect, but everybody laughs at Wilbur, so she solves her problem by turning Wilbur back to black and putting all the colors on her house instead.

Farm Animals

The Animals of Buttercup Farm, by Phoebe and Judy Dunn. Farmer John shows all the children of the neighborhood exactly how the animals live on his farm. Beautiful accurate photos.

Animals on the Farm, illustrated by Feodor Rojankovsky. Artistic but realistic full-page paintings of animals commonly found on farms.

The Big Red Barn, by Margaret Wise Brown, illustrated by Felicia Bond. This is a reprint of a well-loved rhyming story about all the animals and their babies who live in the Big Red Barn on the farm.

The Box with the Red Wheels, by Maud and Miska Petersham. The garden gate is open and all the curious animals come in to look into the strange red box. What's in it?

A Chick Hatches, by Joanna Cole, illustrated by Jerome Wexler. A photographic presentation of what happens inside the egg during the twenty-one-day incubation period before the new little chick appears.

Color Farm, by Lois Ehlert. With center cutouts in the pages, the book uses strong colors to emulate farm animals. A novel approach.

Early Morning in the Barn, by Nancy Tafuri. In a wordless book all of the barnyard animals are pictured making appropriate sounds.

Egg Story, by Anca Hariton. With accurate but charming illustrations, this book follows an egg from the time it is laid, through its incubation under the hen's body, to the chick's birth after twenty-one days.

Emma's Lamb, by Kim Lewis. With realistic illustrations of a sheep farm, we see a girl looking after a lost lamb, playing games with him, and then helping him to find his mother.

Going to Sleep on the Farm, by Wendy Cheyette Lewison, illustrated by Juan Wijngaard. Wonderful illustrations show how different animals go to sleep standing, lying down, sitting on eggs, cuddled with a brood, or, if one is a small boy, in bed with some favorite toy animals.

Hattie and the Fox, by Mem Fox, illustrated by Patricia Mullins. Hattie the Hen spots danger in the bushes when she sees a fox hiding there. She warns the other animals—the goose, the pig, the sheep, and the horse—with varying reactions.

The Little Pig, by Judy Dunn, illustrated by Phoebe Dunn. Michael has a new-born pig, Lucy, as a pet, and she wins a blue ribbon at the fair, even though she is typically self-willed when being judged.

Our Animal Friends at Maple Hill Farm, by Alice and Martin Provensen. The authors have personalized the animals that live at Maple Hill Farm so that the reader understands each one as an individual.

Milk, by Donald Carrick. The story of milk from cow to carton is simply told and beautifully illustrated here.

The Very Busy Spider, by Eric Carle. As a little spider begins her web, each of the farm animals tries without success to divert her. Each strand of the web provides a tactile experience for the very young child as the spider completes her web and catches a fly.

Wild and Zoo Animals

Anansi and the Moss-Covered Rock, retold by Eric Kimmel, illustrated by Janet Stevens. Anansi the Spider is walking through the forest when a strange moss-covered rock with magic powers catches his eye. Anansi then uses the rock to fool Lion, Elephant, Rhinoceros, Hippopotamus, Giraffe, and Zebra. But Little Bush Deer is not fooled and uses the rock to teach Anansi a lesson.

Andy and the Lion, by James Daugherty. This tall tale is a retelling of the classic story of Androcles and the Lion. A boy bravely removes a thorn from the paw of a lion, and later is remembered by the same lion who breaks loose at the circus.

Animal Alphabet, by Bert Kitchen. An oversize book with one-to-a-page paintings of unusual animals which illustrate the twenty-six letters of the alphabet. The reader is invited to guess their identities or check the answers at the back of the book.

Animals Should Definitely Not Wear Clothing, by Judith Barrett, illustrated by Ron Barrett. Very amusing illustrations show why the book's title is true.

Anytime Mapleson and the Hungry Bears, by Mordecai Gerstein, illustrated by Susan Yard Harris. All the Maplesons like pancakes with maple syrup, which they make from the trees on their farm. But bears like the syrup too, so Anytime gives them his clothes and takes them home to eat with the family.

Awful Aardvark, by Mwenye Hadithi, illustrated by Adrienne Kennaway. Why do aardvarks sleep all day and eat termites at night? In this "pourquoi" story we find the answer when Aardvark's snoring annoys his larger fellow animals, who fail to dislodge him from his branch of a tree.

Be Nice to Spiders, by Margaret Bloy Graham. Billy leaves his pet spider Helen at the zoo where she makes all the animals happy by spinning webs and catching flies. Then the webs are all swept away because the mayor is coming for an inspection tour, and the flies are back. But Helen has been hiding and returns in triumph.

The Biggest Bear, by Lynd Ward. Johnny Orchard wants to shoot a bear, but all he finds is a baby cub, which comes home with him only to eat everything in sight and become "the biggest bear." He's a nuisance to the neighbors, but when the boy tries to lose the bear in the woods, it always comes back. Finally, it must be taken to the zoo where Johnny can visit any time with maple sugar treats.

Blueberries for Sal, by Robert McCloskey. Little Sal and her mother go to Blueberry Hill and have quite an adventure when they "get all mixed up" with a bear and her cub.

The Camel Who Took a Walk, by Jack Tworkow, illustrated by Roger Duvoisin. When the beautiful camel does not complete her walk, she unknowingly frustrates not only the tiger who is lying in wait to eat her, but some other animals as well.

Cecily G. and the 9 Monkeys, by H. A. Rey. Both Cecily and the monkeys are lonely, so they join forces to play wonderful games and live happily together.

A Children's Zoo, by Tana Hoban. As each animal is shown, appropriate words accompany the picture—words which capsulate the characteristics of that animal, such as "Giraffe: tall, spotted, silent." A chart at the end of the book shows where the animals come from, where they live, and what foods they eat.

Crafty Chameleon, by Mwenye Hadithi, illustrated by Adrienne Kennaway. Illustrated in bold and exciting patterns, this is a tale of brains over brawn, as the chameleon outwits both the leopard and the crocodile who are threatening him.

Crocodile Beat, by Gail Jorgensen, illustrated by Patricia Mullins. The jungle animals playing by the riverbank have only the crocodile to fear, but the lion saves them by reversing the lion tamer's role and putting a chair in Croc's mouth.

Dear Zoo, by Rod Campbell. Each page of this book for the toddler has a foldout revealing various animals, each unsuitable for a pet, until the last one—a puppy.

Effie, by Beverley Allinson, illustrated by Barbara Reid. When Effie the ant saves other ants from being trampled by an elephant, her loud voice is suddenly appreciated by her friends.

Farewell to Shady Glen, by Bill Peet. A group of woodland animals must leave Shady Glen, which is being bulldozed for more big city buildings. They make a narrow escape on top of a train, and fortunately find another Shady Glen, but the ecological warning is clear.

The Grizzly Sisters, by Cathy Bellows. Mama Bear is careful, but her cubs don't listen to her admonitions. They delight in scaring beavers and wolves, but when they meet humans, Mama must rescue them from the people and their cameras.

Harald and the Great Stag, by Donald Carrick. When Harald, who lives in England during the Middle Ages, hears that the baron and his royal guests are planning to hunt the legendary Great Stag, he devises a clever plan to outwit the hunters and protect the animal.

Have You Seen My Cat?, by Eric Carle. A little boy is looking for his cat and meets all the other "cats": a puma, a jaguar, a cheetah, and so on. Finally, he finds his cat.

Have You Seen My Duckling?, by Nancy Tafuri. A mother duck with seven little ducklings suddenly has only six. She asks all her animal friends about the missing baby who finally shows up.

Hot Hippo, by Mwenye Hadithi, illustrated by Adrienne Kennaway. An African "pourquoi" story which tells why hippos live in water during the day, but come out to eat grass nightly.

Katy-No-Pocket, by Emmy Payne, illustrated by H. A. Rey. Poor Katy Kangaroo has no pocket in which to carry her baby Freddy. She asks all her animal friends how they carry their babies, but nothing works for her until she goes to the city and gets a carpenter's apron with many pockets. Now she can carry Freddy and other baby animals as well.

Listen, Rabbit, by Aileen Fisher, illustrated by Symeon Shimin. A poetic tale of a little boy who tries to make friends with a rabbit through the seasons and ends by finding the rabbit's tiny babies in their nest.

Little Gorilla, by Ruth Bornstein. All the jungle animals love little gorilla when he is a tiny thing. Then he grows into a BIG gorilla, and his friends show their love by giving him a birthday party.

Mousekin's Golden House, by Edna Miller. Mousekin, the whitefoot mouse, makes his home in a discarded pumpkin, and it proves a safe haven from the weather and other animals.

Mousekin's Woodland Sleepers, by Edna Miller. A little white-tailed mouse finds it somewhat difficult to survive in the forest in winter, but finally makes it back to a little birdhouse and is safe from predators.

Over in the Meadow, by John Langstaff and Feodor Rojankovsky, illustrated by Feodor Rojankovsky. A counting song—one to ten—based on all the little animals of the forest and their babies. The music is the one used in the southern Appalachian Mountains.

Owl Moon, by Jane Yolen, illustrated by John Schoenherr. On a winter's night, under a full moon, a father and daughter trek into the woods to see the Great Horned Owl.

Raccoons and Ripe Corn, by Jim Arnosky. A simple tale of how a raccoon family pulls down the corn when it is ripe, eats what they can, and goes back into the woods at sunrise.

Salt Hands, by Jane Chelsea Aragon, illustrated by Ted Rand. A little girl goes into her garden at night when she sees a deer, and he likes both her song and the salt on her hands.

Sam Who Never Forgets, by Eve Rice. At exactly three o'clock Sam feeds each zoo animal what that animal enjoys eating, and Sam never forgets.

"Stand Back," Said the Elephant, "I'm Going to Sneeze," by Patricia Thomas, illustrated by Wallace Tripp. In humorous rhymed verse, each animal asks the elephant not to sneeze, remembering what had happened last time. The

little mouse scares the elephant, so he doesn't sneeze. He laughs instead with the same terrible results.

That's Good! That's Bad!, by Margery Cuyler, illustrated by David Catrow. A little boy has a series of adventures and misadventures when he visits the zoo with his parents.

This Old House, by Karen Ackerman, illustrated by Sylvie Wickstrom. Although an old house seems abandoned, an owl, some squirrels, mice, rabbits, and other woodland animals have made it their home. A charmingly illustrated book.

Veronica, by Roger Duvoisin. This hippopotamus feels that she isn't noticed among all the other hippos on the mud bank where she lives, so she runs away to the city where she is conspicuous and famous, but gets into a lot of trouble. She is glad to go home again.

Wake Up, Vladimir, by Felicia Bond. Vladimir Groundhog runs away from home in late autumn and, after a long winter's nap, wakes up, scares away a monster (his shadow), and runs home never to leave again.

We Hide, You Seek, by Jose Aruego and Ariane Dewey. Poor clumsy rhino always manages to find the other animals because his bumbling behavior startles them into revealing themselves. Then they have to look for him. Whimsical illustrations of animals from Kenya, featuring camouflage.

When Winter Comes, by Pearl Neuman, illustrated by Richard Roe. This book explains how the woodchuck, black bear, red fox, and Canadian goose cope with winter in the northern parts of North America.

Will Spring Be Early? Or Will Spring Be Late?, by Crockett Johnson. The groundhog, about to make his annual prediction, is fooled by a paper flower into saying that spring has already arrived, but the falling snow is just a temporary setback.

Winter Bear, by Ruth Craft, illustrated by Erik Blegvad. A simple rhymed story of children outside just as winter is beginning. They find a little bear and take him home.

The Winter Hedgehog, by Ann and Reg Cartwright. The smallest hedgehog doesn't listen to his mother who warns him that winter is beautiful, yes, but cold and cruel too, so he goes in search of winter and almost comes to harm.

Wombat Stew, by Marcia K. Vaughan, illustrated by Pamela Lofts. When the clever dingo catches a wombat on the banks of a billabong, he plans on stew, but he listens to the advice of other animals, such as the platypus, and adds all kinds of miscellany to the stew before putting the wombat in, so he ends up without his meal.

You Look Ridiculous, Said the Rhinoceros to the Hippopotamus, by Bernard Waber. When the Rhino tells the Hippo that she looks ridiculous because she doesn't have a horn on her nose, it starts Hippo dreaming. Then in her dream each animal she meets tells her she needs what he has—a lion's mane, tiger's spots, elephant's ears, and so on. Now she really looks ridiculous, so she's happy that it was only a dream. She's proud to be what she is.

Zoo, by Gail Gibbons. This book provides a behind-the-scenes look at a working day at the zoo from the moment the workers arrive until the night guard locks the gate.

Various Locales

Because children can learn about settings vicariously, books in which a sense of place is an important element seem to call for such lists. Children who live in cities, for example, may very well never have the opportunity to see rural life firsthand, just as country-bred children may not have the chance to learn personally about city life. So, although reading about other environments is not equal in any sense to actual experience, it is certainly better than nothing. Sense of time and place are not concepts easily grasped by the young child, but illustrations make a Vermont farm a reality for a child who has been raised in Los Angeles, just as they can bring into focus a street in Harlem for a youngster reared on a ranch in Wyoming.

Rural Settings

Ask Mr. Bear, by Marjorie Flack. Danny asks each animal in turn what he should give his mother for her birthday. Finally, Mr. Bear gives him the answer which pleases Danny's mother.

Autumn Harvest, by Alvin Tresselt, illustrated by Roger Duvoisin. A book in praise of autumn in the country, from the first glimmering of cool weather through Halloween and Thanksgiving dinner.

Barn Dance!, by Bill Martin, Jr., and John Archambault, illustrated by Ted Rand. A country boy dreams of a barn dance with the scarecrow as fiddler and the animals participating. Illustrations make the scene come alive.

Bigmama's, by Donald Crews. Visiting his grandmother's house—she is Bigmama—in Cottondale, the author remembers all the fun he had as a boy spending the whole summer vacation with his family on an old-fashioned farm.

The Chick and the Duckling, translated by Mirra Ginsburg, illustrated by Jose and Ariane Aruego. The chick and the duckling eggs hatch at the same time, and the chick copies every action of the duckling even when the duckling decides to swim.

Cotton Mill Town, by Kathleen Hershey, ilustrated by Jeanette Winter. A small girl visits her grandmother in a rural section of North Carolina and savors the leisurely pace of life lived there by her extended family. When summer ends and she must return home to the city, she does take a souvenir, a white kitten named Cotton.

The Day Jimmy's Boa Ate the Wash, by Trinka Hakes Noble, illustrated by Steven Kellogg. The class visits a farm on their field trip, but when Jimmy brings along his pet boa constrictor, the result is mayhem. One thing leads to the next, with unpredictable results.

Farm Alphabet Book, by Jane Miller. Photographs of farm animals and objects accompanied by simple descriptions illustrate the letters of the alphabet.

Farm Counting Book, by Jane Miller. One to ten with some math problems at the end. Great for preschoolers who are just learning their numbers.

Farm Noises, by Jane Miller. This book presents the distinctive noises made by two dozen animals, birds, and machines that are heard on a farm.

Farmer Palmer's Wagon Ride, by William Steig. Farmer Palmer, a pig, and his hired hand Ebenezer go to town with a load of vegetables to sell, but must use all the gifts which Farmer Palmer has for his family to get them back to the farm safely.

The Folks in the Valley: A Pennsylvania Dutch ABC, by Jim Aylesworth, illustrated by Stefano Vitale. With upper- and lower-case letters, this rhyming alphabet book tells about the people and activities of a Pennsylvania Dutch settlement in a rural valley.

Go Tell Aunt Rhody, illustrated by Aliki. More than two hundred years ago in France, Jean Jacques Rousseau wrote an opera called *The Village Soothsayer.* After many years the opera was forgotten, but one melody remained and eventually became an early American folk song celebrating rural life. Music and verses in the back.

The Gollywhopper Egg, by Anne Rockwell. Timothy Todd, a peddler, tries to get rid of a coconut by passing it off as a gollywhopper egg, and he succeeds.

Good Morning, Chick, by Mirra Ginsburg, illustrated by Byron Barton. A very simple book for the toddler about a chick, her mother, and some other barnyard animals.

Ida and Betty and the Secret Eggs, by Kay Chorao. Vacationing in the country, Ida is "best friends" with Betty, and they share a secret. Then along comes Lucinda and trouble brews.

Ladybug, Ladybug, by Ruth Brown. A rhymed extension of the familiar, "Ladybug, ladybug, fly away home!" these imaginative illustrations evoke the countryside on a sun-drenched day.

Mary Had a Little Lamb, by Sarah Josepha Hale, illustrated by Bruce McMillan. A contemporary interpretation of the well-known nineteenth-century nursery rhyme about the lamb that went to school. Accompanied by colored photographs and a sample exercise from a *McGuffy Reader* (1857).

Mr. Gumpy's Outing, by John Burningham. Mr. Gumpy lives near a river and has a boat. He agrees to take the children and a number of animals for a boat ride and all goes well until they start misbehaving.

Mommy, Buy Me a China Doll, by Harve Zemach, illustrated by Margot Zemach. A repetitive song from the Ozarks with charming illustrations.

Moses the Kitten, by James Herriot, illustrated by Peter Barrett. A true story by the famous vet about a stray kitten who finds a very strange mother at the farm.

One Crow, a Counting Rhyme, by Jim Aylesworth, illustrated by Ruth Young. One to ten in rhymed verse, using farm animals and children.

Our Veronica Goes to Petunia's Farm, by Roger Duvoisin. At first Veronica the hippopotamus seems welcome at the farm; then the other animals treat her like an outsider, and she pines away until they show her friendship once again.

The Ox-Cart Man, by Donald Hall, illustrated by Barbara Cooney. This book describes the day-to-day life of an early nineteenth-century New England family throughout the changing seasons.

The Patchwork Farmer, by Craig Brown. This wordless book humorously shows how the farmer rips his overalls again and again in his daily work, and ends with a colorful patchwork pair.

Petunia, by Roger Duvoisin. A silly goose learns that just carrying a book doesn't make her wise after all her barnyard friends follow her advice with negative results. She decides to learn to read.

A Pocketful of Cricket, by Rebecca Caudill, illustrated by Evaline Ness. Jay is a boy who is really in touch with nature. He treasures all the items he saves: leaves, Indian arrowheads, and others, but nothing is like the cricket Jay takes home and then to school.

Rosie's Walk, by Pat Hutchins. In this wordless book the fox is after Rosie the hen, but she doesn't know it. Unwittingly, she leads him into one disaster after another, each funnier than the last.

Sitting on a Farm, by Bob King, illustrated by Bill Slavin. A rollicking song about a little girl who tries to get a bug off her knee by enlisting the aid of larger and larger animals.

Six Crows, by Leo Lionni. The crows and the farmer are at war. The crows eat the farmer's wheat so he builds larger and larger scarecrows, while they frighten him with scarier and scarier kites. Finally the wise owl suggests that they talk, and they settle their differences peaceably before the crop is ruined.

Skip to My Lou, illustrated by Nadine Bernard Westcott. When his parents leave a young boy in charge of the farm for a day, chaos erupts as the animals take over the house, beginning with flies in the sugarbowl. But he gets it all cleaned up before Mom and Dad return.

Squawk to the Moon, Little Goose, by Edna Mitchell Preston, illustrated by Barbara Cooney. Little Goose, who is supposed to stay in bed, goes out to see the moon and is caught by the fox. She cleverly escapes him—but not Mother Goose's spanking.

There's Nothing to Do, by James Stevenson. When Mary Ann and Louie tell Grandpa how bored they are, it reminds him of a time when he and his brother Wainwright were visiting their grandfather's farm, not a boring time.

Who Took the Farmer's Hat?, by Joan L. Nodset, illustrated by Fritz Siebel. When the wind takes the farmer's hat, he runs after it, but the wind runs faster. He asks each animal in turn about his hat, and finally decides to replace it after he finds it being used as a bird's nest.

The Year at Maple Hill Farm, by Alice and Martin Provensen. This is a book describing seasonal changes on a farm and surrounding countryside, showing months, holidays, and activities of animals and small children.

A Year in the Country, by Douglas Florian. A wordless book showing each month with appropriate activities on a farm.

***Yonder,* by Tony Johnston, illustrated by Lloyd Bloom. With very effective artwork, this book shows the cycle of life in nature and for humans as well.

Urban Settings

Abuela, by Arthur Dorros, illustrated by Elisa Kleven. While riding on a bus with her Spanish-speaking grandmother, a little girl imagines that they are flying over New York City, seeing the sights. A glossary is at the end of the book.

The Adventures of Taxi Dog, by Debra and Sal Barracca, illustrated by Mark Buehner. Maxi, a homeless dog, finds taxi driver Jim who invites him to come home and live with him. A humorous dog-eye view of New York, as Maxi goes everywhere with Jim.

Anatole, by Eve Titus, illustrated by Paul Galdone. The most contented mouse in France, Anatole is upset when he hears people say unkind things about mice, and he devises a way to do something nice to change their minds.

Apt 3G, by Ezra Jack Keats. Ben and Sam investigate the sound of music in their tenement and meet the blind man downstairs who plays the harmonica. A touching, unsentimental look at his world.

The Boy Who Didn't Believe in Spring, by Lucille Clifton, illustrated by Brinton Turkle. King Shabazz and his friend Tony Polito do not believe what their teacher says about spring being just around the corner, so they go looking for it. And they find it!

Dreams, by Ezra Jack Keats. Roberto and Archie, city children the author has created in other books, are here, dreaming that the huge shadow of Roberto's paper mouse sails down and scares away the dog that has cornered Archie's cat.

Evan's Corner, by Elizabeth Starr Hill, illustrated by Sandra Speidel. A reissue with contemporary illustrations, this warm story tells of Evan's desire for a corner of his own in the two-room flat he shares with his family.

Friday Night Is Papa Night, by Ruth Sonneborn, illustrated by Emily A. McCully. Papa must have two jobs so that he can take care of his family, but he is able to come home on Friday nights. Mama, Manuela, Carlo, and Ricardo all wait patiently when Papa does not come by dark. But it is Pedro, the youngest child, who lights up the kitchen and greets his father.

Goggles, by Ezra Jack Keats. Peter finds goggles, but he and his friend Archie nearly lose them to some older, tougher boys. Then his dog Willie helps the boys recover the goggles.

Hi, Cat!, by Ezra Jack Keats. Archie only says, "Hi, Cat," but that's all the encouragement the stray cat needs to stick around.

***I Hate English!,* by Ellen Levine, illustrated by Steve Bjorkman. When her family moves to New York from Hong Kong, Mei Mei finds it difficult to adjust to school and the sounds of English until her teacher, Nancy, tries a new tactic.

Left Behind, by Carol Carrick, illustrated by Donald Carrick. When Christopher's class goes to the city to visit the aquarium, they also travel on the subway. When the boy gets separated from the group, he is afraid he'll never be reunited with them.

Madeline, by Ludwig Bemelmans. In rhymed verse the author pictures twelve little girls in a Parisian boarding school, emphasizing the smallest and bravest, Madeline. Poor Miss Clavel must call a doctor in the middle of the night—Madeline has appendicitis. After a visit to the hospital, the other eleven want one too. Accurate drawings of the sights of Paris.

Madeline in London, by Ludwig Bemelmans. The irrepressible Madeline and her eleven schoolmates have an adventure in London, illustrating the sights of that city realistically in the process.

Madeline's Rescue, by Ludwig Bemelmans. Intrepid Madeline almost drowns, but is saved by a dog, Genevieve, who then returns with Miss Clavel's girls to the boarding school. She fits in well until Lord Cucuface, a trustee, insists that she be turned out. The girls have their revenge when Genevieve returns with eleven puppies—one for each girl.

Make Way for Ducklings, by Robert McCloskey. In this gentle tale of a duck family trying to find a safe place to raise their brood, the Mallard family causes quite a stir in Boston before they settle on an island in the Public Garden.

Maxi, the Hero, by Debra and Sal Barracca, illustrated by Mark Buehner. A follow-up to *Maxi, the Taxi Dog,* this book shows him still riding with his friend Jim, and becoming a hero when he catches a thief. Done in rhyme.

Maybelle the Cable Car, by Virginia Lee Burton. Set in San Francisco, the cable cars reminisce about the "old days" before competition from buses almost eliminated them. But the citizens vote to keep the cable cars, and, freshly painted, they still run up and down the steep hills with a merry "clang, clang."

Mirette on the High Wire, by Emily Arnold McCully. In nineteenth-century Paris the Widow Gateau and her daughter Mirette run a high-class boarding house for actors and performers of many kinds. When the Great Bellini, famed high-wire walker, comes to Mme Gateau's, he agrees to teach Mirette, but he also confesses that he now has a fear of performing. However, with Mirette's help, he regains his courage.

Night on Neighborhood Street, by Eloise Greenfield, illustrated by Jan Spivey Gilchrist. A collection of poems exploring the sights, sounds, and emotions enlivening an African-American neighborhood during the course of one evening.

Nothing Ever Happens on My Block, by Ellen Raskin. Chester Filbert imagines all kinds of excitement that could happen on his block, but as he sits on the curb, he misses all that really does happen.

One Monday Morning, by Uri Shulevitz. Skillfully juxtaposing the stark reality of a New York tenement with the make-believe world of a child who imagines royalty in the image of playing cards, this book creates an endearing young hero.

Pet Show!, by Ezra Jack Keats. When the pet show starts, Archie cannot find his cat anywhere, so he brings a germ in a glass jar and gets the prize for the quietest pet, just as an old lady shows up with Archie's cat. The boy lets her keep the blue ribbon, but takes back his cat.

**Ragtime Tumpie, by Alan Schroeder, illustrated by Bernie Fuchs. Tumpie, a young African-American girl who will later become famous as the dancer Josephine Baker, longs to find the opportunity to dance amid the poverty and vivacious street life of St. Louis in the early 1900s, and she wins a silver dollar for her first appearance in a contest.

Tar Beach, by Faith Ringgold. The setting is a New York City apartment house roof, and the story revolves around the quilt on which the girl lies, dreaming of flying over the George Washington Bridge, over the ice cream factory, and into the night sky filled with stars.

The Weather

Along the same line as locale are matters of weather and the seasons. Books which stress these can make other places and times more "real" to children, helping them to understand that youngsters who live in conditions strange to them and who perhaps celebrate holidays they're unfamiliar with are not really very different in terms of behavior, family life, and important relationships.

Bringing the Rain to Kapiti Plain, by Verna Aardema, illustrated by Beatriz Vidal. In rhyme and using the rhythm of "The House That Jack Built," this African folktale tells of a man who shoots an arrow into a big black cloud to end the severe drought that is causing havoc on Kapiti Plain.

Gilberto and the Wind, by Marie Hall Ets. A little boy personifies the wind as he plays with it.

It Looked Like Spilt Milk, by Charles G. Shaw. Fluffy white clouds take on shapes of various animals and ordinary items, but they are only clouds. Good to use with a story board.

My Red Umbrella, by Robert Bright. A little girl finds that her umbrella grows larger as more animals find shelter from the rain under it.

Rain, by Robert Kalan, illustrated by Donald Crews. Blue sky, white clouds, yellow sun. Then grey clouds and rain, rain, rain—ending in a rainbow. Very simple pictures illustrate this phenomenon.

Rain, by Peter Spier. A wordless book showing with splendid illustrations all the activities of a family when it rains.

Rain Drops Splash, by Alvin Tresselt, illustrated by Leonard Weisgard. The rain keeps coming until a little puddle becomes a big lake with big fish, overflows into a river, and finally goes into the sea with an ocean liner and lots of little tugboats. Then the sun comes out and at last the rain stops.

Rain Rain Rivers, by Uri Shulevitz. A simple book illustrating a child's view of the rain from the pattering sound on the roof to the swell in the ocean's waves.

A Rainbow of My Own, by Don Freeman. A little boy goes out into the rain, imagining what it would be like to catch the rainbow he has seen. Then as he comes home, the sun catches the water in his fishbowl and. . . .

The Secret of the Hawaiian Rainbow, by Stacey Kaopuiki, illustrated by Bob Wagstaff. A wizard and a legendary race of small elves gather colors from native sources and make a rainbow to remind the people of how important and beautiful are water and rain.

Skyfire, by Frank Asch. Little Bear and Little Bird do not agree. Is it a rainbow with a pot of golden honey at the end, or is the sky on fire? In any case, Little Bear has his fill of honey after he has put out the fire in the sky.

Umbrella, by Taro Yashima. Momo is impatient for the rain to come, and she is delighted when she can carry her umbrella to nursery school and walk home without holding either her mother or her father's hand.

Where Does the Butterfly Go When It Rains?, by May Garelick, illustrated by Leonard Weisgard. A poetic inquiry with soft illustrations.

The Wind Blew, by Pat Hutchins. A humorous cumulative story in delicious rhyme, this book illustrates what the mischievous wind can do.

Books About the Four Seasons

First Comes Spring, by Anne Rockwell. With a simple text and pictures bursting with fun and familiar activities, this author goes through the four seasons with the Bear family. At the end, we know the cycle will begin again—with spring.

I Was Born in a Tree and Raised By Bees, by Jim Arnosky. Crinkleroot is pictured as a forest-dwelling old man who understands all the plants and animals that surround him. There are intriguing puzzles in the pictures that go through the four seasons of the year.

The Ox-Cart Man, by Donald Hall, illustrated by Barbara Cooney. This book describes the day-to-day life of an early nineteenth-century New England family throughout the changing seasons.

The Seasons of Arnold's Apple Tree, by Gail Gibbons. Going through the four seasons, and including recipes for Arnold's apple pie and apple cider too, this story of what Arnold and the tree experience at each change is easily understood and colorfully illustrated.

Spring Is Here, by Taro Gomi. Going through the four seasons, the artist transforms what the child sees with simple, childlike drawings.

A Tree Is Nice, by Janice May Udry, illustrated by Marc Simont. What good are trees? They are beautiful to see, wonderful to climb or hang a swing from. They give shade in summer, protection from the strong winds in winter, and if they are apple trees, children can enjoy the fruit. Plant trees!

What Comes in Spring?, by Barbara Savadge Horton, illustrated by Ed Young. As a mother goes through the four seasons with her small child, she also gently tells the story of the child's own birth.

The Year at Maple Hill Farm, by Alice and Martin Provensen. This is a book describing seasonal changes on a farm and surrounding countryside, showing months, holidays, and activities of animals and young children.

A Year of Beasts, by Ashley Wolff. Ellie and Peter go through the months, exploring with appropriate woodland animals for each. Shows the cycle in nature with lovely soft illustrations.

A Year in the Country, by Douglas Florian. A wordless book showing each month with appropriate activities on a farm.

Winter and Its Holidays

Animals in Winter, by Henrietta Bancroft and Richard G. Van Gelder, illustrated by Gaetano Di Palma. Simple explanations with drawings which show the way wild animals of the forest survive winter weather.

Anytime Mapleson and the Hungry Bears, by Mordecai Gerstein, illustrated by Susan Yard Harris. All the Maplesons like pancakes with the maple syrup they make from the trees on their farm. But bears like the syrup too, so Anytime gives them his clothes and takes them home to eat with the family.

Arthur's Valentine, by Marc Brown. Arthur makes some wrong guesses about the secret admirer who is sending him valentines, but finds out the truth in time to give her "kisses."

Baboushka and the Three Kings, by Ruth Robbins, illustrated by Nicolas Sidjakov. In this Russian folktale a poor woman, Baboushka, decides to follow the three kings to seek the newborn Babe, but she loses the path in the snow. Now every year she travels through the land with her gifts for small children.

The Best Valentine in the World, by Marjorie Weinman Sharmat, illustrated by Lilian Obligado. Ferdinand Fox makes a magnificent valentine for Florette, but she has supposedly forgotten all about Valentine's Day. Then she gives him an even more elaborate valentine, so all is fine between them.

The Big Snow, by Berta and Elmer Hader. Many of the animals of the forest stay in their warm dens during winter, and kind people put out food for the birds which have not escaped from "the big snow."

The Chanukkah Guest, by Eric A. Kimmel, illustrated by Giora Carmi. In this very humorous story an elderly "bubba" makes the best potato *latkes* in her village, and she expects many guests, including the rabbi, for the holiday feast. However, she doesn't hear or see very well, so she serves all the *latkes* to a bear instead of to the rabbi.

Claude, the Dog, by Dick Gackenbach. A very generous hound, Claude, gives all his Christmas gifts to a less fortunate dog, Bummer. But Claude has the best gift of all at home, his family's love.

Cranberry Valentine, by Wende and Harry Devlin. Maggie, her grandmother, and the whole sewing circle make Cranberryport a brighter place when they secretly make valentines for Old Whiskers. Includes a recipe for Cranberry Upside-Down Cake.

Cross-Country Cat, by Mary Calhoun, illustrated by Erick Ingraham. A very clever Siamese cat, Henry, finds when he is left behind by accident in the snow-covered mountains that he can use the skis the children have made for him.

***The Day Before Christmas,* by Eve Bunting, illustrated by Beth Peck. A really wonderful story of seven-year-old Allie who goes to the city on the train with her grandfather for her first view of *The Nutcracker.* The ballet itself is gorgeous, but even more memorable is that her grandfather tells her how her deceased mother had enjoyed the same ballet when she was seven. Magnificent illustrations.

Emily's Snowball, the World's Biggest, by Elizabeth Keown, illustrated by Irene Trivas. With the help of friends and neighbors, Emily's snowball grows to the size of a small mountain and lasts until spring, when only the sign "World's Biggest" remains.

Ernest and Celestine, by Gabrielle Vincent. Ernest, a bear, and Celestine, a mouse, lose Celestine's stuffed bird Gideon in the snow. But Ernest fixes everything. A sweet story for the very young child.

First Snow, by Emily Arnold McCully. A wordless book in which the little mouse family is going to Grandma's through the first snow of the season. One timid little mouse is afraid to try sledding, but becomes an enthusiast before the story ends.

Geraldine's Big Snow, by Holly Keller. Geraldine has a new sled, but she thinks the snow will never come. Overnight it does, and she happily takes her sled to the top of the highest hill in the park and coasts down.

Gung Hay Fat Choy, by June Behrens. This book with the aid of authentic photographs explains the Chinese New Year and describes its celebration by Chinese Americans.

Habari Gani, by Sundaira Morninghouse, illustrated by Jody Kim. From December 26 to January 1, an African-American family celebrates each day of Kwanzaa, their only nationally celebrated, indigenous, nonheroic holiday, lighting a candle each day to mark the Seven Principles.

How the Grinch Stole Christmas, by Dr. Seuss. The Whos are about to celebrate Christmas, but the crabby Grinch thinks of a way to take away this happy day. Dressed as Santa Claus, he removes all the presents, the trees, and the food. But when the Whos sing anyway, the Grinch reverses his behavior and gives everything back.

It's Snowing, It's Snowing, by Jack Prelutsky, illustrated by Jeanne Titherington. A collection of short poems about snow and children's delight in winter activities.

Katy and the Big Snow, by Virginia Lee Burton. A valiant (female) tractor saves the town when no other vehicle can get through the deep snow.

Lion Dancer: Ernie Wan's Chinese New Year, by Kate Waters and Madeline Slovenz-Low, illustrated by Martha Cooper. Ernie Wan is six and this is to be his first year to dance in the lion costume at Chinese New Year. This book explains many customs associated with this holiday.

Little Runner of the Longhouse, by Betty Baker, illustrated by Arnold Lobel. A charming story of a little boy and his participation in the New Year celebration of his Iroquois family.

Mousekin's Woodland Sleepers, by Edna Miller. A little white-tailed mouse finds it somewhat difficult to survive winter in the forest, but he finally makes it back to a little birdhouse and is safe.

Nine Days to Christmas: A Story of Mexico, by Marie Hall Ets and Aurora Labastida, illustrated by Marie Hall Ets. Ceci, a kindergarten-aged child, is waiting for the *posada,* the Mexican Christmas party at which she will have her first *piñata.* She selects a star and is sad when it is broken. Then she looks to the sky and sees a real star.

One Zillion Valentines, by Frank Modell. Marvin and Milton make valentines for everyone, then sell the rest of them for enough money to buy themselves a heart-shaped box of chocolates.

Owl Moon, by Jane Yolen, illustrated by John Schoenherr. On a winter's night under a full moon, a father and daughter trek into the woods to see the Great Horned Owl.

The Polar Express, by Chris Van Allsburg. While thinking of Santa Claus on Christmas Eve, a child dreams of going to the North Pole on a train. He returns with a broken bell from Santa's reindeer, which has a special ring for him.

Potato Pancakes All Around, by Marilyn Hirsh. In this variation of the traditional folktale in which a stranger comes into a quarrelsome situation and demonstrates making food without using traditional ingredients, here a peddler shows both Grandma Yetta and Grandma Sophie that potato pancakes can be made from an old crust of rye bread, plus, of course. . . .

Sleepy Bear, by Lydia Dabcovich. It's winter and Bear hibernates until spring when the insects, including bees, show up. Then he thinks "honey," and emerges from his cave.

The Snow Party, by Beatrice Schenk De Regniers, illustrated by Bernice Myers. This story tells of a farmer and his lonely wife who would like to have people to talk to. When a heavy snow closes the road, many stranded travelers are invited in and it becomes a really fine party.

The Snowman, by Raymond Briggs. In this charming wordless book a little boy personifies a snowman he has built, and they do everything together.

The Snowy Day, by Ezra Jack Keats. Peter goes out into the snow to play and discovers that he cannot keep a snowball overnight in his pocket. But it snows again the next morning.

Somebody Loves You, Mr. Hatch, by Eileen Spinelli. Mr. Hatch is a somber, solitary figure until he receives a mysterious heart-shaped box of chocolates on Valentine's Day. After that, he becomes outgoing, happy, and helpful to his neighbors. Then the postman confesses that he had delivered the box to Mr. Hatch by mistake.

Take Time to Relax!, by Nancy Carlson. Tina the beaver and her family are constantly "on the go" until a snowstorm keeps them home, and they rediscover how much fun they can have, just the three of them.

The Valentine Bears, by Eve Bunting, illustrated by Jan Brett. The bears are hibernating, but Mrs. Bear sets the alarm for February 14 so she can prepare a Valentine surprise for Mr. Bear, who snores on until she takes drastic measures to awaken him.

Valentine's Day, by Gail Gibbons. A book explaining how this special day is the day for saying "I love you!," with simple directions for making valentines at home.

A Valentine for Cousin Archie, by Barbara Williams, illustrated by Kay Chorao. Responding to the anonymous valentine he receives, Cousin Archie sets off a whole soap opera of valentine giving and receiving.

Wake Up, Vladimir, by Felicia Bond. Vladimir Groundhog runs away from home in late autumn and, after a long winter's sleep, wakes up, scares away a monster (his shadow), and runs home never to leave again.

Why Rat Comes First: The Story of the Chinese Zodiac, by Clara Yen, illustrated by Hideo C. Yoshida. When the Jade King calls all the animals to heaven, twelve come, so there is a twelve-year cycle of years. The Jade King decides to let earthly children choose which animal will be first, and, in a contest between the ox and the rat, through cleverness the rat wins.

When Winter Comes, by Pearl Neuman, illustrated by Richard Roe. This book explains how the woodchuck, black bear, red fox, and Canadian goose cope with winter in the northern parts of North America.

White Snow, Bright Snow, by Alvin Tresselt, illustrated by Roger Duvoisin. When it snows, adults do what they must—tasks like shoveling out their cars and paths. But children exult in the soft white stuff until the sun melts it all away.

Winter, by Ron Hirschi, illustrated by Thomas D. Mangelsen. The natural world in winter is abundantly illustrated with colored photographs.

Winter Bear, by Ruth Craft, illustrated by Erik Blegvad. A simple rhymed story of children outside just as winter is beginning; they find a little bear and take him home.

The Winter Hedgehog, by Ann and Reg Cartwright. The smallest hedgehog doesn't listen to his mother who warns him that winter is beautiful, yes, but cold and cruel too, so he goes in search of winter and almost comes to harm.

Spring and Its Holidays

Arthur's April Fool, by Marc Brown. Arthur manages to beat his nemesis, Binky Barlow, at the school's April Fool show by offering to saw Binky in half as the final trick.

The Boy Who Didn't Believe in Spring, by Lucille Clifton, illustrated by Brinton Turkle. King Shabazz and his friend Tony Polito do not believe what their teacher said about spring being just around the corner, so they go looking for it. And they find it!

Bunny Trouble, by Hans Wilhelm. Bunnies decorate Easter eggs—all except Ralph who cares for nothing but soccer, which gets him into all kinds of trouble.

The Carp in the Bathtub, by Barbara Cohen, illustrated by Joan Halpern. The friendship of Leah and Harry with Joe the carp makes it difficult for their mother to make gefilte fish of the carp. But make it she does, even if the children won't eat it.

The Carrot Seed, by Ruth Krauss, illustrated by Crockett Johnson. Everyone said the carrot seed would not come up, but the little boy faithfully tends it and has his reward in spring.

Chicken Sunday, by Patricia Polacco. Eula Mae Walker, her grandchildren, and their friend whose family comes from Russia have a very special relationship. How the children get Gramma her Easter hat by making Easter eggs in Russian designs—*pysanky* eggs—is a great story.

The Easter Egg Artists, by Adrienne Adams. This is a charming little story of the Abbott family, rabbits who do wonderful things with paint. Their son Orson finally becomes interested in the art business.

Fiesta!, by June Behrens. Here is the description, with photographs, of Cinco de Mayo, the commemoration of the victory of the Mexican army over the French army on May 5, 1862. This is a day of celebration among Mexican Americans.

The Golden Egg Book, by Margaret Wise Brown, illustrated by Leonard Weisgard. A little bunny who finds an egg tries hard to get it open, but falls asleep just as the little yellow duck emerges. The two become friends, and "no one is ever alone again."

Goldie's Purim, by Jane Breskin Zalben. Although Goldie is scared at first, she overcomes her stage fright to play Queen Esther in the synagogue's celebration of Purim.

Happy Mother's Day, by Steven Kroll, illustrated by Marilyn Hafner. When Mother returns home, she finds that Dad and the children have figured a novel way to show her their love and appreciation on Mother's Day.

In a Spring Garden, edited by Richard Lewis, illustrated by Ezra Jack Keats. Haiku verses glorify spring flowers and small animals in the garden.

It's Nesting Time, by Roma Gans, illustrated by Kazue Mizumura. It's spring and birds must build nests in which to lay their eggs. In this book we learn about many different ways varieties of birds accomplish this task.

Jennie's Hat, by Ezra Jack Keats. Jennie is disappointed that the hat which her aunt sends her is so plain. Then her friends, the birds, trim her hat to make it the most beautiful hat in the world.

Look Out, It's April Fool's Day, by Frank Modell. Marvin loves to play jokes on his friend Milton, but on April Fool's Day Milton just won't be fooled until. . . .

The Magician, adapted and illustrated by Uri Shulevitz. On the eve of Passover the prophet Elijah comes to a small village disguised as a magician and gives a poor family everything they need to celebrate the holiday.

Miss Suzy's Easter Surprise, by Miriam Young, illustrated by Arnold Lobel. Miss Suzy, a squirrel who lives in a sturdy oak tree, goes out to get some trimmings for her Easter hat, and finds some orphaned squirrels who need her.

The Mother's Day Mice, by Eve Bunting, illustrated by Jan Brett. Three mice brothers go into the meadow to find presents for their mother, but it is the littlest mouse that comes up with the most unusual gift of all.

My Spring Robin, by Anne Rockwell, illustrated by Harlow and Lizzy Rockwell. A little boy looks in spring for the return of his special robin, and then he hears it singing just for him.

Rechenka's Eggs, by Patricia Polacco. An injured goose, rescued by Babushka, unintentionally breaks the painted eggs intended for the Easter Festival in Moscva, but lays thirteen marvelously colored ones to replace them, then leaves one last egg before rejoining her flock.

St. Patrick's Day in the Morning, by Eve Bunting, illustrated by Jan Brett. Small as he is, Jamie is determined to march in the St. Patrick's Day parade, and he finds a way to prove that he can do it.

Will Spring Be Early? Or Will Spring Be Late?, by Crockett Johnson. The groundhog, about to make his annual prediction, is fooled by a paper flower into saying that spring has already arrived, but the falling snow is just a temporary setback.

Summer and Its Holidays

Summer, by Richard L. Allington and Kathleen Krull, illustrated by Dennis Hockerman. One of a series of four books about the seasons, this book tells of the sights, sounds, and typical activities of summer.

At the Beach, by Anne and Harlow Rockwell. A child experiences enjoyable sights and sounds during a day at the beach.

Fourth of July, by Barbara M. Joosse, illustrated by Emily Arnold McCully. A six-year-old boy marches in the traditional small-town parade holding up his half of a banner and is rewarded by being allowed to write his name in the night sky with sparklers.

The Happy Hippopotami, by Bill Martin, Jr., illustrated by Betsy Everitt. In deliciously droll verse we see the happy hippos enjoying a day at the beach.

I See Something You Don't See, by Robin Michael Koontz. Two children enjoying a summer day at Grandma's entertain each other with rhyming riddles. The pictures give the answers, with an extra answer page at the back of the book.

On a Hot, Hot Day, by Nicki Weiss. Mama and her young son Angel find nice things to do together, no matter the weather.

One Way: A Trip With Traffic Signs, by Leonard Shortall. With humorous illustrations we see the travels of a family going to a Fourth of July celebration, meeting every kind of traffic sign enroute.

Parade, by Donald Crews. This book shows a parade from the No Parking signs at the beginning to the clean-up crew of the Sanitation Department at the end.

A Perfect Father's Day, by Eve Bunting, illustrated by Susan Meddaugh. When four-year-old Susie treats her father to a series of special activities for Father's Day, they just happen to be all of her own favorite things.

Picnic, by Emily Arnold McCully. A wordless book which shows one little mouse missing from the family picnic. But she is found as the truck returns.

Autumn and Its Holidays

Alligator Arrived With Apples: A Potluck Alphabet Feast, by Crescent Dragonwagon, illustrated by Jose Aruego and Ariane Dewey. A wonderfully imaginative and colorful retelling of the alphabet with statements such as "Goose Gave Gravy, Grapes, and Gingerbread" and "Hyena Had the Hiccups, but He Hailed us with Honey and Hazelnuts."

Amanda and the Witch Switch, by John Himmelman. A friendly witch named Amanda gives a toad three wishes, but her good intentions backfire when he uses one of the wishes to become a witch—and not a friendly one either!

Apples and Pumpkins, by Anne Rockwell, illustrated by Lizzy Rockwell. In preparation for Halloween night, a family visits Mr. Comstock's farm to pick apples and pumpkins.

Arthur's Halloween, by Marc Brown. Arthur has to take his little sister trick-or-treating and bravely follows her into the neighborhood "haunted house," which turns out to be a pleasant place after all.

Autumn Days, by Ann Schweninger. Part of a series covering the four seasons, this book answers children's questions such as "Why do the leaves change color?" or "What is frost?" or "Why does it stay warm in Southern California in autumn?" Nice drawings of "little people in fur" and their activities.

Autumn Harvest, by Alvin Tresselt, illustrated by Roger Duvoisin. A book in praise of autumn in the country, from the first glimmering of cool weather through Halloween and Thanksgiving dinner.

Big Pumpkin, by Erica Silverman, illustrated by S. D. Schindler. This is a Halloween story of a witch who grows an enormous pumpkin—too big for her to carry—so she enlists the help of some spooky characters like a ghost, Dracula, a mummy, and others. They help, but she must share with them.

Fall, by Ron Hirschi, illustrated by Thomas D. Mangelsen. This book introduces the characteristics of autumn in simple text and illustrations.

Friendship's First Thanksgiving, by William Accorsi. Friendship, a dog who has crossed the sea with the Pilgrims, describes the colony's first year in the New World, culminating in the first Thanksgiving.

Funnybones, by Janet and Allan Ahlberg. Three skeletons—a big one, a little one, and a dog—decide to go out and scare someone, but cannot find anyone to scare, so they just frolic in the park and return home.

Georgie, by Robert Bright. Georgie is a sweet little ghost in the attic of the Whittakers' house until repairs keep him from making his usual noises, so Georgie runs away. Then the cold winter undoes the repairs, so Georgie returns happily to his home.

Hester, by Byron Barton. Hester Crocodile is dressed as a witch for Halloween and investigates a scary house where she meets a real witch who takes her for a ride on her broom.

**Hist Whist,* by e. e. cummings, illustrated by Deborah Kogan Ray. It's a Halloween party and the children's costumes are the inspiration for the poetry.

**How Many Days to America?,* by Eve Bunting, illustrated by Beth Peck. Refugees from a Caribbean island embark on a dangerous boat trip to America where they have a special reason to celebrate Thanksgiving.

Humbug Witch, by Lorna Balian. This witch has everything witches are supposed to have: a broom, a black cat, a big black hat with long stringy hair falling out of it, and a very big ugly nose. But her magic just doesn't work. She goes nowhere on her broom, her magic potion only makes her black cat sick to his stomach, and her laugh sounds like a giggle. So she takes off her mask and costume and goes to bed.

In the Haunted House, by Eve Bunting, illustrated by Susan Meddaugh. A story where every spooky character that you have ever heard of or seen in a movie is now a resident of the Halloween House. Why is Daddy more frightened than his little girl? Done in rhyme.

**King of the Cats*, by Joseph Jacobs, retold and illustrated by Paul Galdone. A great ghost story about a gravedigger who tells his wife his strange experience, and then finds that it is his own cat who solves the mystery about the identity of Tim Tildrum.

The Little Old Lady Who Was Not Afraid of Anything, by Linda Williams, illustrated by Megan Lloyd. The little old lady does well with all the spooky objects that follow her through the woods, trying to scare her. Youngsters love the repetition and the surprise ending.

***Molly's Pilgrim*, by Barbara Cohen, illustrated by Michael J. Deraney. When Molly is told to make a doll like a Pilgrim for the Thanksgiving display at school, Molly's mother dresses the doll as she herself dressed before leaving Russia to seek religious freedom. Molly is embarrassed; her classmates laugh at her, but Ms. Stickley, a wise teacher, makes things right.

Mousekin's Golden House, by Edna Miller. Mousekin the whitefoot mouse makes his home in a discarded pumpkin, and it proves a safe haven from the weather and predators.

Nanny Noony and the Dust Queen, by Edward Frascino. Nanny Noony the good witch and Cat figure out how to stop the Dust Queen who is causing havoc to the farm with a drought.

Nanny Noony and the Magic Spell, by Edward Frascino. A blackbird tells Cat how to rid the farm of the evil hex supposedly put on it by Nanny Noony, but when Cat finds Nanny, he discovers that it is Blackbird who is guilty. All ends well.

One Terrific Thanksgiving, by Marjorie Weinman Sharmat, illustrated by Lilian Obligado. Irving Morris Bear loves to eat, but when he overbuys for his Thanksgiving dinner, he must ask some friends to hide food to keep himself from eating ahead of time. He then learns that to have a good holiday he must share.

Over the River and Through the Wood, by Lydia Maria Child, illustrated by Iris Van Rynbach. An illustrated version of the well-known song describing the joys of a Thanksgiving visit to grandmother's house. Music on the last two pages.

Popcorn, by Frank Asch. Sam Bear's friends come to his Halloween party and bring popcorn. But when it's all popped, it fills the house, so they eat it all to clean up before Sam's parents return from their Halloweeen party, bringing him a treat—popcorn.

The Pumpkin Patch, by Elizabeth King. Text and photos describe the activities in a pumpkin patch as the pink-colored seeds become fat pumpkins, ready to be carved into jack-o'-lanterns.

Scary, Scary Halloween, by Eve Bunting, illustrated by Jan Brett. A band of trick-or-treaters and a mother cat with her kittens spend a very scary Halloweeen. Done in verse.

Silly Tilly's Thanksgiving Dinner, by Lillian Hoban. Tilly Mole is planning a fine dinner for all her friends, but she is so forgetful that she loses her glasses, confuses the invitations with the recipes, and then falls asleep. But her friends, even Mr. Turkey, come anyway.

Space Case, by Edward Marshall, illustrated by James Marshall. Buddy McGee and his friends are trick-or-treating and believe the "thing from outer space" must be a costume on the new kid on the block. Then they learn differently. It's fun to take The Thing to school, but It decides to go home when It learns that Halloween comes only once a year.

Space Witch, by Don Freeman. Tilly Ipswitch, a witch, makes a space ship and takes off with Kit, her black cat, for other planets. But she and Kit land at home and it's still Halloween.

The Squirrels' Thanksgiving, by Steven Kroll, illustrated by Jeni Bassett. When their naughty cousins come for dinner, Brenda and Buddy realize that they're pretty good squirrels after all, and so do their parents.

Thanksgiving Day, by Gail Gibbons. This book relates the first Thanksgiving Day and its present-day equivalent.

A Tiger Called Thomas, by Charlotte Zolotow, illustrated by Catherine Stock. Thomas is a spectator. He won't venture off the porch of his family's new house until Halloween, when he goes trick-or-treating in his tiger costume. He's surprised that everyone recognizes him, and he decides that everyone likes him after all.

**Washington Irving's the Headless Horseman,* adapted by Natalie Standiford, illustrated by Donald Cook. In language that a second-grade child can understand, this book relates the story of Ichabod Crane, Brom Bones, and the beautiful Katrina Van Tassel, who marries Brom after the superstitious Ichabod is frightened by "the headless horseman."

Winnie the Witch, by Valerie Thomas, illustrated by Korky Paul. Wilbur, Winnie's black cat, can't be easily seen in Winnie's all-black house, so she turns him green, but falls over him in the grass. Then she tries a rainbow effect, but everybody laughs at Wilbur, so Winnie solves her problem but turning Wilbur back to black and putting all the colors on her house instead.

The Witch Next Door, by Norman Bridwell. The children love their neighbor the witch, but some other neighbors are not so tolerant. So when they ask the witch to leave, she casts a spell and makes them a beautiful prince and princess, who now forget about her moving.

Witches Four, by Marc Brown. A simple Halloween story told with humor.

Wobble the Witch Cat, by Mary Calhoun, illustrated by Roger Duvoisin. Wobble gets rid of Maggie's broom because it's too narrow to be comfortable as they ride through the sky on Halloween. Then Maggie decides to substitute the vacuum cleaner and all is well. Wobble is very happy, sitting on the bag.

A Woggle of Witches, by Adrienne Adams. It's Halloween and the witches gather to "do what witches do on that night." Then the children, dressed as monsters, frighten them away.

Books About Birthdays

All children look forward to holidays; as a matter of fact, many youngsters delineate their lives in terms of particular days which will bring special treats. And these are different from one family to the next. But the most important holiday for every child is his own special day—his birthday.

Alfie Gives a Hand, by Shirley Hughes. Alfie goes to his first birthday party at Bernard's, but since his mother and little sister are not going, Alfie takes what's left of his security blanket with him. Then he puts it down to help little Min, another preschooler, and finds he doesn't need it after all.

Angelina's Birthday Surprise, by Katherine Holabird, illustrated by Helen Craig. Angelina the dancing mouse and her friend Alice work very hard to earn enough money to replace Angelina's bicycle, which was wrecked when she was racing Alice on the day of her party. . . .

Arthur's Birthday, by Marc Brown. Their friends must decide which party to attend when Muffy schedules her birthday party for the same day as Arthur's. The boys figure out a way to compromise.

Ask Mr. Bear, by Marjorie Flack. Danny asks each animal in turn what he should give his mother for her birthday. Finally, Mr. Bear gives him the answer which pleases Danny's mom.

Benny Bakes a Cake, by Eve Rice. Benny helps his mother make his birthday cake, but Ralph, his dog, pulls it off the table. Benny's daddy saves the day when he comes home with a birthday cake for Benny.

A Birthday for Frances, by Russell Hoban, illustrated by Lillian Hoban. It's not Frances's birthday; it's Gloria's, and Frances has to borrow two weeks' allowance to buy her little sister some bubble gum and a tasty Chompo bar. It's hard to be an un-birthday girl.

The Birthday Party, by Ruth Krauss, illustrated by Maurice Sendak. A little boy has been everywhere, but he's never been to a birthday party—until. . . .

Dandelion, by Don Freeman. When Dandelion gets an invitation to Jennifer Giraffe's party, he gets so "gussied up" that he is not recognized by his hostess, who shuts the door in his face. Then it rains: his mane becomes straight; he loses his fancy jacket, cap, and cane; but now that he is no longer a stylish dandy, he is welcomed at the party.

Digging to China, by Donna Rawlins. Hearing her friend Marj, the elderly lady next door, speak wistfully of China, Alexis digs a hole all the way through the earth to that exotic country and brings back a postcard for Marj on her birthday.

Go Away, Dog, by Joan L. Nodset, illustrated by Crosby Bonsall. Uncle George sends Jimmy a dog for his birthday, but Jimmy doesn't like dogs. Of course, the dog changes all that.

Happy Birthday, Grampie, by Susan Pearson, illustrated by Ronald Himler. Martha makes a special birthday card for her Swedish grandfather's eighty-ninth birthday, since he is blind. The family goes to visit him in the nursing home, and he "reads" her card, saying in English, "I love you too, Martha."

Happy Birthday, Moon, by Frank Asch. Bear and Moon exchange birthday gifts and both are happy.

Happy Birthday, Rotten Ralph, by Jack Gantos, illustrated by Nicole Rubel. Sarah is going to give a birthday party for Rotten Ralph, even though he does many naughty things. But when she sends him to his room, and he can't find his present, he decides that Sarah has cancelled the party. But she hasn't.

Happy Birthday, Sam, by Pat Hutchins. It is Sam's birthday, but he still cannot reach the light switch, the bathroom taps, or the front-door knob. Then his grandfather's gift arrives and solves his problem.

Happy Birthday, Wombat!, by Kerry Argent. The wombat looks everywhere for his present, as the pages of this book fold out. But he doesn't find it until the last page.

It's My Birthday!, by Shigeo Watanabe, illustrated by Yasuo Ohtomo. It's Bear's fourth birthday, and he looks through the photo album to remember earlier years.

A Letter to Amy, by Ezra Jack Keats. Peter's invitation to Amy almost goes awry, but she does come to his birthday party, the only girl there.

Little Gorilla, by Ruth Bornstein. All the jungle animals love little gorilla when he is a tiny thing. Then he grows into a BIG gorilla, and his friends show their love by giving him a birthday party.

Magical Hands, by Marjorie Barker, illustrated by Yoshi. A lovely, warm story of four men who are friends. William, the barrel maker, secretly does the morning chores for each of his friends on their birthdays, and when his own birthday comes, he finds himself rewarded.

**Me Day,* by Joan L. Lexau, illustrated by Robert Weaver. It's Rafer's birthday, but his parents are divorced, and the boy thinks his father has forgotten him. A realistic, rather somber picture of a ghetto family, even though his dad does come to take him for a "long, long day."

Mr. Rabbit and the Lovely Present, by Charlotte Zolotow, illustrated by Maurice Sendak. A little girl consults her rabbit friend about a birthday gift for her mother and takes his advice about giving something of each color her mother likes—a basket of fruit.

Papa's Panda, by Nancy Willard, illustrated by Lillian Hoban. James and his dad discuss the problems a real panda would cause if James got one as a birthday present, after which James is very pleased with his gift of a toy panda.

Some Birthday!, by Patricia Polacco. A little girl's birthday is celebrated by going with her dad to take photos of a monster which lives in a pond near her grandma's house. But all ends happily.

Something Special for Me, by Vera B. Williams. Rosa is to select something special for her birthday. First, she tries on roller skates, next a new dress, then a sleeping bag, and each seems fine. But when she hears an accordianist, she knows what she really wants, and she gets it.

***The Wednesday Surprise,* by Eve Bunting, illustrated by Donald Carrick. Anna and her grandmother have a very close relationship, especially since Anna is helping Grandma prepare a surprise for Anna's father at his birthday party. Grandma has learned to read.

Which Witch Is Which?, by Pat Hutchins. A simple book about twin girls at a birthday party. Since all the children are in costume, it's difficult to tell which witch is Ella and which witch is Emily. Trying to decide is fun.

Books Featuring Ethnic Groups

Because we should stress commonality rather than differences, citing titles by various ethnic groups might seem something of a contradiction. However, for the convenience of those who might want to use books for particular purposes, some specialized lists follow.

African Americans

Abby, by Jeanette Caines, illustrated by Steven Kellogg. Adopted as a baby, Abby is very happy with her parents and her big brother Kevin, who wants to take her to school for show-and-tell.

Amazing Grace, by Mary Hoffman, illustrated by Caroline Binch. Grace loves to act, and she is determined to play Peter Pan in the school play. Her classmates say that she cannot do it because she is African-American and a girl, but Grace discovers that she can do anything she sets her mind to do.

Apt 3G, by Ezra Jack Keats. Ben and Sam investigate the sound of music in their tenement and meet the blind man downstairs who plays the harmonica. A touching, unsentimental look at his world.

Aunt Flossie's Hats (and Crab Cakes Later), by Elizabeth Fitzgerald Howard, illustrated by James Ransome. Sarah and Susan enjoy going to their great-great-aunt's house to hear her reminisce about past events in her life, evoked by each of her hats, which the little girls try on. Then they all go to eat crab cakes.

**Ben's Trumpet,* by Rachel Isadora. Young Ben wants to be a trumpeter, but plays only an imaginary instrument and is ridiculed by his friends. Then one of the musicians in a neighborhood nightclub discovers his ambition and rectifies the situation.

Bigmama's, by Donald Crews. Visiting his grandmother's house—she is Bigmama—in Cottondale, the author remembers all the fun he had as a boy spending the whole summer vacation with his family on an old-fashioned farm.

Black Is Brown Is Tan, by Arnold Adoff, illustrated by Emily A. McCully. A small child's view of his mixed parentage: an African-American mother and a Caucasian father, apparently a happy home.

The Boy Who Didn't Believe in Spring, by Lucille Clifton, illustrated by Brinton Turkle. King Shabazz and his friend Tony Polito do not believe what their teacher said about spring being just around the corner, so they go looking for it. And they find it!

Bright Eyes, Brown Skin, by Cheryl Willis Hudson and Bernette G. Ford, illustrated by George Ford. Four African-American children romp through this book, telling about their physical characteristics. Based on a poem written by Hudson in 1979.

Chicken Sunday, by Patricia Polacco. Eula Mae Walker, her grandchildren, and their friend, whose family comes from Russia, have a very special relationship. How the children get Gramma her Easter hat by making Easter eggs in Russian designs—*pysanky* eggs—is a great story.

Cornrows, by Camille Yarbrough, illustrated by Carole Bayard. Mama and Great-Grammaw tell stories of African history as they braid Shirley Ann and her brother Mike's hair in cornrows, making meaningful patterns and giving the cornrows names of famous African Americans.

Corduroy, by Don Freeman. The little brown bear has lost a button on his overalls and tries unsuccessfully to find it at night after the department store is closed. But little Lisa loves him just as he is and takes him home.

Dreams, by Ezra Jack Keats. Roberto and Archie, city children the author has created in other books, are here, dreaming that the huge shadow of Roberto's paper mouse sails down and scares away the dog that has cornered Archie's cat.

The Drinking Gourd, by F. N. Monjo, illustrated by Fred Brenner. Tommy Fuller is a mischievous lad, and when he is sent home for disturbing the church service, he discovers some runaway slaves hiding in his father's barn, a station on the Underground Railway. He helps them escape the bounty hunters and learns why his father breaks the law.

Evan's Corner, by Elizabeth Starr Hill, illustrated by Sandra Speidel. A reissue with contemporary illustrations, this warm story tells of Evan's desire for a corner of his own in the two-room flat he shares with his family.

Everett Anderson's Friend, by Lucille Clifton, illustrated by Ann Grifalconi. Everett learns that a little girl, Maria, can be fun to play with, even though she wins when Everett and his three boyfriends let her play ball with them.

Everett Anderson's Nine Month Long, by Lucille Clifton, illustrated by Ann Grifalconi. Everett, first a one-parent child, learns to love Mr. Perry, his new daddy, and to welcome baby Evelyn Perry, who arrives to complete their family.

First Pink Light, by Eloise Greenfield, illustrated by Moneta Barnett. Tyree's mother does not understand why he wants to hide and surprise his daddy, who has been away a whole month, but he follows her suggestion and waits for the dawn in a big comfortable chair with his pillow and blanket. Then Daddy comes home and carries him to his bed.

Flossie and the Fox, by Patricia C. McKissack, illustrated by Rachel Isadora. Told in rural Southern dialect, this is the story of a wily fox notorious for stealing eggs who meets his match when he encounters a bold little girl in the woods. Flossie insists that she must have proof that he is a fox before she will be frightened.

***Follow the Drinking Gourd,* by Jeanette Winter. By following the directions in an old song, "The Drinking Gourd," taught to them by an old sailor, Peg Leg Joe, runaway slaves journey north along the Underground Railway. The Drinking Gourd is the Big Dipper, which points to the North Star.

Goggles!, by Ezra Jack Keats. Peter finds goggles, but he and his friend Archie nearly lose them to some older, tougher boys. Then his dog Willie helps the boys to keep the goggles.

Golden Bear, by Ruth Young, illustrated by Rachel Isadora. Golden Bear and his human companion learn to play the violin, talk to a ladybug, make mudpies, and dream together. Done in simple rhymed verse.

Habari Gani, by Sundaira Morninghouse, illustrated by Jody Kim. From December 26 to January 1, an African-American family celebrates each day of Kwanzaa, their only nationally celebrated, indigenous, nonheroic holiday, lighting a candle each day to mark the Seven Principles.

Jamaica Tag-Along, by Juanita Havill, illustrated by Anne Sibley O'Brien. When her older brother Ossie won't let Jamaica play basketball with him and his friends, she helps a younger child build a sand castle, as she realizes what it feels like to be considered a "tag-along."

John Henry: An American Legend, by Ezra Jack Keats. The great steel-driving man was unusual even as an infant, and the "tall tale" comes alive here.

Just Us Women, by Jeanette Caines, illustrated by Pat Cummings. A young girl and her Aunt Martha drive to North Carolina, doing whatever suits them enroute. It's a lovely trip.

***The Knee-High Man and Other Tales,* retold by Julius Lester, illustrated by Ralph Pinto. In these folktales personified animals subtly represent human relationships, particularly among rural African Americans of earlier times.

A Letter to Amy, by Ezra Jack Keats. Peter's invitation to Amy almost goes awry, but she does come to his birthday party, the only girl there.

Lisa Lou and the Yeller Belly Swamp, by Mercer Mayer. This version of the Little Red Riding Hood story has the quick-thinking Lisa Lou outsmarting all the "haunts," "gobbly-gooks," witches, and devils in the Yeller Belly Swamp.

Mary Had a Little Lamb, by Sarah Josepha Hale, illustrated by Bruce McMillan. A contemporary interpretation of the well-known nineteenth-century nursery rhyme about the lamb who went to school. Accompanied by color photographs and a sample exercise from a *McGuffy Reader* (1857).

***Me Day,* by Joan M. Lexau, illustrated by Robert Weaver. It's Rafer's birthday, but his parents are divorced, and the boy thinks his father has forgotten him. A realistic, rather somber picture of a ghetto family, even though his dad does come to take him for a "long, long day."

Mirandy and Brother Wind, by Patricia C. McKissack, illustrated by Jerry Pinkney. To win first prize in the Junior Cakewalk, Mirandy tries to capture the wind for her partner, and she succeeds. Of course, Ezel, who is usually clumsy, helps a lot.

**Moss Gown,* by William H. Hooks, illustrated by Donald Carrick. Here the characters of Cordelia from Shakespeare's *King Lear* and Cinderella blend seamlessly, with the magic of the Black gris-gris woman acting as catalyst. Really gorgeous paintings bring it all to life.

**Nettie Jo's Friends,* by Patricia C. McKissack, illustrated by Scott Cook. Nettie Jo searches for a needle to sew a dress for Annie Mae, so she can take the doll to the wedding where Nettie Jo will be the flower girl, but the three animals she helps during her search do not seem inclined to reciprocate until the end.

Night on Neighborhood Street, by Eloise Greenfield, illustrated by Jan Spivey Gilchrist. A collection of poems exploring the sights, sounds, and emotions enlivening an African-American neighborhood during the course of one evening.

On a Hot, Hot Day, by Nicki Weiss. Mama and her young son Angel find nice things to do together, no matter the weather.

The Patchwork Quilt, by Valerie Flournoy, illustrated by Jerry Pinkney. Tenderly told, this is the story of the patchwork quilt which Grandmother is making. When she becomes unable to finish it, her granddaughter completes the masterpiece.

Pet Show!, by Ezra Jack Keats. When the pet show starts, Archie cannot find his cat anywhere, so he brings a germ in a glass jar and gets the prize for the quietest pet, just as an old lady shows up with Archie's cat. The boy lets her keep the blue ribbon, but he takes his cat.

Peter's Chair, by Ezra Jack Keats. Now Peter feels displaced by his new baby sister Susie, and so he decides to "run away" by going outside with his dog Willie and his little chair. However, he does not fit in the chair anymore. He has outgrown it.

A Picture Book of Harriet Tubman, by David A. Adler, illustrated by Samuel Byrd. A short life of this African-American woman who was called the "Moses" of her people because she led so many slaves to freedom as a conductor on the Underground Railway. She later became active in the fight for women's rights.

A Picture Book of Martin Luther King, Jr., by David A. Adler, illustrated by Robert Casilla. A very simplified overview of this great African-American leader, with important milestones in his life emphasized.

A Pocket for Corduroy, by Don Freeman. Lisa's little bear thinks he needs a pocket for his overalls, so he tries to find one in the laundromat, getting into all kinds of scrapes until Lisa finds him the next day and makes him a pocket with his name tucked inside.

****Ragtime Tumpie*, by Alan Schroeder, illustrated by Bernie Fuchs. Tumpie, a young African-American girl who will later become famous as the dancer Josephine Baker, longs to find the opportunity to dance amid the poverty and vivacious street life of St. Louis in the early 1900s, and she wins a silver dollar for her first public appearance in a contest.

Sam, by Ann Herbert Scott, illustrations by Symeon Shimen. Sam is lonely because each family member is too busy to pay attention to him. Then when he cries, they all understand, and his mother lets him make his own tart with raspberry jam.

She Come Bringing Me That Little Baby Girl, by Eloise Greenfield, illustrated by John Steptoe. Kevin asked for a baby brother, not a wrinkled little sister who is now the center of attention for all visitors. But his mother makes it clear that he must help her with the baby, and that his mother has two arms, one for each child.

The Snowy Day, by Ezra Jack Keats. Peter goes out into the snow to play and discovers that he cannot keep a snowball overnight in his pocket. But it snows again the next morning!

Spin a Soft Black Song, by Nikki Giovanni, illustrated by Charles Bible. This is a very unusual book, celebrating African-American life in poems based on what children say from infancy through age ten. The author uses her own experiences and those of her brother Charles for verisimilitude.

Stevie, by John Steptoe. Robert is not too thrilled when he hears that little Stevie is coming to stay with his family on weekdays, and the little boy does prove to be something of a pest. Then Stevie's family moves away and Robert finds he misses the little guy.

The Talking Eggs, by Robert D. San Souci, illustrated by Jerry Pinkney. A colorful folktale of the American South, this story deals with two sisters, Rose, who is spoiled and lazy but her mother's favorite, and Blanche, who is forced to fetch and carry and do all the hard work. When Blanche meets a strange old lady in the woods and behaves with her usual kindness, everything is reversed for her, Rose, and their mother.

Tar Beach, by Faith Ringgold. The setting is a New York City apartment house roof, and the story revolves around the quilt on which the girl lies, dreaming of flying over the George Washington Bridge, over the ice cream factory, and into the night filled with stars.

Ten, Nine, Eight, by Molly Bang. In an unusual bedtime book, a little girl counts backward from "ten small toes all washed and warm" through numbers to "one big girl all ready for bed."

Wagon Wheels, by Barbara Brenner, illustrated by Don Bolognese. A true story of the Muldie family, African-American pioneers, who travel to Kansas after the Civil War to take advantage of the Homestead Act. The father and his three children start in Nicodemus, Kansas, but the boys must follow their father to a place 150 miles farther on where the farming is good.

A Weed Is a Flower: The Life of George Washington Carver, by Aliki. An imaginatively illustrated book which tells the inspiring story of the baby born with no hope for the future who became one of the great practical scientists of his country.

What Mary Jo Shared, by Janice May Udry, illustrated by Eleanor Mill. Mary Jo can't find a thing to share with her classmates. When she finds one grasshopper, Jimmy brings a jar full. When she thinks of her umbrella, she finds it is one of many. Finally she shares something no one else has thought of.

When I Am Old With You, by Angela Johnson, illustrated by David Soman. A little girl imagines being old with her beloved Grandaddy and joining him in such activities as playing cards all day, visiting the ocean, and eating bacon on the porch.

Whistle for Willie, by Ezra Jack Keats. Little Peter wants to be able to whistle to call his dog Willie, but he simply can't make the sound. However, practice makes perfect, so Peter eventually learns to whistle.

Wiley and the Hairy Man, by Molly Garrett Bang. A folktale from the South about a boy and his mother who live on a swamp near the Tombigbee River. To avoid the evil of the Hairy Man and get rid of him forever, the two have to trick him three times—and they do.

You're My Nikki, by Phyllis Rose Eisenberg, illustrated by Jill Kastner. Nikki needs reassurance when her mother goes out to work, and she gets it.

Africans

Akimba and the Magic Cow: An African Folktale, retold by Anne Rose, illustrated by Hope Meryman. Akimba, the poorest man in his village, is given a magic cow which gives gold coins, then a magic sheep which gives silver coins, and finally a chicken which gives eggs. Each time he leaves the animals in the care of his friend Bumba, they are stolen. How Akimba uses his magic stick to get his animals back is a very satisfying ending.

**Anancy and Mr. Dry-Bone, by Fiona French. Miss Louise is very clever and very beautiful, but she has never laughed in her whole life. So she vows to marry the first man who can make her laugh. Mr. Dry-Bone does conjuring tricks, but they don't work. Then Anancy comes along with a weird outfit, and Miss Louise makes her decision.

Anansi and the Moss-Covered Rock, retold by Eric Kimmel, illustrated by Janet Stevens. Anansi the Spider is walking through the forest when a strange moss-covered rock with magic powers catches his eye. Anansi then uses the rock to fool Lion, Elephant, Rhinoceros, Hippotamus, Giraffe, and Zebra. But little Bush Deer is not fooled and uses the rock to teach Anansi a lesson.

Anansi Goes Fishing, retold by Eric Kimmel, illustrated by Janet Stevens. Including a "pourquoi" motif showing why spiders spin webs, this folktale tells how the lazy spider Anansi is fooled by his friend Turtle into making a net to catch a fish which is then eaten by Turtle.

Anansi the Spider: A Tale from the Ashanti, adapted and illustrated by Gerald McDermott. The trickster Anansi has six good sons, each with a special talent, which each son uses to rescue Kwaku Anansi when he is in trouble. When Anansi calls upon Nyame, the God of All Things, to help him decide which son shall be rewarded with the globe of white light, Nyame decides it shall remain in the sky for all to see, and so we have the moon.

Ashanti to Zulu: African Traditions, by Margaret Musgrove, illustrated by Leo and Diane Dillon. Going through the alphabet, each page of this very beautiful book has a story about each tribe and its traditions.

Awful Aardvark, by Mwenye Hadithi, illustrated by Adrienne Kennaway. Why do aardvarks sleep all day and eat termites all night? In this "pourquoi" story we find the answer when aardvark's snoring annoys his larger fellow animals, who fail to dislodge him from his branch of a tree.

Bringing the Rain to Kapiti Plain, by Verna Aardema, illustrated by Beatriz Vidal. In rhyme and using the rhythm of "The House That Jack Built," this African folktale tells of a man who shoots an arrow into a big black cloud to end the severe drought that is causing havoc on Kapiti Plain.

Hot Hippo, by Mwenye Hadithi, illustrated by Adrienne Kennaway. An African "pourquoi" story which tells why hippos live in water during the day but come out to eat grass nightly.

Jafta, by Hugh Lewin, illustrated by Lisa Kopper. This is the first of a series about an African child who describes some of his everyday feelings by comparing his actions to those of various animals.

Jambo Means Hello: A Swahili Alphabet Book, by Muriel Feelings, illustrated by Tom Feelings. Each letter of the alphabet is the first letter of a Swahili word (with phonetic pronunciation in parenthesis), and each word is illustrated. For example, "R—rafiki (rah fee key), which means friend. Friends do chores together."

Moja Means One: A Swahili Counting Book, by Muriel Feelings, illustrated by Tom Feelings. Each number is illustrated by a Swahili word, with phonetic pronunciation and pictured explanation.

Mufaro's Beautiful Daughters: An African Folktale, told and illustrated by John Steptoe. Inspired by an African story collection of 1895, this book illustrates kindness rewarded, greed and pride punished, when two sisters travel to the court of their king, who is searching for a worthy bride.

**Shadow,* by Blaise Cendars, translated and illustrated by Marcia Brown. A strange and somewhat frightening book based on African tales about one's shadow. Not for the very young child.

A Story, A Story: An African Tale, retold and illustrated by Gail E. Haley. This Spider Man or Ananse story tells how Ananse fulfills the requirements of the sky god in order to earn the god's golden box filled with stories and bring it back to earth, scattering the stories everywhere.

Two Ways to Count to Ten: A Liberian Folktale, retold by Ruby Dee, illustrated by Susan Meddaugh. King Leopard decides to test all the other animals to see who will succeed him. The one who throws the king's spear into the air and counts to ten before it comes down shall win. How the clever antelope wins makes a delightful story.

The Village of Round and Square Houses, by Ann Grifalconi. A grandmother explains to her listeners why in their village on the side of a volcano (in the remote hills of the Cameroons in Central Africa) the men live in square houses and the women live in round ones.

We Hide, You Seek, by Jose Aruego and Ariane Dewey. Poor, clumsy Rhino always manages to find the other animals because his bumbling behavior startles them into revealing themselves. Then they have to look for him. Whimsical illustrations of animals from Kenya, featuring camouflage.

Who's in Rabbit's House?: A Masai Tale, retold by Verna Aardema, illustrated by Leo and Diane Dillon. Written as though it were a staged play, with masks to show various emotions, this tale tells of a rabbit who cannot get into his house because "the long one" has taken possession of it. Finally, after threatening other animals, the "ferocious creature" opens the door. He is only a caterpillar.

Why Mosquitoes Buzz in People's Ears: A West African Tale, retold by Verna Aardema, illustrated by Diane Dillon. Children enjoy the sequential repetition in this beautifully illustrated "pourquoi" story.

Why the Sun and the Moon Are in the Sky: An African Folktale, by Elphinstone Dayrell, illustrated by Blair Lent. When the water comes to visit the sun and the moon in their house, it fills the house to overflowing and so forces the hosts to go up into the sky, where they remain to the present.

Asian Americans

Angel Child, Dragon Child, by Michelle Maria Surat, illustrated by Vo-Dinh Mai. Ut, a little Vietnamese girl attending school in the United States, is very lonely for her mother, who is still in Vietnam and finds it difficult to adjust. But an "enemy" becomes a friend, and all ends happily.

Chang's Paper Pony, by Eleanor Coerr, illustrated by Deborah Kogan Ray. In San Francisco during the 1850s Gold Rush, Chang, the son of Chinese immigrants, wants a pony but cannot afford one until his friend Big Pete finds a solution.

Gung Hay Fat Choy, by June Behrens. This book with the aid of authentic photographs explains the Chinese New Year and describes its celebration by Chinese Americans.

**I Hate English!, by Ellen Levine, illustrated by Steve Bjorkman. When her family moves to New York from Hong Kong, Mei Mei finds it difficult to adjust to school and the sounds of English until her teacher, Nancy, tries a new tactic.

How My Parents Learned to Eat, by Ina R. Friedman, illustrated by Allen Say. An American sailor courts a Japanese girl and each tries, in secret, to learn the other's way of eating. They succeed and the little girl says her parents now use chopsticks some days and knives, forks, and spoons at other times.

Lion Dancer: Ernie Wan's Chinese New Year, by Kate Waters and Madeline Slovenz-Low, illustrated by Martha Cooper. Ernie Wan is six and this is to be his first year to dance in the lion costume at Chinese New Year. This book explains many customs associated with this holiday.

Momo's Kitten, by Mitsu and Taro Yashima. The little kitten is now a grown cat with babies of her own, each a distinct individual. Momo enjoys seeing them develop and grow.

Umbrella, by Taro Yashima. Momo is impatient for the rain to come, and she is delighted when she can finally carry her umbrella to nursery school and walk home without holding either her mother or her father's hand.

Asians

***The Chinese Mirror,* adapted from a Korean folktale by Mirra Ginsburg, illustrated by Margot Zemach. A villager returns home from a voyage to China with a strange treasure which he keeps in his trunk—a mirror. When his family discovers it, there is wild confusion as each person sees a different stranger peering out.

Cherry Tree, by Ruskin Bond, illustrated by Allan Eitzen. A story from India in which Rakhi, a six-year-old girl, heeds her grandfather's advice and plants the seed of a cherry which survives many mishaps and grows into a lovely tree.

***Crow Boy,* by Taro Yashima. A very tender story of an unusual boy, Chibi, who seems to be slower than other children in his school, but who has a very special talent.

The Empty Pot, by Demi. A charming tale of Ping, a small Chinese boy whose honesty is rewarded by the emperor.

Everyone Knows What a Dragon Looks Like, by Jay Williams, illustrated by Mercer Mayer. The poor boy Han is courteous to the little rotund man who claims to be the dragon come to save the city of Wu from the Wild Horsemen who are threatening. No one else treats him well, but he saves the city anyway for Han's sake. Then he turns into a traditional dragon.

The Funny Little Woman, retold by Arlene Mosel, illustrated by Blair Lent. This Japanese folktale begins with the funny little woman chasing her rice dumpling, reminding the reader of the gingerbread boy who ran away. However, in this story the woman is captured by the evil Oni, who make her cook for them until she escapes, returns home, and cooks rice dumplings with the Oni's magic paddle, becoming the richest woman in Japan.

In a Spring Garden, edited by Richard Lewis, illustrated by Ezra Jack Keats. Haiku verses glorify spring flowers and small animals in the garden.

***The Jade Stone: A Chinese Folktale,* adapted by Caryn Yacowitz, illustrated by Ju-Hong Chen. When the Great Emperor of All China commands him to carve a Dragon of Wind and Fire in a piece of perfect jade, Chan Lo discovers the stone wants to be something else. He braves the displeasure of the emperor by carving what he "hears" from the jade, and almost loses his life.

Lon Po Po, translated from the Chinese and illustrated by Ed Young. In this version of Little Red Riding Hood, it is the mother who goes to visit the grandmother, leaving her three daughters at home to be visited by the wolf who gets into their house by pretending to be Grandma. The eldest girl, however, out-smarts the wolf and saves them all.

Momotaro the Peach Boy: A Japanese Tale, retold and illustrated by Linda Shute. The kind and courageous peach boy, with his dog, his monkey, and his pheasant, beats the wicked Oni and brings back all the silver and gold which the Oni had taken from the poor peasants.

The Monkey and the Crocodile: A Jataka Tale from India, illustrated by Paul Galdone. In the conflict between the monkey and the crocodile who wants to eat him, the monkey outwits the greedy predator.

**The Moon Lady,* by Amy Tan, illustrated by Gretchen Schields. Nai-Nai tells her granddaughters the story of her outing as a seven-year-old in China to see the Moon Lady and being granted a secret wish.

Once a Mouse, by Marcia Brown. An Indian fable illustrates the consequences of conceit as an old hermit with magic powers changes a mouse to a cat, then to a dog, and finally to a tiger—each time to save the mouse from harm. When the tiger threatens to kill the old hermit, he is turned back into a mouse.

**Our Home Is the Sea,* by Ricki Levinson, illustrated by Dennis Luzak. A Chinese boy hurries home from school to his family's houseboat in Hong Kong's harbor. He is very anxious to get back to the sea with his father and grandfather and wishes to remain on the sea for the rest of his life.

Peach Boy, by William H. Hooks, illustrated by June Otani. Found floating on the river inside a peach, Momotaro is a blessing to his childless parents. Then when he is grown, he sets out to rid the village of the evil Oni monsters, and with the help of a dog, a monkey, and a hawk, Momotaro succeeds.

Red Dragon Fly on My Shoulder, translated by Sylvia Cassedy and Kunihiro Suetake, illustrated by Molly Bang. An unusual collection of Haiku poetry with marvelous illustrations.

**Silent Lotus,* by Jeanne M. Lee. Lotus, who is born deaf, cannot speak, and she is a lonely child, playing only with the herons, cranes, and white egrets. Her parents take her to the palace in Khmer kingdom, and she learns to dance so well that she becomes the most famous dancer in the court. Gorgeous illustrations.

**The Stonecutter: A Japanese Folktale,* by Gerald McDermott. When the stonecutter gets his wish to become first the prince, then the sun, the cloud, and ultimately the mountain, he must fear the stonecutter chiseling away at his base.

The Story About Ping, by Marjorie Flack, illustrated by Kurt Wiese. Ping and his family, who live on a Yangtze River boat, go ashore each day to hunt for snails. But when the master calls, they must return, and Ping is always late. To avoid being last back on board, Ping decides to hide, but finds life alone is quite dangerous for a small duck and returns to his family.

**Toad Is the Uncle of Heaven: A Vietnamese Folktale,* retold and illustrated by Jeanne M. Lee. In Vietnam, "Uncle" is a term of respect, and this folktale explains how the toad earns that title when all the animals on earth are dying from a drought. The toad leads the bees, rooster, and a tiger to beg the King of Heaven for rain, which he grants, so when Uncle Toad croaks, it is a sign of rain for the Vietnamese.

Three Strong Women: A Tall Tale from Japan, by Claus Stamm, illustrated by Jean and Mou-sein Tseng. Forever-Mountain is the best sumo wrestler in Japan, but he learns what real strength is when he meets Maru-me, her mother, and her grandmother. Stunningly illustrated with authentically detailed landscapes.

Tikki Tikki Tembo, retold by Arlene Mosel, illustrated by Blair Lent. A delightful "explanation" for the Chinese custom of giving their children short names and a subtle reprimand to parents who show favoritism to one child over another.

The Wave, adapted from Lafcadio Hearn's *Gleaning in Budda-Fields* by Margaret Hodges, illustrated by Blair Lent. In this Japanese folktale Ojiisan, the grandfather who lives at the top of the mountain with his grandson Tada, burns his rice field in order to get the attention of four hundred villagers who live near the shore, so that they may escape the tidal wave which will wreck their little village.

Why Rat Comes First: A Story of the Chinese Zodiac, by Clara Yen, illustrated by Hideo C. Yoshida. When the Jade King calls all the animals to heaven, twelve come, so there is a twelve-year cycle of years. The Jade King decides to let earthly children decide which animal will be first, and in a contest between the ox and the rat, through cleverness the rat wins.

Yeh-Shen, retold by Ai-Ling Louie, illustrated by Ed Young. This unique version of the Cinderella story dates back to tenth-century China, so that it is of historic interest, as well as being an exquisite book on its own.

Latinos

Abuela, by Arthur Dorros, illustrated by Elisa Kleven. While riding on a bus with her Spanish-speaking grandmother, a little girl imagines that they are flying over New York City, seeing the sights. A glossary is at the end of the book.

All of You Was Singing, by Richard Lewis, illustrated by Ed Young. An Aztec myth told lyrically about the world's creation and the advent of music.

And Sunday Makes Seven, by Robert Baden, illustrated by Michelle Edwards. Carlos and Ana are poor, but happy; cousin Ricardo is rich, but selfish. When Carlos makes a rhyme about the days of the week, he is richly rewarded by twelve witches, but Ricardo is punished when he tries to do the same thing. A tale from Costa Rica.

**Atariba and Niguayona,* adapted by Harriet Rohmer and Jesus Guerrero Rea, illustrated by Consuelo Mendez Castillo. With both Spanish and English on each page, this is a legend of a miraculous cure from the native people of Puerto Rico.

A Birthday Basket for Tia, by Pat Mora, illustrated by Cecily Lang. Cecilia and her cat Chica prepare a special surprise for Tia's ninetieth birthday. In the basket Cecilia puts all the special things she shares with her great-aunt.

Borreguita and the Coyote, by Verna Aardema, illustrated by Petra Mathers. A Mexican folktale which tells how a clever little lamb repeatedly outwits the coyote who plans to eat her.

Diego, by Jonah Winter, translated by Amy Prince, illustrated by Jeanette Winter. In both Spanish and English this book describes the childhood and youth in Paris of Diego Rivera and explains how his experiences influenced his art.

***The Flame of Peace: A Tale of the Aztecs,* by Deborah Nourse Lattimore. To prevent the outbreak of war, a young Aztec boy, Two Flint, must outwit nine evil lords of the night to obtain the Flame of Peace from Lord Morning Star. He succeeds, and a great Alliance of Cities marks the beginning of many peaceful decades.

Friday Night Is Papa Night, by Ruth Sonneborn, illustrated by Emily A. McCully. Papa must have two jobs so that he can take care of his family, but he is able to come home on Friday nights. Mama, Manuela, Carlos, and Ricardo all wait patiently when Papa does not come by dark. But it is Pedro, the youngest child, who lights up the kitchen and greets his father.

Gilberto and the Wind, by Marie Hall Ets. A little boy personifies the wind as he plays with it.

How the Birds Changed Their Feathers: A South American Indian Folktale, by Joanna Troughton. In the "pourquoi" tradition this brightly colored book explains how all birds which were completely white in the beginning became so richly colored.

***How We Came to the Fifth World,* adapted by Harriet Rohmer and Mary Anchondo, illustrated by Graciela Carrillo. This book tells an Aztec creation story, using both English and Spanish on each page. Each of the worlds is ruled and then eventually destroyed by gods of the four elements—water, air, fire, and earth—because of evil in the hearts of the people.

I Speak English for My Mom, by Muriel Stanek, illustrated by Judith Friedman. A Mexican widow and her young daughter share life, with the child translating for her mom. Then the woman decides that to get a better job she has to learn English and starts night school.

Jo, Flo and Yolanda, by Carol De Poix. In this subtle picture of a warm, loving Puerto-Rican family living in New York, each of the triplets has her own dream for the future.

The Legend of Food Mountain, adapted by Harriet Rohmer, illustrated by Graciela Carrillo. With very colorful illustrations and both Spanish and English on each page, we learn the legend of how the great god Quetzalcoatl solved the problem of how to feed his people when the great red ant brought corn, but not before he tamed the rain god Tialoc.

Nine Days to Christmas: A Story of Mexico, by Marie Hall Ets and Aurora Labastida, illustrated by Marie Hall Ets. Ceci, a kindergarten-aged child, is waiting for the *posada,* the Mexican Christmas party at which she will have her first *piñata.* She selects a star and is sad when it is broken. Then she looks to the sky and sees a real star.

On the Pampas, by Maria Cristina Brusca. A personal account of the author's summer spent with her grandparents at the Argentine equivalent of a ranch. Life is very different from her world in Buenos Aires, but she learns a lot and loves it.

Perez y Martina: A Puerto Rican Folktale, by Pura Belpre, illustrated by Carlos Sanchez. Martina, a beautiful cockroach, is sought by many animals, but chooses Perez, a debonair mouse.

Rosa and Marco and the Three Wishes, by Barbara Brenner, illustrated by Megan Halsey. A magical fish grants the traditional three wishes to a boy and girl who are fishing. They waste them in comical fashion.

Tortillitas Para Mama and Other Nursery Rhymes, translated by Margot Griego, Betsy L. Bucks, Sharon S. Gilbert, and Laurel H. Kimball, illustrated by Barbara Cooney. A traditional collection of Latin-American nursery rhymes, preserved through the oral tradition. Both Spanish and English on every page.

Uncle Nacho's Hat, adapted by Harriet Rohmer, illustrated by Veg Reisberg. This simple Nicaraguan folktale tells of a lovable old man who tries without success to get rid of his old hat after his niece has bought him a new one. It is a metaphor for all the bad habits he cannot discard until he changes his way of thinking. Spanish and English on each page.

Native Americans

***Annie and the Old One,* by Miska Miles, illustrated by Peter Parnall. In this Navajo family Annie and her grandmother have a very special relationship, so the child tries very hard to avoid the fact that her grandmother will die. She tries to hold back time, but then her grandmother explains the idea of life as a cycle, and Annie takes up her weaving stick again.

Arrow to the Sun: A Pueblo Indian Tale, retold and illustrated by Gerald McDermott. A Native-American version of Christ's birth and rebirth as Boy, child of the Lord of the Sun.

Baby Rattlesnake: An Indian Tale, adapted by Lynn Moroney, illustrated by Veg Reisberg. Willful Baby Rattlesnake throws tantrums because he wants a rattle before he's ready, and he misuses it, learning a valuable lesson.

Corn Is Maize: The Gift of the Indians, by Aliki. This is a simple description of how corn was discovered and used by the Indians, and how it came to be an important food throughout the world.

Crow Chief, by Paul L. Goble. An Indian legend and also a "pourquoi" story of why crows, which were originally white, are now black. It is a punishment for warning the buffalo so that they could not be caught by the Plains Indian hunters who needed them to survive.

The Desert Is Theirs, by Byrd Baylor, illustrated by Peter Parnall. In poetic terms the author speaks of the Papago Indians, a desert people, and the various animals with which they share this very special kind of environment.

Dragonfly's Tale, by Kristina Rodanas. The people waste food and stage a mock battle with it to show off to their neighbors, but the Corn Maidens, disguised as old beggar women, see what is going on and punish the tribe with poor harvests. Then two Ashivi children must regain the blessings of the Maidens, which they do with the aid of a cornstalk toy, a dragonfly.

Dreamcatcher, by Audrey Osofsky, illustrated by Ed Young. A story of the Ojibway Indians of the Great Lakes, who put great store in dreams. There is a dream net to catch the bad dreams so that only the good dreams get through to the sleeping infant. Illustrated with dreamlike pastels.

Everybody Needs a Rock, by Byrd Baylor, illustrated by Peter Parnall. Ten rules for selecting that special rock which will fit in your hand, jingle in your pocket, and become a treasure.

***The Girl Who Loved Wild Horses,* by Paul Goble. Though this Indian girl loves her family, she prefers to live with the wild horses, and Sioux tradition holds that she becomes one of them.

The Goat in the Rug, by Charles L. Blood and Martin Link, illustrated by Nancy Winslow Parker. Geraldine, a goat, describes each step as she and her Navajo friend make a traditional Navajo rug from her hair. The book shows the process from clipping the hair to carding, dyeing, and actually weaving the finished product.

***Hiawatha,* by Henry Wadsworth Longfellow, illustrated by Susan Jeffers. This lavishly illustrated book concentrates on the boyhood of the Indian's life, from his birth through adolescence.

In My Mother's House, by Ann Nolan Clark, illustrated by Velino Herrara. In this reissued classic, the Tewa children of Tesuque Pueblo, near Santa Fe, share poetry about their world. We see the pueblo, the people, fire, fields, water, land, and animals, strung together like beads.

***Knots on the Counting Rope,* by Bill Martin, Jr., and John Archambault, illustrated by Ted Rand. On a cool dark night under the stars, an Indian boy sits with his grandfather before a campfire. "Tell me who I am, Grandfather," pleads the boy, and the old man does. The counting rope is a metaphor for the passage of time and for the boy's emerging confidence in facing the challenge of his blindness. A moving and poignant story.

The Legend of the Indian Paintbrush, retold and illustrated by Tomie De Paola. A dramatically told story of a young Indian boy's Dream-Vision, which when realized results in a magnificent painting of the sunset and the wildflowers called Indian Paintbrush that still cover the hills of Wyoming every spring.

Little Runner of the Longhouse, by Betty Baker, illustrated by Arnold Lobel. A charming story of a little boy and his participation in the New Year celebration of his Iroquois family.

Red Fox and His Canoe, by Nathaniel Benchley, illustrated by Arnold Lobel. Red Fox catches a lot of fish, but uninvited bears join the party. Then some otters come, and a raccoon, but when the moose gets in, the canoe breaks, leaving Red Fox only the front and back which he ties together to get home.

***The Rough-Face Girl,* by Rafe Martin, illustrated by David Shannon. This is the Algonquin version of the Cinderella story, where the heroine and her two beautiful but heartless sisters compete for the affections of the Invisible

Being. Here the wise sister of the Invisible Being replaces the Fairy Godmother, seeing the inner beauty of the rough-face girl.

Small Wolf, by Nathaniel Benchley, illustrated by Joan Sandin. A little Indian boy discovers that settlers have taken over Manhattan, and ultimately learns that the interlopers feel they now own the land, pushing the Indians farther and farther away from their native habitats.

Eskimos

***Nessa's Fish,* by Nancy Luenn, illustrated by Neil Waldmann. Nessa, a brave Eskimo girl, goes fishing with her grandmother, who becomes ill during the night. This leaves Nessa with the responsibility of watching over the woman and also frightening away the animal poachers who try to get the fish. She succeeds, but is glad to see her family in the morning.

On Mother's Lap, by Ann Herbert Scott, illustrated by Glo Coalson. There are two versions of this book—one in sepia tones, the other in soft colors. Both tell the story of little Michael who brings all his toys and his puppy to share mother's lap with him and his new baby sister. There is always room on mother's lap.

Very Last First Time, by Jan Andrews, illustrated by Ian Wallace. A most unusual story of an Inuit family on Ungava Bay in northern Canada. Eva, a young child, has always accompanied her mother in their walks on the bottom of the seabed. This day she goes alone searching for mussels, and almost comes to grief when her candle goes out and the tide starts to come in.

Cajuns

Cajun Alphabet, by James Rice. Cajun *patois* is most interesting, combining as it does English and French. The author-illustrator makes this book very entertaining and quite unusual with Gaston, the green alligator, leading the reader through the alphabet. To give the reader an idea of the humor, it begins with Gaston deciding he wants to go to a university, and since he can't find a football uniform to fit, he might as well learn the alphabet.

Other Cajun books by the same author include: *Gaston, the Green-Nosed Alligator; Cajun Columbus; Gaston Goes to the Mardi Gras;* and as illustrator, *Cajun Night Before Christmas.*

Bilingual Books (English and Spanish)

ABC . . . Z, illustrated by Robert Tallon. A bilingual book which has each letter humorously illustrated by the appropriate word in both languages.

Are You My Mother?, by P. D. Eastman. The little bird that has fallen out of the nest asks everybody and everything thing he meets the same question in two languages until he is back in the nest with his mother again.

Arroz Con Leche: Popular Songs and Rhymes from Latin America, selected and illustrated by Lulu Delacre. With Spanish and English on each page, and suggestions for activities as songs are sung, this colorful book has verses and music from Mexico, Argentina, and Puerto Rico.

**Atariba and Niguayona,* adapted by Harriet Rohmer and Jesus Guerrero Rea, illustrated by Consuelo Mendez Castillo. Here is a legend of a miraculous cure from the native people of Puerto Rico. Both languages on every page.

The Cat in the Hat, by Dr. Seuss. In Spanish and English the cat manages to divert the children with every kind of prank until their mother returns, before which the cat has managed to tidy everything up beautifully.

Diego, by Jonah Winter, translated by Amy Prince, illustrated by Jeanette Winter. The childhood and youth in Paris of Diego Rivera is beautifully shown here in both languages, with reference to how Diego's experiences influenced his art.

**How We Came to the Fifth World,* adapted by Harriet Rohmer and Mary Anchondo, illustrated by Graciela Carrillo. This book tells an Aztec creation story, using both English and Spanish throughout. Each of the worlds is ruled and eventually destroyed by gods of the four elements—water, air, fire, and earth—because of the evil in the hearts of the people.

**The Legend of Food Mountain,* adapted by Harriet Rohmer, illustrated by Graciela Carrillo. With very colorful illustrations and both Spanish and English on each page, we learn the legend of how the great god Quetzalcoatl solved the problem of how to feed his people when the great red ant brought corn, but not before he tamed the rain god Tialoc.

My Mother and I Are Growing Strong, by Inez Maury, translated by Anna Munoz, illustrated by Sandy Speidel. A bilingual story of a family whose father is in prison for hitting someone who had insulted him. Emilita and her mother bravely carry on the father's gardening route alone.

My Mother the Mail Carrier, by Inez Maury, translated by Norah Allemany, illustrated by Lady McCrady. A little girl tells about her mother's life as a mail carrier and describes their warm relationship. In both Spanish and English.

Poemas: Very Very Short Poems, by Ernesto Galarza. A bilingual book illustrated on each page with photographs.

The Tamarindo Puppy and Other Poems, by Charlotte Pomerantz, illustrated by Byron Barton. An illustrated collection of thirteen poems with a sprinkling of Spanish throughout.

Tortillitas Para Mama and Other Nursery Rhymes, translated by Margot Griego, Betsy L. Bucks, Sharon S. Gilbert, and Laurel H. Kimball, illustrated by Barbara Cooney. A traditional collection of Latin-American nursery rhymes, preserved through oral tradition. Both Spanish and English on every page.

Uncle Nacho's Hat, adapted by Harriet Rohmer, illustrated by Veg Reisberg. This simple Nicaraguan folktale tells of a lovable old man who tries without success to get rid of his old hat after his niece has bought him a new one. It is a metaphor for all the bad habits he cannot discard until he changes his way of thinking. Spanish and English on each page.

Other Books Too Good to Miss

If the reader goes through every category, he will find titles listed once, twice, or even three times simply because those books have particular qualities that deserve to be highlighted. On the other hand, there are some books which do not fit neatly into one category or another; still, they are excellent.

Aaron's Shirt, by Deborah Gould, illustrated by Cheryl Harness. Aaron finds a shirt that suits him very well, indeed, so well that no matter what happens to it, he won't give it up. Faced with being too big to wear it, Aaron solves the problem with the help of his brown teddy bear.

The Adventures of Albert, the Running Bear, by Barbara Isenberg and Susan Wolf, illustrated by Dick Gackenbach. Albert, a circus bear, finds himself in the zoo performing for the public in return for snacks which make him fat. When the snacks stop, Albert escapes and then finds himself the winner of a marathon; he returns to the zoo, but runs daily on a special track, with an audience, of course.

Albert's Toothache, by Barbara Williams, illustrated by Kay Chorao. No one will believe that Albert Turtle has a toothache because turtles don't have teeth. Then his wise grandmother figures it out and all is well.

Alistair's Elephant, by Marilyn Sadler, illustrated by Roger Bollen. Alistair Grittle is an unusual ten-year-old. He's very neat, does his homework, and plays games that exercise his mind. However, his life changes radically when an elephant follows him home from the zoo.

Alistair's Time Machine, by Marilyn Sadler, illustrated by Roger Bollen. When Alistair builds a time machine as his entry for the school science competition, he takes on more than he bargains for. He has some strange encounters in past eras, even saving cave people from the woolly mammoths, but the judges don't believe his contraption works.

All Falling Down, by Gene Zion, illustrated by Margaret Bloy Graham. In terms children can understand, the principle of gravity is shown to apply through ordinary happenings, such as flower petals and leaves that fall, snow that falls, and so on. The child doesn't fall when tossed into the air because his daddy catches him in his arms.

Aminal, by Lorna Balian. Little Patrick finds an "aminal" and takes it home, but as gossip about it spreads, it becomes a wild, dangerous thing which could be frightening to children. Then Patrick shows his "aminal" to his friends, and they are surprised.

Babar the King, by Jean De Brunhoff. The story of the famous elephant and his family continues with all the friends who live in Celesteville, including the little monkey Zephir, who is always into mischief.

**** *The Bear Who Loved Puccini,* by Arnold Sundgaard, illustrated by Dominic Catalano. An interesting mixture of a personified bear named Barefoot, who becomes an opera singer at La Scala, and his interaction with humans who become an adoring audience. Tongue-in-cheek humor?

Bearymore, by Don Freeman. Bearymore, a performing circus bear, has trouble hibernating and working up a new act at the same time, but when he wakes up in April, he must get his unicycle out of the rain, which gives him a great idea for a brand new act.

Cassandra Who?, by Iris Hiskey, illustrated by Normand Chartier. When Casandra the cat gets a mysterious invitation to a costume party, she makes a costume and goes as a pig. Then the real pig, Cassandra, enters. But the confusion is cleared up, and everyone has a good time.

Crictor, by Tomi Ungerer. When Madame Louise Bodot's son, who is studying reptiles in Africa, sends her a boa constrictor as a birthday gift, she calls him Crictor and raises him like a child. He repays her kindness.

Cowardly Clyde, by Bill Peet. Set in the days of knights in armor, Sir Galavant rides a horse, Clyde, an abysmal coward. Eventually he decides to act as though he's brave, after scaring off an owl-eyed monster who can't stand the sunlight.

A Dark Dark Tale, by Ruth Brown. Journeying through the dark, dark house, a black cat surprises the only inhabitant. A scary book with a great ending.

Dibble and Dabble, by Dave Saunders. Two white ducks swimming in the river think they sight a furry snake, and they warn all their animal friends, but Pete, a young boy, shows them it's only the tail of Tiger the cat.

Doctor DeSoto, by William Steig. Dr. DeSoto, a mouse dentist, and his wife treat all kinds of animals, except cats and others who are dangerous to mice. They do agree, however, to treat a fox, and they almost regret it, but the fox is outfoxed in the end.

Dragon for Breakfast, by Eunice and Nigel McMullen. Much to his surprise, King Ulf's breakfast egg contains a small dragon who grows up to be a friendly nuisance until the king can find a special job for it.

Earrings!, by Judith Viorst, illustrated by Nola Langner Malone. A young girl tries everything she can think of to convince her parents to allow her to have her ears pierced, but nothing she says or promises works. She will have to wait!

The Escape of Marvin the Ape, by Caralyn and Mark Buehner. When it's feeding time at the zoo, Marvin leaves and finds that life in the big city suits him perfectly. He fits right in.

A Fish for Mrs. Gardenia, by Yossi Abolafia. A series of haphazard events threaten to spoil Mr. Bennett's dinner with Mrs. Gardenia after his fish disappears from the outside grill, but a final accident returns the fish to its rightful place.

Fish Is Fish, by Leo Lionni. When his friend the tadpole becomes a frog and leaves the pond to explore the world, the little minnow decides that maybe he doesn't have to remain in the pond either.

The 500 Hats of Bartholomew Cubbins, by Dr. Seuss. King Darwin is a very proud king whose anger grows when Bartholomew Cubbins does not doff his hat as the king passes. The poor boy thinks his hat is off, but it is replaced again and again—magically—until the five-hundredth hat intrigues the monarch, who buys it for five hundred pieces of gold.

***The Great Round-the-World Balloon Race,* by Sue Scullard. Aunt Harriet takes her niece Rebecca and her nephew William on a hot-air balloon race, and finally parachutes out so that with a lighter load the two children can guide Firebreather into Paris to win the competition.

The Great White Man-Eating Shark: A Cautionary Tale, by Margaret Mahy, illustrated by Jonathan Allen. Marvin has just two talents: swimming and acting. In order to have the ocean for himself, he makes a dorsal fin, straps it on his back, and scares people who think it is a shark. They then leave the water hastily. But one day he meets a real shark and. . . .

***The Heart of the Wood,* by Marguerite W. Davol, illustrated by Sheila Hamanaka. A cumulative tale in which a tree in Winderly Woods that is home to a singing mockingbird continues to be a source of music after it has gone through all the processes necessary to become a violin. Magnificent illustrations and rhymed text.

Hedgehog for Breakfast, by Ann Turner, illustrated by Lisa McCue. A misunderstanding of Papa's request, "I'd like to have Mrs. Hedgehog for breakfast," almost results in tragedy, but Papa and Mama come home in time to show their children what it means to have a guest share a meal.

The House at Pooh Corner, by A. A. Milne, illustrated by Ernest H. Shepard. Adventures continue in the Hundred Acre Wood where all of Christopher Robin's friends live, with Pooh continuing his little songs. Whatever happens it will always remain the enchanted place where a little boy and his bear will be playing.

A House for Hermit Crab, by Eric Carle. Hermit Crab finds a shell and decorates it with the help of other sea animals. Then when it becomes too small, he lets another hermit crab take over, and he moves along, seeking a larger shell.

The House on East 88th Street, by Bernard Waber. When the Primm family moves into their house, they discover an added member of the family, Lyle, a domesticated crocodile, left by Hector P. Valenti, his trainer.

How Droofus the Dragon Lost His Head, by Bill Peet. Droofus is a baby dragon, separated from his group, who grows up to be a gentle herbivore. He helps a farm family, but almost loses his head when the king wants it to mount on the castle wall. However, a happy compromise is reached in time for April 8, the day of the Grand Spring Festival.

Hubert's Hair-Raising Adventure, by Bill Peet. Vain Hubert the lion accidentally burns off his beautiful mane. Only his friend the elephant is willing to go after a cure—crocodile tears. The problem is that the mane keeps on growing until Barber Baboon must cut it to free the animals which have become entwined.

If You Give a Mouse a Cookie, by Laura Joffe Numeroff, illustrated by Felicia Bond. Relating a cycle of requests a mouse is liable to make if you give him a cookie takes the reader through a day in the life of an average small boy.

Inch by Inch, by Leo Lionni. A hungry robin decides to eat an inchworm, but the inchworm explains to the bird how he measures things, so the robin takes the worm to measure other birds. When the nightingale wants him to measure his song, the worm inches out of sight, right off the page.

***Island Child,* by Lisa Wallis, illustrated by Deborah Haeffele. A quiet book of reminiscences about growing up on Nantucket Island and hoping to live there as an adult woman.

It's So Nice to Have a Wolf Around the House, by Harry Allard, illustrated by James Marshall. The man and his pets, Peppy, Ginger, and Lightning, are all very old and tired, so they hire a companion, Cuthbert O. Devine, who turns out to be a wolf. But he is so wonderful that even after they discover his true identity, they keep him, and even move to Arizona for Cuthbert's health.

Johnny Crow's Garden, by Leslie Brooke. A charming, somewhat quaint and comic rhyme about animals in Johnny Crow's garden, drawn as only Brooke can.

Johnny Crow's Party, by Leslie Brooke. Johnny Crow has all his animal friends to a party, with rhyme and wonderful drawings.

Just Plain Fancy, by Patricia Polacco. Naomi, an Amish girl whose elders have impressed upon her the importance of adhering to the simple ways of her people, is horrified when one of her hen's eggs hatches into an extremely fancy bird.

Kermit the Hermit, by Bill Peet. In sprightly verse we read about Kermit, who was a real crab and a miser too. But when a young boy saves him from being buried alive, Kermit rewards him and his impoverished family handsomely.

The Little House, by Virginia Lee Burton. At the beginning the little house is alone in the country; then as the city encroaches, she finds herself lost between two big buildings. When the great-great-granddaughter of the original owner rescues her, she is brought back to the country and restored.

Little Rabbit's Loose Tooth, by Lucy Bate, illustrated by Diane DeGroat. When Little Rabbit's loose tooth finally comes out, she is not convinced that the tooth fairy will really come.

Love from Aunt Betty, by Nancy Winslow Parker. Aunt Betty sends Charlie an old Transylvanian gypsy recipe for chocolate fudge cake which calls for cobwebs and dried Carpathian tree toad flakes. It had been Uncle Clyde's favorite.

Lyle Finds His Mother, by Bernard Waber. Lyle is a very contented crocodile living with the Primm family in the house on East 88th Street, but he falls for the trick which Hector P. Valenti plays on him and agrees to go back to performing with Hector to earn money to travel to see his mother. Big surprise! He finds her and brings her back to the Primms with him.

Lyle, Lyle, Crocodile, by Bernard Waber. Lyle, a lovable crocodile, is very happy in his home on East 88th Street with the Primm family. But Mr. Grumps, who lives next door with his cat Loretta, wants to get rid of Lyle. Everything turns out fine when Lyle saves Mr. Grumps and Loretta from a fire.

Maggie and the Pirate, by Ezra Jack Keats. A rather touching story of Maggie, a little girl whose pet cricket Niki is stolen by a "pirate" who really wants only the cage. How Maggie and her friends solve the mystery makes a satisfying ending.

Magic in the Mist, by Margaret Mary Kimmel, illustrated by Tina Schart Hyman. Thomas is a lonely Welsh boy whose home is a rude hut at the edge of a bog, not far from the sea, and his only company is a toad named Jeremy. Thomas tries unsuccessfully to make magic. Then one day. . . .

Martha the Movie Mouse, by Arnold Lobel. In rhymed verse the author tells about Martha, who finds sanctuary with Dan, the kind projectionist in a movie theater. In the end she is able to repay Dan by entertaining the patrons when the projector won't work.

McElligot's Pool, by Dr. Seuss. In his inimitable rhyme we learn why there's everything in the pool from whales to A THING-A-MA-JIGGER, which is why the boy keeps on fishing there.

Milton the Early Riser, by Robert Kraus, illustrated by Jose Aruego and Ariane Dewey. Milton, a panda, can't get anyone to wake up as early as he does. Even a whirlwind that rearranges everyone doesn't awaken them. So Milton puts them all back where they belong before they wake up, which makes him very tired.

Mr. McMouse, by Leo Lionni. Timothy is surprised one day to find he is dressed like a man, so is taken for one by his fellow mice. He can't pass all their tests, but he does prove his identity when he helps his friend Spinney escape from the cat.

The Moon Jumpers, by Janice May Udry, illustrated by Maurice Sendak. A fanciful look at children who, when the moon comes out, turn into moon jumpers.

Olive and the Magic Hat, by Ellen Christelow. Playing with their father's hat, his birthday present, Olive and Otis Opossum accidentally drop it on Mr. Foxley, who is convinced it is magic. Olive and Otis think of a way to get it back—without magic.

***The Paper Crane,* by Molly Bang. The highway has moved and the restaurant has no customers until a poor stranger enters, is fed, and pays his bill with a paper napkin which turns into a dancing crane.

***The Philharmonic Gets Dressed,* by Karla Kuskin, illustrated by Marc Simont. A really unusual and delightful book showing how the 105 members of the philharmonic orchestra get ready to perform.

The Popcorn Book, by Tomie De Paola. As two little boys make popcorn, one boy reads facts about its history, while the other one prepares the treat. Two great recipes at the end.

Rain Makes Applesauce, by Julian Scheer, illustrated by Marvin Billeck. This is a book of silly talk, using fanciful nonsense combined with intricate pictures, full of sly subtleties and happy surprises.

The Robbery at the Diamond Dog Diner, by Eileen Christelow. Glenda Feathers has a great idea to save the diamonds that Lois always wears to work at her diner. But Glenda talks too much, so the robbers almost get away with their heist.

The Rose in My Garden, by Arnold Lobel, illustrated by Anita Lobel. A lovely rhythmic description of a variety of flowers that surrounds one rose which has a bee sleeping in it until a cat chases a fieldmouse and disturbs the flowers and the bee.

Samuel Todd's Book of Great Inventions, by E. L. Konigsburg. The boy Samuel has interesting ideas of what are important inventions: a mirror, belt loops, velcro, backpacks, and other really important things, like potatoes that are French fried—so they named a whole country after them.

Song of the Swallows, by Leo Politi. On March 19 every year the swallows return to the mission at Capistrano, but this year they are a little late. The old gardener and bell ringer Julian assures his little friend Juan that they will arrive, and at dusk they do.

The Story of Babar, by Jean De Brunhoff. The first book about the elephant who comes to the city after his mother has been killed. He has great adventures and is married to Celeste by the end of this story.

The Tooth Witch, by Nurit Karlin. The tooth witch is bored after six hundred years of doing the same thing, so she assigns a helper who takes over as the Tooth Fairy.

**The Velveteen Rabbit,* by Margery Williams, illustrated by William Nicholson. Few illustrations, but a wonderful story for children of first- and second-grade level. How do toys become "real" through the power of love?

We're Back: A Dinosaur Story, by Hudson Talbott. Creatures from prehistoric times win a trip to the twentieth century, and just get to the Museum of Natural History in time for Dr. Bleeb to save them from a fear-ridden mob. They pose as a diorama and decide to stay awhile.

Whose Mouse Are You?, by Robert Kraus, illustrated by Jose Aruego. A charming tale for the very young of a "deserted" mouse who rescues his mother, his father, and his sister, and then finds he has a "brand-new" brother too.

Winnie-the-Pooh, by A. A. Milne, illustrated by Ernest H. Shepard. Christopher Robin's friends—Pooh Bear, Piglet, Eeyore, Rabbit, Tigger, Kanga, Roo, and Owl—all represent people with certain personality traits, which makes their adventures very enjoyable for adults to read to children.

The Wolf's Chicken Stew, by Keiko Kasza. A wolf with a tremendous appetite decides to take goodies to the chicken's house to fatten her up before cooking her, but he has a surprise coming when he goes to pick her up.

Yummers Too: The Second Course, by James Marshall. Emily is having a terrible time resisting or trying to resist food. She does not succeed.

Poetry

When dealing with young children, it is acceptable to interpret broadly the definition of poetry as "a work in metrical form," so that we may include the simplest nursery rhymes for the diaper set and go on to unrhymed verse for the older child. Perhaps the most important point to keep in mind when dealing with this form is to include poetry as an integral part of literature, rather than setting it apart as something "special" or different, once the patty-cake period has passed. The negative attitudes so commonly encountered when poetry is mentioned to upper-elementary or secondary-school children may be forestalled if a young child has been presented with sufficient poetic expression without comment, simply as a book to hear read. A very useful technique in this regard is to tie a poem into a prose selection on the same subject, with animals or weather or seasons of the year, in such a way as to make it seem less extraordinary.

One of the main features of this kind of writing is its potential for lyrical expression, so that even adults may enjoy the musical aspects of poetry, sometimes without full intellectual comprehension. Therefore, if the reader chooses well and prepares carefully, he should be able to stress this aspect, resulting in the child's enjoyment of poetic form along with prose at each level of his development.

Another mark of good poetry is strong use of imagery, which for young children is helped by copious illustration in their books. Especially after the age of four, many youngsters appreciate humor, and the compressed language which is so often a part of poetic expression can easily come into play here.

As in all literature, in choosing poetry we must select the best available, taking special care here to avoid sentimentalism, a trap into which it seems particularly easy to fall when dealing with verses written especially for children.

We will also want to avoid didacticism, common prior to the period of William Blake's "Songs of Innocence" (first published in 1789), and continuing well into the modern era. It is obvious not only that such pieces are poor poetry, but also that their purpose—to teach proper behavior—might quite possibly have the opposite effect on a youngster today. As an example, consider two poems on the same subject. First, a poem called "Dreams" from the Victorian period:

> If children have been good all day,
>   And kept their tongues and lips quite clean,
> They dream of flowers that nod and play,
>   And fairies dancing on the green.
> But if they've spoken naughty words,

> Or told a lie, they dream of rats,
> Of crawling snakes, and ugly birds,
> Of centipedes and vampire bats.*

Then, contrast it with a piece by Louise Driscoll called "Hold Fast Your Dreams":

> Hold fast your dreams!
> Within your heart
> Keep one still, secret spot
> Where dreams may go,
> And sheltered so,
> May thrive and grow—
> Where doubt and fear are not.
> Oh, keep a place apart
> Within your heart,
> For little dreams to go.†

In terms of imagery alone, it is not difficult to understand the difference between these two, and the response each would be likely to get from a youngster.

Some of the following books of poetry are humorous; some are actually nonsense verse; some are serious. All for this age range are appropriately illustrated.

The Adventures of Isabel, by Ogden Nash, illustrated by James Marshall. Meet the intrepid Isabel, who handles the most hair-raising encounters with ease and aplomb. Nash's verses are delightful.

All the Pretty Horses, by Susan Jeffers. A lullaby, this beautifully illustrated book pictures all the horses the child can dream of as she sleeps. (No music included)

Anna Banana: 101 Jump-Rope Rhymes, by Joanna Cole, illustrated by Alan Tiegreen. An illustrated collection of jump-rope rhymes arranged according to the type of jumping they are meant to accompany.

A Child's Garden of Verses, by Robert Louis Stevenson, illustrated by Brian Wildsmith. The ageless poetry of Robert Louis Stevenson is lavishly and lovingly illustrated in this don't-miss edition.

Egg Thoughts and Other Frances Songs, by Russell Hoban, illustrated by Lillian Hoban. Short, humorous poems that are very appealing, just as Frances is.

---

*"Dreams" from *The Child World,* 3d ed. (London: John Lane, 1886).

†Louise Driscoll, *Hold Fast Your Dreams* (New York: The New York Times Company, 1916).

Every Time I Climb a Tree, by David McCord, illustrated by Marc Simont. Short poems, most of them in a comical vein, are appropriately illustrated.

Father Fox's Pennyrhymes, by Clyde Watson, illustrated by Wendy Watson. With musical lilt these exuberant rhymes sing of American country life. There are lullabies, counting-rhymes, sly and funny jingles all set forth by Father Fox in overalls.

Good Books, Good Times!, selected by Lee Bennett Hopkins, illustrated by Harvey Stevenson. This delightful anthology of poems about the joys of books and reading includes selections by David McCord, Karla Kuskin, Myra Cohn Livingston, and Jack Prelutsky.

A Great Big Ugly Man Came Up and Tied His Horse to Me: A Book of Nonsense Verse, by Wallace Tripp. Some of the poems are clever and mischievous, and others are just plain silly, but with the wonderful illustrations all will touch a child's funny bone.

Hailstones and Halibut Bones, by Mary O'Neill. Newly illustrated by John Wallner. These lovely poems describing colors have been enhanced in this new edition by vibrant drawings which make them leap off the page.

A Hippopotamustn't, by J. Patrick Lewis, illustrated by Victoria Chess. More than thirty mostly humorous poems about animals of every kind, with appropriately funny illustrations.

**Hiawatha,* by Henry Wadsworth Longfellow, illustrated by Susan Jeffers. This lavishly illustrated book concentrates on the boyhood of this Indian's life, from his birth through adolescence.

**Hist Whist,* by e. e. cummings, illustrated by Deborah Kogan Ray. It's a Halloween party, and the children's costumes are the inspiration for the poetry.

In a Spring Garden, edited by Richard Lewis, illustrated by Ezra Jack Keats. Haiku verses glorify spring flowers and small animals in the garden.

Inner Chimes: Poems on Poetry, selected by Bobbye S. Goldstein, illustrated by Jane Breskin Zalben. A delightful anthology celebrating the mysterious process of writing poetry. The illustrations are charming and witty.

It's Snowing! It's Snowing!, by Jack Prelutsky, illustrated by Jeanne Titherington. A collection of short poems about snow and children's delight in winter activities.

Lullabies and Night Songs, edited by William Engvick, music by Alec Wilder, illustrated by Maurice Sendak. Many of the poems in this book have been set to music for the first time, and they seem to ask to be sung as well as read. Some are lullabies, but some are rollicking songs meant to end the day with laughter. A truly wonderful selection enhanced by Sendak's illustrations.

Monster Poems, edited by Daisy Wallace, illustrated by Kay Chorao. Seventeen poems by various authors describe different kinds of monsters.

Night on Neighborhood Street, by Eloise Greenfield, illustrated by Jan Spivey Gilchrist. A collection of poems exploring the sights, sounds, and emotions enlivening an African-American neighborhood during the course of one evening.

Now We Are Six, by A. A. Milne, illustrated by Ernest H. Shepard. More verses by Christopher Robin about his friends from the Hundred Acre Wood, other people, and other things of interest to children.

Poemas: Very Very Short Nature Poems, by Ernesto Galarza. A bilingual book, Spanish and English, illustrated on each page with photographs.

The Pelican's Chorus & the Quangle Wangle's Hat, by Edward Lear, illustrated by Kevin W. Maddison. In two poems the grand King and Queen of the Pelicans live a joyous life on the banks of the Nile, and a strange creature's vast hat attracts a wide variety of nesters. Nonsense verse with great pictures.

Poems for Fathers, edited by Myra Cohn Livingston, illustrated by Robert Casilla. Some serious, some comical poems about fathers of all kinds and their behavior.

Poems to Read to the Very Young, edited by Josette Frank, illustrated by Eloise Wilkin. An excellent selection of short poems by well-known poets from Robert Louis Stevenson to Aileen Fisher, with lovely illustrations.

The Quangle Wangle's Hat, by Edward Lear, illustrated by Helen Oxenbury. All of the traditional animals come to build on the Quangle Wangle's hat, as rhymed nonsense and great illustrations combine.

Read-Aloud Rhymes for the Very Young, selected by Jack Prelutsky, illustrated by Marc Brown. An excellent collection of short poems and little songs, which parents can share with the youngest child. The comic illustrations keep it all together.

Red Dragon Fly on My Shoulder, translated by Sylvia Cassedy and Kunihiro Suetake, illustrated by Molly Bang. An unusual collection of haiku with marvelous illustrations.

Rolling Harvey Down the Hill, by Jack Prelutsky, illustrated by Victoria Chess. A collection of humorous poems about the narrator's four friends, one of whom is the obnoxious Harvey.

Spin a Soft Black Song, by Nikki Giovanni, illustrated by Charles Bible. This is a very unusual book, celebrating African-American life in poems based on what children say from infancy through age ten. The author uses her own experience and that of her brother Charles for verisimilitude.

Street Rhymes Around the World, edited by Jane Yolen. A glorious collection of thirty-two street rhymes from seventeen nations with artwork by native artists. Shown in each language with English translations.

The Tamarindo Puppy and Other Poems, by Charlotte Pomerantz, illustrated by Byron Barton. An illustrated collection of thirteen poems with a sprinkling of Spanish throughout.

Under the Sunday Tree, by Eloise Greenfield, illustrated by Amos Ferguson. In this collection of poems and paintings there is a charming view of life in the Bahamas.

The Walrus and the Carpenter, by Lewis Carroll, illustrated by Jane Breskin Zalben. Originally part of *Alice Through the Looking Glass,* this poem, recited by Tweedledee and Tweedledum, tells of the portly Walrus, the dour Carpenter, and the naive Oysters, with magnificent illustrations that make it come to life.

When It Comes to Bugs, by Aileen Fisher, illustrated by Chris and Bruce Degen. Sixteen original poems show us a new way to look at the world— from a bug's point of view.

When We Were Very Young, by A. A. Milne, illustrated by Ernest H. Shepard. A book of poems written for Christopher Robin, including some Pooh songs and hums.

A Zooful of Animals, edited by William Cole, illustrated by Lynn Munsinger. A great collection of short poems about animals—all kinds—with delightful, humorous illustrations. For example, "The Raccoon" reads, "The raccoon wears a mask at night and has a brown-ringed tail. That's how I recognize him when he dumps my garbage pail."

Songs with Music

Abiyoyo: South African Lullaby and Folk Story, by Pete Seeger, illustrated by Michael Hays. Banished from town for making mischief, a little boy who plays the ukelele and his father, a magician, are welcomed back when they find a way to make the dreaded giant, Abiyoyo, disappear.

All God's Critters Got a Place in the Choir, words and music by Bill Staines, illustrated by Margot Zemach. Charming illustrations show animals with their many sounds, blended into a joyful cacophony.

Always Room for One More, by Sorche Nic Leodhas, illustrated by Nonny Hogrogian. This is an old Scottish song about a generous family which keeps growing by inviting all passing travelers to join them. Then when the house literally bursts, all the strangers rebuild the house—twice the size it was. Music at the end of the book.

Arroz Con Leche: Popular Songs and Rhymes from Latin America, selected and illustrated by Lulu Delacre. With Spanish and English on each page, and suggestions for activities, this colorful book has verses and music from Mexico, Argentina, and Puerto Rico.

Baby Beluga, by Raffi, illustrated by Ashley Wolff. This is an illustrated text to Raffi's song about the little white whale who swims wild and free. Music in back of the book.

The Erie Canal, illustrated by Peter Spier. The old song is charmingly illustrated, and there is a page of information about the canal's construction and use as an aid to opening up the Old West.

Five Little Ducks, illustrated by Jose Aruego and Ariane Dewey. A simple counting song, each duck leaving, then finally reunited with Mama Duck. Music in back.

Fox Went Out on a Chilly Night, illustrated by Peter Spier. Interesting illustrations and the music to an old song with seven verses.

Frog Went A-Courtin', by John Langstaff, illustrated by Feodor Rojankovsky. Until the cat spoils the wedding, all the animals are having a great time with Frog and his mouse bride. Music at the back.

Go Tell Aunt Rhody, illustrated by Aliki. More than two hundred years ago in France, Jean Jacques Rousseau wrote an opera called *The Village Soothsayer.* After many years the opera was forgotten, but one melody remained, and eventually it became an early American folk song celebrating rural life. Music and verses in back.

Hush Little Baby, illustrated by Aliki. Starting in England and moving to the Appalachians, this old folk lullaby is charmingly illustrated here with music in back.

I Know an Old Lady Who Swallowed a Fly, illustrated by Nadine Bernard Westcott. An English folk song showing in cumulative rhyme how each solution to the old lady's problem proves worse than the one before. Music is included.

Knick Knack Paddywack, by Marissa Moss. In this variation and extension of the traditional counting song, "this old man" ends up blasting off and flying to the moon.

The Lap-Time Song and Play Book, edited by Jane Yolen, musical arrangements by Adam Stemple, illustrated by Margot Tomes. This charming book is a collection of favorite lap games to be played by a child and an adult.

With each selection are brief directions for parents who may not recall the exact movements involved, and there is music for those who wish to use it.

London Bridge Is Falling Down, illustrated by Peter Spier. An interesting history of London Bridge, or rather London Bridges, is in the back of this charming book, as is the music for the well-known song.

Lullabies and Night Songs, edited by William Engvick, music by Alec Wilder, illustrated by Maurice Sendak. Many of the poems in this book have been set to music for the first time, and they seem to ask to be sung as well as read. Some are lullabies, but some are rollicking songs meant to end the day with laughter. A truly wonderful selection enhanced by Sendak's illustrations.

Mommy, Buy Me a China Doll, by Harve Zemach, illustrated by Margot Zemach. A repetitive song from the Ozarks with lovely illustrations.

Oh, A-Hunting We Will Go, by John Langstaff, illustrated by Nancy Winslow Parker. To the familiar strains of the old song (music at the end of the book), the children catch a fox and put him in a box, catch a bear and put him in his underwear, catch even a brontosaurus and put him in the chorus—but always let them go. Excellent for group participation.

Old MacDonald Had a Farm, illustrated by Carol Jones. The old song enhanced by peek-a-boo holes in each page, so the reader can guess the next animal.

Old MacDonald Had a Farm, illustrated by Glen Rounds. The inhabitants of Old MacDonald's farm are described verse by verse, illustrated by childlike drawings. The music is on the last page.

Over in the Meadow, by John Langstaff, illustrated by Feodor Rojankovsky. A counting song—one to ten—based on all the little animals of the forest and their babies. The music is the one used in the southern Appalachian Mountains.

Over the River and Through the Wood, by Lydia Maria Child, illustrated by Iris Van Rynbach. An illustrated version of the well-known song describing the joys of a Thanksgiving visit to grandmother's house. Music on the last two pages.

Play Rhymes, collected and illustrated by Marc Brown. Old favorites with music at the end of the book makes this a handy collection.

Singing Bee! A Collection of Favorite Children's Songs, edited by Jane Hart, illustrated by Anita Lobel. One hundred twenty-five songs, arranged according to origins, with piano music and guitar chords indicated. Two indexes at the back, one by song title, one by subject, make this a very useful book with groups.

Sitting on a Farm, by Bob King, illustrated by Bill Slavin. A rollicking song about a little girl who tries to get a bug off her knee by enlisting the aid of larger and larger animals.

Skip to My Lou, illustrated by Nadine Bernard Westcott. When his parents leave a young boy in charge of the farm for a day, chaos erupts as the animals take over the house, beginning with flies in the sugarbowl. But he gets it all cleaned up before Mom and Dad return.

The Teddy Bears' Picnic, by Jimmy Kennedy, illustrated by Prue Theobalds. Illustrates the texts of the familiar song about the festivities at the teddy bears' picnic. They do everything small children do at a picnic.

There's a Hole in the Bucket, illustrated by Nadine Bernard Westcott. With hilarious illustrations and music at the end of the book, this old song is very entertaining, as poor Henry tries without success to fix the hole in the bucket.

This Old Man, illustrated by Carol Jones. With peepholes at each number, one to ten, this song is fun to read and/or sing. Music at the end of the book.

This Old Man: The Counting Song, illustrated by Robin Michael Koontz. With very humorous drawings, this is the knick-knack, paddy-whack way of counting from one to ten. With music and play instructions at the back of the book.

Waltzing Matilda, by A. B. Paterson, illustrated by Desmond Digby. With a glossary of terms at the back, this Australian song is beautifully illustrated. Unfortunately, there is no music included. Supposedly everyone knows the tune.

The Wheels on the Bus, by Maryann Kovalski. This is a modern adaptation (with music) of the traditional song. This grandmother and her two granddaughters miss the bus and take a taxi home.

Play One—Play All: Books for Participation

Children enjoy playing with other children and also with adults, so we have listed some titles to use together.

A—My Name Is Alice, by Jane Bayer, illustrated by Steven Kellogg. Never before have the letters of the alphabet been viewed so inventively. "My name is Gertrude and my husband's name is George. We come from Glasgow and we sell giggles" is a typical example. Gertrude is a goose, George is a gorilla. The game and less familiar animals are explained at the back of the book.

***A Basket Full of White Eggs: Riddle-Poems,* by Brian Swann, illustrated by Ponder Goembel. Very interesting concepts for these riddles, which are pictured as double-spread paintings. For example, "I run, I run. When I arrive I bend down and let fall all my white hairs" is on a page with a breaking wave. Many different ethnic sources for the question, "Who am I?" and answers in back of the book, if needed.

Bus Stops, by Taro Gomi. This simple text details the bus's path and its riders while the subtext challenges children to find a variety of objects and people sprinkled throughout the pictures.

But Where Is the Green Parrot?, by Thomas Zacharias, illustrated by Wanda Zacharias. Very young readers will play a lively game of hide-and-seek as they search for the green parrot on every page of this interactive picture book.

Caps for Sale, retold and illustrated by Esphyr Slobodkina. This story of the peddler, his caps, and the monkeys who take them has everything young children love: plot, drama, suspense, humor, warmth, and simplicity. They enjoy acting out this story.

Clap Your Hands, by Lorinda Bryan Cauley. Sing-along, act-along rhymes and bright pictures for the toddler set.

Demi's Find the Animal A B C, by Demi. With answers in the back of the book in case a child needs them, this book combines the alphabet with sharpening observational skills. In a group of many, can the reader pick out the exact duplicate of a single one pictured in the corner?

Each Peach, Pear, Plum, by Janet and Allan Ahlberg. Rhymed text and illustrations invite the reader to play "I spy" with a variety of Mother Goose and other folklore characters.

Finger Rhymes, by Marc Brown. Many familiar rhymes, such as "The Eensy, Weensy Spider," and some less well-known ones. With illustrations of how to use fingers as the rhymes are repeated.

Five Little Monkeys Jumping on the Bed, retold and illustrated by Eileen Christelow. After their bedtime baths the five little monkeys are supposed to lie quietly, waiting to fall asleep. However, they begin jumping on the bed, each in turn falling off and getting hurt. Finally, Mama gets them all tucked in and can go to bed herself.

Five Little Monkeys Sitting in a Tree, by Eileen Christelow. These mischievous monkeys tease Mr. Crocodile, who seems to snap them up one by one, but they escape to a tree and have their picnic supper with their mama.

Hand Rhymes, by Marc Brown. A collection of thirty-one nursery rhymes with accompanying diagrams for hand play.

Have You Seen My Duckling?, by Nancy Tafuri. A mother duck with seven little ducklings suddenly has only six. She asks all her animal friends about the missing baby, who finally shows up.

Here Are My Hands, by Bill Martin, Jr., and John Archambault, illustrated by Ted Rand. In rhyme, a very simple book naming parts of the body, ending with skin "bundling me in."

I See Something You Don't See, by Robin M. Koontz. Two children enjoying a summer day at Grandma's entertain each other with rhyming riddles. The pictures give the answers, with an extra answer page at the back.

I Unpacked My Grandmother's Trunk, by Susan Ramsay Hoguet. This is a word game for two or more players, based on the alphabet. For example, "I unpacked my grandmother's trunk and took out an acrobat," followed by the second player saying, "I unpacked . . . and took out an acrobat and a bear," and so on with each player reciting the whole list in correct order. Colorfully illustrated suggestions for each letter.

It Does Not Say Meow, by Beatrice Schenk De Regniers, illustrated by Paul Galdone. Rhymed riddles about animals, with answers pictured on each page following the riddle.

It Looked Like Spilt Milk, by Charles G. Shaw. This can be used with a group of children who suggest what each cloud "looks like," as the fluffy white clouds take on shapes of animals and so on.

Jump, Frog, Jump, by Robert Kalan, illustrated by Byron Barton. In a cumulative story about a frog catching a fly and then almost being caught himself, the audience participates on every other page, by shouting, "Jump, Frog, jump!" Great for groups.

Knick Knack Paddywack, by Marissa Moss. In this variation of the traditional counting song, "this old man" ends up blasting off and flying to the moon.

The Lap-Time Song and Play Book, edited by Jane Yolen, musical arrangements by Adam Stemple, illustrated by Margot Tomes. This charming book is a collection of favorite lap games to be played by a child and an adult. With each selection are brief directions for parents who may not recall the exact movements involved, and there is music for those who wish to use it.

Little Rabbit Foo Foo, by Michael Rosen, illustrated by Arthur Robins. Naughty Rabbit Foo Foo, who mistreats the other forest creatures, receives his just deserts from the Good Fairy.

****The Little Red Riding Hood Rebus Book*, retold by Ann Morris, illustrated by Ljiljana Rylands. A charming puzzle book which tells the traditional tale by substituting pictures for some words or parts of words. There's a "dictionary" in back for those who need it.

***Little Sister and the Month Brothers,* retold by Beatrice Schenk De Regniers, illustrated by Margot Tomes. This Slavic fairy tale shows the twelve month brothers helping Little Sister to thwart the schemes of her stepmother and stepsister. There are interesting small pictures with added dialogue on each page which makes this ideal for use in a creative dramatics group.

Look Again, by Tana Hoban. Each page features a cutout showing part of the next page. But when the child sees the entire page which follows, he gets the idea that all is not what it seems at first.

***Look Again!,* illustrated by April Wilson. The reader is encouraged to spot the differences in twelve seemingly identical pairs of illustrations depicting a variety of the world's plants and animals that use shape and color to ensure their survival. There's a key to answers at the end, if needed.

Mouse Around, by Pat Schories. In a wordless book we follow a tiny mouse who gets separated from his family and find him in each picture until they are reunited.

Nothing at All, by Wanda Gag. In a forgotten corner of an old forgotten farm stand three little doghouses in which three orphan puppies live. One has pointed ears, one has curly ears, the third is invisible. But little Nothing-at-all (on the advice of a jackdaw with a book) repeats a magic chant for nine days, each day becoming more "real," until he can join his brothers and play with the children who have adopted them. Youngsters love his chant, "I'm busy getting dizzy," meanwhile whirling round and round, and will join in as the puppy works hard to materialize.

Oh, A-Hunting We Will Go, by John Langstaff, illustrated by Nancy Winslow Parker. To the familiar strains of the old song (with music at the end of the book), the children catch a fox, put him in a box, catch a bear and put him in his underwear, and so on—but always let him go. Excellent for group participation.

Old Mother Hubbard, by Colin and Jacqui Hawkins. A "Lift the Flap" Book. As the old rhyme proceeds, each page has a lift-up flap revealing a humorous picture beneath.

Peanut Butter and Jelly: A Play Rhyme, illustrated by Nadine Bernard Westcott. Humorous text and illustrations explain how to make a peanut butter and jelly sandwich. This book includes instructions for accompanying hand and foot motions.

Pierre: A Cautionary Tale, by Maurice Sendak. No matter what is said to Pierre, he has only one retort, "I don't care!" Then a lion changes his mind.

Play Rhymes, collected and illustrated by Marc Brown. Old favorites with music at the end of the book make this a handy collection.

Roar and More, by Karla Kuskin. This colorful reissue of a notable book presents rhyming text showing behavior and noises of each animal. Children can imitate these.

Take Another Look, by Tana Hoban. With holes in the middle of the pages, one might guess at what's on the next page and be wrong. Seeing the whole picture is the clue.

This Old Man, illustrated by Carol Jones. With peepholes at each number—one to ten—this song is fun to read and/or sing. Music at the end of the book.

This Old Man: The Counting Song, illustrated by Robin M. Koontz. With very humorous drawings, this is the knick-knack, paddy-whack way of counting from one to ten. With music and play instructions at the back.

Tom and Annie Go Shopping, by Barry Smith. In this book children are given a shopping list and must find (along with the reader) the listed items in each store.

**Upside-Downers, by Mitsumasa Anno. This is the sequel to *Topsy-Turvies.* Here again the artist uses rhyme, and with playing cards shows that what is up in one view is down in another.

We're Going on a Bear Hunt, by Michael Rosen, illustrated by Helen Oxenbury. Brave bear hunters, a daddy and his four children, go through tall grass, deep mud, a blinding snowstorm, a dark forest, and cross a river, until finally they spy their quarry in a cave and turn back toward home with the bear in pursuit.

What Am I? Very First Riddles, by Stephanie Calmenson, illustrated by Karen Gundersheimer. With the answers on the page following each riddle, this is a simple way to involve a youngster in finding answers.

What's Missing?, by Niki Yektai, illustrated by Susannah Ryan. As parents, a child, and a dog go through their day, there is a missing part of each picture, with the answer on the following page. A simple way to foster imagination.

The Wheels on the Bus, by Maryann Kovalski. This is a modern adaptation (with music) of the traditional song. The grandmother and her two granddaughters miss the bus and take a taxi home.

Where's Wallace?, by Hilary Knight. An orangutan and his keeper, Mr. Frumbee, conspire so that Wallace is able to make numerous escapes from his cage at the zoo, which challenges the reader to find him in many unusual places.

Whose Hat?, by Margaret Miller. Children will have fun guessing the professions which are represented by a variety of hats.

INFORMATIONAL BOOKS

In this category there is a great range of subject matter, and in order to find material written at a level comprehensible to young children, some titles designated as *I Can Read* or *Let's Read and Find Out* have been included. This does not mean that these can be called literature in the strict sense. It signifies only that in order to satisfy the curiosity of a four-year-old about the natural sciences or history, for example, it is sometimes necessary to choose books written to be read independently by children in an older age range.

The general heading "Informational" refers to the main objective of certain books, that is, the imparting of factual material, but in this category too there will be some titles which could be called "fiction" where the author has constructed a "story" in the traditional sense, with plot, characters, and setting, in order to catch and hold the interest of the average youngster. Where the book has this format, the same rules apply about a straightforward, exciting story, vividly drawn characters, and a clear sense of time and place characteristic of any superior work of fiction. And, of course, the illustrations must be both literally accurate and aesthetically pleasing.

Furthermore, whether an informational book is done as a story, or as what we might call straight nonfiction, it must meet one more criterion, perhaps the most significant one for this kind of book—it must be factually accurate at whatever level it is written.

What do we mean by "whatever level it is written"?

Informational books in almost all categories can be individually designed so that they are appropriate for different age levels. For instance, alphabet books all have a single subject—the twenty-six letters in the English alphabet—but they range widely in complexity. For the youngest child, we might want a single capital letter presented on each page, with a clear and literal rendition of an object which is spelled beginning with that letter, say an "A" and an apple. For a child nearing school age, however, we might prefer an alphabet book which shows both the upper- and lower-case letters, with a less obvious example, such as "aardvark," maybe modifed by adjectives. The point is that whatever is presented as factual may be simple or quite complex, but it must never be incorrect.

There is also an opportunity in this area to consider concepts of a more philosophical nature, as in the section entitled "World View," where we have a book like Peter Spier's *People* which is completely accurate but which by implication suggests that there is an underlying factor of our common humanity that should be taken into account in dealing with others.

If we consider an all-time favorite like *The Very Hungry Caterpillar,* we see how fictional elements can work in an informational book that is basically factual. Without doubt, a great part of this book's attractiveness is due to the magificent illustrations which combine stylization of the sun and moon, for example, with pictures of edibles that capture the essence of each item.

There is some fantasy here too, since the "very hungry caterpillar" eats through "one apple on Monday, two pears on Tuesday," and so on, and he finally ends up with a stomach ache on Saturday after he's eaten through everything from "one piece of chocolate cake" to "one slice of watermelon," tasting many foods in between. Nevertheless, the days of the week are correctly ordered; it's a counting book, it teaches colors, and the process of metamorphosis is basically accurate.

In the lists that follow, every effort has been made to select books which can be considered "informational" whether or not the manner of presentation is "fictional." Titles are grouped in two general categories: first, those which merely inform about particular subjects, such as animals, plants, and the environment; and second, those which involve particular skills, such as color recognition, counting, and concept books. All have been chosen to expand the youngster's knowledge of himself, the world in which he lives, and the animate and inanimate objects with which he shares that world. As explained earlier, a title may appear in more than one list if its contents fit into more than a single group.

In this area of information, there is so much material that we could not do more than indicate some possible choices. As the child becomes curious about some particular subject, there are many additional titles which may be explored. Librarians can be very helpful in this regard.

World View

**Basket Full of White Eggs: Riddle-Poems, by Brian Swann, illustrated by Ponder Goembel. Very interesting concepts for these riddles, which are pictured as double-spread paintings. For example, "I run, I run. When I arrive I bend down and let fall all my white hairs" is on a page with a breaking wave. Many different ethnic sources for the question, "Who am I?" and answers in back of the book, if needed.

Bread Bread Bread, by Ann Morris, illustrated by Ken Heyman. This book celebrates the many kinds of bread, explains how they are made, and emphasizes culinary enjoyment.

Life Story, by Virginia Lee Burton. Using the metaphor of a drama, the author presents factually "the story of life on our earth from its beginnings up to now" in a very interesting way, with her own inimitable drawings throughout. She closes with a memorable sentence,"The drama of life is a continuous story—ever new, ever changing, and ever wondrous to behold."

People, by Peter Spier. With more than four billion people in the world, it is sometimes hard for any one of us to feel special, but this book reminds us of our uniqueness, deserving the respect of others. This author-artist covers every facet of life from differences in appearance, tastes, home styles, and climate to differences in races, religions, and socio-economic circumstances. This is virtually a one-volume picture encyclopedia.

Street Rhymes Around the World, edited by Jane Yolen. A glorious collection of thirty-two street rhymes from seventeen nations with artwork by native artists. Each rhyme is shown in both its original language and an English translation.

History and Biography

Araminta's Paint Box, by Karen Ackerman, illustrated by Betsy Lewin. When her family moves from Boston to California in 1847, Araminta treasures the paintbox given her by an uncle, but the box is lost and goes through many hands until it is by coincidence brought back to her father, Dr. Darling, by an old miner who has been using it to collect gold nuggets.

By George, Bloomers!, by Judith St. George, illustrated by Margot Tomes. In the mid-nineteenth century no women wore slacks. Then Mrs. Amelia Bloomer started something as an early feminist. In this fictional story a little girl, Hannah, is able to save her little brother Jamie because she can climb onto the roof in her "bloomers."

Chang's Paper Pony, by Eleanor Coerr, illustrated by Deborah Kogan Ray. In San Francisco during the 1850s Gold Rush, Chang, the son of Chinese immigrants, wants a pony but cannot afford one until his friend Big Pete finds a solution.

****Diego,* by Jonah Winter, translated by Amy Prince, illustrated by Jeanette Winter. In both Spanish and English this book describes the childhood and youth in Paris of Diego Rivera and tells how his experiences influenced his art.

****The Drinking Gourd,* by F. N. Monjo, illustrated by Fred Brenner. Tommy Fuller is a mischievous lad, and when he is sent home for disturbing the church service, he discovers some runaway slaves hiding in his father's barn— a station on the Underground Railway. He helps them escape the bounty hunters and learns why his father breaks the law.

****Follow the Drinking Gourd,* by Jeanette Winter. By following directions in an old song, "The Drinking Gourd," taught to them by an old sailor, Peg Leg Joe, runaway slaves journey north along the Underground Railway. The Drinking Gourd is the Big Dipper, which points to the North Star.

Friendship's First Thanksgiving, by William Accorsi. Friendship, a dog who has crossed the sea with the Pilgrims, describes the colony's first year in the New World, culminating in the first Thanksgiving.

The House on Maple Street, by Bonnie Pryor, illustrated by Beth Peck. During the course of three hundred years, many people have lived where the house stands today. Items lost long ago turn up when the latest family digs the ground to plant a garden.

The Josefina Story Quilt, by Eleanor Coerr, illustrated by Bruce Degen. While traveling west with her family in 1850, a young girl makes a patchwork quilt chronicling the experiences of the journey and reserves two special patches for her pet hen Josefina.

A Picture Book of Martin Luther King, Jr., by David A. Adler, illustrated by Robert Casilla. A very simplified overview of this great African-American leader, with important milestones in his life emphasized.

A Picture Book of Abraham Lincoln, by David A. Adler, illustrated by John and Alexandra Wallner. This book follows the life of this popular president from his childhood on the frontier to his assassination after the end of the Civil War.

A Picture Book of Eleanor Roosevelt, by David A. Adler, illustrated by Robert Casilla. Touching on the high spots of her life as a girl, her marriage to Franklin Delano Roosevelt, then as first lady, Eleanor Roosevelt comes across as an important historical figure, working until the time of her death for human rights.

A Picture Book of Harriet Tubman, by David A. Adler, illustrated by Samuel Byrd. A short life of this African-American woman who was called the "Moses" of her people because she led so many slaves to freedom as a conductor on the Underground Railway. She later became active in the fight for women's rights.

A Picture Book of George Washington, by David A. Adler, illustrated by John and Alexandra Wallner. A simplified history of Washington from young surveyor to soldier and then leader of the army in the Revolution, finally becoming president of the United States.

Sam the Minuteman, by Nathaniel Benchley, illustrated by Arnold Lobel. A young boy goes with his father, a Minuteman, at the beginning of the American Revolution, and sees firsthand how terrible fighting is when his friend is shot by a British soldier.

Small Wolf, by Nathaniel Benchley, illustrated by Joan Sandin. A little Indian boy discovers that settlers have taken over Manhattan, and ultimately learns that the interlopers feel they now own the land, pushing the Indians farther and farther away from their native habitats.

Snowshoe Thompson, by Nancy Smiler Levinson, illustrated by Joan Sandin. A true story of a man who brought the idea of skis to the United States in the 1850s, and successfully carried mail across the Sierra Nevada Mountains in winter.

The Story of Johnny Appleseed, by Aliki. In this version the legendary Johnny loves the land and roams near and far to spread the seeds of apple trees.

Wagon Wheels, by Barbara Brenner, illustrated by Don Bolognese. A true story of the Muldie family, African-American pioneers who travel to Kansas after the Civil War to take advantage of the Homestead Act. The father and his three children start in Nicodemus, Kansas, but the boys must follow their father to a place 150 miles farther on where the farming is good.

A Weed Is a Flower: The Life of George Washington Carver, by Aliki. An imaginatively illustrated book which tells the inspiring story of the baby born with no hope for the future who becomes one of the great practical scientists of his country.

Who Came Down That Road?, by George-Ella Lyon, illustrated by Peter Catalanotto. A small boy's question leads to answers that go backward in time from Union soldiers, to Indians, to plains animals, to woolly mammoths, and to the sea which covered everything.

Dinosaurs and Prehistoric Life

Bones, Bones, Dinosaur Bones, by Byron Barton. A very simple book picturing the search for dinosaur bones. After they're dug up, cleaned, and shipped to the museum, the reconstruction of Tyrannosaurus Rex begins.

Dinosaur Chase, by Carolyn Otto, illustrated by Thacher Hurd. A madcap romp through a fantastic world in which dinosaur thieves steal a precious necklace as a mother reads her baby dinosaur to sleep.

Dinosaur Days, by Joyce Milton, illustrated by Richard Roe. This book covers dinosaur bones, their use in reconstructing what the dinosaurs looked like, and detailed descriptions of various dinosaurs, including the meanings of their names.

Dinosaurs, Dinosaurs, by Byron Barton. In prehistoric times there were many kinds of dinosaurs, big and small, those with spikes, and those with long sharp teeth. A good introduction for the very young child.

A Dinosaur Named After Me, by Bernard Most. Here the author draws parallels between the physical characteristics and capabilities of particular dinosaurs and specific children, and incorporates the name of each child into that of the dinosaur.

Dinosaur Time, by Peggy Parish, illustrated by Arnold Lobel. Shows each dinosaur and explains what it looked like, what it ate, and so on, in "dinosaur time."

The First Dog, by Jan Brett. Set in the Pleistocene Age, Kip the cave boy meets Paleowolf, who warns him just in time when fierce animals are in the area, and the first boy-dog friendship becomes reality. Imaginatively illustrated with pages that reproduce cave drawings.

If Dinosaurs Came Back, by Bernard Most. A child imagines ways dinosaurs could be useful in this modern world. Different dinosaurs are accurately labeled at the back of the book.

The Littlest Dinosaurs, by Bernard Most. Not all dinosaurs were enormous—some were only eight inches long—and this book combines fact with fancy to show some of the smaller models in various modern settings, such as a telephone booth, a school orchestra, and a bathtub.

Mik's Mammoth, by Roy Gerrard. A great story told in rhyme of a little boy who is left behind when the rest of the tribe of cavemen go off in search of food. He finds a baby mammoth, Rumm, and the two survive very well, saving the tribe from fierce warriors who pursue them when they return.

My Visit to the Dinosaurs, by Aliki. A small boy goes to the museum and sees reconstructed dinosaurs of many varieties, with explanations of how they were discovered, what they ate, and so on.

Patrick's Dinosaurs, by Carol Carrick, illustrated by Donald Carrick. Hank and Patrick go to the zoo, and when Hank tells his younger brother about dinosaurs, the younger boy's imagination goes wild.

Prehistoric Animals, by Gail Gibbons. After the dinosaurs disappeared, other animals remained, and in this factual book youngsters can get some idea of their world, what they looked like, what they ate, and so forth. Simply demonstrates evolution and paleontology.

Wild and Woolly Mammoths, by Aliki. This artist has pictured the mammoths which lived thousands of years ago with simple, scientifically correct explanations.

Animals

Animals in Winter, by Henrietta Bancroft and Richard G. Van Gelder, illustrated by Gaetano Di Palma. Simple explanations with drawings which show the way wild animals of the forest survive winter weather.

Bees and Beelines, by Judy Hawes, illustrated by Aliki. How do the bees know where to find flowers filled with nectar? Then, how do they make a "beeline" for their hives? And finally, how do they communicate with other bees to go and gather the nectar? Answers are found in this book.

Bird, by Moira Butterfield, illustrated by Paul Johnson. At a very simple level this gaily illustrated book shows the development of an egg until it becomes a bird and flies away.

Birds, by Brian Wildsmith. Each variety of bird is exquisitely painted and given the correct name, as in "a wedge of swans" and "a bevy of quail." These collective terms, a mixture of the archaic and the current, are amusing and tantalizing.

Busy Beavers, by Lydia Dabcovich. The simple text follows the activities of a beaver family as they swim, play, and build a sturdy dam.

Butterfly, by Moira Butterfield, illustrated by Paul Johnson. A beginning book to explain how butterflies go through a metamorphosis, starting from eggs and becoming butterflies.

A Chick Hatches, by Joanna Cole, illustrated by Jerome Wexler. A photographic presentation of what happens inside the egg during the twenty-one day incubation period before the new little chick appears.

Chickens Aren't the Only Ones, by Ruth Heller. In verse and beautifully illustrated, this book explains that many animals lay eggs to reproduce, including fish, insects, and even two mammals, the spiny anteater and the platypus.

Ducks Don't Get Wet, by Augusta Goldin, illustrated by Leonard Kessler. Ducks are waterproof. How does this happen? This elementary science book shows the different varieties of ducks, what each one eats, and how they fly south when the water is frozen. Simple experiments are included to show how oily feathers work.

Egg Story, by Anca Hariton. With accurate but charming illustrations, this book follows an egg from the time it is laid through its incubation under the hen's body, to the chick's birth after twenty-one days.

Fishes, by Brian Wildsmith. Again, this author has done research and given all the "schools" of fish their proper names. And he gives us full double-spread paintings of many varieties found in both salt and fresh water.

Frog, by Moira Butterfield, illustrated by Paul Johnson. Frogs spawn eggs that grow into tadpoles, then into frogs, which after about three years are ready to repeat the process. Good simple explanation.

It's Nesting Time, by Roma Gans, illustrated by Kazue Mizumura. It's spring and birds must build nests in which to lay their eggs. In this book we learn about the many ways different varieties of birds accomplish this task.

Lily Pad Pond, by Bianca Lavies. This book goes through the life cycle of a tadpole, which becomes a bullfrog. With this, there is other life on the lily pad that becomes either predator or victim.

Look for a Bird, by Edith Thacher Hurd, illustrated by Clement Hurd. A nicely illustrated beginning book for birdwatchers. It tells a little about each variety and how to recognize each one.

My Puppy Is Born, by Joanna Cole, photos by Jerome Wexler. An informational book showing the first eight weeks in the life of a miniature dachshund, Sausage.

Seahorse, by Robert A. Morris, illustrated by Arnold Lobel. An interesting and factual account of the seahorse and its life in the ocean.

Sharks, by Gail Gibbons. This book explains clearly and simply the 350 varieties of sharks, with their physical characteristics, differences in size, and uses for mankind.

Sleepy Bear, by Lydia Dabcovich. It's winter and the bear hibernates until spring when the insects, including bees, show up. Then he thinks "honey," and emerges from his cave.

Tree Trunk Traffic, by Bianca Lavies. Text and colored photos show life on a seventy-year-old maple tree. Squirrels, birds, and insects share life here.

The Very Hungry Caterpillar, by Eric Carle. How do butterflies come into being? Here the author imaginatively combines the process of metamorphosis with the days of the week, numbers of fruits, and ten foods dear to the hearts of children.

Who Lives Here?, by Dot and Sy Barlowe. The homes of animals of the pond, forest, prairie, desert, mountains, meadow, and swamp are pictured in their native habitats and clearly identified.

The Wildlife ABC, by Jan Thornhill. Upper- and lower-case letters, great pictures, and some rhyme make this an outstanding book. For example, "Gg— G is for goose, paddling under a bridge." And on the facing page, "Hh— H is for housefly, inspecting your fridge." There are Nature Notes at the back, explaining each entry in detail.

Plants

A B Cedar: An Alphabet of Trees, by George-Ella Lyon, illustrated by Tom Parker. An unusual alphabet book which introduces the leaves from various trees to illustrate the letters.

Corn Is Maize: The Gift of the Indians, by Aliki. This is the simple description of how corn was discovered and used by the Indians and how it came to be an important food throughout the world.

Counting Wildflowers, by Bruce McMillan. From one to twenty, this book combines colors and the recognition of common wildflowers, done in beautiful photographs.

Crinkleroot's Guide to Knowing the Trees, by Jim Arnosky. An illustrated introduction to trees and woodlands with information on how to identify the bark and leaves, the many ways animals use trees, and how to read the individual history that shapes each tree.

Flower, by Moira Butterfield, illustrated by Paul Johnson. A seed, which may have been dropped by a passing bird or carried by the wind, grows into a plant with flowers that may become fruit. A simple book of information.

A Flower Grows, by Ken Robbins. This book shows the growth of an amaryllis through its entire life cycle from an ugly bulb called a Hippeastrum to its flowers, then dying back to flower again next season.

From Seed to Plant, by Gail Gibbons. Here the mystery of how seeds are formed and grow into plants is simply and colorfully solved. Includes an illustrated project at the back of the book.

How a Seed Grows, by Helene J. Jordan, illustrated by Loretta Krupinski. Clear introduction to how seeds grow into flowers, vegetables, and even trees. Simple pictures help.

How My Garden Grew, by Anne and Harlow Rockwell. With pride and pleasure, a little girl describes how she planted and took care of a vegetable garden all by herself. A very first look at gardening.

Once There Was a Tree, by Natalia Romanova, illustrated by Gennady Spirin. A book of rare simplicity and luminous beauty that tells of a tree stump which attracts many living creatures, even man, and when it is replaced by a new tree, attracts the same creatures who need it.

The Pumpkin Patch, by Elizabeth King. Text and photos describe the activities in a pumpkin patch as pink-colored seeds become fat pumpkins, ready to be carved into jack-o'-lanterns.

The Reason for a Flower, by Ruth Heller. A simple but informative book about flowers, seeds, and the whole cycle of plant growth.

The Tiny Seed, by Eric Carle. Colorful collage illustrations dramatize the fascinating story of the life cycle of a flower from its beginning as a tiny seed to a giant flower, which in turn showers tiny seeds everywhere.

Tree Trunk Traffic, by Bianca Lavies. Text and colored photos show life on a seventy-year-old maple tree. Squirrels, birds, and insects share life here.

Trees: A Poem, by Harry Behn, illustrated by James Endicott. A beautifully illustrated book telling what trees do for the world and its inhabitants.

Environment and Ecology

Berenstain Bears Don't Pollute Anymore, by Stan and Jan Berenstain. The young Berenstain Bears learn about pollution in school and finally galvanize their parents into action with the Earth Savers Club.

Cherry Tree, by Ruskin Bond, illustrated by Allan Eitzen. A story from India in which Rakhi, a six-year-old girl, heeds her grandfather's advice and plants the seed of a cherry which survives many mishaps and grows into a lovely tree.

The Desert Is Theirs, by Byrd Baylor, illustrated by Peter Parnall. In poetic terms the author speaks of the Papago Indians, a desert people, and the various animals with which they share this very special kind of environment.

Farewell to Shady Glen, by Bill Peet. A group of small woodland animals must leave Shady Glen, which is being bulldozed for more big city buildings. They make a narrow escape on top of a train, and fortunately find another Shady Glen, but the ecological warning is clear.

The Great Trash Bash, by Loreen Leedy. Mayor Hippo and the animal citizens of Beaston realize that what is ruining their city is too much trash, and they set about changing the situation. A list of ideas for cutting down on trash is on the last page of the book. Children, take notice!

Harald and the Great Stag, by Donald Carrick. When Harald, who lives in England during the Middle Ages, hears that the baron and his royal guests are planning to hunt the legendary Great Stag, he devises a clever plan to outwit the hunters and protect the animal.

Hey, Get Off Our Train, by John Burningham. A really clever book in which a young boy goes to bed and dreams that his toy train really runs. But as he and his dog are traveling around the world, an elephant, a seal, and other endangered animals board the train to avoid extinction. Simply wonderful imaginative illustrations and a surprise ending.

How to Hide a Butterfly, by Ruth Heller. Simple, informational book, beautifully illustrated, which demonstrates camouflage from predators such as moths and inchworms.

How to Hide an Octopus and Other Sea Creatures, by Ruth Heller. Camouflage is masterfully painted in this book which illustrates a fact of nature most artistically.

I Was Born in a Tree and Raised by Bees, by Jim Arnosky. Crinkleroot is pictured as a forest-dwelling old man who understands all the plants and animals that surround him. There are intriguing puzzles in the pictures which go through the four seasons of the year.

In the Tall, Tall Grass, by Denise Fleming. This is a backyard tour conducted by a fuzzy caterpillar. Rhymes and double-spread pictures make this a delightful trip from early morning until firefly time.

Just a Dream, by Chris Van Allsburg. When Walter has a dream about a future Earth devastated by pollution, he begins to understand the importance of taking care of the environment now.

The Lady and the Spider, by Faith McNulty, illustrated by Bob Marstall. A spider who lives in a head of lettuce is saved when the lady who finds her puts her back into the garden, showing respect for all living things, no matter how small.

Miss Rumphius, by Barbara Cooney. Alice Rumphius wants to grow up to travel the world and then live by the sea, as her grandfather had. But first she must make the world more beautiful, which she does by scattering flower seeds everywhere so that the countryside is ablaze with color every spring and fall.

Mother Earth, by Nancy Luenn, illustrated by Neil Waldman. This book describes the gifts the earth gives us and the gifts we can give back. Simply shown—ecological responsibility.

Once There Was a Tree, by Natalia Romanova, illustrated by Gennady Spirin. A book of rare simplicity and luminous beauty that tells of a tree stump which attracts many living creatures, even man, and when it is replaced by a new tree attracts the same creatures who need it.

A Tree Is Nice, by Janice May Udry, illustrated by Marc Simont. What good are trees? They are beautiful to see, wonderful to climb or hang a swing from. They give shade in summer, protection from strong winds in winter, and if they are apple trees, children can enjoy the fruit. Plant trees!

Trees: A Poem, by Harry Behn, illustrated by James Endicott. A beautifully illustrated book telling what trees do for the world and its inhabitants.

The World That Jack Built, by Ruth Brown. An eloquent plea for taking care of our environment and a warning of its imminent endangerment.

The Wump World, by Bill Peet. When the Pollutians come roaring out of the sky onto the peaceful agrarian Wump world, the Wumps are forced to go underground until the Pollutians finally ruin their world completely and leave to ruin the next one.

Other Sciences

The Big Dipper, by Franklyn M. Branley, illustrated by Molly Coxe. This book explains basic facts about the Big Dipper, including which stars make up the constellation, how its position changes in the sky, and how it points to the North Star.

Earth, by David Bennett, illustrated by Rosalinda Kightley. A very simple book, using a little bear to tell about the earth, its evolution over time, and some basic facts about the necessity for saving our planet.

Gregg's Microscope, by Millicent E. Selsam, illustrated by Arnold Lobel. After Greg's father gives him a microscope of his own, he and the whole family begin to use it to discover how different common things like salt and hair look when truly magnified.

How We Learned the Earth Is Round, by Patricia Lauber, illustrated by Megan Lloyd. An excellent book with very simple experiments which show how we know the earth is round, not flat, as people believed prior to the Greeks about twenty-five hundred years ago. The voyages of Columbus and Magellan are also mentioned as proof that the world is not flat.

I Want to Be an Astronaut, by Byron Barton. A small boy tells what will happen if he gets his wish. He will eat ready-to-eat food, experience zero gravity, and go for space walks when he becomes an astronaut.

Is There Life in Outer Space?, by Franklyn M. Branley, illustrated by Don Madden. At a very simple level this book shows the child that it is improbable that there is life on any of the planets in our galaxy, but leaves the question open about the possibility that life exists in some form in other solar systems. Skillfully combines drawings with photographs of the moon, Mars, and other planets to which we've sent probes.

Light, by Donald Crews. This book begins with daylight and goes through the various kinds of lights which brighten the dark in city and country until the dawn comes again—daylight.

The Magic School Bus at the Waterworks, by Joanna Cole, illustrated by Bruce Degen. In the popular comic-book format used for all the "Magic School Bus" stories, facts about water from its position in the clouds to its final destination in the school's water pipes are made clear with humor.

The Magic School Bus Inside the Earth, by Joanna Cole, illustrated by Bruce Degen. At a very elementary level, and using a comic-book format, this book accurately describes various formations above and below the surface of the earth. There is a question-and-answer section at the end.

The Planets in Our Solar System, by Franklyn M. Branley, illustrated by Don Madden. Here the solar system and its nine planets are introduced. This book includes directions for making two models, one showing the relative sizes of the planets and the other their relative distance from the sun.

Prove It!, by Rose Wyler and Gerald Ames, illustrated by Talivaldis Stubis. Here the reader is shown very simple experiments to prove scientific facts about water, air, sounds, and magnets. "If it's true, you can prove it" is a very good basis for critical thinking.

The Sky Is Full of Stars, by Franklyn M. Branley, illustrated by Felicia Bond. This book explains how to view the stars and ways to locate star pictures, known as constellations, throughout the year. It includes directions for simple projects.

Sun Up, Sun Down, by Gail Gibbons. A little girl is awakened in the morning by the sun shining into her bedroom and goes through the day with her moving shadow, clouds, rain, and a rainbow. Simple explanations, but scientifically accurate.

The Tree of Life: The Wonders of Evolution, by Ellen Jackson, illustrated by Judeanne Winter. Necessarily simplified, this book does convey the fundamentals of evolution without didacticism. The emphasis is on the almost infinite variety of living forms and the continuity of life itself.

Human Biology and Health Services

Alligator's Toothache, by Diane DeGroat. A wordless book which shows a party at which alligator cannot enjoy himself until after the dentist has pulled his aching tooth.

Arthur's Eyes, by Marc Brown. Arthur needs glasses, but although he sees better with them, he can't take the ridicule from his classmates, so he hides them in his lunchbox. However, his poor eyesight causes havoc when he enters the girls' restroom by mistake.

Arthur's Tooth, by Marc Brown. Arthur is seven, but he still has all his baby teeth. The dentist reassures him that one is loose, and then by accident Francine hits him and out it comes.

A Baby Starts to Grow, by Paul Showers, illustrated by Rosalind Fry. Tastefully done with clear illustrations, this book begins with conception and continues to the birth of a new baby.

Bellybuttons Are Navels, by Mark Schoen, illustrated by M. J. Quay. Robert and his sister Mary are taking a bath and discuss their bodies: each has two eyes, two ears, and so on, including the correct anatomical terms for genitals.

Bodies, by Barbara Brenner, illustrated by George Ancona. With simple explanations, this book covers concepts of cells, bodily functions, and what makes each individual different from every other human being.

Did the Sun Shine Before You Were Born?, by Sol and Judith Gordon, illustrated by Vivien Cohen. An interesting approach for young children, this book shows various families and relationships, then segues gracefully into the specifics of pregnancy and birth in answer to the question posed in the title. Very nice illustrations.

A Drop of Blood, by Paul Showers, illustrated by Don Madden. Concise and correct explanation of blood, at the level which is completely understandable to a first- or second-grade child.

Ears Are for Hearing, by Paul Showers, illustrated by Holly Keller. This book describes the process of hearing, during which sound waves travel through the ear and become signals which the brain interprets as individual sounds. Clearly and simply illustrated in color.

Even Little Kids Get Diabetes, by Connie White Pirner, illustrated by Nadine Bernard Westcott. This book explains in simple terms the diagnosis and treatment of a little girl's diabetes, including taking daily injections of insulin, the correct diet, and daily checking of the blood. But it is reassuring; she is a very normal, active child.

Faces, by Barbara Brenner, illustrated by George Ancona. Every face has two eyes, a nose, two ears, and a mouth. With photos we become aware of all the senses, and of talking with a friend "face to face."

Going to the Dentist, by Fred Rogers, illustrated by Jim Judkis. A factual book with photographs to take the mystery out of the child's first visit to the dentist.

Grandfather's Nose: Why We Look Alike or Different, by Dorothy Hinshaw Patent, illustrated by Diane Palmisciano. This book discusses basic genetics, explaining how the combination of genes passed on from our parents makes each of us a unique individual. Very clearly explained and illustrated.

I'm Growing, by Aliki. In simple words and delightful pictures the child can understand the principle of growth, inside and outside the body.

The Magic School Bus Inside the Human Body, by Joanna Cole, illustrated by Bruce Degen. Part of a series of informational books which make learning fun. There are True/False questions at the end of an almost comic-book format, but with a point.

Me and My Family Tree, by Paul Showers, illustrated by Don Madden. A very clear explanation of genetics picturing Mendel's work and illustrating how we all have genes from those who lived and died long before we were born.

My Dentist, by Harlow Rockwell. A simple, pleasant visit to the dentist's office takes the fear out of such an occurrence, and there's a "prize drawer" at the end.

My Doctor, by Harlow Rockwell. This is a reassuring look at what a small child can expect when he visits his pediatrician.

My Hands, rev. ed. by Aliki. This book gives a child an awareness of left and right, what different fingers are used for, and explains with bright illustrations the many uses humans have for these all-important parts of our anatomy.

Spectacles, by Ellen Raskin. Because she sees everything quite differently from what it really is, the little girl finally agrees to wear glasses, which is a good thing.

When I See My Doctor, by Susan Kuklin. This four-year-old boy is at Dr. Mitchell's office for a general checkup, and all is clearly explained in terms small children can understand.

Your Skin and Mine, by Paul Showers, illustrated by Paul Galdone. The amusing and informative illustrations tell the story of skin, the largest bodily organ.

Occupational Opportunities

All I Am, by Eileen Roe, illustrated by Helen Cogancherry. A small boy tells all the things he is: a friend, an artist, a dancer, and so on, and then contemplates what he will be in the future as he gazes at the stars.

The Biggest Truck, by David Lyon. The biggest truck has to get strawberries to Woosterville, a seven-hour drive away, and the driver makes it by dawn.

Building a House, by Byron Barton. Covering all essentials in building construction, this gives a young child a simple overview with pictures.

The Busy Day of Mamma Pizza, by Anne-Marie Dalmais, illustrated by Graham Percy. Mamma Pizza is a kind elephant who runs an Italian restaurant, and this book goes through both luncheon and dinner with all the animals coming to dine, each with a peculiarity just as human customers might have.

Cowboys, by Glen Rounds. These are real cowboys, and we see their day from sunup to sundown: rounding up cattle, killing a rattlesnake, and finally relaxing after dinner. Unusual childlike illustrations.

Daddies at Work, by Eve Merriam, illustrated by Eugenie Fernandes. A companion to *Mommies at Work,* this book shows daddies at many kinds of jobs, and also tending and loving their children.

Fill It Up!: All About Service Stations, by Gail Gibbons. This book describes a typical day at a service station with cars coming in for gas or repairs.

Fire Engines, by Anne Rockwell. Using all dalmatians as characters, this is a very simple book describing all kinds of fire engines and explaining their uses to fight different sorts of fires.

Fire! Fire!, by Gail Gibbons. This book explains different kinds of fires and those who fight them—in cities, in the country, and on water. These people may have firefighting as a job or be unpaid volunteers.

Frank and Ernest, by Alexandra Day. Two friends—a bear and an elephant—take over Sally's diner while she's away and learn some very special language about food. The humorous "dictionary" is at the front of the book.

Handy Hank Will Fix It, by Anne Rockwell. Hank the handyman does a variety of jobs during a typical day's work. A chimney damper, a clogged sink, a broken window, and other jobs require his attention. Repairs are accurately described.

I Want to Be a Fire Fighter, by Edith Kunhardt. Molly's father is a volunteer firefighter, and she learns all about fighting fires which helps her to choose her future job. This author has a series on different occupations.

I Want to Be an Astronaut, by Byron Barton. A small boy tells what will happen if he gets his wish. He will eat ready-to-eat food, experience zero gravity, and go for space walks when he becomes an astronaut.

Little Nino's Pizzeria, by Karen Barbour. Tony likes to help his father at their small family restaurant, but everything changes when Little Nino's Pizzeria becomes a fancier place. Now Tony just seems to be in the way. Then Nino decides to return to the smaller place, but now it is to be called Tony's Pizzeria.

Marge's Diner, by Gail Gibbons. This is the story of a small-town diner which is open twenty-four hours a day. We learn about all the customers who make it their favorite place to eat.

Mommies at Work, by Eve Merriam, illustrated by Eugenie Fernandes. Here we see a great many occupations and professions now commonly done by working women who are also mothers.

Mommy's Office, by Barbara Shook Hazen, illustrated by David Soman. Emily accompanies her mother downtown to see where she works. A very friendly look at an executive mother.

Mothers Can Do Anything, by Joe Lasker. The text and illustrations demonstrate many occupations of modern mothers, including plumber, dentist, subway conductor, and others.

My Dentist, by Harlow Rockwell. A simple, pleasant visit to the dentist's office takes the fear out of such an occurrence, and there's a "prize drawer" at the end.

My Doctor, by Harlow Rockwell. This is a reassuring look at what a small child can expect when he visits his pediatrician.

People Working, by Douglas Florian. Here we have brief descriptions of where and how people work, indoors and out, alone or together, with plants, animals, or machines.

A Visit to the Fire Station, by Dotti Hannum, photos by Dave Holme, Sue Markson, and Tom Wolf. A realistic view of a fire station and firefighters, equipment, training and all.

A Visit to the Police Station, by Dotti Hannum, photos by Romie Flanagen. This book describes the activities that take place at a police station and explains the various duties of the policemen and policewomen.

When We Grow Up, by Anne Rockwell. Pictures demonstrate the various jobs children want when they grow up. Nonsexist and nondidactic.

Whose Hat?, by Margaret Miller. Children will have fun guessing the professions that are represented by a variety of hats.

Zoo, by Gail Gibbons. This book provides a behind-the-scenes look at a working day at the zoo, from the moment the workers arrive until the night guard locks the gate.

Machines

Airplane Ride, by Douglas Florian. A pilot and his small plane soar, loop, and cruise over cities, forests, deserts, and mountains across the country.

Airport, by Byron Barton. From arrival at the airport through the take-off of a jet, this book explains quite simply what goes on at an airport.

All Aboard ABC, by Doug Magee and Robert Newman. An alphabet book introducing the world of trains from Amtrak to subways.

The Big Book of Fire Trucks and Fire Fighting, by Teddy Slater, illustrated by Mones. This book includes a brief history of fire fighting with pictures of old fire engines, and then comes to modern day equipment of every kind and methods of fighting fires.

The Biggest Truck, by David Lyon. The biggest truck has to get strawberries to Woosterville, a seven-hour drive away, and the driver makes it by dawn.

Boat Book, by Gail Gibbons. Here the child is introduced to many kinds of boats and ships, including rowboats, canoes, sailboats, speedboats, cruise ships, submarines, tugboats, and tankers.

Boats, by Anne Rockwell. Using little bears as characters, this is a simple book describing boats of all kinds, large and small.

Choo Choo, by Virginia Lee Burton. Choo Choo, a steam engine, is tired of pulling the other cars from the country into the city, and she runs away, causing a lot of havoc until she is recovered and resumes her normal run.

Fill It Up! All About Service Stations, by Gail Gibbons. This book describes a typical day at a service station with cars coming in for gas or repairs.

Fire Engines, by Anne Rockwell. Using all dalmatians as characters, this is a very simple book describing all kinds of fire engines and explaining their uses to fight different kinds of fires.

Fire! Fire!, by Gail Gibbons. This book explains different kinds of fires and those who fight them—in cities, in the country, and on water. These people are firefighters as a job or they are unpaid volunteers.

Flying, by Donald Crews. From take-off to landing, this simple book shows what airplane travel is like.

Freight Train, by Donald Crews. An easy-to-understand and colorful explanation of freight trains.

Harbor, by Donald Crews. Simply and with accuracy, this book shows all of the types of boats and ships usually found in a harbor, from a tugboat to a passenger ship.

How Many Trucks Can a Tow Truck Tow?, by Charlotte Pomerantz, illustrated by R. W. Alley. A sturdy little tow truck comes to the rescue when the three other tow trucks in town all break down on the same day. Rhyme and colorful illustration make this book comical.

Katy and the Big Snow, by Virginia Lee Burton. A valiant (female) tractor saves the town when no other vehicle can get through the deep snow.

The Little Engine That Could, by Watty Piper. When the train filled with toys and goodies breaks down, the Passenger Train and the Freight Train feel too important to help, and the Rusty Old Engine is too tired. So it is the Little Blue Engine who saves the day.

Little Toot, by Hardie Gramatky. Little Toot comes from a long line of tugboats, but he doesn't like work and is frightened of the sea which lies outside the channel. All he wants to do is blow smoke bubbles. Then when he changes his mind, no ship wants him, until he becomes a hero by saving a huge liner stuck between two rocks.

Machines, by Anne and Harlow Rockwell. With one picture to a page, this book illustrates at a very basic level various machines, beginning with a wheel and a lever and going on to show what makes them work, from feet on a bicycle to gasoline for an automobile.

Machines at Work, by Byron Barton. Down comes the old building, up goes the new—all with the construction crew using machines of every variety.

Maybelle, the Cable Car, by Virginia Lee Burton. Set in San Francisco, the cable cars reminisce about the "old days" before competition from buses almost eliminated them. But the citizens vote to keep the cable cars, and, freshly painted, they still run up and down the steep hills with a merry "clang, clang."

Mike Mulligan and His Steam Shovel, by Virginia Lee Burton. Mary Anne, Mike's steam shovel, has dug canals, cut through mountains, and dug deep holes for the cellars of skyscrapers. But now Mary Anne is considered old-fashioned, until in Popperville she digs the cellar for the new town hall and remains there as the new furnace.

Mr. Little's Noisy Plane, by Richard Fowler. Mr. Little is trying to take off, but one noise after another indicates a problem under this and under that, and flaps in the book must be lifted to correct each problem.

Planes, by Anne Rockwell. A simple explanation of flying in planes, with rabbits as the characters.

Sam Goes Trucking, by Henry Horenstein. Using photographs, this book shows a young boy going with his trucker father in a sixteen-wheeler as they haul fish to the big city, a full day's ride round trip.

Scuffy the Tugboat, by Gertrude Crampton, illustrated by Tibor Gergely. Scuffy thinks he is too big to play with the little boy in the bathtub, so he goes on an adventure down the stream, which goes into the river, and is almost lost at sea. But he is rescued by the boy and his dad and then decides that the bathtub is the place "for a red-painted tugboat" after all.

The Toolbox, by Anne Rockwell, illustrated by Harlow Rockwell. Done very simply, the ordinary hand tools found in a toolbox are shown, one picture to a page.

Train Song, by Diane Siebert, illustrated by Mike Wimmer. In rhyme which evokes the sounds of a train going across the country, this book tells all about the different cars that make up a train, the tracks it travels on, and the passengers who watch the world go by from the window.

Train Whistles: A Language in Code, by Helen Roney Sattler, illustrated by Tom Funk. With lively illustrations, this book shows what each train whistle means and includes light and telephone signals too.

Trains, by Byron Barton. With childlike drawings, this book explains about steam and electric trains, stations, crossings, and so on.

Trucks, by Donald Crews. A very colorful wordless book about trucks—all kinds of trucks.

Trucks, by Anne Rockwell. Using animal characters, this book illustrates many kinds of trucks: refrigerator trucks, snowplows, dump trucks, fire trucks, and even campers.

A Visit to the Fire Station, by Dotti Hannum. Photos by Dave Holme, Sue Markson, and Tom Wolf. A realistic view of a fire station and firefighters, equipment, training and all.

BOOKS TO EMPHASIZE SKILLS

Alphabet

A Is for Aloha, by Stephanie Feeney, illustrated by Hella Hammid. An alphabet book with the pictures as examples, concentrating on Hawaii and life there.

A Is for Angry: An Animal and Adjective Alphabet Book, by Sandra Boynton. What separates this alphabet book from others is that it stresses adjectives which describe the noun (name) of each animal, and illustrates it with humor.

A Is for Annabelle, by Tasha Tudor. Using Grandmother's doll, Annabelle, as the opening of this charming alphabet book, the author/artist goes through the alphabet with Annabelle's clothing and possessions.

A—My Name Is Alice, by Jane Bayer, illustrated by Steven Kellogg. Never before have the letters of the alphabet been viewed so inventively. "My name is Gertrude and my husband's name is George. We come from Glasgow and we sell giggles" is a typical example. Gertrude is a goose, George is a gorilla. The game and less familiar animals are explained in back.

A, B, See!, by Tana Hoban. A collection of objects which begin with a particular letter of the alphabet, pictured in white on a black background. A very striking and unusual alphabet book.

The ABC Bunny, by Wanda Gag. With music at the back of the book, it is easy to sing about the adventures of a little bunny as she goes from *A* to *Z.*

ABC . . . Z, illustrated by Robert Tallon. A bilingual book, Spanish and English, with each letter humorously illustrated by an appropriate word in both languages.

A B Cedar: An Alphabet of Trees, by George-Ella Lyon, illustrated by Tom Parker. An unusual alphabet book which introduces the leaves from various trees to illustrate the letters.

Albert's Alphabet, by Leslie Tryon. Clever Albert, a goose, uses all the wood in his workshop to build an alphabet for the school playground, and then he goes on to use other materials.

All Aboard ABC, by Doug Magee and Robert Newman. An alphabet book introducing the world of trains from Amtrak to subways.

Alligators Arrived with Apples: A Potluck Alphabet Feast, by Crescent Dragon-wagon, illustrated by Jose Aruego and Ariane Dewey. A wonderfully imaginative and colorful retelling of the alphabet with statements such as "Goose Gave Gravy, Grapes, and Gingerbread," and "Hyena Had the Hiccups, but He Hailed us with Honey and Hazelnuts."

Alligators All Around, by Maurice Sendak. Alligators go through the alphabet humorously, even x-raying x-rays.

Alphabears, by Kathleen Hague, illustrated by Michael Hague. Here we see a bear for each letter of the alphabet and each bear's special quality is described in rhyme. Very original verse and drawings.

The Alphabet Book, by P. D. Eastman. This is a comical book with pictures such as "Kangeroo with keys" or "Skunk on a scooter" to illustrate the letters.

Alphabet Soup, by Scott Gustafson. Otter invites all his friends to a potluck and each one brings food according to the first letter of his name. Double-spread pictures captivate the reader. For example, "Lion's lentils. Lighthouse Lion licked his lips and laughed. 'I love lentils—loads and loads.' "

The Alphabet Tree, by Leo Lionni. Each letter has a favorite leaf, but a strong wind blows them in every direction. Then the word bug shows them how letters can form words, and the purple caterpillar shows the next step, sentences—important sentences, like "Peace on Earth."

**Animal Alphabet,* by Bert Kitchen. An oversize book with one-to-a-page paintings of unusual animals which illustrate the twenty-six letters. The reader is invited to guess their identities or check the answers at the back of the book.

**Animalia,* by Graeme Base. This is an alphabet book with a difference—best for older children. Each double-page spread has much more than animal illustrations. For example, "Crafty crimson cats carefully catching crusty crayfish" illustrates *C,* and under the water there are other items, such as a comb, a cornflakes box, a clarinet, and a crab. Very challenging.

**Anno's Alphabet: An Adventure in Imagination,* by Mitsumasa Anno. A very sophisticated alphabet book with one picture to a page, plus borders which also illustrate each letter. There is a guide at the back which will prove useful.

Ashanti to Zulu: African Traditions, by Margaret W. Musgrove, illustrated by Leo and Diane Dillon. Going through the alphabet, each page of this very beautiful book has a story about each tribe and its traditions.

Aster Aardvark's Alphabet Adventures, by Steven Kellogg. This is a really clever vocabulary book with a story. For example, the letter *O* reads, "Outraged by the otter's outburst, Oliver, the old orangutan from Ohio, ordered the obnoxious oaf and his offensive oboe out of the orchestra." Amusing illustrations on every page.

Chicka Chicka Boom Boom, by Bill Martin, Jr., and John Archambault, illustrated by Lois Ehlert. The letters of the alphabet get mixed up as they all try to climb the coconut tree. In rhyme and vivid color.

Cajun Alphabet, by James Rice. Gaston, the green-nosed alligator who first appeared in *Cajun Night Before Christmas,* illustrates the alphabet with words used by Cajun people and pictures unique to this area of Louisiana. This vocabulary mixes English and French without apology and includes some words which are neither.

Curious George Learns the Alphabet, by H. A. Rey. The man in the yellow hat shows George how to form the letters of the alphabet using humorous pictures. Both upper- and lower-case letters are included.

Demi's Find the Animal ABC, by Demi. With answers in the back of the book in case a child needs them, this book combines the alphabet with sharpening observational skills. In a group of many, can the reader pick out the exact duplicate of a single one pictured in the corner?

The Dragon ABC Hunt, by Loreen Leedy. Ten little dragons go on a scavenger hunt to find objects for each letter of the alphabet. Done in rhyme, using both upper- and lower-case letters.

Eating the Alphabet: Fruits and Vegetables from A to Z, by Lois Ehlert. "Apple to Zucchini, come take a look. Start eating your way through this alphabet book" is the invitation on the first page of this colorful array, which includes some less well-known fruits and veggies.

An Edward Lear Alphabet, by Edward Lear, illustrated by Carol Newsom. Beginning with "A a—A was once an apple-pie, Pidy, Widy, Tidy, Pidy, Nice Insidy, Apple-pie!" this charming book goes through the alphabet with drawings that Lear would have loved. A really different alphabet book.

Everyday ABC, by Jenny Williams. Modern children are pictured in scenes which illustrate the alphabet in both upper- and lower-case letters.

Farm Alphabet Book, by Jane Miller. Photographs of farm animals and objects, accompanied by simple descriptions illustrate the letters of the alphabet.

**A Farmer's Alphabet*, by Mary Azarian. Beautiful woodcuts grace each oversize page, which concentrates on rural themes and traditions. Both upper- and lower-case letters are shown.

The Folks in the Valley: A Pennsylvania Dutch ABC, by Jim Aylesworth, illustrated by Stefano Vitale. With upper- and lower-case letters, this rhyming alphabet book tells about the people and activities of a Pennsylvania Dutch settlement in a rural valley.

The Guinea Pig ABC, by Kate Duke. This alphabet book does not use nouns to illustrate the letters, but concentrates instead on adjectives and concepts, as the guinea pig demonstrates each letter.

Helen Oxenbury's ABC of Things, by Helen Oxenbury. With inimitable illustrations, this ABC book has wonderfully comic pictures for each letter of the alphabet. For example, for the letter *G, g,* there is a goat shopping with a goose in a grocery store.

In a Pumpkin Shell, by Joan Walsh Anglund. This is the alphabet book which gives a Mother Goose rhyme for each letter, such as "Hickety Pickety, my black hen" for *H.*

Jambo Means Hello: A Swahili Alphabet Book, by Muriel Feelings, illustrated by Tom Feelings. Each letter of the alphabet is the first letter of a Swahili word (with the phonetic pronunciation in parenthesis), and each word is illustrated. For example, "R—rafiki (rah fee key), which means friend. Friends do chores together."

Mousekin's ABC, by Edna Miller. In verse and with charming pictures Mousekin and all the woodland animals go through the alphabet *A* to *Z.*

Old Black Fly, by Jim Aylesworth, illustrated by Stephen Gammell. Rhyming text and illustrations follow a mischievous old black fly through the alphabet as he has a very busy bad day landing where he should not be.

On Beyond Zebra, by Dr. Seuss. A very unusual alphabet book for children who are already familiar with their ABCs.

A Peaceable Kingdom: The Shaker Abecedarius, illustrated by Alice and Martin Provensen. A quaintly illustrated rhyme that includes the animals from alligator to zebra.

Quentin Blake's ABC, by Quentin Blake. Rhyming from letter to letter, this delightful alphabet book has both upper- and lower-case letters and very humorous illustrations.

***Twenty-six Letters and Ninety-nine Cents,* by Tana Hoban. Letters with unnamed objects for each, and, if the book is turned around, money is used to illustrate numbers, with nickels, dimes, and quarters shown. For example,

5 shows five pennies and also one nickel; 30 shows a quarter and a nickel, and so on. Very unusual and helpful for children learning monetary equivalent values.

The Wildlife ABC, by Jan Thornhill. Upper- and lower-case letters, great pictures, and some rhyme make this an outstanding book. For example, "G g—G is for goose, paddling under a bridge." And, on the facing page, "H h—H is for housefly, inspecting your fridge." There are Nature Notes at the back, explaining each entry in detail.

Numbers

Babies Have Fun With Numbers, by Eileen McCarney-Muldoon and Mary Bennett O'Brien. Very appealing photos of babies and items one to ten should encourage toddlers to count the things pictured, such as four bibs and six teddy bears.

Chicken Little Count-to-Ten, by Margaret Friskey, illustrated by Katherine Evans. Chicken Little is thirsty, so he asks one cow, two elephants, three camels, and finally ten foxes how to get a drink. Then he learns the right way. Numerals and words for each number.

Count and See, by Tana Hoban. One to ten, eleven to twenty, then on up to one hundred with photographs of familiar, everyday items.

Counting Wildflowers, by Bruce McMillan. From one to twenty, this book combines colors and the recognition of common wildflowers done in beautiful photographs.

Dollars and Cents for Harriet, by Betsy and Giulio Maestro. With the aim of teaching concepts about money, the authors have created a problem for Harriet, the elephant, who wants to buy a kite, but has only one hundred pennies toward the five dollars she needs. She works for twenty nickels, ten dimes, four quarters, two half dollars, and is then able to make her purchase.

Farm Counting Book, by Jane Miller. One to ten with math problems at the end. Great for preschoolers just learning their numbers.

Five Little Ducks, illustrated by Jose Aruego and Ariane Dewey. A simple counting song, each duck leaving, then finally being reunited with Mama Duck. With music at the end of the book.

From One to One Hundred, by Teri Sloat. A spectacular, fun-filled parade of numbers with each one cleverly incorporated into each picture. An intriguing book for readers of all ages.

Harriet Goes to the Circus, by Betsy and Giulio Maestro. In this book children are exposed to ordinal numbers when Harriet rushes to be first in line, followed by Mouse second, Duck third, and so on. Then the line reverses and Harriet becomes last.

Helen Oxenbury's Numbers of Things, by Helen Oxenbury. A clever book illustrating numbers one through fifty with charming paintings, and ending by looking at the stars, asking "How many?"

How Much Is a Million?, by David M. Schwartz, illustrated by Steven Kellogg. Humorous illustrations and examples answer the question in the title. For example, "If a goldfish bowl were big enough for a million goldfish, it would be large enough to hold a whale." Then it continues with a billion and a trillion, with some notes from Marvelosissimo in the back for those interested in math.

Knick Knack Paddywack, by Marissa Moss. In this variation and extension of the traditional counting song, "this old man" ends up blasting off and flying to the moon.

Moja Means One: A Swahili Counting Book, by Muriel Feelings, illustrated by Tom Feelings. Each number is illustrated by a Swahili word, with phonetic pronunciation and pictured explanations.

A Number of Dragons, by Loreen Leedy. Ten through one and one through ten, the little dragons go out to play ball, climb walls, and bury a bone. All done in rhymed verse.

Numbers, by John J. Reiss. From 1, with a single boy, to 1000, with raindrops as the example, this book colorfully illustrates numerical concepts.

On the River: An Adding Book, by Sheila White Samton. As each page is turned, the river fills with animals in this colorful counting book.

One Ballerina Two, by Vivian French, illustrated by Jan Ormerod. A little sister copies her older sister's ballet movements, counting backward ten to one.

One Crow: A Counting Rhyme, by Jim Aylesworth, illustrated by Ruth Young. One to ten in rhymed verse, using farm animals and children.

One Duck, Another Duck, by Charlotte Pomerantz, illustrated by Jose Aruego and Ariane Dewey. A charming counting book—one to ten—for Danny, his grandmother, and very young children.

One Hunter, by Pat Hutchins. One hunter walks through the jungle observed by two elephants, three giraffes, and so on—one through ten.

1 Is One, by Tasha Tudor. A variety of animals, children, trees, and flowers, as well as the easy-to-remember verses will encourage young readers to learn numbers one through twenty.

One Little Teddy Bear, by Mark Burgess. A counting book from one to ten with clever peek-a-boo pages and rhymes to help a child's memory.

One Was Johnny, by Maurice Sendak. A novel counting book, one to ten and then back to one again.

Over in the Meadow, by John Langstaff, illustrated by Feodor Rojankovsky. A counting song, one to ten, based on all the little animals of the forest and their babies. The music is the one used in the southern Appalachian Mountains.

Playtime 1 2 3, by Jenny Williams. A brightly colored counting book, one through twenty.

Richard Scarry's Best Counting Book Ever, by Richard Scarry. From one to one hundred with the possibility of addition and subtraction included. Little Willy Bunny counts all the things he sees in one day.

Ten, Nine, Eight, by Molly Bang. In an unusual bedtime book a little girl counts from "ten small toes all washed and warm" backward through numbers to "one big girl all ready for bed."

Ten Potatoes in a Pot and Other Counting Rhymes, edited by Michael Jay Katz, illustrated by June Otani. From one cinnamon bun warming in the sun to ten potatoes bubbling in a pot to a hillside fifteen hundred berries deep, these charming pieces make a perfect read-aloud rhyming and counting book for the youngest child.

This Old Man, illustrated by Carol Jones. With peepholes at each number—one to ten—this song is fun to read and/or sing. Music at the end of the book.

This Old Man: The Counting Song, illustrated by Michael Koontz. With very humorous drawings, this is the knick-knack, paddy-whack way of counting one to ten. With music and play instructions at the back of the book.

**Twenty-six Letters and Ninety-nine Cents,* by Tana Hoban. Upper- and lower-case letters with unnamed objects for each letter, and, if the book is turned around, money is used to illustrate numbers with pennies, nickels, dimes, and quarters shown. For example, the number 5 shows five pennies and also one nickel; 30 shows a quarter and a nickel, and so on. Very unusual and helpful for children learning monetary equivalents.

Two Ways to Count to Ten: A Liberian Folktale, retold by Ruby Dee, illustrated by Susan Meddaugh. King Leopard decides to test all the other animals to see who will succeed him. The one who throws the king's spear into the air and counts to ten before it comes down shall win. How the clever antelope wins makes a delightful story.

The Very Hungry Caterpillar, by Eric Carle. How do butterflies come into being? Here the author imaginatively combines the process of metamorphosis with the days of the week, numbers of fruits, and ten foods dear to the hearts of children.

What Comes In Twos, Threes, and Fours?, by Suzanne Aker, illustrated by Bernie Karlin. This book introduces the numbers two, three, and four by enumerating the ways in which they occur in everyday life, from two eyes and two arms to the four seasons of the year.

Who's Counting?, by Nancy Tafuri. In double-spread pages the numbers one to ten are beautifully illustrated with familiar animals, such as rabbits and puppies.

Willy Can Count, by Anne Rockwell. A simple counting book—one to ten.

Shapes

Circles, Triangles and Squares, by Tana Hoban. Photographs of ordinary scenes, people, and objects illustrate these shapes clearly. They are everywhere.

My First Look at Shapes, illustrated by Stephen Oliver. Here the concepts of shapes are explored, including squares, circles, rectangles, diamonds, ovals, and others, using items which are familiar to children.

Round and Round and Round, by Tana Hoban. Illustrating the concept of roundness in this wordless book, the author has pictured everything from green peas to tires.

Shapes, by Gwenda Turner. Here there are cutout shapes in the center of each page, so that the child can guess what the whole picture will reveal.

Shapes, by John J. Reiss. This book illustrates common shapes, such as triangles and squares, and some less common as well. Brings across the idea that shapes are everywhere, not just in math books.

What Shape?, by Debbie MacKinnon, illustrated by Anthea Sieveking. Brief text and colorful photos introduce a variety of shapes as curious toddlers explore the world around them.

The Wing on a Flea: A Book About Shapes, by Ed Emberley. Using rhyme, this book covers triangles, rectangles, and circles, showing the many places each shape may be found.

Colors

Brown Bear, Brown Bear, What Do You See?, by Bill Martin, Jr., illustrated by Eric Carle. A great book to teach colors with humor.

The Chalk Box Story, by Don Freeman. Eight sticks of magic chalk draw the sky, sea, an island, a turtle, and a boy waiting to be rescued. But the ship doesn't see the boy, so the turtle takes things in hand.

Color Farm, by Lois Ehlert. With center cutouts in the pages, the book uses strong colors to represent farm animals. This is a novel approach.

A Color of His Own, by Leo Lionni. The sad chameleon has no color of his own, but he finds a partner and they change colors together.

Colors, by John J. Reiss. Each color—red, orange, yellow, black, blue, green, brown, and purple—is shown in vibrant color with examples of items having that color.

Freight Train, by Donald Crews. A simple and very colorful explanation of freight trains.

Green Says Go, by Ed Emberley. This clever book deals with common connotations of colors, such as "purple with rage," or "white with fear," and so on, challenging children to think of additional feelings expressed in this way.

Growing Colors, by Bruce McMillan. Cleverly combining colors with fruits and vegetables, the vivid photographs make the reader hungry.

Hailstones and Halibut Bones, by Mary O'Neill, newly illustrated by John Wallner. These lovely poems describing colors have been enhanced in this new edition by vibrant drawings which make them leap off the page.

Is It Red? Is It Yellow? Is It Blue?, by Tana Hoban. A wordless book to help young children identify colors.

Hawaii Is a Rainbow, by Stephanie Feeney, illustrated by Jeff Reese. The colors of a rainbow—red, orange, yellow, green, blue, and purple—are used to organize pictures of the people, places, plants, and animals of Hawaii. Almost wordless.

Little Blue and Little Yellow, by Leo Lionni. Personifying colors, the author has them hugging and becoming green, but their families don't recognize them, so they cry until they are all blue and yellow tears. Then everyone understands and all ends happily.

Mr. Rabbit and the Lovely Present, by Charlotte Zolotow, illustrated by Maurice Sendak. A little girl consults her rabbit friend about a birthday gift for her mother and takes his advice about giving something of each color her mother likes—a basket of fruit.

My First Look at Colors, Toni Rann, art editor. Vivid realistic photographs illustrate every common color with everyday items easily recognized by preschoolers.

Of Colors and Things, by Tana Hoban. Photographs of toys, food, and other common objects are grouped by color in such a way that a child can practice pointing out one color in a group of many.

Planting a Rainbow, by Lois Ehlert. A child and her mother plant a flower garden with bulbs, seeds, and seedling plants, and every year they reap a rainbow of colors.

Samuel Todd's Book of Great Colors, by E. L. Konigsburg. Sometimes different things can be the same color; other times the same things can be different colors, and some things are colorless, like hugs, kisses, and songs.

Who Said Red?, by Mary Serfozo, illustrated by Keiko Narahashi. A dialogue between two speakers, one of whom must keep insisting on an interest in the color red, introduces that hue, as well as green, blue, yellow, and others.

Winnie the Witch, by Valerie Thomas, illustrated by Korky Paul. Wilbur, Winnie's black cat, can't be easily seen in Winnie's all-black house, so she turns him green, but falls over him in the grass. Next, she tries a rainbow effect, but everybody laughs at Wilbur, so Winnie solves the problem by turning Wilbur back to black and putting all the colors on her house instead.

Verbal Skills

American Heritage Picture Dictionary, by Robert L. Hillerich, illustrated by Maggie Swanson. For the child beginning to grasp the idea of "looking up" meanings, this is a very good way to start.

***American Heritage First Dictionary,* edited by Stephen Krensky, illustrated by George Ulrich. For the first or second grader who has "graduated" from the picture dictionary.

Busy Buzzing Bumblebees and Other Tongue Twisters, by Alvin Schwartz, illustrated by Kathie Abrams. These are short, simple, and usually silly, just the kind of thing first graders love.

Green Eggs and Ham, by Dr. Seuss. Sam-I-Am tries to persuade the reluctant reader to try green eggs and ham, so he finally gives in and finds that he likes them! In rhyme, of course.

Herds of Words, by Patricia MacCarthy. Text and colorful illustrations provide examples of named groups of animals, people, and things, including such phrases as "a parliament of owls," "a crew of sailors," and "a fleet of ships."

Hop on Pop, by Dr. Seuss. In a comic fashion with his special kind of drawing, the author shows the phonetic sounding of words, as in "Red, Ned, Ted, and Ed in bed."

I Read Signs, by Tana Hoban. Signs which surround the young child will actually result in what we call "reading" before we are aware of it.

I Read Symbols, by Tana Hoban. With clear photographs we see that children read without words all the time, as they interpret picture signs, for example, like the outline of a woman or a man on a rest-room door.

Kitten Can, by Bruce McMillan. Using all verbs to describe what is pictured as the kitten stares, climbs, clings, jumps, and. . . . Very good way to show action words.

***Messages in the Mailbox: How to Write a Letter,* by Loreen Leedy. This book discusses (in a humorous manner) how to write different kinds of letters, tells who can be a potential correspondent, and provides examples. For first or second graders.

My First Word Book, by Angela Wilkes. A really inclusive picture dictionary for the young child. It has divisions which tell the child about himself, his family, various locales, colors, shapes, opposites, and just about anything he or she may be curious to investigate. The photography makes it all very clear.

One Sun: A Book of Terse Verse, by Bruce McMillan. This interesting book describes a day at the beach in a series of two monosyllabic words that rhyme. For example, as the child is having lemonade, we read "Pink drink."

One Way: A Trip With Traffic Signs, by Leonard Shortall. With humorous illustrations we see the travels of a family going to a Fourth of July celebration, meeting every kind of traffic sign enroute.

Open House for Butterflies, by Ruth Krauss, illustrated by Maurice Sendak. Childlike sayings and original words carry quite a bit of subtle meaning, as in "A little tree is not a good thing to be because you might grow up to be a telephone pole," or "Lovabye is a good thing to know."

Squeeze a Sneeze, by Bill Morrison. Some very funny ways to use rhyming words, such as "Can you tickle a pickle for a nickel?" or "Hit a fly in the eye with a blueberry pie" make this a great way to start a game with children making up their own "funnies."

Super Super Superwords, by Bruce McMillan. With great photos of children, this book shows adjectives with their positive, comparative, and superlative forms. Excellent for language development.

Concepts

All Year Long, by Nancy Tafuri. A charming way to teach the days of the week and the months of the year through illustration.

Bear Child's Book of Hours, by Anne Rockwell. From eight in the morning when his alarm rings until eight at night when he goes to bed, each hour of the day is shown with bear child's activity at that time.

Becca Backward, Becca Frontward: A Book of Concept Pairs, illustrated by Bruce McMillan. Many common concept pairs are shown by photographs of one child and her activities.

Chicken Soup With Rice: A Book of Months, by Maurice Sendak. In rhyme a little boy tells what he will do each month of the year with his chicken soup and rice.

Dawn, by Uri Shulevitz. An old man and his grandson sleep by a lake and awake to put their rowboat into the lake. Then everything dramatically turns green because of the sunrise.

Demi's Opposites: An Animal Game Book, by Demi. As children go through this unusual book of imaginatively pictured animals, they learn the meaning of opposing terms, such as fat-thin, rich-poor, and open-shut. All done in rhyme.

Fast-Slow-High-Low: A Book of Opposites, by Peter Spier. Many concepts are included in this clearly illustrated book, including wide-narrow, quiet-noisy, and a multitude of others done with humor.

For Strawberry Jam or Fireflies, by Gail Hartman, illustrated by Ellen Weiss. Many items have multiple uses and this book illustrates some of the less obvious ones, such as a mason jar for jam or to keep fireflies in, and raisins for a snack or a funny face on a cookie. Good concept book.

The Guinea Pig ABC, by Kate Duke. This ABC book doesn't use nouns to illustrate the letters, but concentrates instead on adjectives and concepts, as the guinea pig demonstrates each letter.

Here a Chick, There a Chick, by Bruce McMillan. Photographs of baby chicks are used to illustrate such opposite concepts as inside-outside, asleep-awake, and alone-together. A charming idea.

A House Is a House for Me, by Mary Ann Hoberman, illustrated by Betty Fraser. With lilting, rhythmic verse and lovely illustrations, this book subtly teaches spatial concepts and some novel ways of looking at the world.

Is It Dark? Is It Light?, by Mary D. Lankford, illustrated by Stacey Schuett. While describing the moon's appearance, two children introduce pairs of opposites.

Maybe Right, Maybe Wrong, by Dan Barker, illustrated by Brian Strassburg. Without sermonizing, this book is a good guide to ethical behavior, showing as it does the difference bewtween rules and principles, and illustrating clearly how choices can be made—sometimes right, sometimes wrong—but always by using one's mind to make the best decisions possible.

Maybe Yes, Maybe No, by Dan Barker, illustrated by Brian Strassburg. Subtitled "A Guide for Young Skeptics," this useful book stresses the scientific method in nontechnical language and emphasizes the need for critical thinking even at a young age. It could be useful in combating the barrage of questionable material on television.

My First Look at Sizes, illustrated by Stephen Oliver. Using Russian nesting dolls, for example, this book gives ideas of small, large, larger, with many items included and growth shown by picturing human hands.

Nice or Nasty: A Book of Opposites, by Nick Butterworth and Mick Inkpen. Colorful and humorous drawings illustrate clearly the idea of opposites, such as rough-smooth, weak-strong, and so on.

Over and Over, by Charlotte Zolotow, illustrated by Garth Williams. A little girl who is too young to understand concepts of time asks her mother, "What comes next?" as they go through the year. Her birthday wish is for it all to happen again, which, her mother assures her, it will.

Over, Under and Through: And Other Spatial Concepts, by Tana Hoban. Using photographs of children, this book illustrates the concepts which adults often take for granted—the meaning of simple prepositions.

Pigs Say Oink, by Martha Alexander. This first book of sounds includes farm animals, zoo animals, and common country and city sounds with simple illustrations.

Push, Pull, Empty, Full: A Book of Opposites, by Tana Hoban. Using action photos of children, this book illustrates concepts such as thick-thin, whole-broken, and empty-full. An easy way to explain prepositions and adjectives.

Traffic: A Book of Opposites, by Betsy and Giulio Maestro. Using a little car journeying from the city to the country, this book introduces antonyms, such as over the bridge and under it, passing a full truck and an empty one, and so forth.

Time To . . . , by Bruce McMillan. Through clearly sequenced activities, this book shows the passing of time, hour by hour, as a child wakes, goes through his day, and then goes to sleep.

The Very Hungry Caterpillar, by Eric Carle. How do butterflies come into being? Here the author imaginatively combines the process of metamorphosis with the days of the week, numbers of fruits, colors, and ten foods dear to the hearts of children.

Part Three

Reading Aloud

SOME GENERAL HINTS

There are some specific differences to be noted between reading to one or two children, usually in a home setting, and reading to a group of perhaps eight or ten youngsters in a more formal atmosphere of a school, library, or child-care center. On the other hand, some of the basic "rules" for successfully reading aloud are quite apt to be consistently applicable.

The Differences

When reading to one child or to a very small number, it is possible to offer suggestions, and then allow the final decision about what book or books are chosen to be up to the child or children. When there are a greater number of children, however, there are apt to be a greater number of preferences, which can set up a poor initial atmosphere for a story and may even result in a behavior problem with a child whose book is not the majority choice. Therefore, with a group, it is best for the adult who is reading to make the selections in advance.

Then, secondly, there is the matter of interruptions. Assuming that one or two children are being read to at home (ignoring such common nuisances as telephones and doorbells which might interrupt the reading), the adult is able to stop and explicate more often in answer to a child's questions than he would be able to do in a group setting. Anyone who has read to a group of three-year-olds knows how easily a reading about zoo animals, for example, may be sidetracked by a child's recital about *his* trip to the zoo. Practice in incorporating such comment into the reading without allowing the discussion to become too general—with the book forgotten—is a good way to deal with this problem.

Next, in groups there is often a wider age spread than there is when reading in the home setting, and this may be difficult to deal with. In general, it is a good idea to read to a rather limited number of children within a similar age frame, and then go on with the next group, rather than try to interest children who range from age three to six in the same story at one sitting.

There is also the practical matter of book size to consider. For one or two children, a very small book held in the reader's lap is quite cozy. For a group, however, it is necessary to select a book which is large enough to be easily seen by all, and it must be held so that it is facing the youngsters at all times. Since 1988 Scholastic Inc. has done a great deal to help in this regard, by reprinting over one hundred of the best titles for younger children in really large books—at least 15″ by 18″—so that they are visible with a very large group, and this publisher offers study guides for additional activities as well.

Finally, although in all situations the child or children need to be comfortably settled before being read to, and extraneous noise kept at a minimum, the practice of reading only as a prelude to rest, nap, or bedtime is undesirable. Such a time slot suggests that reading is an activity meant to put one to sleep, certainly not an idea we want to promote.

In the case of children who resist a cessation of physical activity, we must be careful to avoid the impression that reading is being used as though it were a sedative. Ideally, of course, an available adult should acquiesce to every child's request to be read to at any time such a request is made, and in the home this is quite possible within limits. In a group situation, however, it is less likely that at any given moment it is convenient for a teacher or aide to stop whatever activity is under way to read to one child. In any case, promising to read a story as a kind of reward for completing a task or doing a good job of tidying up after an art project, for example, sets the scene for a favorable attitude toward books and reinforces positive feelings about reading.

SOME RULES FOR SUCCESSFUL READ-ALOUDS

In spite of the differences in reading aloud at home or in a group situation, there are some very basic rules for success in making literature live for children under any circumstances:

1. Choose a book that you like, one appropriate to the age of the child/children. Your enthusiasm will be contagious.

2. Handle the book carefully, as an example to your listeners.

3. Be thoroughly familiar with the book beforehand, especially with what are called the "hinges" of the plot, that is, the points at which the story progresses from one situation to the next. This will help with point 4.

4. If reading to more than three children, seat them in a semicircle in front of you and sit on a very low chair, facing them. Then hold the book toward the children at all times. Practice beforehand so that you can read "upside down" or by glancing sideways at the text.

5. Make as much eye contact as possible with your listeners.

6. If there are any explanations necessary before starting to read, make them. For instance, if you are reading a folktale from far away Indonesia, you might want to mention this, calling attention to the illustrations.

7. In the same way, if there is an unfamiliar word which is not made self-explanatory through context or illustration, stop and paraphrase it. However, do not "read down" or change the author's words to simplify the material since this would preclude the acquisition of new vocabulary words. For example, in Leo Lionni's book *Frederick* the word "granary" is used, but not pictured. Read the word as written; then explain its meaning very simply, as "A granary is like a barn, a big building on a farm, but the animals stay in the barn and the grain is put in the granary."

8. Make certain that you are reading at an appropriate speed, taking time to show the illustrations and varying the tempo as the story calls for such variation.

9. Make sure that you are audible at all times.

10. Possibly the most important point in an effective read-aloud may be called "animation," or what might loosely approximate "acting."

   a. Be sure that your voice and tone are appropriate to the story: if it is a serious story, be serious; if it is a funny story, take a light tone, and so on.

   b. If there are several characters, try to differentiate among them by using different voices, if possible. For example, if there is a small mouse speaking, make your voice a bit "squeaky." If the character is a huge troll, make your voice loud and booming. One word of caution: don't attempt a book with too many characters at first.

   c. Make good use of the built-in stylistic devices provided by the author. For instance, if a character is running quickly, try to simulate some sense of breathlessness and speed. If a character is described as a "teeny, tiny" person, emphasize the words "teeny" and "tiny."

11. Remember that what you may consider somewhat "hammy" behavior while reading will probably delight your audience. Nothing fails as completely or quickly as a drab rendition.

12. Certain stories lend themselves well to oral participation by children, which increases their sense of immediate involvement. For instance, the books listed under the category "Play one—Play All" will elicit responses, as will a story with a cumulative or repetitive text. Encourage this.

13. Individual books adapt well as bases for creative dramatics, a topic discussed separately in the following section.

14. Particular books lend themselves to the use of story boards and/or simple hand puppets as visual reinforcements. These will also be discussed in the following section.

15. Be prepared for success, which means that you will have requests to read and reread the same books to the same child or children. As anyone who has read to youngsters knows, this is the highest form of praise both for the material and for its interpreter. If you have chosen a book you like in the first place, you will still enjoy it when asked for repeated renditions.

But remember, even if you are bored by the fifth repetition, don't let down on your "performance." Suggest another book tactfully, for a change of pace, and then cheerfully do all the encores of the original book requested by your listeners. The child or children may have a special reason for wanting a particular story, even though that reason is never verbalized.

CREATIVE DRAMATICS

Before beginning a detailed discussion of this way of reinforcing literary values, we must first be aware that this activity bears little resemblance to the presentation of "plays" in the usual sense. No sets are used, except as informal arrangements may occur to the children themselves; no costumes or makeup is involved, no audience of doting adults is allowed, and there are no speeches or lines to be learned. Actually, creative dramatics parallels what in adult theater would be called "improvisation," with the concomitant benefits of that form and the necessity of introducing certain "performance techniques" to the children before any reference is made to literature.

If we examine those "techniques," the advantages of participation will become clear. First, for youngsters to whom playing and making believe are such common activities, impromptu responses to imagined situations seem a natural kind of behavior. For example, children will listen to music and "act out" a march of elephants or a circle of merry-go-round horses at the slightest suggestion, and pretraining for creative dramatics can start with simple movements like these.

Then, gradually, additional games can be added to stimulate imaginative thinking. For instance, if the youngsters are seated in a circle, told to close their eyes, and then told to put their hands on the floor next to them, they will respond to suggestions regarding supposed changes in that floor. If the adult now says that it has become sticky, so that they cannot pick up their hands without tremendous effort, they will enter into the game and do some very realistic tugging and pulling. If the floor is then supposed to become a pool of ice water, the children will react appropriately, and so on.

Obviously, there is no limit to the kinds of situations that the adult leader might want to suggest.

Going from group activity to individual children, the teacher could then pretend to put something into each child's mouth, varying the item with each one. As one child blows an imaginary bubble with his "bubble gum," another will realistically react with a puckered mouth while "eating" a sour dill pickle. All of these exercises are done without any props at all, so that the activities may vary according to the adult's imagination, and they will stimulate without limit the imaginative faculties of the children.

Returning to the group, the children may be given a "make-believe" situation, such as getting ready to go to the beach for a day's outing or packing to move to a new house, with the adult briefly suggesting progressive activities in the pretended situations, if needed.

As anyone who has worked with groups of children knows, they will assign roles to each other, pantomime behavior, and interact freely with a mimimum of direction from the sidelines. This kind of "performance" again stimulates formation of original mental images and, in addition, sharpens listening skills. After the children have mastered a number of these "situation" scenes, they can be directed toward characterization.

This is easily done by instructing individuals to enact various tasks, as the rest of the group watches. For instance, one child may be told to "walk like an old person going outside in the rain," or another may be told to "walk like a princess going to your throne," while a third may be directed to "walk in a dark woods, trying to find the way home." After they have mastered to some degree the idea of acting out individual roles, they can work together in pairs in similar kinds of "scenes."

For example, a child could play the dog who doesn't want to come into the house for the old person going out in the rain to fetch him. Or in the second situation, a child could pick up the princess's train as she walked toward her throne, while in the third scene, a second "actor" could become an owl in the dark woods where his partner is "lost." After a few sessions, sometimes with children suggesting roles for themselves, most youngsters over age four should be ready for creative dramatics in the more formal sense.

At this juncture particularly, the books chosen must have specific qualities. First, they should be stories with rather simple plot lines—even some already familiar to the youngsters. Secondly, the "characters" in the book should be equal in number to the participants, since young children find it difficult to sit as "audience" while others in their group perform. In regard to this, certain flexibility may be derived by choosing stories in which some "characters" may or may not be used. Trees, for example, can be "acted out" or not, depending on the number of children in the group. Or in a story such as *Caps for Sale,* the number of monkeys is indeterminate.

Next, stories that have action but which do not require forceful physical contact between characters are literally the safest, since small children may become so involved that their interactions could become dangerous to other participants.

Finally, stories with a variety of characterizations will provide the broadest scope for the youngsters. As a footnote, it may be noticed that children who have watched a lot of television will tend at first to imitate cliches they've seen, but as they become more familiar with this form, they will learn to draw more and more on their own creativity in regard to both action and dialogue.

As an introduction to children who have been doing the kinds of improvisations suggested above, it is usually enough merely to announce that a story will now be the basis for their "play." It is important that the children be seated in a semicircle and told that they will resume the same seats when the activity is completed; we shall see the reason for this shortly. At this point, the adult reads the story in the usual way, with the book held toward the children so that they can see the illustrations.

When the story is over, the adult reviews the "hinges" so that they are kept in the correct order when being dramatized. This may be done by asking the children to retell the plot, point by point; then, if any important action is left out, the teacher can gently remind the group of the omission. After the story line is firmly set in the minds of the youngsters, the characters should be reviewed in the same way, and beginning from the left side of the semicircle, each child asked to say what "part" he or she would like to try. If there is a shy child in the group, the adult may want to assign a role which does not require more than a minimum of effort, perhaps a part which does not call for any speaking lines at all.

When all roles have been assigned, the next item is the "setting." If more than one locale is called for, the children may need a little prompting before they can decide which part of the space will be designated as one place, which another. When all is ready, the adult need only coach from the sidelines, and the rule of "less is better" should apply.

The first time a story is done this way, whole sections may be inadvertently omitted and the characterizations may not be too well done. But no matter. After the action has been completed, the children take their same places in the semicircle and an informal critique is initiated. Questions such as, "Did we forget any parts of the story?" or "Did the lion sound really fierce when she roared?" will elicit responses, and then, beginning from the other side (the right-hand side) of the semicircle, parts are again assigned—this time to different children, of course—and the whole story is acted out again.

Usually a group will want to do the play at least three times in succession, so that after the second "critique" the teacher can assign roles beginning with the middle child and going toward each end alternately. This may seem picayune, but the repeat performances make it mandatory that the children resume their original seats after each time through, to avoid having the same child ask to play a major role each time.

Once the children become familiar with this kind of activity, they not only grow to appreciate the literature involved, but also they learn to speak extemporaneously, to listen to each other, and to answer appropriately since they make up all the dialogue as they go along. They also learn to objectively criticize performance. And, additionally, the youngsters who are very shy in the beginning frequently gain in self-confidence as they go along, while those who customarily expect to be the center of attention come to understand the value of being a supporting player, so to speak. In this way, consistently including creative dramatics in the literature program for all ages can be worthwhile as a painless way to modify behavior as well as a method of reinforcing literary values.

Some Suggested Titles for Creative Dramatics

Three Billy Goats Gruff (p. 74)
Angus and the Ducks (p. 166)
Caps for Sale (p. 58)
The Three Bears (p. 74)
Dandelion (p. 129)
Sylvester and the Magic Pebble (p. 83)
Ira Sleeps Over (p. 82)
The Ugly Duckling (p. 77)
One Fine Day (p. 69)
Lon Po Po (p. 67)
Liza Lou and the Yeller Belly Swamp (p. 67)
Tico and the Golden Wings (p. 75)
Stone Soup (p. 73)
The Little Red Hen (p. 66)
Six-Dinner Sid (p. 172)
Too Much Noise (p. 76)
Two Ways to Count to Ten (p. 76)

Many of these books have animals as characters, frequently an indeterminate number, which makes casting less of a problem. The more familiar the story, such as *The Little Red Hen,* for example, the easier it will be to get started with children under age four. Some of the more complex stories, like *Tico and the Golden Wings* or *Lon Po Po* might best be used with more mature children. But basically, any book with a fairly simple plot line and some action involving a number of interesting characters can be used. What is important to keep in mind is that if a story doesn't work well for any reason, it should simply be dropped from the repertoire, and conversely, if it is asked for repeatedly, it should be redone.

Creative dramatics, then, can be a popular reinforcement tool in the presentation of literature to young children.

THE STORY BOARD

Another way in which we can make literature "come alive" for children is the story board. This can be used even with a few children in a home situation. Once the board has been constructed, youngsters themselves can often do the "art work" necessary to add to the enjoyment of stories in this way.

To make the board, first, using a piece of ¼-inch plywood, cut (or have the lumber yard cut) a board to a suitable size: two by one and a half feet for home use, three by two feet for use with a larger group. Then using a staple gun, cover the board with black felt, securing the material firmly to the plywood all around the edges, after covering both sides. This is easily done, since felt is commonly available in 72-inch width at most fabric stores, has no right/wrong side, and no "straight of the goods" to complicate its handling.

There are several alternatives, however. Flannel may be substituted for felt, but it is less durable, wrinkles easily, and has less surface nap on which to make the cutouts stick. One may also use an inexpensive indoor-outdoor carpeting and glue it to the wood instead of using the staple gun. If the larger size board is used, a strap handle (a piece of a discarded belt will do) should then be attached to the middle of the top edge to make the board portable. At any rate, there is little difficulty involved in making this "background" ready for use.

From this point on, the procedure can be extremely simple or, if one is an artist, it can become quite complex. Assuming no particular artistic ability at all, let us illustrate how to use the story board for an uncomplicated book, such as *It Looked Like Spilt Milk*. This book features royal blue pages, each with a white shape in outline form. These shapes—one to a page—resemble single objects, such as a mitten, an ice-cream cone, a woolly lamb, and so on. Each of these can easily be traced onto white felt, cut out, and used "as is" since the felt pieces will adhere to the board's covering material. As the adult reads the book aloud, each piece can then be placed by a child, insuring immediate involvement. In this book questions are repeatedly asked, such as,"Is it a mitten?" or "Is it a rabbit?" and so on, as each page is turned, and each time, of course, the answer is negative. Finally, we learn that each shaped white blob only seems to be a particular object, but that they are all really just white cloud shapes in a blue sky.

Many activities may well follow such a reading. For instance, the children could go outside and make up their own items by looking at real white clouds in a blue sky; then they might attempt outline drawings of their own to be translated into additional felt pieces. In any case, this sort of book stretches the child's imagination while still remaining a suitable choice for those who are at a very literal level of understanding in regard to illustration.

With a more complicated book there will be some drawing necessary as each individual piece is cut out, but felt-tip pens work well directly on pellon or felt. And if appropriate, figures may be trimmed with sequins, small buttons, or whatever will make them seem like the characters in the story.

Another way to replicate characters is by cutting out pictures from old magazines or discarded books and stiffening them with pellon, which will adhere well to the felt or carpet-covered board. There are commercially produced sets of certain classics, such as *Little Red Riding Hood*, which can be purchased, but these are not inexpensive, and generally, it is better to have the children involved in the entire art project from the beginning.

Even if adults have to help make some of the characters in a story, four- and five-year-olds can make some of the background objects, such as the green pastures which the billy goats want to reach in *Three Billy Goats Gruff*, or the maple trees for a story like *Anytime Mapleson and the Hungry Bears*. The possibilities are almost limitless for using this aid to appreciating books, and many times there is added benefit from the "construction" of the art work involved.

PUPPETS

We know that children relate very well to puppets, sometimes holding conversations with them when talking to real live people seems threatening. Puppets can therefore often provide a bridge over which real communication can take place between an adult and a child or between one child and another. For example, a child whose native language is not English may be shy about speaking to others but that same child will frequently "talk" to a puppet particularly if it "answers" through the ingenuity of a sensitive adult.

Almost any story can be enhanced by the use of a single puppet, perhaps "turning the pages" of the book or just "listening" to the story, and of course complete sets of characters may be used as well. In the latter case, the story chosen, particularly for beginning puppeteers, should have a limited number of characters in order to facilitate using a different voice for each one.

Books which lend themselves to putting on a puppet show usually have a great deal of action (remember the old Punch and Judy shows?), and with multiple characters, it may be wise to prerecord the story on tape (at least for inexperienced puppeteers) so that "working" the puppets has the adult's full attention.

No attempt will be made here to discuss details of the art of puppetry itself, since that is quite beyond the scope of this book. Several basics, however, might be helpful. First, hand puppets are not the same as marionettes, and so there is no need to fear using them because of difficulty in manipulation.

Secondly, puppets should be kept simple and durable so that they do not become showpieces which children cannot touch and use at will. Next, we should remember that while puppets are available commercially, they are quite easy to construct with a basic "body" pattern, some styrofoam balls, and a little imagination.

Equally easy to create are puppets made from old gloves, socks, discarded stuffed animals with the stuffing removed, and even paper bags. Some can be made and manipulated by the children themselves. Finally, in order to make the fullest use of puppets, interested adults might find it useful and great fun to enroll in a course in beginning puppetry.

Unfortunately, many books on this subject seem to be more complicated than necessary for the neophyte, but the Puppeteers of America do have a service called "The Puppetry Store" at 1525 24th S.E., Auburn, WA 98002-7837, which offers a catalog that might be helpful. In any case, puppets can add zest to read-alouds, so if they can be added, especially for classroom and library use, they are well worth the effort.

CONCLUSION

The modern world is a busy place, and it is understandable that adults who interact with young children find themselves having to make choices constantly regarding the best use of time. They are urged at every turn to involve the child in play experiences so that he can "act out" his feelings; they are encouraged to provide the child with physical activities so that he can develop his musculature; and they are concerned that the child interact with other children so that he can become "socialized." Furthermore, adults find themselves with many claims on their own time, claims which have little or nothing to do with the children in their care.

And tempting them too often is the all-too-convenient electronic babysitter, the television set, which promises to enlarge the scope of the child's learning while simultaneously providing free time for supervising adults.

Somewhat analogous to the expenditure of money in a limited budget, then, is the expenditure of time which is also somewhat scarce. Therefore, adults must become convinced of the benefits of exposing young children to literature before they decide to expend the time necessary for wise book selection and for sharing the process itself. However, just reading about the benefits to be gained and the ways in which children can profit from exposure to literature will never convince anyone as completely as experience with real live youngsters! It is earnestly hoped that this book will encourage its readers to participate with children in the enjoyment of literature. Remember, they're never too young for books.

Bibliography

Aardema, Verna
Borreguita and the Coyote
Illustrated by Petra Mathers
Alfred A. Knopf, 1991

Aardema, Verna
Bringing the Rain to Kapiti Plain
Illustrated by Beatriz Vidal
Dial, 1981

Aardema, Verna
Who's in Rabbit's House?
Illustrated by Leo and Diane Dillon
Dial, 1977

Aardema, Verna
*Why Mosquitos Buzz in People's
Ears: An African Tale*
Illustrated by Leo and Diane Dillon
Dial, 1975

Abolafia, Yossi
A Fish for Mrs. Gardenia
Greenwillow, 1988

Accorsi, William
Friendship's First Thanksgiving
Holiday House, 1992

Ackerman, Karen
Araminta's Paint Box
Illustrated by Betsy Lewin
Atheneum, 1990

Ackerman, Karen
Song and Dance Man
Illustrated by Stephen Gammell
Alfred A. Knopf, 1988

Ackerman, Karen
This Old House
Illustrated by Sylvie Wickstrom

Atheneum, 1992

Adams, Adrienne
The Easter Egg Artists
Scribner, 1976

Adams, Adrienne
A Woggle of Witches
Scribner, 1971

Adler, David A.
A Picture Book of Abraham Lincoln
Illustrated by John and Alexandra
Wallner
Holiday House, 1989

Adler, David A.
A Picture Book of Eleanor Roosevelt
Illustrated by Robert Casilla
Holiday House, 1991

Adler, David A.
*A Picture Book of George
Washington*
Illustrated by John and Alexandra
Wallner
Holiday House, 1989

Adler, David A.
A Picture Book of Harriet Tubman
Illustrated by Samuel Byrd
Holiday House, 1992

Adler, David A.
*A Picture Book of Martin Luther
King, Jr.*
Illustrated by Robert Casilla
Holiday House, 1989

Adoff, Arnold
Black Is Brown Is Tan
Illustrated by Emily A. McCully

Harper-Collins, 1973

Adorjan, Carol
I Can! Can You?
Illustrated by Miriam Nerlove
Albert Whitman, 1990

Aesop
Aesop's Fables
Illustrated by Michael Hague
Holt, Rinehart and Winston, 1985

Aesop
Three Aesop Fables (Fox and Grapes, Stork, Crow)
Illustrated by Paul Galdone
Seabury, 1971

Aesop
Town Mouse and the Country Mouse
Illustrated by Janet Stevens
Holiday House, 1987

Ahlberg, Janet, and Allan Ahlberg
The Baby's Catalogue
Little, Brown, 1982

Ahlberg, Janet, and Allan Ahlberg
Each Peach, Pear, Plum
Viking, 1979

Ahlberg, Janet, and Allan Ahlberg
Funnybones
Greenwillow, 1980

Aker, Suzanne
What Comes in Twos, Threes, and Fours?
Illustrated by Bernie Karlin
Simon & Schuster, 1990

Alexander, Ellen
Llama and the Great Flood: A Folktale from Peru
Thomas Y. Crowell, 1989

Alexander, Martha
And My Mean Old Mother Will Be Sorry, Blackboard Bear
Dial, 1972

Alexander, Martha
Blackboard Bear
Dial, 1969

Alexander, Martha
Bobo's Dream
Dial, 1970

Alexander, Martha

Nobody Asked Me If I Wanted a Baby Sister
Dial, 1971

Alexander, Martha
Out! Out! Out!
Dial, 1968

Alexander, Martha
Pigs Say Oink
Random House, 1978

Alexander, Martha
Sabrina
Dial, 1971

Alexander, Martha
We Never Get to Do Anything
Dial, 1970

Alexander, Sue
Nadia the Willful
Illustrated by Lloyd Bloom
Pantheon, 1983

Aliki
At Mary Bloom's
Greenwillow, 1976

Aliki
Corn Is Maize: The Gift of the Indians
Thomas Y. Crowell, 1976

Aliki
Feelings
Greenwillow, 1984

Aliki
Go Tell Aunt Rhody
Macmillan, 1974

Aliki
Hush Little Baby
Prentice-Hall, 1987

Aliki
I'm Growing
Harper Collins, 1992

Aliki
Jack and Jake
Greenwillow, 1986

Aliki
Keep Your Mouth Closed, Dear
Dial, 1966

Aliki
My Hands
Thomas Y. Crowell, 1962

Aliki
My Visit to the Dinosaurs
Thomas Y. Crowell, 1969
Aliki
Overnight at Mary Bloom's
Greenwillow, 1987
Aliki
Story of Johnny Appleseed
Prentice-Hall, 1963
Aliki
The Two of Them
Greenwillow, 1979
Aliki
Use Your Head, Dear
Greenwillow, 1983
Aliki
*A Weed Is a Flower: The Life of
George Washington Carver*
Prentice-Hall, 1965
Aliki
Wild and Woolly Mammoths
Thomas Y. Crowell, 1977
Allard, Harry
*It's So Nice to Have a Wolf Around
the House*
Illustrated by James Marshall
Doubleday, 1977
Allard, Harry
Miss Nelson Has a Field Day
Illustrated by James Marshall
Houghton Mifflin, 1985
Allard, Harry
Miss Nelson Is Back
Illustrated by James Marshall
Houghton Mifflin, 1982
Allard, Harry
The Stupids Step Out
Illustrated by James Marshall
Houghton Mifflin, 1977
Allard, Harry, and James Marshall
Miss Nelson Is Missing!
Illustrated by James Marshall
Houghton Mifflin, 1977
Allen, Jeffrey
Nosey Mrs. Rat
Illustrated by James Marshall
Viking, 1985

Allen, Pamela
Who Sank the Boat?
Coward-McCann, 1982
Allen, Patricia
My Cat Maisie
Viking, 1990
**Allington, Richard L., and Kathleen
Krull**
Summer
Illustrated by Dennis Hockerman
Raintree, 1981
Allinson, Beverley
Effie
Illustrated by Barbara Reid
Scholastic, 1990
Andersen, Hans Christian
The Emperor's New Clothes
Illustrated by Virginia L. Burton
Houghton Mifflin, 1949
Andersen, Hans Christian
The Nightingale
Translated by Eva Le Gallienne
Illustrated by Nancy Ekholm Burkert
Harper, 1965
Andersen, Hans Christian
The Princess and the Pea
Illustrated by Paul Galdone
Seabury, 1978
Andersen, Hans Christian
Thumbelina
Retold by Amy Ehrlich
Illustrated by Susan Jeffers
Dial, 1979
Andersen, Hans Christian
Thumbelina
Retold by Deborah Hautzig
Illustrated by Kaarina Kaila
Alfred A. Knopf, 1990
Andersen, Hans Christian
The Ugly Duckling
Retold and Illustrated by Lorinda
Bryan Cauley
Harcourt Brace Jovanovich, 1979
Andersen, Hans Christian
The Ugly Duckling
Retold by Lilian Moore
Illustrated by Daniel San Souci

Scholastic, 1987
Anderson, Karen Born
What's the Matter, Sylvie, Can't You Ride?
Dial, 1981
Andrews, Jan
Very Last First Time
Illustrated by Ian Wallace
Atheneum, 1985
Anglund, Joan Walsh
In a Pumpkin Shell
Harcourt Brace Jovanovich, 1960
Anholt, Catherine
Aren't You Lucky!
Little, Brown, 1990
Anholt, Catherine, and Laurence Anholt
All About You
Viking, 1991
Anno, Mitsumasa
Anno's Alphabet: An Adventure in Imagination
Thomas Y. Crowell, 1975
Anno, Mitsumasa
Topsy-Turvies: Pictures to Stretch the Imagination
Weatherhill, 1970
Anno, Mitsumasa
Upside-Downers: More Pictures to Stretch the Imagination
Translated by M. Wetherby and S. Trumbull
Weatherhill, 1971
Apy, Deborah, Retold by
Beauty and the Beast
Illustrated by Michael Hague
Holt, Rinehart, Winston, 1983
Aragon, Jane Chelsea
Lullaby
Illustrated by Kandy Radzinski
Chronicle Books, 1989
Aragon, Jane Chelsea
Salt Hands
Illustrated by Ted Rand
E. P. Dutton, 1989
Argent, Kerry
Happy Birthday, Wombat!
Little, Brown, 1989

Arnold, Tedd
Ollie Forgot
Dial, 1988
Arnold, Tedd
The Signmaker's Assistant
Dial, 1992
Arnosky, Jim
Crinkleroot's Guide to Knowing Trees
Bradbury, 1992
Arnosky, Jim
I Was Born in a Tree and Raised by Bees
Bradbury, 1988
Arnosky, Jim
Raccoons and Ripe Corn
Lothrop, Lee & Shepard, 1987
Arnstein, Helen S.
Billy and Our New Baby
Illustrated by M. Jane Smyth
Human Sciences Press, 1973
Arthur, Catherine
My Sister's Silent World
Illustrated by Nathan Talbot
Children's Press, 1979
Aruego, Jose, and Ariane Dewey, illustrators
Five Little Ducks
Crown, 1989
Aruego, Jose, and Ariane Dewey
We Hide, You Seek
Greenwillow, 1979
Asbjornsen, P. C.
The Three Billy Goats Gruff
Illustrated by Marcia Brown
Harcourt Brace Jovanovich, 1957
Asbjornsen, P. C.
The Three Billy Goats Gruff
Illustrated by Paul Galdone
Seabury, 1973
Asch, Frank
Baby in the Box
Holiday House, 1989
Asch, Frank
Bear Shadow
Prentice-Hall, 1985
Asch, Frank
Bread and Honey

Parents Magazine Press, 1982
Asch, Frank
Goodbye House
Simon & Schuster, 1986
Asch, Frank
Happy Birthday, Moon
Simon & Schuster, 1988
Asch, Frank
Just Like Daddy
Simon & Schuster, 1981
Asch, Frank
Moongame
Prentice-Hall, 1984
Asch, Frank
Popcorn
Parents Magazine Press, 1979
Asch, Frank
Skyfire
Simon & Schuster, 1984
Aylesworth, Jim
The Folks in the Valley: A Pennsylvania Dutch ABC
Illustrated by Stefano Vitale
Harper Collins, 1992
Aylesworth, Jim
Mr. McGill Goes to Town
Illustrated by Thomas Graham
Henry Holt, 1989
Aylesworth, Jim
Old Black Fly
Illustrated by Stephen Gammell
Henry Holt, 1992
Aylesworth, Jim
One Crow: A Counting Rhyme
Illustrated by Ruth Young
J. P. Lippincott, 1988
Azarian, Mary
A Farmer's Alphabet
David R. Godine, 1981
Babbitt, Natalie
The Something
Farrar, Straus, and Giroux, 1970
Baden, Robert
And Sunday Makes Seven
Illustrated by Michelle Edwards
Albert Whitman, 1990
Baker, Betty

Little Runner of the Longhouse
Illustrated by Arnold Lobel
Harper-Collins, 1962
Baker, Leslie
The Third-Story Cat
Little, Brown, 1987
Balian, Lorna
Aminal
Abingdon, 1972
Balian, Lorna
Humbug Witch
Abingdon, 1965
Balian, Lorna
Leprechauns Never Lie
Abingdon, 1980
Bancroft, Henrietta, and Richard G. Van Gelder
Animals in Winter
Illustrated by Gaetano DiPalma
Thomas Y. Crowell, 1963
Bang, Molly
The Paper Crane
Greenwillow, 1985
Bang, Molly
Ten, Nine, Eight
Morrow, 1991
Bang, Molly
Wiley and the Hairy Man
Macmillan, 1976
Barbour, Karen
Little Nino's Pizzeria
Harcourt Brace Jovanovich, 1987
Barker, Dan
Maybe Right, Maybe Wrong
Illustrated by Brian Strassburg
Prometheus Books, 1992
Barker, Dan
Maybe Yes, Maybe No
Illustrated by Brian Strassburg
Prometheus Books, 1990
Barker, Marjorie
Magical Hands
Illustrated by Yoshi
Picture Book Studio, 1989
Barlowe, Dot, and Sy Barlowe
Who Lives Here?
Random House, 1978

Barracca, Debra, and Sal Barracca
The Adventures of Taxi Dog
Illustrated by Mark Buehner
Dial, 1990

Barracca, Debra, and Sal Barracca
Maxi, the Hero
Illustrated by Mark Buehner
Dial, 1991

Barrett, Judith
Animals Should Definitely Not Wear Clothing
Illustrated by Ron Barrett
Atheneum, 1974

Barrett, Judith
Cloudy With a Chance of Meatballs
Illustrated by Ron Barrett
Atheneum, 1978

Barton, Byron
Airport
Thomas Y. Crowell, 1982

Barton, Byron
Bones, Bones, Dinosaur Bones
Thomas Y. Crowell, 1990

Barton, Byron
Building a House
Greenwillow, 1981

Barton, Byron
Dinosaurs, Dinosaurs
Harper-Collins, 1989

Barton, Byron
Hester
Greenwillow, 1975

Barton, Byron
I Want To Be an Astronaut
Harper-Collins, 1988

Barton, Byron
Machines At Work
Thomas Y. Crowell, 1987

Barton, Byron
Trains
Thomas Y. Crowell, 1986

Bartos-Hoppner, Barbara, adaptation by
Pied Piper of Hamelin
Illustrated by Anne Gert Fuchshuber
Harper, 1987

Base, Graeme
Animalia

Harry N. Abrams, 1986

Bate, Lucy
Little Rabbit's Loose Tooth
Illustrated by Diane De Groat
Crown, 1975

Baum, Louis
One More Time
Illustrated by Paddy Bouma
William Morrow, 1986

Bayer, Jane
A—My Name Is Alice
Illustrated by Steven Kellogg
Dial, 1984

Baylor, Byrd
The Desert Is Theirs
Illustrated by Peter Parnall
Scribner, 1975

Baylor, Byrd
Everybody Needs a Rock
Illustrated by Peter Parnall
Macmillan, 1974

Behn, Harry
Trees: A Poem
Illustrated by James Endicott
Henry Holt, 1992

Behrens, June
Fiesta!
Illustrated by Scott Taylor
Childrens Press, 1978

Behrens, June
Gung Hay Fat Choy
Illustrated by Terry Behrens
Childrens Press, 1982

Bellows, Cathy
The Grizzly Sisters
Macmillan, 1991

Bellows, Cathy
Toad School
Macmillan, 1990

Belpre, Pura
Perez y Martina: A Puerto Rican Folktale
Illustrated by Carlos Sanchez
Viking, 1991

Bemelmans, Ludwig
Madeline
Viking, 1939

Bemelmans, Ludwig
Madeline and the Bad Hat
Viking, 1959
Bemelmans, Ludwig
Madeline in London
Viking, 1961
Bemelmans, Ludwig
Madeline's Rescue
Viking, 1953
Benchley, Nathaniel
Red Fox and His Canoe
Illustrated by Arnold Lobel
Harper-Collins, 1964
Benchley, Nathaniel
Sam the Minuteman
Illustrated by Arnold Lobel
Harper-Collins, 1969
Benchley, Nathaniel
Small Wolf
Illustrated by Joan Sandin
Harper-Collins, 1972
Bennett, David
Earth
Illustrated by Rosalinda Kightley
Bantam, 1988
Bennett, Jill
Teeny Tiny
Illustrated by Tomie DePaola
Putnam, 1986
Berenstain, Stan, and Jan Berenstain
The Berenstain Bears Don't Pollute Anymore
Random House, 1981
Bernhard, Durga
What's Maggie Up To?
Holiday House, 1992
Beskow, Elsa
Pelle's New Suit
Scholastic, 1974
Bider, Djemma
A Drop of Honey: An Armenian Folktale
Illustrated by Armen Kojoyian
Simon & Schuster, 1989
Blaine, Marge
The Terrible Thing That Happened at Our House

Illustrated by John Wallner
Parents Magazine Press, 1975
Blake, Quentin
Mrs. Armitage on Wheels
Alfred A. Knopf, 1987
Blake, Quentin
Quentin Blake's ABC
Alfred A. Knopf, 1989
Blake, Robert J.
The Perfect Spot
Philomel, 1992
Blegvad, Lenore
Anna Banana and Me
Illustrated by Erik Blegvad
Atheneum, 1985
Blood, Charles L., and Martin Link
The Goat in the Rug
Illustrated by Nancy Winslow Parker
Parents Magazine Press, 1976
Blos, Joan W.
Old Henry
Illustrated by Stephen Gammell
Wm. Morrow, 1987
Bodsworth, Nan
A Nice Walk in the Jungle
Viking, 1989
Bond, Felicia
Poinsetta and Her Family
Harper-Collins, 1981
Bond, Felicia
Poinsetta and the Firefighters
Thomas Y. Crowell, 1984
Bond, Felicia
Wake Up, Vladimir
Thomas Y. Crowell, 1987
Bond, Ruskin
Cherry Tree
Illustrated by Allan Eitzen
Caroline House, 1991
Bonsall, Crosby N.
And I Mean It, Stanley
Harper-Collins, 1974
Bonsall, Crosby N.
Mine's the Best
Harper-Collins, 1973
Boon, Emilie
Belinda's Balloon

Alfred A. Knopf, 1985

Borack, Barbara
Grandpa
Illustrated by Ben Shecter
Harper-Collins, 1967

Bornstein, Ruth
Little Gorilla
Seabury, 1976

Bottner, Barbara
Messy
Delacorte, 1979

Bourque, Nina
The Best Trade of All
Illustrated by Jackie Urbanovic
Raintree, 1985

Boyd, Lizi
Sam Is My Half Brother
Viking, 1990

Boynton, Sandra
*A Is for Angry: An Animal and
   Adjective Alphabet*
Workman, 1983

Brandenberg, Franz
Aunt Nina's Visit
Illustrated by Aliki
Greenwillow, 1984

Brandenberg, Franz
I Wish I Was Sick, Too!
Illustrated by Aliki
Greenwillow, 1976

Brandenberg, Franz
Otto Is Different
Illustrated by James Stevenson
Greenwillow, 1985

Branley, Franklyn M.
The Big Dipper
Illustrated by Molly Coxe
Harper-Collins, 1991

Branley, Franklyn M.
Is There Life in Outer Space?
Illustrated by Don Madden
Thomas Y. Crowell, 1984

Branley, Franklyn M.
The Planets in Our Solar System
Illustrated by Don Madden
Harper-Collins, 1981

Branley, Franklyn M.

The Sky Is Full of Stars
Illustrated by Felicia Bond
Harper-Collins, 1981

Breinburg, Petronella
Shawn Goes to School
Illustrated by Errol Lloyd
Thomas Y. Crowell, 1974

Brenner, Barbara
Bodies
Illustrated by George Ancona
Dutton, 1973

Brenner, Barbara
Faces
Illustrated by George Ancona
Dutton, 1977

Brenner, Barbara
*Rosa and Marco and the Three
   Wishes*
Illustrated by Megan Halsey
Macmillan, 1992

Brenner, Barbara
Wagon Wheels
Illustrated by Don Bolognese
Harper-Collins, 1978

Brett, Jan
Annie and the Wild Animals
Houghton Mifflin, 1985

Brett, Jan
Beauty and the Beast
Clarion, 1989

Brett, Jan
The First Dog
Harcourt Brace Jovanovich, 1988

Brett, Jan
Goldilocks and the Three Bears
Putnam, 1987

Brett, Jan
The Mitten
Putnam, 1990

Bridwell, Norman
Clifford, the Big Red Dog
Scholastic, 1988

Bridwell, Norman
The Witch Next Door
Scholastic, 1971

Briggs, Raymond
Jim and the Beanstalk

Coward-McCann, 1970
Briggs, Raymond
Mother Goose Treasury
Coward, 1966
Briggs, Raymond
The Snowman
Random House, 1978
Bright, Robert
Georgie
Doubleday, 1959
Bright, Robert
My Red Umbrella
Morrow, 1959
Brillhart, Julie
Story Hour—Starring Megan!
Albert Whitman, 1992
Brinckloe, Julie
Playing Marbles
Wm. Morrow, 1988
Brooke, Leslie L.
Johnny Crow's Garden
Frederick Warne, 1903
Brooke, Leslie L.
Johnny Crow's Party
Frederick Warne, 1967
Brown, Craig
The Patchwork Farmer
Greenwillow, 1989
Brown, Laurene K., and Marc Brown
Dinosaurs Divorce
Little, Brown, 1988
Brown, M. K.
Let's Go Swimming With Mr. Sillypants
Crown, 1986
Brown, Marc
Arthur Meets the President
Little, Brown, 1991
Brown, Marc
Arthur's April Fool
Little, Brown, 1983
Brown, Marc
Arthur's Baby
Little, Brown, 1987
Brown, Marc
Arthur's Birthday
Little, Brown, 1989

Brown, Marc
Arthur's Eyes
Little, Brown, 1979
Brown, Marc
Arthur's Halloween
Little, Brown, 1982
Brown, Marc
Arthur's Tooth
Little, Brown, 1985
Brown, Marc
Arthur's Valentine
Little, Brown, 1987
Brown, Marc
D. W. All Wet
Little, Brown, 1988
Brown, Marc
Finger Rhymes
E. P. Dutton, 1980
Brown, Marc
Hand Rhymes
E. P. Dutton, 1985
Brown, Marc
Play Rhymes
E. P. Dutton, 1987
Brown, Marc
The True Francine
Little, Brown, 1981
Brown, Marc
Witches Four
Parents Magazine Press, 1980
Brown, Marc
Perfect Pigs: An Introduction to Manners
Little, Brown, 1983
Brown, Marc, and Stephen Krensky
Dinosaurs Beware! A Safety Guide
Little, Brown, 1984
Brown, Marcia
Dick Whittington and His Cat
Scribner, 1950
Brown, Marcia
Once a Mouse
Scribner, 1961
Brown, Marcia
Stone Soup
Scribner, 1947
Brown, Margaret Wise

Big Red Barn
Illustrated by Felicia Bond
Harper-Collins, 1989

Brown, Margaret Wise
Dead Bird
Illustrated by Remy Charlip
A-W, 1958

Brown, Margaret Wise
The Golden Egg Book
Illustrated by Leonard Weisgard
Western, 1976

Brown, Margaret Wise
Good Night, Moon
Illustrated by Clement Hurd
Harper-Collins, 1977

Brown, Margaret Wise
Little Fur Family
Illustrated by Garth Williams
Harper-Collins, 1968

Brown, Margaret Wise
The Runaway Bunny
Illustrated by Clement Hurd
Morrow, 1954

Brown, Ruth
A Dark Dark Tale
Dial, 1981

Brown, Ruth
Ladybug, Ladybug
E. P. Dutton, 1988

Brown, Ruth
The World That Jack Built
Dutton, 1991

Browne, Anthony
Changes
Alfred A. Knopf, 1990

Browne, Anthony
Piggybook
Alfred A. Knopf, 1986

Browne, Anthony
Willy and Hugh
Alfred A. Knopf, 1991

Browne, Anthony
Willy the Champ
Alfred A. Knopf, 1985

Browne, Anthony
Willy the Wimp
Alfred A. Knopf, 1984

Browning, Robert
The Pied Piper of Hamelin
Illustrated by Terry Small
Harcourt Brace Jovanovich, 1988

Brusca, Maria Cristina
On the Pampas
Henry Holt, 1991

Buehner, Caralyn, and Mark Buehner
The Escape of Marvin the Ape
Dial, 1992

Bunting, Eve
The Day Before Christmas
Illustrated by Beth Peck
Houghton Mifflin, 1992

Bunting, Eve
Fly Away Home
Illustrated by Ronald Himler
Houghton Mifflin, 1991

Bunting, Eve
Ghost's Hour, Spook's Hour
Illustrated by Donald Carrick
Houghton Mifflin, 1987

Bunting, Eve
How Many Days to America?
Illustrated by Beth Peck
Ticknor & Fields, 1988

Bunting, Eve
In the Haunted House
Illustrated by Susan Meddaugh
Houghton Mifflin, 1990

Bunting, Eve
The Mother's Day Mice
Illustrated by Jan Brett
Houghton Mifflin, 1986

Bunting, Eve
No Nap
Illustrated by Susan Meddaugh
Houghton Mifflin, 1989

Bunting, Eve
Our Teacher's Having a Baby
Illustrated by Diane De Groat
Houghton Mifflin, 1992

Bunting, Eve
A Perfect Father's Day
Illustrated by Susan Meddaugh
Houghton Mifflin, 1991

Bunting, Eve

St. Patrick's Day in the Morning
Illustrated by Jan Brett
Houghton Mifflin, 1980
Bunting, Eve
Scary, Scary Halloween
Illustrated by Jan Brett
Houghton Mifflin, 1986
Bunting, Eve
Terrible Things
Illustrated by Stephen Gammell
Jewish Publication Society, 1989
Bunting, Eve
The Valentine Bears
Illustrated by Jan Brett
Houghton Mifflin, 1983
Bunting, Eve
The Wall
Illustrated by Ronald Himler
Clarion, 1990
Bunting, Eve
The Wednesday Surprise
Illustrated by Donald Carrick
Houghton Mifflin, 1989
Burgess, Mark
One Little Teddy Bear
Viking, 1991
Burningham, John
Avocado Baby
Harper-Collins, 1982
Burningham, John
Come Away from the Water, Shirley
Harper-Collins, 1977
Burningham, John
The Friend
Harper-Collins, 1976
Burningham, John
Hey! Get Off Our Train
Crown, 1989
Burningham, John
John Patrick Norman McHennessy:
The Boy Who Was Always Late
Crown, 1987
Burningham, John
Mr. Gumpy's Motor Car
Harper-Collins, 1976
Burningham, John
Mr. Gumpy's Outing

Holt, Rinehart & Winston, 1971
Burningham, John
Time to Get Out of the Bath, Shirley
Harper-Collins, 1979
Burton, Virginia Lee
Choo Choo
Houghton Mifflin, 1946
Burton, Virginia Lee
Katy and the Big Snow
Houghton Mifflin, 1943
Burton, Virginia Lee
Life Story
Houghton Mifflin, 1962
Burton, Virginia Lee
The Little House
Houghton Mifflin, 1942
Burton, Virginia Lee
Maybelle the Cable Car
Houghton Mifflin, 1952
Burton, Virginia Lee
Mike Mulligan and His Steam Shovel
Houghton Mifflin, 1977
Butler, Dorothy
My Brown Bear Barney
Illustrated by Elizabeth Fuller
Greenwillow, 1988
Butterfield, Moira
Bird
Illustrated by Paul Johnson
Simon & Schuster, 1991
Butterfield, Moira
Butterfly
Illustrated by Paul Johnson
Simon & Schuster, 1991
Butterfield, Moira
Flower
Illustrated by Paul Johnson
Simon & Schuster, 1991
Butterfield, Moira
Frog
Illustrated by Paul Johnson
Simon & Schuster, 1991
Butterworth, Nick, and Mick Inkpen
Nice or Nasty: A Book of Opposites
Little, Brown, 1987
Caines, Jeanette
Abby

Illustrated by Steven Kellogg
Harper-Collins, 1973

Caines, Jeanette
Just Us Women
Illustrated by Pat Cummings
Harper-Collins, 1982

Calhoun, Mary
Cross-Country Cat
Illustrated by Erick Ingraham
Morrow, 1979

Calhoun, Mary
High-Wire Henry
Illustrated by Erick Ingraham
Morrow, 1991

Calhoun, Mary
Hot-Air Henry
Illustrated by Erick Ingraham
Morrow, 1981

Calhoun, Mary
The Hungry Leprechaun
Illustrated by Roger Duvoisin
Morrow, 1962

Calhoun, Mary
Wobble the Witch Cat
Illustrated by Roger Duvoisin
Morrow, 1958

Calmenson, Stephanie
The Principal's New Clothes
Illustrated by Denise Brunkus
Scholastic, 1989

Calmenson, Stephanie
What Am I? Very First Riddles
Illustrated by Karen Gundersheimer
Harper-Collins, 1989

Campbell, Rod
Dear Zoo
Four Winds, 1982

Caple, Kathy
The Coolest Place in Town
Houghton Mifflin, 1990

Carle, Eric
Do You Want to Be My Friend?
Harper-Collins, 1971

Carle, Eric
The Grouchy Ladybug
Harper-Collins, 1977

Carle, Eric

Have You Seen My Cat?
Watts, 1973

Carle, Eric
A House for Hermit Crab
Picture Book Studio, 1987

Carle, Eric
I See a Song
Harper-Collins, 1973

Carle, Eric
Pancakes! Pancakes!
Alfred A. Knopf, 1970

Carle, Eric
Rooster's Off to See the World
Picture Book Studio, 1972

Carle, Eric
The Tiny Seed
Picture Book Studio, 1987

Carle, Eric
The Very Busy Spider
Putnam, 1989

Carle, Eric
The Very Hungry Caterpillar
Collins-World, 1969

Carlson, Nancy
Arnie and the Stolen Markers
Viking, 1987

Carlson, Nancy
I Like Me!
Viking, 1988

Carlson, Nancy
Take Time to Relax
Viking, 1991

Carlstrom, Nancy White
Better Not Get Wet, Jesse Bear
Illustrated by Bruce Degen
Macmillan, 1988

Carlstrom, Nancy White
Blow Me a Kiss, Miss Lilly
Illustrated by Amy Schwartz
Harper-Collins, 1990

Carlstom, Nancy White
I'm Not Moving, Mama
Illustrated by Thor Wickstrom
Macmillan, 1990

Carlstrom, Nancy White
No Nap for Benjamin Badger
Illustrated by Dennis Nolan

Macmillan, 1991
Carrick, Carol
The Accident
Illustrated by Donald Carrick
Seabury, 1976
Carrick, Carol
The Foundling
Illustrated by Donald Carrick
Seabury, 1977
Carrick, Carol
Left Behind
Illustrated by Donald Carrick
Clarion, 1988
Carrick, Carol
Lost in the Storm
Illustrated by Donald Carrick
Seabury, 1974
Carrick, Carol
Patrick's Dinosaurs
Illustrated by Donald Carrick
Houghton Mifflin, 1983
Carrick, Donald
Harald and the Giant Knight
Clarion, 1982
Carrick, Donald
Harald and the Great Stag
Houghton Mifflin, 1988
Carrick, Donald
Milk
Greenwillow, 1985
Carroll, Lewis
The Walrus and the Carpenter
Illustrated by Jane Breskin Zalben
Henry Holt, 1986
Cartwright, Ann, and Reg Cartwright
The Winter Hedgehog
Macmillan, 1990
Caseley, Judith
Ada Potato
Greenwillow, 1989
Cassedy, Sylvia, and Kunihiro Suetake,
  translators
Red Dragon Fly on My Shoulder
Illustrated by Molly Bang
Harper-Collins, 1992
Castle, Caroline
The Hare and the Tortoise

Illustrated by Peter Weevers
Dial, 1985
Caudill, Rebecca
A Pocketful of Cricket
Illustrated by Evaline Ness
Holt, Rinehart & Winston, 1964
Cauley, Lorinda Bryan
Clap Your Hands
Putnam, 1992
Cauley, Lorinda Bryan
The Pancake Boy: An Old Norwegian
  Folktale
Putnam, 1988
Cauley, Lorinda Bryan
The Town Mouse and the Country
  Mouse
Putnam, 1984
Cendars, Blaise
Shadow
Translated and illustrated by Marcia
  Brown
Chas. Scribner, 1982
Chalmers, Mary
Throw a Kiss, Harry
Harper-Collins, 1986
Chapman, Carol
The Tale of Meshka the Kvetch
Illustrated by Arnold Lobel
Dutton, 1980
Charlip, Remy, and Burton Supree
Harlequin and the Gift of Many
  Colors
Illustrated by Remy Charlip
Parents Magazine Press, 1973
Chaucer, Geoffrey
Chanticleer and the Fox
Adapted and illustrated by Barbara
  Cooney
Thomas Y. Crowell, 1961
Cherry, Lynne
Archie, Follow Me
Dutton, 1990
Child, Lydia Maria
Over the River and Through the
  Wood
Illustrated by Iris Van Rynbach
Little, Brown, 1989

Chorao, Kay
The Baby's Lap Book
Dutton, 1977
Chorao, Kay
The Child's Story Book
Dutton, 1987
Chorao, Kay
Ida and Betty and the Secret Eggs
Houghton Mifflin, 1991
Christelow, Eileen
Five Little Monkeys Jumping on the Bed
Houghton Mifflin, 1990
Christelow, Eileen
Five Little Monkeys Sitting in a Tree
Houghton Mifflin, 1991
Christelow, Eileen
Henry and the Red Stripes
Houghton Mifflin, 1982
Christelow, Eileen
Jerome the Babysitter
Houghton Mifflin, 1985
Christelow, Eileen
Olive and the Magic Hat
Ticknor & Fields, 1987
Christelow, Eileen
The Robbery at the Diamond Dog Diner
Houghton Mifflin, 1986
Christiansen, C. B.
Mara in the Morning
Illustrated by Catherine Stock
Atheneum, 1991
Christiansen, C. B.
My Mother's House, My Father's House
Illustrated by Irene Trivas
Atheneum, 1989
Clark, Ann Nolan
In My Mother's House
Illustrated by Velino Herrara
Viking, 1941
Cleary, Beverly
The Real Hole
Illustrated by Mary Stevens
Morrow, 1986
Clifton, Lucille

Clifton, Lucille
The Boy Who Didn't Believe in Spring
Illustrated by Brinton Turkle
Dutton, 1973
Clifton, Lucille
Everett Anderson's Friend
Illustrated by Ann Grifalconi
Holt, Rinehart & Winston (n.d.)
Clifton, Lucille
Everett Anderson's Nine Month Long
Illustrated by Ann Grifalconi
Holt, Rinehart & Winston, 1978
Climo, Shirley
The Egyptian Cinderella
Illustrated by Ruth Heller
Harper-Collins, 1989
Coerr, Eleanor
Chang's Paper Pony
Illustrated by Deborah Kogan Ray
Harper-Collins, 1988
Coerr, Eleanor
The Josefina Quilt Story
Illustrated by Bruce Degen
Harper-Collins, 1986
Cohen, Barbara
The Carp in the Bathtub
Illustrated by Joan Halpern
Lothrop, 1972
Cohen, Barbara
Molly's Pilgrim
Illustrated by Michael J. Deraney
Morrow, 1983
Cohen, Miriam
Best Friends
Illustrated by Lillian Hoban
Macmillan, 1971
Cohen, Miriam
Jim's Dog Muffins
Illustrated by Lillian Hoban
Greenwillow, 1984
Cohen, Miriam
The New Teacher
Illustrated by Lillian Hoban
Macmillan, 1974
Cohen, Miriam
Will I Have a Friend?
Illustrated by Lillian Hoban

Macmillan, 1971

Cohen, Miriam
When Will I Read?
Illustrated by Lillian Hoban
Greenwillow, 1977

Cohn, Janice
I Had a Friend Named Peter
Illustrated by Gail Owens
Morrow, 1987

Cole, Babette
The Trouble with Grandad
Putnam, 1988

Cole, Joanna
*Anna Banana: One Hundred and One
Jump-Rope Rhymes*
Illustrated by Alan Tiegreen
Morrow, 1989

Cole, Joanna
Bony-Legs
Illustrated by Dirk Zimmer
Four Winds Press, 1983

Cole, Joanna
A Chick Hatches
Illustrated by Jerome Wexler
Morrow, 1976

Cole, Joanna
Don't Call Me Names!
Illustrated by Lynn Munsinger
Random House, 1990

Cole, Joanna
Don't Tell the Whole World!
Illustrated by Kate Duke
Thomas Y. Crowell, 1990

Cole, Joanna
*The Magic School Bus at the
Waterworks*
Illustrated by Bruce Degen
Scholastic, 1986

Cole, Joanna
*The Magic School Bus Inside the
Earth*
Illustrated by Bruce Degen
Scholastic, 1987

Cole, Joanna
*The Magic School Bus Inside the
Human Body*
Illustrated by Bruce Degen

Scholastic, 1989

Cole, Joanna
My Puppy is Born
Illustrated by Jerome Wexler
Morrow, 1973

Cole, Joanna
Your New Potty
Photos by Margaret Miller
Morrow, 1989

Cole, William
A Zooful of Animals
Illustrated by Lynn Munsinger
Houghton Mifflin, 1992

Cooney, Barbara
Miss Rumphius
Viking, 1982

Corrin, Stephen, and Sara Corrin, adaptation by
The Pied Piper of Hamelin
Illustrated by Errol Le Cain
Harcourt Brace and Jovanovich, 1989

Craft, Ruth
Winter Bear
Illustrated by Eric Blegvad
Atheneum, 1975

Craig, Helen
*Susie and Alfred in The Knight, the
Princess, and the Dragon*
Alfred A. Knopf, 1985

Crampton, Gertrude
Scuffy the Tugboat
Illustrated by Tibor Gergely
Western, 1973

Crews, Donald
Bigmama's
Greenwillow, 1991

Crews, Donald
Flying
Greenwillow, 1986

Crews, Donald
Freight Train
Greenwillow, 1978

Crews, Donald
Harbor
Greenwillow, 1982

Crews, Donald
Light

Greenwillow, 1981
Crews, Donald
Parade
Greenwillow, 1983
Crews, Donald
Trucks
Greenwillow, 1980
Crowe, Robert L.
Clyde Monster
Illustrated by Kay Chorao
Dutton, 1976
cummings, e. e.
Hist Whist
Illustrated by Deborah Kogan Ray
Crown, 1989
Cummings, Phil
Goodness Gracious!
Illustrated by Craig Smith
Orchard, 1989
Cuyler, Margery
That's Good! That's Bad!
Illustrated by David Catrow
Henry Holt, 1991
Dabcovich, Lydia
Busy Beavers
Dutton, 1988
Dabcovich, Lydia
Sleepy Bear
Dutton, 1982
Dalmais, Anne-Marie
The Busy Day of Mamma Pizza
Illustrated by Graham Percy
Farrar, Straus and Giroux, 1990
Daugherty, James
Andy and the Lion
Viking, 1938
Davol, Marguerite
The Heart of the Wood
Illustrated by Sheila Hamanaka
Simon & Schuster, 1992
Day, Alexandra
Carl Goes Shopping
Farrar, Straus and Giroux, 1989
Day, Alexandra
Carl's Afternoon in the Park
Farrar, Straus and Giroux, 1991
Day, Alexandra

Frank and Ernest
Scholastic, 1988
Dayrell, Elphinstone, and Blair Lent
*Why the Sun and the Moon Live in
the Sky: An African Folktale*
Illustrated by Blair Lent
Houghton Mifflin, 1968
De Brunhoff, Jean
Babar the King
Random, 1937
De Brunhoff, Jean
The Story of Babar
Random House, 1960
Dee, Ruby
*Two Ways to Count to Ten: A Liber-
ian Folktale*
Illustrated by Susan Meddaugh
Henry Holt, 1990
Degen, Bruce
Jamberry
Harper & Row, 1983
DeGroat, Diane
Alligator's Toothache
Crown, 1977
Delacre, Lulu, ed. and illustrator
*Arroz Con Leche: Popular Songs and
Rhymes from Latin America*
Scholastic, 1989
De La Mare, Walter
Molly Whuppie
Illustrated by Errol Le Cain
Farrar, Straus and Giroux, 1983
Delton, Judy
I'm Telling You Now
Illustrated by Lillian Hoban
Dutton, 1983
Delton, Judy
My Mother Lost Her Job Today
Illustrated by Irene Trivas
Albert Whitman, 1980
Delton, Judy
Rabbit's New Rug
Illustrated by Marc Brown
Parents Magazine Press, 1979
Delton, Judy, and Dorothy Tucker
My Grandma's in a Nursing Home
Illustrated by Charles Robinson

Albert Whitman, 1986

Demarest, Chris L.
No Peas for Nellie
Macmillan, 1988

Demi
Demi's Find the Animal ABC
Grosset & Dunlop, 1985

Demi
Demi's Opposites: An Animal Game Book
Grosset & Dunlop, 1987

Demi
The Empty Pot
Henry Holt, 1990

Denton, Kady MacDonald
Granny Is a Darling
Macmillan, 1988

DePaola, Tomie
Andy—That's My Name
Prentice-Hall, 1973

DePaola, Tomie
Big Anthony and the Magic Ring
Harcourt Brace Jovanovich, 1979

DePaola, Tomie
Bill and Pete
Putnam, 1978

DePaola, Tomie
Charlie Needs a Cloak
Prentice-Hall, 1974

DePaola, Tomie
Favorite Nursery Tales
Putnam, 1986

DePaola, Tomie
Fin M'Coul, the Giant of Knockmany Hill
Holiday House, 1981

DePaola, Tomie
Jamie O'Rourke and the Big Potato
Putnam, 1992

DePaola, Tomie
The Knight and the Dragon
Putnam, 1980

DePaola, Tomie
The Legend of the Indian Paintbrush
Putnam, 1991

DePaola, Tomie
Nana Upstairs and Nana Downstairs

Putnam, 1973

DePaola, Tomie
Now One Foot, Now the Other
Putnam, 1981

DePaola, Tomie
The Popcorn Book
Holiday House, 1978

DePaola, Tomie
Quicksand Book
Holiday House, 1977

DePaola, Tomie
Strega Nona
Prentice-Hall, 1975

DePaola, Tomie
Strega Nona's Magic Lessons
Harcourt Brace and Jovanovich, 1984

DePaola, Tomie
Watch Out for the Chicken Feet in Your Soup
Prentice-Hall, 1974

DePoix, Carol
Jo, Flo and Yolanda
Illustrated by Stephanie Sove Ney
Lollipop Power, 1973

De Regniers, Beatrice Schenk
It Does Not Say Meow
Illustrated by Paul Galdone
Seabury, 1972

De Regniers, Beatrice Schenk
Little Sister and the Month Brothers
Illustrated by Margo Tomes
Seabury, 1976

De Regniers, Beatrice Schenk
May I Bring a Friend?
Illustrated by Beni Montresor
Atheneum, 1964

De Regniers, Beatrice Schenk
The Snow Party
Illustrated by Bernice Myers
Pantheon, 1989

Devlin, Wende, and Harry Devlin
Cranberry Valentine
Macmillan, 1986

Dodd, Lynley
Hairy Maclary—Scattercat
Gareth Stevens, 1988

Dodd, Lynley

Slinky Malinki
Gareth Stevens, 1991

Domanska, Janina, illustrator
If All the Seas Were One Sea
Macmillan, 1971

Dorer, Ann
Mother Makes a Mistake
Illustrated by Ellen Anderson
Gareth Stevens, 1991

Dorros, Arthur
Abuela
Illustrated by Elisa Kleven
Dutton, 1991

Dragonwagon, Crescent
Alligator Arrived with Apples
Illustrated by Jose Aruego and Ariane
Dewey
Macmillan, 1987

Drescher, Joan
My Mother's Getting Married
Dial, 1986

Du Bois, William Pene
Bear Party
Viking, 1963

Dubanevich, Arlene
Tom's Tail
Viking, 1990

Duke, Kate
The Guinea Pig ABC
Dutton, 1983

Dunbar, Joyce
A Cake for Barney
Illustrated by Emilie Boon
Orchard Books, 1987

Dunn, Judy
The Animals of Buttercup Farm
Illustrated by Phoebe Dunn
Random House, 1981

Dunn, Judy
The Little Pig
Illustrated by Phoebe Dunn
Random House, 1987

Dunn, Phoebe
Busy, Busy Toddlers
Random House, 1987

Duplaix, Georges
The Big Brown Bear

Illustrated by Gustaf Tenggren
Western, 1976

Duvoisin, Roger
Our Veronica Goes to Petunia's Farm
Alfred A. Knopf, 1962

Duvoisin, Roger
Petunia
Alfred A. Knopf, 1950

Duvoisin, Roger
Veronica
Alfred A. Knopf, 1961

Eastman, P. D.
The Alphabet Book
Random House, 1974

Eastman, P. D.
Are You My Mother?
Harper-Collins, 1961

Eastman, P. D.
Are You My Mother? (Engish and Spanish)
Random House, 1960

Ehlert, Lois
Color Farm
J. B. Lippincott, 1990

Ehlert, Lois
Eating the Alphabet: Fruits and Vegetables from A to Z
Harcourt Brace Jovanovich, 1989

Ehlert, Lois
Growing Vegetable Soup
Harcourt Brace Jovanovich, 1987

Ehlert, Lois
Planting a Rainbow
Harcourt Brace Jovanovich, 1988

Ehrlich, Amy, retold by
Rapunzel
Illustrated by Kris Waldherr
Dial, 1989

Eisenberg, Phyllis Rose
You're My Nikki
Illustrated by Jill Kastner
Dial, 1992

Elkin, Benjamin
Six Foolish Fishermen
Illustrated by Katherine Evans
Children's Press, 1957

Emberley, Barbara

Drummer Hoff
Illustrated by Ed Emberley
Prentice-Hall, 1967
Emberley, Ed
Green Says Go
Little, Brown, 1968
Emberley, Ed
Klippity Klop
Little, Brown, 1974
Emberley, Ed
The Wing on a Flea: A Book About Shapes
Little, Brown, 1961
Emberley, Michael
Ruby
Little, Brown, 1990
Emmert, Michelle
I'm the Big Sister Now
Illustrated by Gail Owens
Albert Whitman, 1989
Engvick, William, editor
Lullabies and Night Songs
Illustrated by Maurice Sendak
Harper-Collins, 1965
Ernst, Lisa Campbell
Nattie Parsons' Good-Luck Lamb
Viking, 1988
Ernst, Lisa Campbell
Sam Johnson and the Blue Ribbon Quilt
Morrow, 1983
Ets, Marie Hall
Gilberto and the Wind
Viking, 1963
Ets, Marie Hall, and Aurora Labastida
Nine Days to Christmas
Illustrated by Marie Hall Ets
Viking, 1959
Fassler, Joan
Howie Helps Himself
Illustrated by Joe Lasker
Albert Whitman, 1975
Feelings, Muriel
Jambo Means Hello: A Swahili Alphabet Book
Illustrated by Tom Feelings
Dial, 1974

Feelings, Muriel
Moja Means One: A Swahili Counting Book
Illustrated by Tom Feelings
Dial, 1971
Feeney, Stephanie
A Is for Aloha
Illustrated by Hella Hammid
University of Hawaii Press, 1980
Feeney, Stephanie
Hawaii Is a Rainbow
Illustrated by Jeff Reese
University of Hawaii Press, 1980
Feldman, Eve
The Squire Takes a Wife
Illustrated by Bari Weissman
Raintree, 1990
Fisher, Aileen
Listen, Rabbit
Illustrated by Symeon Shimin
Harper-Collins, 1964
Fisher, Aileen
When It Comes to Bugs
Illustrated by Chris and Bruce Degen
Harper-Collins, 1986
Flack, Marjorie
Angus and the Cat
Doubleday, 1989
Flack, Marjorie
Angus and the Ducks
Doubleday, 1989
Flack, Marjorie
Angus Lost
Doubleday, 1989
Flack, Marjorie
Ask Mr. Bear
Macmillan, 1958
Flack, Marjorie
Story About Ping
Illustrated by Kurt Wiese
Viking, 1977
Fleischman, Paul
Rondo in C
Illustrated by Janet Wentworth
Harper-Collins, 1988
Fleming, Denise
In the Tall, Tall Grass

Houghton Mifflin, 1987
Gackenbach, Dick
Harry and the Terrible Whatzit
Seabury, 1977
Gackenbach, Dick
Harvey, the Foolish Pig
Houghton Mifflin, 1988
Gackenbach, Dick
Hound and Bear
Seabury, 1976
Gackenbach, Dick
Mag the Magnificent
Houghton Mifflin, 1985
Gackenbach, Dick
Poppy the Panda
Houghton Mifflin, 1984
Gag, Wanda
The ABC Bunny
Putnam, 1978
Gag, Wanda
Millions of Cats
Putnam, 1977
Gag, Wanda
Nothing at All
Putnam, 1941
Galarza, Ernesto
*Poemas: Very Very Short Nature
Poems*
Pan American, 1972
Galdone, Joanna
The Little Girl and the Big Bear
Illustrated by Paul Galdone
Houghton Mifflin, 1980
Galdone, Paul
The Amazing Pig
Houghton Mifflin, 1981
Galdone, Paul
Cinderella
McGraw Hill, 1978
Galdone, Paul
The Elves and the Shoemaker
Houghton Mifflin, 1984
Galdone, Paul
The Gingerbread Boy
Houghton Mifflin, 1983
Galdone, Paul
Henny Penny

Seabury, 1968
Galdone, Paul
King of the Cats: A Ghost Story
Houghton Mifflin, 1980
Galdone, Paul
Little Red Hen
Seabury, 1973
Galdone, Paul
Little Red Riding Hood
McGraw Hill, 1974
Galdone, Paul
*The Monkey and the Crocodile: A
Jataka Tale from India*
Seabury, 1969
Galdone, Paul
The Monster and the Tailor
Houghton Mifflin, 1982
Galdone, Paul
Puss in Boots
Seabury, 1976
Galdone, Paul
The Table, the Donkey and the Stick
McGraw Hill, 1976
Galdone, Paul
The Teeny-Tiny Woman
Houghton Mifflin, 1984
Galdone, Paul
The Three Bears
Seabury, 1972
Galdone, Paul
Three Little Kittens
Houghton Mifflin, 1986
Galdone, Paul
The Three Little Pigs
Seabury, 1970
Galdone, Paul
*The Turtle and the Monkey: A Philip-
pine Tale*
Clarion, 1983
Gans, Roma
It's Nesting Time
Illustrated by Kazue Mizumura
Thomas Y. Crowell, 1964
Gantos, Jack
Happy Birthday, Rotten Ralph
Illustrated by Nicole Rubel
Houghton Mifflin, 1990

Gantos, Jack
Rotten Ralph
Illustrated by Nicole Rubel
Houghton Mifflin, 1976

Garelick, May
Where Does the Butterfly Go When It Rains?
Illustrated by Leonard Weisgard
Addison-Wesley, 1961

Garland, Sarah
All Gone!
Viking, 1990

Garza, Carmen Lomas
Family Pictures
Children's Book Press, 1990

Gauch, Patricia Lee
Bravo, Tanya
Illustrated by Satomi Ichikawa
Philomel, 1992

Gauch, Patricia Lee
Christina Katerina and the Time She Quit the Family
Illustrated by Elise Primavera
Putnam, 1987

Gauch, Patricia Lee
Dance, Tanya
Illustrated by Satomi Ichikawa
Philomel, 1989

George, Lindsay Barrett
William and Boomer
Greenwillow, 1987

Gerrard, Roy
Mik's Mammoth
Farrar, Straus and Giroux, 1990

Gerstein, Mordecai
Anytime Mapleson and the Hungry Bears
Illustrated by Susan Yard Harris
Harper-Collins, 1990

Gibbons, Gail
Boat Book
Holiday House, 1983

Gibbons, Gail
Fill It Up! All About Service Stations
Thomas Y. Crowell, 1985

Gibbons, Gail
Fire! Fire!
Thomas Y. Crowell, 1984

Gibbons, Gail
From Seed to Plant
Holiday House, 1991

Gibbons, Gail
Marge's Diner
Thomas Y. Crowell, 1989

Gibbons, Gail
Prehistoric Animals
Holiday House, 1988

Gibbons, Gail
The Seasons of Arnold's Apple Tree
Harcourt Brace Jovanovich, 1984

Gibbons, Gail
Sharks
Holiday House, 1992

Gibbons, Gail
Sun Up, Sun Down
Harcourt Brace Jovanovich, 1983

Gibbons, Gail
Thanksgiving Day
Holiday House, 1983

Gibbons, Gail
Valentine's Day
Holiday House, 1986

Gibbons, Gail
Zoo
Thomas Y. Crowell, 1987

Ginsburg, Mirra, translator
The Chick and the Duckling
Illustrated by Jose and Ariane Aruego
Macmillan, 1972

Ginsburg, Mirra
The Chinese Mirror
Illustrated by Margot Zemach
Harcourt Brace and Jovanovich, 1988

Ginsburg, Mirra
Good Morning, Chick
Illustrated by Byron Barton
Greenwillow, 1980

Ginsburg, Mirra
Mushroom in the Rain
Illustrated by Jose Aruego and Ariane Dewey
Macmillan, 1987

Ginsburg, Mirra
Two Greedy Bears

Illustrated by Jose Aruego and Ariane
  Dewey
Macmillan, 1976
Giovanni, Nick
  Spin a Soft Black Song
  Illustrated by Charles Bible
  Hill & Wang, 1971
Girard, Linda Walvoord
  Jeremy's First Haircut
  Illustrated by Mary Jane Begin
  Albert Whitman, 1986
Goble, Paul
  Crow Chief
  Orchard, 1992
Goble, Paul
  The Girl Who Loved Wild Horses
  Bradbury, 1978
Goldin, Augusta
  Ducks Don't Get Wet
  Illustrated by Leonard Kessler
  Thomas Y. Crowell, 1965
Goldman, Susan
  Cousins Are Special
  Albert Whitman, 1978
Goldstein, Bobbye
  Inner Chimes: Poems on Poetry
  Illustrated by Jane Breskin Zalben
  Wordsong-Boyd Mills Press, 1992
Gomi, Taro
  Bus Stops
  Chronicle Books, 1988
Gomi, Taro
  Spring Is Here
  Chronicle Books, 1989
Goodall, John
  Adventures of Paddy Pork
  Harcourt Brace Jovanovich, 1968
Goodall, John
  Little Red Riding Hood
  Macmillan, 1988
Goodall, John
  Paddy's Evening Out
  Atheneum, 1973
Gordon, Sol, and Judith Gordon
  A Better Safe Than Sorry Book
  Illustrated by Vivien Cohen
  Prometheus Books, 1992

Gordon, Sol, and Judith Gordon
  *Did the Sun Shine Before You Were
  Born?*
  Illustrated by Vivien Cohen
  Prometheus Books, 1992
Gould, Deborah
  Aaron's Shirt
  Illustrated by Cheryl Harness
  Bradbury, 1989
Graham, Margaret B.
  Be Nice to Spiders
  Harper-Collins, 1967
Graham, Margaret B.
  Benjy and the Barking Bird
  Harper-Collins, 1971
Graham, Margaret B.
  Benjy's Boat Trip
  Harper-Collins, 1977
Graham, Margaret B.
  Benjy's Dog House
  Harper-Collins, 1973
Graham, Richard
  Jack and the Monster
  Illustrated by Susan Varley
  Houghton Mifflin, 1989
Gramatky, Hardie
  Little Toot
  Putnam, 1978
Greaves, Margaret
  Tattercoats
  Illustrated by Margaret Chamberlain
  Crown, 1990
Green, Norma, retold by
  The Hole in the Dike
  Illustrated by Eric Carle
  Thomas Y. Crowell, 1974
Greenfield, Eloise
  First Pink Light
  Illustrated by Moneta Barnett
  Thomas Y. Crowell, 1976
Greenfield, Eloise
  Night on Neighborhood Street
  Illustrated by Jan Spivey Gilchrist
  Dial, 1991
Greenfield, Eloise
  *She Come Bringing Me That Little
  Baby Girl*

Illustrated by John Steptoe
Lippincott, 1974
Greenfield, Eloise
Under the Sunday Tree
Illustrated by Amos Ferguson
Harper-Collins, 1988
Grifalconi, Ann
*The Village of Round and Square
Houses*
Little, Brown, 1986
**Griego, Margot, Betsy L. Bucks, Sharon
S. Gilbert, and Laurel H. Kimball,
translators**
*Tortillitas Para Mama & Other
Nursery Rhymes*
Illustrated by Barbara Cooney
Henry Holt, 1981
Grimm Brothers
The Bremen Town Musicians
Illustrated by Josef Palecek
Picture Book Studio, 1988
Grimm Brothers
The Frog Prince
Illustrated by Robert Baxter
Troll Associates, 1979
Grimm Brothers
Hansel and Gretel
Illustrated by Susan Jeffers
Dial, 1980
Grimm Brothers
Little Red Riding Hood
Illustrated by Harriet Pincus
Harcourt Brace Jovanovich, 1968
Grimm Brothers
Snow White
Translated by Paul Heins
Illustrated by Trina Schart Hyman
Little, Brown, 1974
Grimm Brothers
Snow White and Rose Red
Illustrated by Gennady Spirin
Philomel, 1992
Grimm Brothers
Snow White and the Seven Dwarfs
Translated by Randall Jarrell
Illustrated by Nancy Ekholm Burkert
Farrar, Straus and Giroux, 1972

Gustafson, Scott
Alphabet Soup
Kipling Press, 1990
Hader, Berta, and Elmer Hader
The Big Snow
Macmillan, 1948
Hadithi, Mwenye
Awful Aardvark
Illustrated by Adrienne Kennaway
Little, Brown, 1989
Hadithi, Mwenye
Crafty Chameleon
Illustrated by Adrienne Kennaway
Little, Brown, 1987
Hadithi, Mwenye
Hot Hippo
Illustrated by Adrienne Kennaway
Little, Brown, 1986
Hague, Kathleen
Alphabears
Illustrated by Michael Hague
Holt, Rinehart and Winston, 1984
Hague, Kathleen, and Michael Hague
The Man Who Kept House
Illustrated by Michael Hague
Harcourt Brace Jovanovich, 1981
Hale, Sara Josepha
Mary Had a Little Lamb
Illustrated by Bruce McMillan
Scholastic, 1990
Haley, Gail E.
A Story, A Story: An African Tale
Atheneum, 1976
Hall, Donald
Ox-Cart Man
Illustrated by Barbara Cooney
Viking, 1979
Hallinan, P. K.
*We're Very Good Friends, My
Brother and I*
Childrens Press, 1973
Hamm, Diane Johnston
Laney's Lost Momma
Illustrated by Sally G. Ward
Albert Whitman, 1991
Hannum, Dotti
A Visit to the Fire Station

Photos by Dave Holmes, Sue Markson, and Tom Wolf
Childrens Press, 1985

Hannum, Dotti
A Visit to the Police Station
Photos by Romie Flanagen
Childrens Press, 1985

Hariton, Anca
Egg Story
Dutton, 1992

Harper, Wilhelmina, retold by
Gunniwolf
Illustrated by William Wiesner
Dutton, 1967

Harshman, Marc, and Bonnie Collins
Rocks in My Pockets
Illustrated by Toni Goffe
Dutton, 1991

Hart, Jane, collector
Singing Bee!
Illustrated by Anita Lobel
Lothrop, Lee and Shepard, 1989

Hartman, Gail
For Strawberry Jam or Fireflies
Illustrated by Ellen Weiss
Bradbury, 1989

Haugaard, Erik Christian
Princess Horrid
Illustrated by Diane Dawson Hearn
Macmillan, 1990

Hautzig, Deborah
A Visit to the Sesame Street Library
Illustrated by Joe Mathieu
Random House, 1986

Havill, Juanita
Jamaica Tag-Along
Illustrated by Anne Sibley O'Brien
Houghton Mifflin, 1989

Hawes, Judy
Bees and Beelines
Illustrated by Aliki
Thomas Y. Crowell, 1964

Hawkins, Colin, and Jacqui Hawkins
Old Mother Hubbard
Putnam, 1985

Hayes, Sarah
Mary Mary

Illustrated by Helen Craig
Macmillan, 1990

Hazen, Barbara Shook
Fang
Illustrated by Leslie Holt Morrill
Atheneum, 1987

Hazen, Barbara Shook
The Gorilla Did It
Illustrated by Ray Cruz
Atheneum, 1974

Hazen, Barbara Shook
Mommy's Office
Illustrated by David Soman
Atheneum, 1992

Hazen, Barbara Shook
Tight Times
Illustrated by Trina Schart Hyman
Viking, 1979

Hazen, Barbara Shook
Wally, the Worry-Warthog
Illustrated by Janet Stevens
Houghton Mifflin, 1990

Hedderwick, Mairi
Katie Morag and the Tiresome Ted
Little, Brown, 1986

Hedderwick, Mairi
*Katie Morag and the Two
    Grandmothers*
Little, Brown, 1985

Heller, Ruth
Chickens Aren't the Only Ones
Grosset & Dunlop, 1985

Heller, Ruth
How to Hide a Butterfly
Platt & Munk, 1992

Heller, Ruth
*How to Hide an Octopus and Other
    Sea Creatures*
Platt & Munk, 1992

Heller, Ruth
The Reason for a Flower
Grosset & Dunlop, 1983

Hennessy, B. G.
School Days
Illustrated by Tracey Campbell
    Pearson
Viking, 1990

Hennessy, B. G.
Sleep Tight
Illustrated by Anthony Carnabuci
Viking, 1992

Herriot, James
Moses the Kitten
Illustrated by Peter Barrett
St. Martin's Press, 1984

Hershey, Kathleen
Cotton Mill Town
Illustrated by Jeanette Winter
Dutton, 1993

Hest, Amy
The Best-Ever Good-Bye Party
Illustrated by DyAnne DiSalvo-Ryan
Morrow, 1989

Hest, Amy
The Crack-of-Dawn Walkers
Illustrated by Amy Schwartz
Macmillan, 1984

Hest, Amy
The Purple Coat
Illustrated by Amy Schwartz
Four Winds Press, 1986

Hewitt, Kathryn, retold and illustrated by
King Midas and the Golden Touch
Harcourt Brace Jovanovich, 1987

Heyer, Carol, retold and illustrated by
Beauty and the Beast
Ideals, 1989

Hickman, Martha Whitmore
My Friend William Moved Away
Illustrated by Bill Myers
Abingdon, 1979

Hill, Elizabeth Starr
Evan's Corner
Illustrated by Sandra Speidel
Viking, 1991

Hill, Eric
Spot's First Walk
Interlink, 1988

Hillerich, Robert L.
The American Picture Dictionary
Illustrated by Maggie Swanson
Houghton Mifflin, 1986

Hilton, Nette

The Long Red Scarf
Illustrated by Margaret Power
Carolrhoda, 1987

Himmelman, John
Amanda and the Witch Switch
Viking, 1985

Hines, Anna Grossnickle
Daddy Makes the Best Spaghetti
Houghton Mifflin, 1986

Hirsch, Marilyn
Could Anything Be Worse?
Holiday House, 1974

Hirsch, Marilyn
Potato Pancakes All Around
Bonim, 1978

Hirschi, Ron
Fall
Illustrated by Thomas D. Mangelsen
Dutton, 1991

Hirschi, Ron
Winter
Illustrated by Thomas D. Mangelsen
Dutton, 1990

Hiskey, Iris
Cassandra Who?
Illustrated by Normand Chartier
Simon & Schuster, 1992

Hoban, Lillian
Mr. Pig and Sonny Too
Harper-Collins, 1977

Hoban, Lillian
Silly Tilly's Thanksgiving Dinner
Harper-Collins, 1990

Hoban, Russell
A Baby Sister for Frances
Illustrated by Lillian Hoban
Harper-Collins, 1976

Hoban, Russell
A Bargain for Frances
Illustrated by Lillian Hoban
Harper-Collins, 1970

Hoban, Russell
Bedtime for Frances
Illustrated by Garth Williams
Harper-Collins, 1960

Hoban, Russell
Best Friends for Frances

Illustrated by Lillian Hoban
Harper-Collins, 1969
Hoban, Russell
Birthday for Frances
Illustrated by Lillian Hoban
Harper-Collins, 1976
Hoban, Russell
Bread and Jam for Frances
Illustrated by Lillian Hoban
Harper-Collins, 1964
Hoban, Russell
Egg Thoughts and Other Frances
Songs
Illustrated by Lillian Hoban
Harper-Collins, 1972
Hoban, Russell
Harvey's Hideout
Illustrated by Lillian Hoban
Parents Magazine Press, 1969
Hoban, Tana
A, B, See!
Greenwillow, 1982
Hoban, Tana
A Children's Zoo
Greenwillow, 1985
Hoban, Tana
Circles, Triangles and Squares
Macmillan, 1974
Hoban, Tana
Count and See
Macmillan, 1972
Hoban, Tana
I Read Signs
Greenwillow, 1983
Hoban, Tana
I Read Symbols
Greenwillow, 1983
Hoban, Tana
Is It Red? Is It Yellow? Is It Blue?
Greenwillow, 1979
Hoban, Tana
Look Again!
Macmillan, 1971
Hoban, Tana
Of Colors and Things
Greenwillow, 1989
Hoban, Tana

Over, Under, Through and Other
Spatial Concepts
Macmillan, 1973
Hoban, Tana
Push, Pull, Empty, Full: A Book of
Opposites
Macmillan, 1972
Hoban, Tana
Round and Round and Round
Greenwillow, 1983
Hoban, Tana
Take Another Look
Greenwillow, 1981
Hoban, Tana
26 Letters and 99 Cents
Greenwillow, 1987
Hoban, Tana
What Is It?
Greenwillow, 1985
Hoban, Tana
Where Is It?
Macmillan, 1974
Hoberman. Mary Ann
A House Is a House for Me
Illustrated by Betty Fraser
Viking, 1979
Hodges, Margaret
Saint George and the Dragon
Illustrated by Trina Schart Hyman
Little, Brown, 1984
Hodges, Margaret
The Wave
Illustrated by Blair Lent
Houghton Mifflin, 1964
Hoellwarth, Cathryn Clinton
The Underbed
Illustrated by Sibyl Graber Gerig
Good Books, 1990
Hoffman, Mary
Amazing Grace
Illustrated by Caroline Binch
Dial, 1991
Hogrogian, Nonny
The Cat Who Loved to Sing
Alfred A. Knopf, 1988
Hogrogian, Nonny
The Contest: An Armenian Folktale

Greenwillow, 1976

Hogrogian, Nonny
One Fine Day
Macmillan, 1971

Hoguet, Susan Ramsay
I Unpacked My Grandmother's Trunk
Dutton, 1983

Holabird, Katherine
Angelina Ballerina
Illustrated by Helen Craig
Crown, 1983

Holabird, Katherine
Angelina's Birthday Surprise
Illustrated by Helen Craig
Crown, 1989

Hooks, William H.
Moss Gown
Illustrated by Donald Carrick
Houghton Mifflin, 1987

Hooks, William H.
Peach Boy
Illustrated by June Otani
Doubleday, 1992

Hooks, William H.
The Three Little Pigs and the Fox
Illustrated by S. D. Schindler
Macmillan, 1989

Hopkins, Lee Bennett, Editor
Good Books, Good Times
Illustrated by Harvey Stevenson
Harper-Collins, 1990

Horenstein, Henry
Sam Goes Trucking
Houghton Mifflin, 1989

Hort, Lenny
The Boy Who Held Back the Sea
Illustrated by Thomas Locker
Dial, 1987

Horton, Barbara Savadge
What Comes in Spring?
Illustrated by Ed Young
Alfred A. Knopf, 1992

Horwitz, Elinor Lander
When the Sky Is Like Lace
Illustrated by Barbara Cooney
Lippincott, 1975

Howard, Elizabeth Fitzgerald
Aunt Flossie's Hats (and Crab Cakes Later)
Illustrated by James Ransome
Houghton Mifflin, 1991

Hudson, Cheryl Willis, and Bernette G. Ford
Bright Eyes, Brown Skin
Illustrated by George Ford
Just Us Books, 1990

Hughes, Shirley
Alfie Gives a Hand
Lothrop, Lee and Shepard, 1983

Hughes, Shirley
Alfie's Feet
Lothrop, Lee and Shepard, 1982

Hughes, Shirley
Moving Molly
Prentice-Hall, 1979

Hurd, Edith Thacher
I Dance in My Red Pajamas
Illustrated by Emily A. McCully
Harper-Collins, 1982

Hurd, Edith Thacher
Look for a Bird
Illustrated by Clement Hurd
Harper-Collins, 1977

Hutchins, Pat
Changes, Changes
Macmillan, 1973

Hutchins, Pat
Clocks and More Clocks
Macmillan, 1973

Hutchins, Pat
Don't Forget the Bacon
Macmillan, 1972

Hutchins, Pat
Goodnight Owl
Macmillan, 1972

Hutchins, Pat
Happy Birthday, Sam
Greenwillow, 1978

Hutchins, Pat
One Hunter
Greenwillow, 1982

Hutchins, Pat
Rosie's Walk

Macmillan, 1968
Hutchins, Pat
Surprise Party
Macmillan, 1969
Hutchins, Pat
Titch
Macmillan, 1971
Hutchins, Pat
Which Witch Is Which?
Greenwillow, 1989
Hutchins, Pat
The Wind Blew
Macmillan, 1974
Hutton, Warwick, retold and illustrated by
Beauty and the Beast
Atheneum, 1985
Hyman, Trina Schart, retold and illustrated by
Sleeping Beauty
Little, Brown, 1977
Isadora, Rachel
Ben's Trumpet
Greenwillow, 1979
Isadora, Rachel
I Hear
Greenwillow, 1985
Isadora, Rachel
I See
Greenwillow, 1985
Isadora, Rachel
I Touch
Greenwillow, 1985
Isadora, Rachel
My Ballet Class
Greenwillow, 1980
Isadora, Rachel
Opening Night
Greenwillow, 1984
Isenberg, Barbara, and Susan Wolf
The Adventures of Albert, the Running Bear
Illustrated by Dick Gackenbach
Houghton Mifflin, 1982
Ives, Penny
Goldilocks and the Three Bears
Putnam, 1992

Jabar, Cynthia
Alice Ann Gets Ready for School
Little, Brown, 1989
Jackson, Ellen
The Tree of Life: The Wonders of Evolution
Illustrated by Judeanne Winter
Prometheus Books, 1993
Jackson, Kathryn
The Tawny Scrawny Lion
Illustrated by Gustav Tenggren
Western, 1952
Jacobs, Joseph, editor
Tattercoats
Illustrated by Margot Tomes
Putnam, 1989
James, Betsy
He Wakes Me
Illustrated by Helen K. Davis
Orchard, 1991
Jeffers, Susan
All the Pretty Horses
Macmillan, 1974
Johnson, Angela
One of Three
Illustrated by David Soman
Orchard, 1991
Johnson, Angela
When I Am Old With You
Illustrated by David Soman
Orchard, 1990
Johnson, Crockett
Harold and the Purple Crayon
Harper-Collins, 1981
Johnson, Crockett
Will Spring Be Early or Will Spring Be Late?
Harper-Collins, 1961
Johnston, Tony
Grandpa's Song
Illustrated by Brad Sneed
Dial, 1991
Johnston, Tony
Yonder
Illustrated by Lloyd Bloom
Dial, 1988
Jonas, Ann

The Trek
Greenwillow, 1985
Jones, Carol, illustrator
Hickory Dickory Dock
Houghton Mifflin, 1990
Jones, Carol, illustrator
Old MacDonald Had a Farm
Houghton Mifflin, 1989
Jones, Carol, illustrator
This Old Man
Houghton Mifflin, 1990
Joosse, Barbara M.
Better With Two
Illustrated by Catherine Stock
Harper-Collins, 1988
Joosse, Barbara M.
Fourth of July
Illustrated by Emily A. McCully
Alfred A. Knopf, 1985
Jordan, Helene J.
How a Seed Grows
Illustrated by Loretta Krupinski
Harper-Collins, 1992
Jorgensen, Gail
Crocodile Beat
Illustrated by Patricia Mullins
Macmillan, 1988
Joyce, William
George Shrinks
Harper-Collins, 1985
Jukes, Mavis
Like Jake and Me
Illustrated by Lloyd Bloom
Knopf, 1984
Kalan, Robert
Jump, Frog, Jump
Illustrated by Byron Barton
Greenwillow, 1981
Kalan, Robert
Rain
Illustrated by Donald Crews
Greenwillow, 1978
Kaldhol, Marit
Goodbye, Rune
Translated by Michael Crosby-Jones
Illustrated by Wenche Yen
Kane/Miller, 1987

Kandoian, Ellen
Maybe She Forgot
Dutton, 1990
Kantrowitz, Mildred
Maxie
Illustrated by Emily A. McCully
Parents Magazine Press, 1970
Kantrowitz, Mildred
Willy Bear
Illustrated by Nancy Winslow Parker
Parents Magazine Press, 1976
Kaopuiki, Stacey
The Secret of the Hawaiian Rainbow
Illustrated by Bob Wagstaff
Hawaiian Island Concepts, 1991
Karlin, Nurit
The Tooth Witch
J. S. Lippincott, 1985
Kasza, Keiko
The Wolf's Chicken Stew
Putnam, 1987
Katz, Michael Jay
Ten Potatoes in a Pot and Other
  Counting Rhymes
Illustrated by June Otani
Harper-Collins, 1990
Keats, Ezra Jack
Apt. 3G
Macmillan, 1971
Keats, Ezra Jack
Dreams
Macmillan, 1974
Keats, Ezra Jack
Goggles!
Macmillan, 1969
Keats, Ezra Jack
Hi, Cat!
Macmillan, 1972
Keats, Ezra Jack
Jennie's Hat
Harper-Collins, 1966
Keats, Ezra Jack
John Henry: An American Legend
Alfred A. Knopf, 1965
Keats, Ezra Jack
Kitten for a Day
Watts, 1974

Keats, Ezra Jack
Letter to Amy
Harper-Collins, 1968

Keats, Ezra Jack
Louie
Greenwillow, 1975

Keats, Ezra Jack
Maggie and the Pirate
Scholastic, 1979

Keats, Ezra Jack
Pet Show!
Macmillan, 1974

Keats, Ezra Jack
Peter's Chair
Harper-Collins, 1967

Keats, Ezra Jack
The Snowy Day
Viking, 1962

Keats, Ezra Jack
Whistle for Willie
Viking, 1977

Keller, Holly
Geraldine's Big Snow
Greenwillow, 1988

Kellogg, Steven
Aster Aardvark's Alphabet Adventures
Morrow, 1987

Kellogg, Steven
Best Friends
Dial, 1986

Kellogg, Steven
Can I Keep Him?
Dial, 1971

Kellogg, Steven
Island of the Skog
Dial, 1973

Kellogg, Steven
Johnny Appleseed: A Tall Tale
Morrow, 1988

Kellogg, Steven
Paul Bunyan
Morrow, 1984

Kellogg, Steven
Pecos Bill
Morrow, 1986

Kellogg, Steven

Pinkerton, Behave!
Dial, 1979

Kennedy, Jimmy
The Teddy Bears' Picnic
Illustrated by Prue Theobalds
Peter Bedrick, 1987

Kent, Jack
The Caterpillar and the Polliwog
Prentice-Hall, 1982

Keown, Elizabeth
Emily's Snowball, the World's Biggest
Illustrated by Irene Trivas
Atheneum, 1992

Ketner, Mary Grace
Ganzy Remembers
Illustrated by Barbara Sparks
Atheneum, 1991

Kibby, Marsha
My Grammy
Illustrated by Karen Ritz
Carolrhoda, 1988

Kilbourne, Frances
Overnight Adventure
Illustrated by Ann Powell
Canadian Women's Educational
    Press, 1977

Kimmel, Eric, retold by
Anansi and the Moss-Covered Rock
Illustrated by Janet Stevens
Holiday House, 1990

Kimmel, Eric, retold by
Anansi Goes Fishing
Illustrated by Janet Stevens
Holiday House, 1992

Kimmel, Eric
Baba Yaga: A Russian Folktale
Illustrated by Megan Lloyd
Holiday House, 1991

Kimmel, Eric
The Chanukkah Guest
Illustrated by Giora Carmi
Holiday House, 1990

Kimmel, Eric
Charlie Drives the Stage
Illustrated by Glen Rounds
Holiday House, 1989

Kimmel, Eric

I Took My Frog to the Library
Illustrated by Blanche Sims
Viking, 1990
Kimmel, Margaret M.
Magic in the Mist
Illustrated by Trina Schart Hyman
Atheneum, 1974
King, Bob
Sitting on a Farm
Illustrated by Bill Slavin
Orchard, 1991
King, Elizabeth
The Pumpkin Patch
Dutton, 1990
Kipling, Rudyard
The Elephant's Child
Illustrated by Jan Mogensen
Crocodile Books, 1988
Kitchen, Bert
Animal Alphabet
Dial, 1984
Klein, Norma
Visiting Pamela
Illustrated by Kay Chorao
Dial, 1979
Kline, Suzy
Don't Touch!
Illustrated by Dora Leder
Albert Whitman, 1985
Knight, Hilary
Where's Wallace?
Harper-Collins, 1964
Koller, Jackie French
Mole and Shrew Step Out
Illustrated by Stella Ormai
Atheneum, 1992
Konigsburg, E. L.
Samuel Todd's Book of Great Colors
Atheneum, 1990
Konigsburg, E. L.
*Samuel Todd's Book of Great
Inventions*
Atheneum, 1991
Koontz, Robin M.
I See Something You Don't See
Dutton, 1992
Koontz, Robin M., illustrator

This Old Man: The Counting Song
Dodd, Mead, 1988
Kovalski, Maryann
The Wheels on the Bus
Little, Brown, 1987
Kraus, Robert
Herman the Helper
Illustrated by Jose Aruego and Ariane
Dewey
Dutton, 1977
Kraus, Robert
Leo the Late Bloomer
Illustrated by Jose Aruego
Dutton, 1971
Kraus, Robert
Milton the Early Riser
Illustrated by Jose Aruego and Ariane
Dewey
Dutton, 1972
Kraus, Robert
Noel the Coward
Illustrated by Jose Aruego and Ariane
Dewey
Dutton, 1977
Kraus, Robert
Owliver
Illustrated by Jose Aruego and Ariane
Dewey
Dutton, 1974
Kraus, Robert
Whose Mouse Are You?
Illustrated by Jose Aruego
Macmillan, 1972
Krauss, Ruth
Birthday Party
Illustrated by Maurice Sendak
Harper-Collins, 1957
Krauss, Ruth
Carrot Seed
Illustrated by Crockett Johnson
Harper-Collins, 1945
Krauss, Ruth
Open House for Butterflies
Illustrated by Maurice Sendak
Harper-Collins, 1960
Krementz, Jill
Jack Goes to the Beach

Random House, 1986

Krensky, Stephen, editor
American Heritage First Dictionary
Houghton Mifflin, 1986

Kroll, Steven
Happy Mother's Day
Illustrated by Marylin Hafner
Holiday House, 1985

Kroll, Steven
The Squirrels' Thanksgiving
Illustrated by Jeni Bassett
Holiday House, 1991

Kroll, Steven
The Tyrannosaurus Game
Illustrated by Tomie DePaola
Holiday House, 1976

Kuklin, Susan
Going to My Nursery School
Bradbury, 1990

Kuklin, Susan
When I See My Doctor
Bradbury, 1988

Kunhardt, Dorothy
Pat the Bunny
Western, 1962

Kunhardt, Edith
I Want to Be a Firefighter
Grosset & Dunlop, 1989

Kuskin, Karla
The Philharmonic Gets Dressed
Illustrated by Marc Simont
Harper-Collins, 1982

Kuskin, Karla
Roar and More
Harper-Collins, 1990

La Fontaine, Jean de
The Hare and the Tortoise
Illustrated by Brian Wildsmith
Franklin Watts, 1966

La Fontaine, Jean de
The Lion and the Mouse
Illustrated by Brian Wildsmith
Franklin Watts, 1963

La Fontaine, Jean de
The North Wind and the Sun
Illustrated by Brian Wildsmith
Franklin Watts, 1964

La Fontaine, Jean de
The Miller, the Boy and the Donkey
Illustrated by Brian Wildsmith
Franklin Watts, 1969

Lang, Andrew, retold by
Aladdin and the Wonderful Lamp
Illustrated by Errol LeCain
Viking, 1981

Langley, Jonathan
Rumpelstiltskin
Harper-Collins, 1991

Langstaff, John
Frog Went A-Courtin'
Illustrated by Feodor Rojankovsky
Harcourt Brace Jovanovich, 1955

Langstaff, John
Oh, A-Hunting We Will Go
Illustrated by Nancy Winslow Parker
Atheneum, 1974

Langstaff, John, and Feodor
  Rojankovsky
Over in the Meadow
Illustrated by Feodor Rojankovsky
Harcourt Brace Jovanovich, 1967

Lankford, Mary D.
Is It Dark? Is It Light?
Illustrated by Stacey Schuett
Alfred A. Knopf, 1991

Lapsley, Susan
I Am Adopted
Illustrated by Michael Charlton
Bradbury, 1975

Larranga, Robert
King's Shadow
Illustrated by Joe Greenwald
Carolrhoda, 1970

Lasker, Joe
He's My Brother
Albert Whitman, 1974

Lasker, Joe
Mothers Can Do Anything
Albert Whitman, 1972

Lasky, Kathryn
*I Have Four Names for My
  Grandfather*
Illustrated by Christopher G. Knight
Little, Brown, 1976

Parnassus, 1976
Lewin, Hugh
Jafta
Illustrated by Lisa Kopper
Carolrhoda, 1983
Lewis, Kim
Emma's Lamb
Macmillan, 1991
Lewis, J. Patrick
A Hippopotamusn't
Illustrated by Victoria Chess
Dial, 1990
Lewis, Richard
All of You Was Singing
Illustrated by Ed Young
Atheneum, 1991
Lewis, Richard
In a Spring Garden
Illustrated by Ezra Jack Keats
Dial, 1976
Lewison, Wendy Cheyette
Going to Sleep on the Farm
Illustrated by Juan Wijngaard
Dial, 1992
Lewison, Wendy Cheyette
Say Thank You, Theodore
Illustrated by Juli Kangas
Platt and Munk, 1992
Lexau, Joan
*Emily and the Clunky Baby and the
   Next-Door Dog*
Illustrated by Martha Alexander
Dial, 1972
Lexau, Joan
Me Day
Illustrated by Robert Weaver
Dial, 1971
Lindgren, Barbro
Sam's Car
Illustrated by Eva Eriksson
Morrow, 1982
Lindgren, Barbro
The Wild Baby
Illustrated by Eva Eriksson
Greenwillow, 1981
Lionni, Leo
Alexander and the Wind-Up Mouse

Pantheon, 1974
Lionni, Leo
The Alphabet Tree
Pantheon, 1968
Lionni, Leo
The Biggest House in the World
Pantheon, 1968
Lionni, Leo
A Color of His Own
Pantheon, 1976
Lionni, Leo
Cornelius
Pantheon, 1983
Lionni, Leo
Fish Is Fish
Pantheon, 1970
Lionni, Leo
Frederick
Pantheon, 1966
Lionni, Leo
The Greentail Mouse
Pantheon, 1973
Lionni, Leo
Inch by Inch
Astor-Honor, 1960
Lionni, Leo
Little Blue and Little Yellow
Astor-Honor, 1959
Lionni, Leo
Matthew's Dream
Alfred A. Knopf, 1991
Lionni, Leo
Mr. McMouse
Alfred A. Knopf, 1992
Lionni, Leo
*On My Beach There Are Many
   Pebbles*
Astor-Honor, 1961
Lionni, Leo
Six Crows
Alfred A. Knopf, 1988
Lionni, Leo
Swimmy
Pantheon, 1963
Lionni, Leo
Tico and the Golden Wings
Pantheon, 1964

Lionni, Leo
Tillie and the Wall
Alfred A. Knopf, 1989

Lipkind, William, and Nicolas Mordvinoff
Finders Keepers
Illustrated by Nicolas Mordvinoff
Harcourt Brace Jovanovich, 1951

Livingston, Myra Cohn, editor
Poems for Fathers
Illustrated by Robert Casilla
Holiday House, 1989

Lobato, Arcadio
The Greatest Treasure
Picture Book Studio, 1989

Lobel, Anita
Potatoes, Potatoes
Harper-Collins, 1967

Lobel, Arnold
Fables
Harper-Collins, 1980

Lobel, Arnold
Frog and Toad Together
Harper-Collins, 1972

Lobel, Arnold
Giant John
Harper-Collins, 1964

Lobel, Arnold
Martha, the Movie Mouse
Harper-Collins, 1966

Lobel, Arnold
Mouse Soup
Harper-Collins, 1977

Lobel, Arnold
Owl at Home
Harper-Collins, 1975

Lobel, Arnold
Prince Bertram the Bad
Harper-Collins, 1963

Lobel, Arnold
The Rose in My Garden
Illustrated by Anita Lobel
Greenwillow, 1984

Lobel, Arnold
A Treeful of Pigs
Illustrated by Anita Lobel
Greenwillow, 1979

Longfellow, Henry Wadsworth
Hiawatha
Illustrated by Susan Jeffers
Dutton, 1983

Lord, John Vernon, and Janet Burroway
The Giant Jam Sandwich
Houghton Mifflin, 1973

Louie, Ai-Ling
Yeh-Shen
Illustrated by Ed Young
Putnam, 1990

Lowrey, Janette S.
Poky Little Puppy
Illustrated by Gustaf Tenggren
Western, 1973

Luenn, Nancy
Mother Earth
Illustrated by Neil Waldman
Atheneum, 1992

Luenn, Nancy
Nessa's Fish
Illustrated by Neil Waldman
Atheneum, 1990

Lyon, David
The Biggest Truck
Lothrop, Lee and Shepard, 1988

Lyon, George-Ella
A B Cedar: An Alphabet of Trees
Illustrated by Tom Parker
Franklin Watts, 1989

Lyon, George-Ella
Together
Illustrated by Vera Rosenberry
Orchard, 1989

Lyon, George-Ella
Who Came Down That Road?
Illustrated by Peter Catalanotto
Orchard, 1992

McCarthy, Patricia
Herds of Words
Dial, 1991

McCloskey, Robert
Blueberries for Sal
Viking, 1948

McCloskey, Robert
Burt Dow, Deep-Water Man
Viking, 1963

McCloskey, Robert
Lentil
Viking, 1940
McCloskey, Robert
Make Way for Ducklings
Viking, 1941
McCloskey, Robert
One Morning in Maine
Viking, 1952
McCloskey, Robert
Time of Wonder
Viking, 1957
McCord, David
Every Time I Climb a Tree
Illustrated by Marc Simont
Little, Brown, 1967
McCully, Emily A.
First Snow
Harper-Collins, 1985
McCully, Emily A.
Mirette on the High Wire
Putnam, 1992
McCully, Emily A.
New Baby
Harper-Collins, 1988
McCully, Emily A.
Picnic
Harper-Collins, 1984
McCully, Emily A.
School
Harper-Collins, 1987
McDermott, Gerald
Anansi the Spider: A Tale from the Ashanti
Holt, Rinehart and Winston, 1977
McDermott, Gerald
Arrow to the Sun: A Pueblo Indian Tale
Viking, 1974
McDermott, Gerald
The Stone Cutter: A Japanese Folktale
Viking, 1975
McDermott, Gerald
Tim O'Toole and the Wee Folk
Viking, 1990
McGovern, Ann

Too Much Noise
Illustrated by Simms Taback
Houghton Mifflin, 1967
MacKinnon, Debbie
What Shape?
Illustrated by Anthea Sieveking
Dial, 1992
McKissack, Patricia C.
Flossie and the Fox
Illustrated by Rachel Isadora
Dial, 1986
McKissack, Patricia C.
Mirandy and Brother Wind
Illustrated by Jerry Pinkney
Alfred A. Knopf, 1988
McKissack, Patricia C.
Nettie Jo's Friends
Illustrated by Scott Cook
Alfred A. Knopf, 1989
MacLachlan, Patricia
Mama One, Mama Two
Illustrated by Ruth Lercher Bornstein
Harper-Collins, 1982
McLeod, Emilie Warren
The Bear's Bicycle
Illustrated by David McPhail
Little, Brown, 1975
McMillan, Bruce
Becca Backward, Becca Frontward
Lothrop, Lee and Shepard, 1986
McMillan, Bruce
Counting Wildflowers
Lothrop, Lee and Shepard, 1986
McMillan, Bruce
Growing Colors
Lothrop, Lee and Shepard, 1988
McMillan, Bruce
Here a Chick, There a Chick
Lothrop, Lee and Shepard, 1983
McMillan, Bruce
Kitten Can . . .
Lothrop, Lee and Shepard, 1984
McMillan, Bruce
One Sun: A Book of Terse Verse
Holiday House, 1990
McMillan, Bruce
Super, Super, Superwords

Lothrop, Lee and Shepard, 1989
McMillan, Bruce
Time to . . .
Lothrop, Lee and Shepard, 1989
McMullen, Eunice, and Nigel McMullen
Dragon for Breakfast
Carolrhoda, 1990
McNaughton, Colin
Anton B. Stanton and the Pirats
Doubleday, 1979
McNaughton, Colin
If Dinosaurs Were Cats and Dogs
Scholastic, 1981
McNulty, Faith
The Lady and the Spider
Illustrated by Bob Marstall
Harper-Collins, 1986
McPhail, David
Bear's Toothache
Little, Brown, 1972
McPhail, David
Emma's Pet
Dutton, 1985
McPhail, David
First Flight
Little, Brown, 1987
McPhail, David
Pig Pig Grows Up
Dutton, 1980
Maestro, Betsy, and Giulio Maestro
Dollars and Cents for Harriet
Crown, 1988
Maestro, Betsy, and Giulio Maestro
Harriet Goes to the Circus
Crown, 1977
Maestro, Betsy, and Giulio Maestro
Traffic, a Book of Opposites
Crown, 1981
Magee, Doug, and Robert Newman
All Aboard ABC
Dutton, 1990
Magorian, Michelle
Who's Going to Take Care of Me?
Illustrated by James Graham Hale
Harper-Collins, 1990
Mahy, Margaret
The Great White Man-Eating Shark

Illustrated by Jonathan Allen
Dial, 1990
Manushkin, Fran
The Best Toy of All
Illustrated by Robin Ballard
Dutton, 1992
Marron, Carol A.
Mother Told Me So.
Illustrated by George Karn
Raintree, 1983
Marshall, Edward
Space Case
Illustrated by James Marshall
Dial, 1980
Marshall, James
The Cut-Ups
Viking, 1984
Marshall, James
George and Martha
Houghton Mifflin, 1972
Marshall, James
Goldilocks and the Three Bears
Dial, 1988
Marshall, James
The Guest
Houghton Mifflin, 1975
Marshall, James, illustrator
Mother Goose
Farrar, Straus and Giroux, 1979
Marshall, James
Old Mother Hubbard and Her Wonderful Dog
Farrar, Straus and Giroux, 1991
Marshall, James
Red Riding Hood
Dial, 1991
Marshall, James
Willis
Houghton Mifflin, 1974
Marshall, James
Yummers!
Houghton Mifflin, 1973
Marshall, James
Yummers Too: The Second Course
Houghton Mifflin, 1986
Martin, Ann
Rachel Parker, Kindergarten Show-Off

Illustrated by Nancy Poydar
Holiday House, 1992
Martin, Bill, Jr.
*Brown Bear, Brown Bear, What Do
    You See?*
Illustrated by Eric Carle
Holt, Rinehart and Winston, 1983
Martin, Bill, Jr.
The Happy Hippopotami
Illustrated by Betsy Everitt
Harcourt Brace Jovanovich, 1991
Martin, Bill, Jr.
*Polar Bear, Polar Bear, What Do
    You Hear?*
Illustrated by Eric Carle
Henry Holt, 1991
Martin, Bill, Jr., and John Archambault
Barn Dance!
Illustrated by Ted Rand
Henry Holt, 1986
Martin, Bill, Jr., and John Archambault
Chicka Chicka Boom Boom
Illustrated by Lois Ehlert
Simon & Schuster, 1989
Martin, Bill, Jr., and John Archambault
Here Are My Hands
Illustrated by Ted Rand
Henry Holt, 1985
Martin, Bill, Jr., and John Archambault
Knots on the Counting Rope
Illustrated by Ted Rand
Henry Holt, 1987
Martin, Bill, Jr., and John Archambault
White Dynamite and Curly Kidd
Illustrated by Ted Rand
Henry Holt, 1989
Martin, C. L. G.
The Dragon Nanny
Illustrated by Robert Rayevsky
Macmillan, 1988
Martin. C. L. G.
Three Brave Women
Illustrated by Peter Elwell
Macmillan, 1991
Martin, Rafe
The Rough-Face Girl
Illustrated by David Shannon

Putnam, 1992
Maury, Inez
My Mother and I Are Growing Strong
Translated by Anna Munoz
Illustrated by Sandy Speidel
New Seed, 1978
Maury, Inez
My Mother the Mail Carrier
Translated by Norah Allemany
Illustrated by Lady McCrady
Feminist Press, 1976
Mayer, Marianna
Beauty and the Beast
Illustrated by Mercer Mayer
Four Winds Press, 1978
Mayer, Mercer
Ah-Choo
Dial, 1977
Mayer, Mercer
A Boy, a Dog, and a Frog
Dial, 1985
Mayer, Mercer
Hiccup
Dial, 1978
Mayer, Mercer
Just for You
Western, 1975
Mayer, Mercer
Liza Lou and the Yeller Belly Swamp
Macmillan, 1984
Mayer, Mercer, illustrator
Pied Piper of Hamelin
Macmillan, 1987
Mayer, Mercer
The Terrible Troll
Dial, 1968
Mayer, Mercer
There's a Nightmare in My Closet
Dial, 1968
Mayer, Mercer
There's an Alligator Under My Bed
Dial, 1987
Mayer, Mercer
There's Something in My Attic
Dial, 1988
Mayer, Mercer
You're the Scaredy-Cat

Rainbird, 1991

Merriam, Eve
Daddies at Work
Illustrated by Eugenie Fernandes
Simon & Schuster, 1989

Merriam, Eve
Mommies at Work
Illustrated by Eugenie Fernandes
Simon & Schuster, 1961

Miles, Sally
Alfi and the Dark
Illustrated by Errol LeCain
Chronicle Books, 1988

Miles, Miska
Annie and the Old One
Illustrated by Peter Parnall
Little, Brown, 1971

Miller, Edna
Mousekin's ABC
Prentice-Hall, 1972

Miller, Edna
Mousekin's Golden House
Prentice-Hall, 1964

Miller, Edna
Mousekin's Woodland Sleepers
Prentice-Hall, 1977

Miller, Jane
Farm Alphabet Book
Prentice-Hall, 1983

Miller, Jane
Farm Counting Book
Simon & Schuster, 1983

Miller, Jane
Farm Noises
Simon & Schuster, 1989

Miller, Margaret
Whose Hat?
Greenwillow, 1988

Milne, A. A.
The House at Pooh Corner
Illustrated by Ernest H. Shepard
Dutton, 1988

Milne, A. A.
Now We Are Six
Illustrated by Ernest H. Shepard
Dutton, 1988

Milne, A. A.

When We Were Very Young
Illustrated by Ernest H. Shepard
Dutton, 1988

Milne, A. A.
Winnie the Pooh
Illustrated by Ernest H. Shepard
Dutton, 1988

Milton, Joyce
Dinosaur Days
Illustrated by Richard Roe
Random House, 1985

Minarik, Else H.
Little Bear
Illustrated by Maurice Sendak
Harper-Collins, 1957

Modell, Frank
Look Out, It's April Fool's Day
Greenwillow, 1985

Modell, Frank
One Zillion Valentines
Greenwillow, 1981

Monjo, F. N.
The Drinking Gourd
Illustrated by Fred Brenner
Harper-Collins, 1969

Monsell, Mary Elise
Underwear!
Illustrated by Lynn Munsinger
Albert Whitman, 1988

Moore, Inga
Six-Dinner Sid
Simon & Schuster, 1991

Mora, Pat
A Birthday Basket for Tia
Illustrated by Cecily Lang
Macmillan, 1992

Morninghouse, Sundaira
Habari Gani
Illustrated by Jody Kim
Open Hand, 1992

Moroney, Lynn, adapted by
Baby Rattlesnake
Illustrated by Veg Reisberg
Children's Book Press, 1989

Morris, Ann
Bread, Bread, Bread
Illustrated by Ken Heyman

Lothrop, Lee and Shepard, 1989
Morris, Ann
*The Little Red Riding Hood Rebus
Book*
Illustrated by Ljiljana Rylands
Orchard, 1987
Morris, Robert A.
Seahorse
Illustrated by Arnold Lobel
Harper-Collins, 1972
Morrison, Bill
Squeeze a Sneeze
Houghton Mifflin, 1977
Mosel, Arlene
The Funny Little Woman
Illustrated by Blair Lent
Dutton, 1972
Mosel, Arlene
Tikki Tikki Tembo
Illustrated by Blair Lent
Holt, Rinehart and Winston, 1968
Moss, Marissa
Knick Knack Paddywack
Houghton Mifflin, 1992
Most, Bernard
A Dinosaur Named After Me
Harcourt Brace Jovanovich, 1991
Most, Bernard
If Dinosaurs Came Back
Harcourt Brace Jovanovich, 1978
Most, Bernard
The Littlest Dinosaurs
Harcourt Brace Jovanovich, 1989
Muldoon, Kathleen M.
Princess Pooh
Illustrated by Linda Shute
Albert Whitman, 1989
**Muldoon, Kathleen M., and Mary B.
O'Brien**
Babies Have Fun With Numbers
Macmillan, 1992
Musgrove, Margaret W.
Ashanti to Zulu: African Traditions
Illustrated by Leo and Diane Dillon
Dial, 1976
Myers, Bernice
Sidney Rella and the Glass Sneaker

Macmillan, 1985
Nash, Ogden
The Adventures of Isabel
Illustrated by James Marshall
Little, Brown, 1991
Nash, Ogden
Custard the Dragon
Illustrated by Linell Nash Smith
Little, Brown, 1973
Naylor, Phyllis Reynolds
King of the Playground
Illustrated by Nola Langer Malone
Atheneum, 1991
Nelson, Vaunda Micheaux
Always Gamma
Illustrated by Kimanne Uhler
Putnam, 1988
Nerlove, Miriam
I Meant to Clean My Room Today
Macmillan, 1988
Ness, Evaline
Sam, Bangs and Moonshine
Holt, Rinehart and Winston, 1966
Neuman, Pearl
When Winter Comes
Illustrated by Richard Roe
Raintree, 1989
Newberry, Clare T.
Marshmallow
Harper-Collins, 1990
Nichol, B. P.
Once: A Lullaby
Illustrated by Anita Lobel
Greenwillow, 1983
Noble, Trinka Hakes
The Day Jimmy's Boa Ate the Wash
Illustrated by Steven Kellogg
Dial, 1984
Noble, Trinka Hakes
Hansy's Mermaid
Dial, 1983
Noble, Trinka Hakes
Jimmy's Boa Bounces Back
Illustrated by Steven Kellogg
Dial, 1984
Noble, Trinka Hakes
Meanwhile, Back at the Ranch

Illustrated by Tony Ross
Dial, 1987
Nodset, Joan
Go Away, Dog
Illustrated by Crosby Bonsall
Harper-Collins, 1963
Nodset, Joan
Who Took the Farmer's Hat?
Illustrated by Fritz Siebel
Harper-Collins, 1963
Nolan, Madeena Spray
My Daddy Don't Go to Work
Illustrated by Jim LaMarche
Carolrhoda, 1978
Numeroff, Laura Joffe
If You Give a Mouse a Cookie
Illustrated by Felicia Bond
Harper-Collins, 1985
Oliver, Stephen, illustrator
My First Look at Shapes
Random House, 1990
Oliver, Stephen, illustrator
My First Look at Sizes
Random House, 1990
O'Neill, Mary
Hailstones and Halibut Bones
Illustrated by John Wallner
Doubleday, 1989
Ormerod, Jan
Moonlight
Lothrop, Lee and Shepard, 1982
Ormerod, Jan
Sunshine
Lothrop, Lee and Shepard, 1981
Ormondroyd, Edward
Broderick
Illustrated by John Larrecq
Houghton Mifflin, 1969
Ormondroyd, Edward
Theodore
Illustrated by John Larrecq
Houghton Mifflin, 1984
Osofsky, Audrey
Dreamcatcher
Illustrated by Ed Young
Orchard, 1992
Otto, Carolyn

Dinosaurs Chase
Illustrated by Thacher Hurd
Harper-Collins, 1991
Oxenbury, Helen
Friends
Simon & Schuster, 1981
Oxenbury, Helen
Helen Oxenbury's ABC of Things
Delacorte, 1983
Oxenbury, Helen
Helen Oxenbury's Numbers of Things
Delacorte, 1983
Oxenbury, Helen
I See
Random House, 1986
Oxenbury, Helen
Tom and Pippo Make a Friend
Macmillan, 1989
Palmer, Helen
A Fish Out of Water
Illustrated by P. D. Eastman
Random House, 1967
Parish, Peggy
Amelia Bedelia
Illustrated by Fritz Siebel
Harper-Collins, 1963
Parish, Peggy
Dinosaur Time
Illustrated by Arnold Lobel
Harper-Collins, 1974
Parker, Nancy Winslow
Love From Aunt Betty
Dodd Mead, 1983
Pasternak, Carol, and Allen Sutterfield
Stone Soup
Illustrated by Hedy Campbell
Canadian Women's Educational Press
(n.d.)
Patent, Dorothy Hinshaw
*Grandfather's Nose: Why We Look
    Alike or Different*
Illustrated by Diane Palmisciano
Franklin Watts, 1989
Paterson, A. B.
Waltzing Matilda
Illustrated by Desmond Digby
Holt, Rinehart and Winston, 1970

Patron, Susan
Burgoo Stew
Illustrated by Mike Shenon
Orchard, 1991
Patron, Susan
Five Bad Boys, Billy Que, and the Dustdobbin
Illustrated by Mike Shenon
Orchard, 1992
Payne, Emmy
Katy No-Pocket
Illustrated by H. A. Rey
Houghton Mifflin, 1989
Pearson, Susan
Everybody Knows That!
Illustrated by Diane Paterson
Dial, 1978
Pearson, Susan
Happy Birthday, Grampie
Illustrated by Ronald Himler
Dial, 1987
Pearson, Susan
Jack and the Beanstalk
Illustrated by James Warhola
Simon & Schuster, 1989
Peet, Bill
The Ant and the Elephant
Houghton Mifflin, 1972
Peet, Bill
Big Bad Bruce
Houghton Mifflin, 1977
Peet, Bill
Cowardly Clyde
Houghton Mifflin, 1979
Peet, Bill
Farewell to Shady Glen
Houghton Mifflin, 1966
Peet, Bill
How Droofus the Dragon Lost His Head
Houghton Mifflin, 1971
Peet, Bill
Hubert's Hair-Raising Adventure
Houghton Mifflin, 1959
Peet, Bill
Huge Harold
Houghton Mifflin, 1961

Peet, Bill
Kermit the Hermit
Houghton Mifflin, 1965
Peet, Bill
Pinkish, Purplish, Bluish Egg
Houghton Mifflin, 1963
Peet, Bill
Randy's Dandy Lions
Houghton Mifflin, 1964
Peet, Bill
The Spooky Tail of Prewitt Peacock
Houghton Mifflin, 1973
Peet, Bill
The Whingdingdilly
Houghton Mifflin, 1980
Peet, Bill
The Wump World
Houghton Mifflin, 1981
Peppe, Rodney
The House That Jack Built
Delacorte, 1970
Perrault, Charles
Cinderella
Illustrated by Marcia Brown
Scribner, 1954
Petersham, Maud, and Miska Petersham
The Box With the Red Wheels
Illustrated by Miska Petersham
Macmillan, 1986
Petersham, Maud, and Miska Petersham
Circus Baby
Illustrated by Miska Petersham
Macmillan, 1989
Peterson, Jeanne Whitehouse
I Have a Sister: My Sister Is Deaf
Illustrated by Deborah Ray
Harper-Collins, 1984
Pinkwater, Manus
Big Orange Splot
Hastings House, 1977
Piper, Watty
The Little Engine That Could
Platt and Munk, 1954
Pirner, Connie White
Even Little Kids Get Diabetes
Illustrated by Nadine B. Westcott
Albert Whitman, 1991

Pryor, Ainslie
The Baby Blue Cat Who Said No
Viking, 1988
Pryor, Bonnie
The House on Maple Street
Illustrated by Beth Peck
Morrow, 1987
Rabe, Berniece
The Balancing Girl
Illustrated by Lillian Hoban
Dutton, 1981
Rabe, Berniece
Where's Chimpy?
Illustrated by Diane Schmidt
Albert Whitman, 1988
Raffi
Baby Beluga
Illustrated by Ashley Wolff
Crown, 1990
Rann, Toni, editor
My First Look at Colors
Random House, 1990
Ransome, Arthur
*The Fool of the World and the Flying
  Ship: A Russian Folktale*
Illustrated by Uri Shulevitz
Farrar, Strauss and Giroux, 1968
Raskin, Ellen
Nothing Ever Happens on My Block
Atheneum, 1966
Raskin, Ellen
Spectacles
Atheneum, 1969
Rawlins, Donna
Digging to China
Orchard, 1988
Rayner, Mary
Garth Pig and the Ice Cream Lady
Atheneum, 1977
Rayner, Mary
Mr. and Mrs. Pig's Night Out
Atheneum, 1976
Redhead, Janet Slater
The Turkeygobbling Frog Show
Illustrated by Tracey Clark
Nelson Price Milburn Ltd., New Zea-
  land, 1989

Reid, Barbara
Zoe's Windy Day
Scholastic, 1991
Reiss, John J.
Colors
Bradbury, 1969
Reiss, John J.
Numbers
Bradbury, 1971
Reiss, John J.
Shapes
Bradbury, 1974
Rey, H. A.
Cecily G. and the Nine Monkeys
Houghton Mifflin, 1977
Rey, H. A.
Curious George
Houghton Mifflin, 1941
Rey, H. A.
Curious George Learns the Alphabet
Houghton Mifflin, 1963
Rey, Margaret, and H. A. Rey
Curious George Goes to the Hospital
Illustrated by H. A. Rey
Houghton Mifflin, 1966
Rice, Eve
Benny Bakes a Cake
Morrow, 1989
Rice, Eve
Oh Lewis!
Macmillan, 1974
Rice, Eve
Once in a Wood: Ten Tales from Aesop
Greenwillow, 1979
Rice, Eve
Peter's Pockets
Illustrated by Nancy W. Parker
Greenwillow, 1989
Rice, Eve
Sam Who Never Forgets
Greenwillow, 1977
Rice, Eve
What Sadie Sang
Greenwillow, 1976
Rice, James
Cajun Alphabet
Pelican, 1976

Richardson, Judith Benet
The Way Home
Illustrated by Salley Mavor
Macmillan, 1991

Ringgold, Faith
Tar Beach
Crown, 1991

Robbins, Ken
A Flower Grows
Dial, 1990

Robbins, Ruth
Babushka and the Three Kings
Illustrated by Nicholas Sidjakov
Parnassus, 1960

Robertus, Polly M.
The Dog Who Had Kittens
Illustrated by Janet Stevens
Holiday House, 1991

Rockwell, Anne
Apples and Pumpkins
Illustrated by Lizzy Rockwell
Macmillan, 1989

Rockwell, Anne
Bear Child's Book of Hours
Thomas Y. Crowell, 1987

Rockwell, Anne
Boats
Dutton, 1982

Rockwell, Anne
Fire Engines
Dutton, 1986

Rockwell, Anne
First Comes Spring
Thomas Y. Crowell, 1985

Rockwell, Anne
Gollywhopper Egg
Macmillan, 1974

Rockwell, Anne
Handy Hank Will Fix It
Henry Holt, 1988

Rockwell, Anne
My Spring Robin
Illustrated by Harlow and Lizzy
Rockwell
Macmillan, 1989

Rockwell, Anne
Planes

Dutton, 1985

Rockwell, Anne
Tool Box
Illustrated by Harlow Rockwell
Macmillan, 1974

Rockwell, Anne
Trucks
Dutton, 1984

Rockwell, Anne
When We Grow Up
Dutton, 1981

Rockwell, Anne
Willy Can Count
Little, Brown, 1989

Rockwell, Anne, and Harlow Rockwell
At the Beach
Macmillan, 1987

Rockwell, Anne, and Harlow Rockwell
The Emergency Room
Macmillan, 1985

Rockwell, Anne, and Harlow Rockwell
How My Garden Grew
Macmillan, 1982

Rockwell, Anne, and Harlow Rockwell
Machines
Macmillan, 1972

Rockwell, Anne, and Harlow Rockwell
Sick in Bed
Macmillan, 1982

Rockwell, Harlow
My Dentist
Greenwillow, 1975

Rockwell, Harlow
My Doctor
Macmillan, 1973

Rockwell, Harlow
My Nursery School
Greenwillow, 1976

Rodanas, Kristina
Dragonfly's Tale
Houghton Mifflin, 1992

Roe, Eileen
All I Am
Illustrated by Helen Cogancherry
Bradbury, 1990

Roffey, Maureen
Here Kitty Kitty!

Houghton Mifflin, 1991
Rogers, Fred
Going to Day Care
Putnam, 1985
Rogers, Fred
Going to the Dentist
Illustrated by Jim Judkis
Putnam, 1989
Rogers, Paul
From Me to You
Illustrated by Jane Johnson
Orchard, 1987
Rogers, Paul and Emma Rogers
Zoe's Tower
Illustrated by Robin Bell Corfield
Simon & Schuster, 1991
Rohmer, Harriet
The Legend of Food Mountain
Illustrated by Graciela Carrillo
Childrens Book Press, 1988
Rohmer, Harriet
Uncle Nacho's Hat
Illustrated by Veg Reisberg
Childrens Book Press, 1989
Rohmer, Harriet, and Jesus G. Rea
Atariba and Niguayona
Illustrated by Consuelo Mendez
   Castillo
Childrens Book Press, 1988
Rohmer, Harriet, and Mary Anchondo
How We Came to the Fifth World:
   An Aztec Myth
Illustrated by Graciela Carrillo
Childrens Book Press (n.d.)
Rojankovsky, Feodor
Animals on the Farm
Alfred A. Knopf, 1967
Romanova, Natalia
Once There Was a Tree
Illustrated by Gennady Spirin
Dial, 1985
Root, Phyllis
Soup for Supper
Illustrated by Sue Truesdell
Harper-Collins, 1986
Rose, Anne, retold by
Akimba and the Magic Cow

Illustrated by Hope Meryman
Scholastic, 1979
Rosen, Michael
Little Rabbit Foo Foo
Illustrated by Arthur Robins
Simon & Schuster, 1990
Rosen, Michael
We're Going on a Bear Hunt
Illustrated by Helen Oxenbury
Macmillan, 1989
Ross, Katherine
Grover, Grover, Come on Over
Illustrated by Tom Cooke
Random House, 1991
Ross, Katherine
When You Were a Baby
Illustrated by Phoebe Dunn
Random House, 1988
Roth, Susan L.
We'll Ride Elephants Through
   Brooklyn
Farrar, Straus and Giroux, 1989
Rounds, Glen
Cowboys
Holiday House, 1991
Rounds, Glen, illustrator
Old MacDonald Had a Farm
Holiday House, 1989
Rowland, Jada
The Elves and the Shoemakers
Kipling, 1989
Rowland, Jada, retold and illustrated by
Rapunzel
Contemporary, 1989
Russo, Marisabina
Waiting for Hannah
Greenwillow, 1989
Russo, Marisabina
Why Do Grown-ups Have All the
   Fun?
Greenwillow, 1987
Ryan, Cheli D.
Hildilid's Night
Illustrated by Arnold Lobel
Macmillan, 1971
Rylant, Cynthia
All I See

Illustrated by Peter Catalanotto
Franklin Watts, 1988
Sadler, Marilyn
Alistair's Elephant
Illustrated by Roger Bollen
Prentice-Hall, 1983
Sadler, Marilyn
Alistair's Time Machine
Illustrated by Roger Bollen
Simon & Schuster, 1986
St. George, Judith
By George, Bloomers!
Illustrated by Margot Tomes
Coward, 1976
Samton, Sheila White
On the River: An Adding Book
Caroline House, 1991
San Souci, Robert D.
The Firebird
Illustrated by Kris Waldherr
Dial, 1992
San Souci, Robert D.
The Talking Eggs
Illustrated by Jerry Pinkney
Dial, 1989
Sattler, Helen R.
Train Whistles: A Language in Code
Illustrated by Tom Funk
Lothrop, Lee & Shepard, 1977
Saunders, Dave
Dibble and Dabble
Bradbury Press, 1990
Saunders, Susan
Fish Fry
Illustrated by S. D. Schindler
Viking, 1982
Sawyer, Ruth
Journey Cake, Ho!
Illustrated by Robert McCloskey
Viking, 1953
Scarry, Richard
Richard Scarry's Best Counting Book Ever
Random House, 1975
Scheer, Julian
Rain Makes Applesauce
Illustrated by Marvin Bileck

Holiday House, 1964
Schoen, Mark
Bellybuttons Are Navels
Illustrated by M. J. Quay
Prometheus Books, 1990
Schories, Pat
Mouse Around
Farrar, Straus and Giroux, 1991
Schroeder, Alan
Ragtime Tumpie
Illustrated by Bernie Fuchs
Little, Brown, 1989
Schwartz, Alvin
Busy Buzzing Bumblebees and Other Tongue Twisters
Illustrated by Kathie Abrams
Harper-Collins, 1982
Schwartz, Amy
Oma and Bobo
Bradbury Press, 1987
Schwartz, David M.
How Much Is a Million?
Illustrated by Steven Kellogg
Scholastic, 1985
Schweninger, Ann
Autumn Days
Viking, 1991
Schweninger, Ann
Off to School!
Viking, 1987
Scott, Ann Herbert
On Mother's Lap
Illustrated by Glo Coalson
McGraw-Hill, 1972
Scott, Ann Herbert
Sam
Illustrated by Symeon Shimin
McGraw-Hill, 1967
Scott, Ann Herbert
Someday Rider
Illustrated by Ronald Himler
Houghton Mifflin, 1989
Scullard, Sue
The Great Round-the-World Balloon Race
Dutton, 1990
Scullard, Sue

*Miss Fanshawe and the Great Dragon
Adventure*
St. Martin's, 1986
Seeger, Pete
*Abiyoyo: South African Lullaby and
Folk Story*
Illustrated by Michael Hays
Macmillan, 1986
Selsam, Millicent
Greg's Microscope
Illustrated by Arnold Lobel
Harper-Collins, 1963
Sendak, Maurice
Alligators All Around
Harper-Collins, 1962
Sendak, Maurice
*Chicken Soup With Rice: A Book of
Months*
Harper-Collins, 1962
Sendak, Maurice
In the Night Kitchen
Harper-Collins, 1970
Sendak, Maurice
One Was Johnny
Harper-Collins, 1962
Sendak, Maurice
Pierre: A Cautionary Tale
Harper-Collins, 1962
Sendak, Maurice
Where the Wild Things Are
Harper-Collins, 1963
Sendak, Maurice, and Matthew Margolis
Some Swell Pup
Illustrated by Maurice Sendak
Farrar, Straus and Giroux, 1989
Serfozo, Mary
Who Said Red?
Illustrated by Keiko Narahashi
Macmillan, 1988
Seuling, Barbara
*Teeny Tiny Woman: An Old English
Ghost Tale*
Viking, 1976
Seuss, Dr.
*And to Think That I Saw It on Mul-
berry Street*
Random House, 1937

Seuss, Dr.
The Butter Battle Book
Random House, 1984
Seuss, Dr.
The Cat in the Hat
Random House, 1957
Seuss, Dr.
*The Five Hundred Hats of Bartho-
lomew Cubbins*
Random House, 1938
Seuss, Dr.
Green Eggs and Ham
Random House, 1960
Seuss, Dr.
Hop on Pop
Random House, 1963
Seuss, Dr.
Horton Hatches the Egg
Random House, 1968
Seuss, Dr.
Horton Hears a Who
Random House, 1954
Seuss, Dr.
How the Grinch Stole Christmas
Random House, 1957
Seuss, Dr.
McElligot's Pool
Random House, 1947
Seuss, Dr.
On Beyond Zebra!
Random House, 1955
Sharmat, Marjorie Weinman
The Best Valentine in the World
Illustrated by Lilian Obligado
Holiday House, 1982
Sharmat, Marjorie Weinman
A Big Fat Enormous Lie
Illustrated by David McPhail
Dutton, 1978
Sharmat, Marjorie Weinman
Gladys Told Me to Meet Her Here
Illustrated by Edward Frascino
Harper-Collins, 1970
Sharmat, Marjorie Weinman
I'm Terrific
Illustrated by Kay Chorao
Holiday House, 1977

Sharmat, Marjorie Weinman
I'm the Best!
Illustrated by Will Hillenbrand
Holiday House, 1991

Sharmat, Marjorie Weinman
Mooch the Messy
Illustrated by Ben Shecter
Harper-Collins, 1976

Sharmat, Marjorie Weinman
One Terrific Thanksgiving
Illustrated by Lilian Obligado
Holiday House, 1985

Sharmat, Marjorie Weinman
Walter the Wolf
Illustrated by Kelly Oechsli
Holiday House, 1975

Sharmat, Mitchell
Gregory the Terrible Eater
Illustrated by Ariane Dewey and Jose
    Aruego
Scholastic, 1980

Shaw, Charles G.
It Looked Like Spilt Milk
Harper-Collins, 1947

Sherman, Josepha
Vassilisa the Wise: A Tale of Medieval
    Russia
Illustrated by Daniel San Souci
Harcourt Brace Jovanovich, 1988

Shortall, Leonard
One Way: A Trip With Traffic Signs
Prentice-Hall, 1975

Showers, Paul
A Baby Starts to Grow
Illustrated by Rosalind Fry
Thomas Y. Crowell, 1969

Showers, Paul
A Drop of Blood
Illustrated by Don Madden
Thomas Y. Crowell, 1972

Showers, Paul
Ears Are For Hearing
Illustrated by Holly Keller
Thomas Y. Crowell, 1990

Showers, Paul
Me and My Family Tree
Illustrated by Don Madden

Thomas Y. Crowell, 1978

Showers, Paul
Your Skin and Mine
Illustrated by Paul Galdone
Thomas Y. Crowell, 1965

Shub, Elizabeth, adapted from the
    Brothers Grimm
Clever Kate
Illustrated by Anita Lobel
Macmillan, 1986

Shulevitz, Uri
Dawn
Farrar, Straus and Giroux, 1974

Shulevitz, Uri
The Magician
Macmillan, 1973

Shulevitz, Uri
One Monday Morning
Scribner, 1967

Shulevitz, Uri
Rain Rain Rivers
Farrar, Straus and Giroux, 1969

Shulevitz, Uri
The Treasure
Farrar, Straus and Giroux, 1978

Shute, Linda
Clever Tom and the Leprechaun
Lothrop, Lee and Shepard, 1988

Shute, Linda
Momotaro the Peach Boy: A Japa-
    nese Tale
Lothrop, Lee and Shepard, 1986

Siebert, Diane
Train Song
Illustrated by Mike Wimmer
Thomas Y. Crowell, 1990

Sieveking, Anthea
What's Inside?
Dial, 1989

Silverman, Erica
Big Pumpkin
Illustrated by S. D. Schindler
Macmillan, 1992

Simon, Norma
All Kinds of Families
Illustrated by Joe Lasker
Albert Whitman, 1975

Simon, Norma
I Know What I Like
Illustrated by Dora Leder
Albert Whitman, 1971

Simon, Norma
I Was So Mad!
Illustrated by Dora Leder
Albert Whitman, 1974

Simon, Norma
The Saddest Time
Illustrated by Jacqueline Rogers
Albert Whitman, 1986

Slater, Teddy
*The Big Book of Real Fire Trucks
and Fire Fighting*
Illustrated by Mones
Grosset & Dunlop, 1987

Slepian, Jan, and Ann Seidler
*The Cat Who Wore a Pot on Her
Head*
Illustrated by Richard E. Martin
Scholastic, 1967

Sloat, Teri
From One to One Hundred
Dutton, 1991

Slobodkina, Esphyr
Caps for Sale
Harper-Collins, 1987

Small, David
Imogene's Antlers
Crown, 1985

Smith, Barry
Tom and Annie Go Shopping
Houghton Mifflin, 1989

Smith, William Jay
Ho for a Hat!
Illustrated by Lynn Munsinger
Little, Brown, 1989

Sobel, Harriet Langsam
*We Don't Look Like Our Mom and
Dad*
Illustrations by Patricia Agre
Coward-McCann, 1984

Sonneborn, Ruth
Friday Night Is Papa Night
Illustrated by Emily A. McCully
Viking, 1970

Spier, Peter
The Erie Canal
Doubleday, 1970

Spier, Peter
*Fast-Slow, High-Low: A Book of
Opposites*
Doubleday, 1972

Spier, Peter
Fox Went Out on a Chilly Night
Doubleday, 1961

Spier, Peter
Gobble, Growl, Grunt
Doubleday, 1971

Spier, Peter
London Bridge Is Falling Down
Doubleday, 1972

Spier, Peter
Oh, Were They Ever Happy!
Doubleday, 1978

Spier, Peter
People
Doubleday, 1980

Spier, Peter
Rain
Doubleday, 1982

Spinelli, Eileen
Somebody Loves You, Mr. Hatch
Illustrated by Paul Yalowitz
Macmillan, 1991

Staines, Bill
*All God's Critters Got a Place in the
Choir*
Illustrated by Margot Zemach
Dutton, 1989

Stamm, Claus
*Three Strong Women: A Tall Tale
from Japan*
Illustrated by Jean and Mou-sien
Tseng
Viking, 1990

Standiford, Natalie
*Washington Irving's The Headless
Horseman*
Illustrated by Donald Cook
Random House, 1992

Stanek, Muriel
I Speak English for My Mom

Illustrated by Judith Friedman
Albert Whitman, 1989
Stanek, Muriel
Starting School
Illustrated by Betty and Tony De
Luna
Albert Whitman, 1981
Steig, William
The Amazing Bone
Farrar, Straus and Giroux, 1976
Steig, William
Amos and Boris
Farrar, Straus and Giroux, 1977
Steig, William
Brave Irene
Farrar, Straus and Giroux, 1986
Steig, William
Caleb and Kate
Farrar, Straus and Giroux, 1977
Steig, William
Doctor DeSoto
Farrar, Straus and Giroux, 1982
Steig, William
Farmer Palmer's Wagon Ride
Farrar, Straus and Giroux, 1974
Steig, William
Roland, the Minstrel Pig
Harper-Collins, 1968
Steig, William
Sylvester and the Magic Pebble
Harper-Collins, 1969
Steptoe, John, told and illustrated by
*Mufaro's Beautiful Daughters: An
African Folktale*
Lothrop, Lee and Shepard, 1987
Steptoe, John
Stevie
Harper-Collins, 1969
Stevenson, James
Could be Worse!
Greenwillow, 1977
Stevenson, James
Grandpa's Too-Good Garden
Morrow, 1989
Stevenson, James
Monty
Greenwillow, 1979

Stevenson, James
There's Nothing to Do!
Greenwillow, 1986
Stevenson, Robert Louis
A Child's Garden of Verses
Illustrated by Brian Wildsmith
Franklin Watts, 1966
Stewig, John Warren
Stone Soup
Holiday House, 1991
Stow, Jenny, illustrator
The House That Jack Built
Dial, 1992
Sundgaard, Arnold
The Bear Who Loved Puccini
Illustrated by Dominic Catalano
Philomel, 1992
Surat, Michele Maria
Angel Child, Dragon Child
Illustrated by Vo-Dinh Mai
Carnival, 1983
Sutherland, Harry A.
Dad's Car Wash
Illustrated by Maxie Chambliss
Atheneum, 1988
Swann, Brian
*A Basket Full of White Eggs: Riddle
Poems*
Illustrated by Ponder Goembel
Orchard, 1988
Tafuri, Nancy
All Year Long
Greenwillow, 1983
Tafuri, Nancy
Early Morning in the Barn
Greenwillow, 1983
Tafuri, Nancy
Have You Seen My Duckling?
Greenwillow, 1984
Tafuri, Nancy
Who's Counting?
Greenwillow, 1986
Talbott, Hudson
We're Back!
Crown, 1987
Tallon, Robert, illustrator
ABC . . . Z (English and Spanish)

Sayre, 1981
Tan, Amy
The Moon Lady
Illustrated by Gretchen Schields
Macmillan, 1992
Tarcov, Edith
The Frog Prince
Illustrated by James Marshall
Four Winds, 1974
Taylor, Mark
Henry the Explorer
Illustrated by Graham Booth
Atheneum, 1966
Tester, Sylvia Root
We Laughed a Lot, My First Day of School
Illustrated by Frances Hook
Child's World, 1979
Thayer, Jane
The Popcorn Dragon
Illustrated by Lisa McCue
Morrow, 1989
Thomas, Marlo
Free To Be You and Me
McGraw-Hill, 1974
Thomas, Patricia
"Stand Back," Said the Elephant, "I'm Going to Sneeze!"
Illustrated by Wallace Tripp
Lothrop, Lee and Shepard, 1971
Thomas, Valerie
Winnie the Witch
Illustrated by Korky Paul
Kane-Miller, 1987
Thornhill, Jan
The Wildlife ABC: A Nature Alphabet Book
Simon & Schuster, 1988
Thurber, James
Many Moons
Illustrated by Louis Slobodkin
Harcourt Brace Jovanovich, 1973
Titus, Eve
Anatole
Illustrated by Paul Galdone
McGraw-Hill, 1956
Tobias, Tobi

Moving Day
Illustrated by William Pene Du Bois
Alfred A. Knopf, 1976
Tompert, Ann
Little Fox Goes to the End of the World
Illustrated by John Wallner
Crown, 1976
Tresselt, Alvin R.
Autumn Harvest
Illustrated by Roger Duvoisin
Morrow, 1990
Tresselt, Alvin R.
The Mitten
Illustrated by Yaroslava Mills
Lothrop, Lee and Shepard, 1964
Tresselt, Alvin R.
Rain Drop Splash
Illustrated by Leonard Weisgard
Morrow, 1990
Tresselt, Alvin R.
White Snow, Bright Snow
Illustrated by Roger Duvoisin
Lothrop, Lee and Shepard, 1989
Trezise, Percy, and Dick Roughsey
Gidja the Moon
Gareth Stevens, 1984
Trezise, Percy, and Dick Roughsey
Turramulli the Giant Quinkin
Gareth Stevens, 1982
Tripp, Wallace
Granfa' Grig Had a Pig and Other Rhymes Without Reason from Mother Goose
Little, Brown, 1976
Tripp, Wallace
A Great Big Ugly Man Came Up and Tied His Horse to Me
Little, Brown, 1974
Trivas, Irene
Annie . . . Anya: A Month in Moscow
Orchard, 1992
Troughton, Joanna
How the Birds Changed Their Feathers: A South American Indian Folktale

Peter Bedrick, 1986

Tryon, Leslie
Albert's Alphabet
Macmillan, 1991

Tudor, Tasha
A Is For Annabelle
Macmillan, 1988

Tudor, Tasha
Mother Goose
Random House, 1980

Tudor, Tasha
One Is One
Macmillan, 1988

Turkle, Brinton
Deep in the Forest
Dutton, 1976

Turkle, Brinton
Do Not Open
Dutton, 1981

Turkle, Brinton
Obadiah the Bold
Viking, 1965

Turkle, Brinton
Rachel and Obadiah
E. P. Dutton, 1978

Turkle, Brinton
Thy Friend, Obadiah
Viking, 1969

Turner, Ann
Hedgehog for Breakfast
Illustrated by Lisa McCue
Macmillan, 1989

Turner, Gwenda
Shapes
Viking, 1991

Tworkov, Jack
The Camel Who Took a Walk
Illustrated by Roger Duvoisin
Dutton, 1974

Udry, Janice
Let's Be Enemies
Illustrated by Maurice Sendak
Harper-Collins, 1961

Udry, Janice
Moon Jumpers
Illustrated by Maurice Sendak
Harper-Collins, 1959

Udry, Janice
A Tree Is Nice
Illustrated by Marc Simont
Harper-Collins, 1987

Udry, Janice
What Mary Jo Shared
Illustrated by Eleanor Mill
Albert Whitman, 1966

Ungerer, Tomi
Crictor
Harper-Collins, 1958

Ungerer, Tomi
Zeralda's Ogre
Doubleday, 1991

Van Allsburg, Chris
The Garden of Abdul Gasazi
Houghton Mifflin, 1979

Van Allsburg, Chris
Jumanji
Houghton Mifflin, 1981

Van Allsburg, Chris
Just a Dream
Houghton Mifflin, 1990

Van Allsburg, Chris
The Polar Express
Houghton Mifflin, 1985

Van Allsburg, Chris
Two Bad Ants
Houghton Mifflin, 1988

Van Laan, Nancy
People, People, Everywhere!
Illustrated by Nadine B. Westcott
Alfred A. Knopf, 1992

Van Woerkom, Dorothy
*The Queen Who Couldn't Bake
Gingerbread*
Illustrated by Paul Galdone
Knopf, 1975

Vaughan, Marcia
Wombat Stew
Illustrated by Pamela Lofts
Silver Burdett, 1984

Vigna, Judith
I Wish Daddy Didn't Drink So Much
Albert Whitman, 1988

Vigna, Judith
She's Not My Real Mother

Albert Whitman, 1980
Vincent, Gabrielle
Ernest and Celestine
Greenwillow, 1982
Viorst, Judith
Alexander and the Terrible, Horrible,
No Good, Very Bad Day
Illustrated by Ray Cruz
Atheneum, 1976
Viorst, Judith
Earrings!
Illustrated by Langner Malone
Atheneum, 1990
Viorst, Judith
The Good-Bye Book
Illustrated by Kay Chorao
Atheneum, 1988
Viorst, Judith
I'll Fix Anthony
Illustrated by Arnold Lobel
Harper-Collins, 1969
Viorst, Judith
My Mama Says There Aren't Any
Zombies, Ghosts, Vampires, Crea-
tures, Demons, Monsters, Fiends,
Goblins, or Things
Illustrated by Kay Chorao
Atheneum, 1973
Viorst, Judith
The Tenth Good Thing About Barney
Illustrated by Erik Blegved
Atheneum, 1975
Waber, Bernard
An Anteater Named Arthur
Houghton Mifflin, 1967
Waber, Bernard
The House on 88th Street
Houghton Mifflin, 1962
Waber, Bernard
I Was All Thumbs
Houghton Mifflin, 1975
Waber, Bernard
Ira Says Goodby
Houghton Mifflin, 1991
Waber, Bernard
Ira Sleeps Over
Houghton Mifflin, 1972

Waber, Bernard
Lyle Finds His Mother
Houghton Mifflin, 1974
Waber, Bernard
Lyle, Lyle Crocodile
Houghton Mifflin, 1965
Waber, Bernard
You Look Ridiculous Said the Rhi-
noceros to the Hippopotamus
Houghton Mifflin, 1966
Wagner, Elaine Knox
My Grandpa Retired Today
Illustrated by Charles Robinson
Albert Whitman, 1982
Wagner, Karen
Chocolate Chip Cookies
Illustrated by Leah P. Preiss
Henry Holt, 1990
Wagner, Karen
Silly Fred
Illustrated by Normand Chartier
Macmillan, 1989
Wahl, Jan
Doctor Rabbit's Foundling
Illustrated by Cyndy Szekeres
Pantheon, 1977
Wahl, Jan
Humphrey's Bear
Illustrated by William Joyce
Henry Holt, 1987
Wahl, Jan
Rabbits on Roller Skates
Illustrated by David Allender
Crown, 1986
Wallace, Daisy, editor
Monster Poems
Illustrated by Kay Chorao
Holiday House, 1976
Wallis, Lisa
Island Child
Illustrated by Deborah Haeffele
Dutton, 1991
Ward, Lynd
The Biggest Bear
Houghton Mifflin, 1952
Ward, Sally G.
What Goes Around Comes Around

Doubleday, 1991
Wasson, Valentina P.
The Chosen Baby
Illustrated by Glo Coalson
Lippincott, 1977
Watanabe, Shigeo
How Do I Put It On?
Illustrated by Yasuo Ohtomo
Putnam, 1991
Watanabe, Shigeo
I Can Build a House!
Illustrated by Yasuo Ohtomo
Putnam, 1983
Watanabe, Shigeo
I Can Ride It!
Illustrated by Yasuo Ohtomo
Philomel, 1981
Watanabe, Shigeo
I Can Take a Walk!
Illustrated by Yasuo Ohtomo
Philomel, 1983
Watanabe, Shigeo
It's My Birthday!
Illustrated by Yasuo Ohtomo
Philomel, 1988
Watanabe, Shigeo
What a Good Lunch!
Illustrated by Yasuo Ohtomo
Philomel, 1978
Watanabe, Shigeo
Where's My Daddy?
Illustrated by Yasuo Ohtomo
Putnam, 1982
Waters, Kate, and Madeline Slovenz-Low
Lion Dancer: Ernie Wan's Chinese New Year
Illustrated by Martha Cooper
Scholastic, 1990
Watson, Clyde
Father Fox's Pennyrhymes
Illustrated by Wendy Watson
Thomas Y. Crowell, 1971
Watson, Richard Jesse
Tom Thumb
Harcourt Brace Jovanovich, 1989
Weiss, Nicki

On a Hot, Hot Day
Putnam, 1992
Weiss, Nicki
Where Does the Brown Bear Go?
Puffin, 1990
Wells, Rosemary
Benjamin and Tulip
Dial, 1973
Wells, Rosemary
Hazel's Amazing Mother
Dial, 1985
Wells, Rosemary
Max's Bath
Dial, 1985
Wells, Rosemary
Max's Dragon Shirt
Dial, 1991
Wells, Rosemary
Noisy Nora
Dial, 1973
Wells, Rosemary
Peabody
Dutton, 1983
Wells, Rosemary
Shy Charles
Dial, 1988
Wells, Rosemary
Timothy Goes to School
Dial, 1981
Westcott, Nadine Bernard
The Giant Vegetable Garden
Little, Brown, 1981
Westcott, Nadine Bernard
I Know an Old Lady Who Swallowed a Fly
Little, Brown, 1980
Westcott, Nadine Bernard
Peanut Butter and Jelly: A Play Rhyme
Dutton, 1987
Westcott, Nadine Bernard, illustrator
Skip to My Lou
Little, Brown, 1989
Westcott, Nadine Bernard, illustrator
There's a Hole in the Bucket
Harper-Collins, 1990
Wiesner, David

Free Fall
Lothrop, Lee and Shepard, 1988
Wiesner, David
Tuesday
Houghton Mifflin, 1991
Wijngaard, Juan
Bear
Crown, 1990
Wijngaard, Juan
Dog
Crown, 1990
Wijngaard, Juan
Duck
Crown, 1990
Wildsmith, Brian
Brian Wildsmith's Birds
Oxford, 1967
Wildsmith, Brian
Brian Wildsmith's Fishes
Oxford, 1987
Wildsmith, Brian
The Hunter and His Dog
Oxford, 1979
Wildsmith, Brian
The Little Wood Duck
Oxford, 1987
Wilhelm, Hans
Bunny Trouble
Scholastic, 1985
Wilkes, Angela
My First Word Book
Houghton Mifflin, 1991
Willard, Nancy
Papa's Panda
Illustrated by Lillian Hoban
Harcourt Brace Jovanovich, 1979
Willhoite, Michael
Daddy's Roommate
Alyson Publications, 1991
Williams, Barbara
Albert's Toothache
Illustrated by Kay Chorao
Dutton, 1974
Williams, Barbara
Kevin's Grandma
Illustrated by Kay Chorao
Dutton, 1975

Williams, Barbara
A Valentine for Cousin Archie
Illustrated by Kay Chorao
Dutton, 1981
Williams, Jay
*Everyone Knows What a Dragon
    Looks Like*
Illustrated by Mercer Mayer
Four Winds, 1976
Williams, Jenny
Everyday ABC
Dial, 1992
Williams, Jenny
Playtime 1, 2, 3
Dial, 1992
Williams, Linda
*The Little Old Lady Who Was Not
    Afraid of Anything*
Illustrated by Megan Lloyd
Thomas Y. Crowell, 1986
Williams, Margery
The Velveteen Rabbit
Illustrated by William Nicholson
Doubleday, 1991
Williams, Vera B.
A Chair for My Mother
Greenwillow, 1982
Williams, Vera B.
Music, Music for Everyone
Greenwillow, 1984
Williams, Vera B.
Something Special for Me
Greenwillow, 1983
Williams, Vera B.
*Three Days on a River in a Red
    Canoe*
Greenwillow, 1981
Willoughby, Elaine Macmann
Boris and the Monsters
Illustrated by Lynn Munsinger
Houghton Mifflin, 1980
Wilson, April
Look Again!
Dial, 1992
Winter, Jeanette
Follow the Drinking Gourd
Alfred A. Knopf, 1988

Winter, Jonah
Diego
Translated by Amy Prince
Illustrated by Jeanette Winter
Alfred A. Knopf, 1991

Winthrop, Elizabeth
Maggie and the Monster
Illustrated by Tomie DePaola
Holiday House, 1987,

Winthrop, Elizabeth
Vasilissa the Beautiful: A Russian Folktale
Illustrated by Alexander Koshkin
Harper-Collins, 1991

Wittman, Sally
A Special Trade
Illustrated by Karen Gundersheimer
Harper-Collins, 1985

Wolde, Gunilla
Betsy and the Chicken Pox
Random House, 1976

Wolde, Gunilla
Betsy's Baby Brother
Random House, 1975

Wolde, Gunilla
Betsy's First Day at Day Care
Random House, 1982

Wolde, Gunilla
This Is Betsy
Random House, 1975

Wolff, Ashley
A Year of Beasts
Dutton, 1986

Wood, Audrey
Elbert's Bad Word
Illustrated by Audrey and Don Wood
Harcourt Brace Jovanovich, 1988

Wood, Audrey
Heckedy Peg
Illustrated by Don Wood
Harcourt Brace Jovanovich, 1987

Wood, Audrey
King Bidgood's in the Bathtub
Illustrated by Don Wood
Harcourt Brace Jovanovich, 1985

Wood, Audrey
The Napping House
Illustrated by Don Wood
Harcourt Brace Jovanovich, 1984

Wood, Don, and Audrey Wood
The Little Mouse, the Red, Ripe Strawberry and the Big Hungry Bear
Illustrated by Don Wood
Child's Play, 1984

Wood, Jakki
Dads Are Such Fun
Illustrated by Rog Bonner
Simon & Schuster, 1992

Woodruff, Elvira
Show and Tell
Illustrated by Denise Brunkus
Holiday House, 1991

Wright, Betty Ren
The Cat Next Door
Illustrated by Gail Owens
Holiday House, 1991

Wright, Blanche Fisher
The Real Mother Goose
Rand McNally, 1965

Wright, Jill
The Old Woman and the Willy Nilly Man
Illustrated by Glen Rounds
Putnam, 1987

Wright, Friere, and Michael Foreman
Seven in One Blow
Random House, 1978

Wyler, Rose, and Gerald Ames
Prove It!
Illustrated by Talivaldis Stubis
Harper-Collins, 1963

Yacowitz, Caryn
The Jade Stone: A Chinese Folktale
Illustrated by Ju-Hong Chen
Holiday House, 1992

Yarbrough, Camille
Cornrows
Illustrated by Carole Byard
Coward, 1979

Yashima, Mitsu, and Taro Yashima
Momo's Kitten
Illustrated by Taro Yashima
Viking, 1961

Yashima, Taro
Crow Boy
Viking, 1955
Yashima, Taro
Umbrella
Viking, 1958
Yektai, Niki
What's Missing?
Illustrated by Susannah Ryan
Houghton Mifflin, 1987
Yen, Clara
*Why Rat Comes First: The Story of
the Chinese Zodiac*
Illustrated by Hideo C. Yoshida
Childrens Book Press, 1991
Yolan, Jane, editor
Lap-Time Song and Play Book
Illustrated by Margot Tomes
Musical Arrangements by Adam
Stemple
Harcourt Brace Jovanovich, 1989
Yolen, Jane
Owl Moon
Illustrated by John Schoenherr
Putnam, 1987
Yolen, Jane
Sleeping Ugly
Illustrated by Diane Stanley
Putnam, 1981
Yolen, Jane, editor
Street Rhymes Around the World
Boyds Mill Press, 1992
Yorinks, Arthur
Hey, Al
Illustrated by Richard Egielski
Farrar, Straus and Giroux, 1986
Young, Ed, translator and illustrator
Lon Po Po
Putnam, 1989
Young, Miriam
Miss Suzy's Easter Surprise
Illustrated by Arnold Lobel
Parents Magazine Press, 1972
Young, Ruth
Golden Bear
Illustrated by Rachel Isadora
Viking, 1992

Zacharias, Thomas
Where Is the Green Parrot?
Illustrated by Wanda Zacharias
Delacorte, 1968
Zalben, Jane Breskin
Goldie's Purim
Henry Holt, 1991
Zelinsky, Paul O.
Rumpelstiltskin
Dutton, 1986
Zemach, Harve
The Judge: An Untrue Tale
Illustrated by Margot Zemach
Farrar, Straus and Giroux, 1969
Zemach, Harve
Mommy, Buy Me a China Doll
Illustrated by Margot Zemach
Farrar, Straus and Giroux, 1975
Zemach, Margot
It Could Always Be Worse
Farrar, Straus and Giroux, 1977
Zemach, Margot
The Three Little Pigs
Farrar, Straus and Giroux, 1989
Zemach, Margot
The Three Wishes
Farrar, Straus and Giroux, 1986
Zemach, Harve, and Margot Zemach
Duffy and the Devil
Farrar, Straus and Giroux, 1973
Zemach, Harve, and Margot Zemach
A Penny a Look
Farrar, Straus and Giroux, 1971
Zemach, Harve, and Margot Zemach
Salt: A Russian Tale
Illustrated by Margot Zemach
Farrar, Straus and Giroux, 1976
Ziefert, Harriet
I Want to Sleep in Your Bed
Illustrated by Mavis Smith
Harper-Collins, 1990
Ziefert, Harriet
A New Coat for Anna
Illustrated by Anita Lobel
Alfred A. Knopf, 1986
Ziefert, Harriet
When Daddy Had the Chicken Pox

Illustrated by Lionel Kalish
Harper-Collins, 1991
Zindel, Paul
I Love My Mother
Illustrated by John Melo
Harper-Collins, 1975
Zion, Gene
All Falling Down
Illustrated by Margaret B. Graham
Harper-Collins, 1951
Zion, Gene
Dear Garbage Man
Illustrated by Margaret B. Graham
Harper-Collins, 1957
Zion, Gene
Harry by the Sea
Illustrated by Margaret B. Graham
Harper-Collins, 1965
Zion, Gene
Harry the Dirty Dog
Illustrated by Margaret B. Graham
Harper-Collins, 1956
Zion, Gene
No Roses for Harry
Illustrated by Margaret B. Graham
Harper-Collins, 1975
Zion, Gene
The Plant Sitter
Illustrated by Margaret B. Graham
Harper-Collins, 1959
Zolotow, Charlotte
Big Brother
Illustrated by Mary Chalmers
Harper-Collins, 1960
Zolotow, Charlotte
Big Sister and Little Sister
Illustrated by Martha Alexander
Harper-Collins, 1966
Zolotow, Charlotte
A Father Like That
Illustrated by Ben Shecter
Harper-Collins, 1971
Zolotow, Charlotte
The Hating Book
Illustrated by Ben Shecter
Harper-Collins, 1969
Zolotow, Charlotte

I Know a Lady
Illustrated by James Stevenson
Greenwillow, 1984
Zolotow, Charlotte
If It Weren't for You
Illustrated by Ben Shecter
Harper-Collins, 1966
Zolotow, Charlotte
Mister Rabbit and the Lovely Present
Illustrated by Maurice Sendak
Harper-Collins, 1962
Zolotow, Charlotte
My Friend John
Illustrated by Ben Shecter
Harper-Collins, 1968
Zolotow, Charlotte
My Grandson Lew
Illustrated by William Pene Du Bois
Harper-Collins, 1974
Zolotow, Charlotte
Over and Over
Illustrated by Garth Williams
Harper-Collins, 1957
Zolotow, Charlotte
The Quarreling Book
Illustrated by Arnold Lobel
Harper-Collins, 1963
Zolotow, Charlotte
Sleepy Book
Illustrated by Ilse Plume
Harper-Collins, 1990
Zolotow, Charlotte
The Summer Night
Illustrated by Ben Shecter
Harper-Collins, 1991
Zolotow, Charlotte
A Tiger Called Thomas
Illustrated by Catherine Stock
Lothrop, 1988
Zolotow, Charlotte
When I Have a Little Girl
Illustrated by Hilary Knight
Harper-Collins, 1965
Zolotow, Charlotte
William's Doll
Illustrated by William Pene Du Bois
Harper-Collins, 1972